"YOU GOT ON ABOUT
YOUR BUSINESS."

Good-bye was heavy in her flatly delivered statement, and suddenly the thought of
riding out and not seeing this willful woman
again was not acceptable to heart or mind.
"And what if I decide to make you my
business, Miss Amos?"

"You won't. I'm not the kind of woman
you want, Dalton, and you've got nothing to
offer that I need."

His eyes narrowed in objection to that cold
truth. She was right. He was no good for her,
or for anyone, and that had never bothered
him before. Instead, he countered her claim
with an observation of his own.

"Afraid you'll get swept off your feet, Miss
Amos?"

"Yes, Mr. MacKenzie, I am. And I can't
afford to be. Not by you."

Her brutal honesty tore the heart from his
chest, making it her humbled trophy as she
turned and proudly walked into the house
that would never be his home.

To Marilyn Dickmann,
a woman of tremendous courage

Chapter 1

❝**T**wo hundred a month.❞

The rasp of a match head across the tabletop punctuated that demand. A pungent bite of sulfur gave way to a bright flare. Eyes as direct as blued gunmetal were briefly illuminated, then veiled behind a curtain of smoke. That glimpse was long enough to assure the rancher sitting opposite that the amount was no joke.

"Two hundred," he muttered uneasily, considering the consequences of a sum so vast. "I'm not hiring you to kill them."

For a long moment there was no response from the man cloaked by corner shadows. His features were concealed within the hazy darkness, framed in anonymity about the glow of his cigarillo. While his manner was nonthreatening and his tone polite, the rancher who'd joined him at the table was sweating—had been even before he sat down to voice his proposition. There had never been a question as to who was in control of the situation. It all rested in the mysterious figure. When he finally spoke, his words were cushioned by a gentle drawl from out of the Oklahoma Territory or maybe Texas.

1

Soft or not, they were backed by a .45-caliber reputation.

"You're hiring me to eliminate an unpleasant problem. That's what I do. I'm the one men like you come to when you can't get your way and don't want to get your own hands dirty."

"Now see here," the rancher sputtered, objecting as strenuously as he dared. He would have spouted on about his own honorable intentions, but the man still wreathed in smoke with the sinister silhouette interrupted almost wearily to state his own hard-edged philosophies.

"Mr. Jamison, you don't need to convince me of your noble causes. Right and wrong aren't my concerns. I'm not interested in your politics. You hire me to do a job, and I take care of it. Obviously you want the best, and that's why you went to so much trouble to bring me up here. I hope I didn't lead you to believe that extricating me from that legal problem would replace my usual fee. I'm not sentimental, sir, and to me, this is business. The best doesn't come cheap. If you don't want to meet my price, there are others in this room who'd gladly work for less. I could point them out to you, if you'd like."

It was the way he said it, without the slightest hint of boastfulness. The calm, indifferent claim did more than the preceding reputation to convince Patrick Jamison he hadn't made a mistake in using his far-reaching influence to snatch Dalton MacKenzie off the New Mexico gallows, and that he wasn't making a mistake now in pulling out his money pouch. He'd heard things about MacKenzie, chilling things, but he wasn't sure he believed them until he heard the matter-of-fact summation from the man himself. He'd heard MacKenzie was methodically ruthless, that he never stepped so far across the line of the law as to draw attention to it, that he applied whatever measures necessary to get the job done. And he always got the job done. He was quick, he was clean, and he was efficient. He didn't hide behind the fancy moniker of cattle detective or stock inspector, though he preferred the term "arbitrator" to "hired killer." Jamison didn't care what he called himself or how much he charged, as long as he did what he was paid to do and didn't involve him in any sticky complications. With his own political ambitions, he couldn't afford them. That's why he'd come to the best and why he'd pay for it without a further quibble.

He started counting out bills on the tabletop while MacKenzie calmly finished his smoke.

"Killing's not what I have in mind, Mr. MacKenzie," Jamison explained as the stack of cash continued to increase. "If you can avoid violence and just bully them with your reputation, I'd prefer it. Just knowing you're on my payroll might be enough to send them scattering." Then he glanced up at the gunman hopefully, so anxious himself, the scent of fear was almost as strong as that of the whiskey he'd used to buck up his bravery before crossing the barroom.

"We need to come to an understanding, sir." The man's politeness gave before a tug of impatient explanation. "If I take your money, I won't ask questions of you and you won't ask any of me. If these folks were easy to spook, you could have done the job yourself. You take me on, I do things my way. I'm not out to spill blood, but if it comes to that, I won't shy off from it. And neither will you. Are we agreed?"

Jamison swallowed hard, forcing down the bitter taste of what he was doing. "Yes."

Two hundred in greenbacks lay in a stack on the table between them. MacKenzie made no move to take it, and Jamison began a nervous fidgeting.

"Another thing," came the deceivingly quiet drawl. "Once we start this, we finish it. No backing out on either side. I have a reputation to uphold, and I happen to think a lot more of it than I do of you and your private dealings. I pride myself on being a man of my word, and once given, I will honor it to the death. I will expect the same from you, sir."

Had the man's stare been less direct, Jamison might have laughed over the idea of integrity in a hired gun. But because MacKenzie's gaze never flickered, the rancher kept his opinions to himself. Wisely.

MacKenzie's big hand flattened the pile of bills beneath it, making a firm claim. Jamison exhaled noisily in relief, grateful to get the business end behind him. He was a rancher, not a man given to violence. He'd done all he could to avoid it, but the time for talk was past. Action was called for, and as the gunman so aptly put it, he didn't want any of the blood to stain his hands—at least not directly.

Jamison nodded, eager to leave now that the unsavory task was done. "When can I expect you, Mr. MacKenzie?"

"I'll be there shortly. I have some business to tie up first."

Jamison waited for him to say more, but the big man was silent, his stare unnerving in its dismissal. "Well, then," the rancher rumbled, "I guess that's that."

"Good day, sir."

Dalton MacKenzie watched the anxious rancher wind his way through the crowded Deadwood barroom. Only after the bat-wing doors swung shut did he begin to count the money again, smiling wryly. He had little care for those who depended on others to command respect for them, even if the man had saved him from an unpleasant drop. That didn't mean he had to feel beholden. Even if he did, business was business. He hadn't asked the man to save his life and would cut no special deals because of it. The best he could do to even the score was to do the job for which he was paid. And paid handsomely.

Two hundred was a lot of money for a man to claim on word of mouth alone. At one time he would have gloated over it, letting the figure inflate his pride, but now the amount seemed unimportant. Too many miles and too much bloodshed dulled the onetime thrill. Now it was just another job to do, one of an endless many for as long as he could intimidate with his very presence and maintain a faster hand and cooler head. It paid to remain detached; it kept the mind more sharp, the hand steadier. And it helped him sleep at night after he rode away.

As if any man in his occupation rested well.

He picked up the wad of bills and folded them away in the pocket of his coat, shaking off his odd mood as he did so. Maybe he would take some time off when this piece of work was done. He had a brimming bank account, enough to support the orphanage that had fostered him well into the next century, if he chose to forgive them for their reluctant charity. Or he could go to San Francisco and realize a long-held dream of shedding his image for a respectable life.

"Respectable" was what they called men like Jamison, men who hired gun-handy strangers to settle their affairs. What he had was better than that. At least there was honor in not pretending to be other than what he was.

The very final conclusion to any argument.

He heard the man's approach long before he actually lifted his gaze to acknowledge it. Out of habit one hand disappeared off the tabletop. The gesture was one of unconscious self-preservation which met both friend and foe.

"Hey, Mac. Ranging kinda far north, ain'cha?"

Latigo Jones paused next to the empty chair, waiting for the reappearance of that right hand to signal it was all right to have a seat. With a welcoming smile, Dalton waved him into it.

"I go where there's money to be made. Besides, I got the feeling I was wearing thin on my welcome down in New Mexico. Man has to mind his instincts about when it's time to move on unless he wants to stay planted permanently. If you know what I mean."

Latigo grinned. He did. He dropped into the chair and provided his own bottle and two glasses. He filled both without being asked, with the casual assumption that friends of long standing had between them. That's what the two of them were, friends, unless their job of the moment required them to be otherwise. Even if and when the situation called for them to pull guns upon each other, it wasn't something they took personally. They'd been in the business too long to think that. They drank and took some time to reminisce, both enjoying the moment the way they enjoyed the whiskey.

"How much you asking for up front these days, Mac?" Jones gave a soft whistle when he was told. "Hell, you must be close to a millionaire by now, as busy as you been keeping. Guess I'll probably hear any day now that you done gone and retired and headed for that good life you're always talking about out in California."

Dalton didn't return the smile because there was more than just a trace of mockery in his friend's words. Latigo was a firm believer that retirement for their kind came in one form: horizontal. But some day, maybe soon, Dalton meant to prove him wrong. He lifted his glass in a toast. "You be watching for that telegram from the coast."

"I will. Until then, you be watching your back."

And they both drank to that.

Latigo set down his glass with a satisfied sigh then pushed back from the table. "Sorry I can't sit a spell and spin some windies with you, but I got some place to be."

"Working?"

Latigo grinned wide. "It's either working or whoring, and I can't do one until I finish the other."

Dalton returned the smile. "Maybe we'll run into each other again some day soon."

Latigo Jones's eyes took on a flat black sheen even as his face held to its jovial expression. "Maybe we will, old friend. Maybe we will."

There was nothing the least bit enjoyable about riding in a Concord Coach on its run from Deadwood to Cheyenne. Jude Amos grabbed for the overhead strap as the lumbering conveyance struck another rut. She tried not to wince as her neighbor's elbow caught her smartly in the ribs. The next time she had to go to Fort Laramie on business, she'd remember to wear more padding. Surely she'd be black and blue for weeks after this trip over the washboard someone had the wry humor to call a road. More like the ever-rolling Black Hills in miniature, she thought as another bounce launched her into the air.

Just then, before she had settled once more, a mighty forward jolt sent her flying over the knees of the man seated opposite.

To catch her balance, her hands flung outward and, to her humiliation, clamped down immodestly upon a brace of rock-hewn thighs. The momentum was too great to stop her from colliding, head first, with a form as yielding as a canyon wall. For a moment she was drowning in the heavy fleece of his coat lapels, sucking up the scent of wool and warm man as she drew a startled gasp. Awareness of him slammed through her, harder than the initial impact, and stunned breathless, she lingered a moment longer than proper, lost to those potently male aromas.

"Are you all right, ma'am?"

The sound of his husky voice shocked her from her daze of discovery. Coming to her senses, Jude began to push away. When she tried to sit back for a breath and a little dignity, her sensible hat pulled cruelly on her hair and pins jabbed at her scalp. In her fretful struggle her hands groped all over the poor man's lap and chest in search of the source of her ensnarement. As she wriggled like a trout on a line, mortification only made her movements more inefficient.

"Here. Let me," came a soft command from

above, and she froze as he worked the netting free from his shirt button. Immediately her apologies spilled forth at a babbling rate—and were stilled by the intensity of his gaze. His smile appeared through a dark stubble of beard, and as charmed as a rabbit beneath the spell of a snake, she found she couldn't move.

"Don't trouble yourself, ma'am. Just one of the hazards of overland travel."

With his big hands circling her upper arms, he eased her back upon her own seat. Then, after tipping his hat, he went back to his dozing, dismissing her from his mind.

After casting a quick glance at the four others sharing their face-to-face accommodations and finding them equally indifferent to her blushes, Jude knotted her shaking hands together and grappled for a sense of calm. Her palms still tingled from the firmly contoured feel of warm denim. It was ridiculous, of course, for a woman of her years and her pragmatic disposition to be so girlishly flustered by accidental contact with the opposite sex. However, years that lent vast experience in life held no such stockpile when it came to love.

Jude Amos was an unkissed spinster of twenty-five.

She sat stiffly on the seat, denying herself another look across the coach. Instead, pretending her heart wasn't yet pounding, she stared out the window toward a landscape shrouded by trail dust, out over the rugged land that was her home.

Everyone thought Bart Amos was a fool when he moved his family out into the middle of a desolate no-man's-land and tried raising a crop in wind-raked soil. They'd been right about the farm. Not much grew in the stingy Wyoming clime, other

than thick bunch grass. But Amos was no quitter,
and his vision proved he was no fool either. When
the Cheyenne and Black Hills Stage and Express
Line answered the call of gold fever and started
setting up a five-day route, Amos's property was
sitting as the crow flies between them. He wasted no
time bidding for the chance to operate a way station.
He managed to turn a floundering farm into a
lucrative business—one Jude opted to continue
when her father passed away. That had been two
years ago. The hard work it demanded suited her
demeanor, just as a sense of purpose filled her
otherwise empty days. Wyoming was progressive in
its thoughts on a woman doing a man's job, and as
soon as she proved herself capable, no one had a
problem with her running the station. It was a good
life, a secure one—until Patrick Jamison sought to
change things.

Jamison made no secret about wanting every inch
of land butting up against the Chugwater River to
host his ever-growing herd of cattle. His bid for her
acreage was both curse and blessing to her. His
buyout would bring her the money to escape the
desolation of her lonely station, to experience some
of the life she'd been denied. But she hung back
from accepting, her reluctance stemming from more
than her own personal fears of leaving her sheltered
life behind. She had her brother to consider. At
twenty, Sammy Amos had a man's body wrapped
around a young boy's mind. He had no memory of
their earlier years when they'd lived in the city,
when Sammy had been ridiculed mercilessly for
being different. But Jude's memory was painfully
clear. At the station he had the chance to feel useful.
What opportunities would he have if she wrested
him from the security of the only home he knew,

forcing him into an environment where differences were greeted with hostility?

None. Which was why she hadn't given Jamison his answer.

Now, if she were to believe what the others were saying, the offer wouldn't be made again. Patrick Jamison wasn't a patient man. He would ask first, and when he didn't hear the answer he wanted, he would take.

Jude had been uneasy about this trip to Fort Laramie. She didn't like leaving Sammy alone with just their elderly Sioux cook, Joseph Otaktay, to watch over things; things were growing ever more dangerous in their isolated little valley since Jamison had begun his push to gobble up all the land. So far she'd tried to stay uninvolved, standing firm against the violence other small ranchers were demanding, and so far they had listened to her reasonings. A time would come when they wouldn't, a time she was dreading. If she could have postponed the trip, she would have, but supplies were low. An absence of four days was necessary, and she was anxious to return to the familiar.

At least she had been until the handsome gunman had settled across from her and reminded her of the special things in life she was missing.

She'd seen him in Fort Laramie as the stage had begun its boarding. He was coming down the outside stairs of one of the saloons, and Jude became intrigued by his struggle to descend with a half-dressed woman latched determinedly to his lips. He'd take a step, pause for a bit of tongue tangling, take another, then reacquaint himself with his scantily clad armful. Jude should have looked away in modest horror, but her gaze and her imagi-

nation were caught by the way the man's big hands
stroked up long, stockinged legs to grasp a mound
of silk-covered buttock. The woman responded by
winding both arms and legs about him as he fought
the drag of gravity that would carry them both end
over frilled and gartered end to the dusty street
below. It was a shamelessly bold display, and Jude
was shamelessly enthralled. Imagine, in broad daylight. Imagine the feel of those roving hands and
seeking lips right out where anyone could be
watching.

Imagine . . .

And Jude was, because no man had ever grabbed
her in a brazen embrace. And she was wondering,
breathlessly, what it would be like.

The woman was obviously a prostitute, no one a
decent female should envy. Yet, in that moment,
Jude did because it seemed to her that the red-
haired harlot was enjoying the kissing as well as the
being kissed.

Scandalous. Fascinating.

Then, before Jude had the sense to look away, the
big man disengaged the woman's hold on him and
indiscreetly tucked a roll of greenbacks down the
top of one stocking with the playful snap of a
ribboned garter. And, to Jude's dismay, he turned
and started right for the stage, where she sat with
cheeks flaming, breath chugging, and imagination
careening out of control. He never once looked back
to where he'd left the sated whore, in nearly undressed disarray on the stairs, but rather sauntered
across the street with the long, slightly bowlegged
stride of a rugged man who lived mostly out of the
saddle. His strongly chiseled features were set upon
other matters, the night of passion already forgotten.

And that's when Jude stopped envying the other woman. To have had such a man, only to let him walk away unhampered by either conscience or commitment, to be merely a way station between two points, always the brief stopover but never the destination, that wasn't for her.

The colorful yellow-and-red coach had filled quickly, the backseat with a family by the name of Brockman—a man, woman, and child—and she, the only female wedged onto the two opposing benches. Luggage was lashed in a mountain to the top rack since both boots were already filled with mail, small express freight items, and gold, she supposed from the bristling appearance of a well-armed guard who rode up top with the cheerfully profane driver. Jude was squashed up against the window, a boon since her companion to the left had an apparent aversion to bathing or changing his clothes. And the big man was settled opposite her, his long legs bent and straddled to accommodate her skirts. Those long, sturdy legs around which the whore had been wrapped.

Those muscle-hardened thighs she'd felt beneath her palms.

Jude shifted in her seat, trying to rid her mind of what she'd seen on the stairs, trying to close the man out of her thoughts. Difficult business when knee to knee with him and with darned little else to observe, as the wheels churned up a thick dust that obscured the scenery. Restless and disturbed by her odd mood, she studied him covertly through the fringe of her lashes.

He'd given her a polite glance when boarding, that quick obliging acknowledgment that men bestowed upon females who were either too old or too plain to hold any allure for them. He had murmured a genteel greeting and then leaned back with eyes closed, probably to catch up on all the sleep he'd missed while in that upstairs room. With his hat brim tipped low, he seemed determined to continue it now.

She could tell by looking at him that he was trouble. It was the air of bold confidence he exuded as much as the fast rig he wore cut low and strapped down tight. He was a man who paved his way with the bone-handled six-guns he toted butts forward. No cowboy was so finely garbed or meticulously groomed. She'd breathed in no scent of horse or saddle when pressed to his bosom. He smelled of fresh starch, a good cigar . . . and of the woman's cloying perfume. A gun for hire. She'd seen them often enough to know the signs: hands that never strayed too far from the holster, an aura of watchfulness that remained even behind closed eyes. And Jude found herself hoping he was passing through to business elsewhere.

That didn't stop her from wishing frivolously that such a man would pay her more than a moment's notice.

For one painful moment Jude Amos wished she'd been blessed with a pretty, feminine helplessness which would snag a man's protective interest the way her veil had his pearl button.

She wasn't a homely female. There was nothing about her regular features to make one wince and avert the eyes. Her face was round, her mouth a trifle wide, her skin a deep, unmarred gold. Her hair was brown and worn knotted sensibly at her nape. It had neither riots of curls nor thick, heavy waves but hung straight and fine when unbound, stubbornly refusing either. She'd always thought her clear gray eyes were her best attribute, along with the full, dark lashes she'd inherited from the mother she could barely remember. But eyelashes alone couldn't overcome the fact that she was plain, plain and simple. Nothing that would hurt the eyes but nothing to attract them either.

She thought of the saloon woman and pictured the same shocking costume as it would look if she wore it. Without the long, shapely legs and fleshy breasts, it would be just so much fabric and lace. Her own bosom was nicely rounded though hardly ample, but she lacked womanly softness. Her father had proudly pronounced her to be as sturdy as a pack mule. He'd meant it as a compliment, but that's not how a painfully shy and awkward young woman had taken it. After years of hard physical labor, her limbs were defined by muscle, not by cushiony, white flesh. She could slap the traces on three pair of horses as fast as any man. But that wasn't something that would inspire him to passion.

As if plain looks and angular build weren't bad enough, she was situated out in the middle of nowhere, tied down to a lonesome job and the care of her brother. If a man could overlook the one, he wouldn't be so charitable about the other. Those of slow wit like Sammy were thought better off shut away from the world, but Bart Amos hadn't agreed. And neither did Jude. She was fiercely protective of her younger sibling. What man would take on a plain woman and the burden of a man/child as well? Better she leave wishes alone and keep to practical purposes.

Jude was jerked from her dreaming by a sudden change in the coach's rhythm. The team had been whipped up into a gallop, and the stage plunged and pitched behind them. Inside, the passengers were tossed to and fro as if the Wyoming road had become a high-breaking sea. Jude clutched at the window frame, jaw clenched tight and muscles braced as she fought against the whip of motion. Was their driver crazy to go at such a dangerous pace? Or was it danger he was thinking to avoid? She thought of the gold in the boot and the armed guard on top, and her heart hurried at the possible consequences of both.

"What's happening?" the woman behind her cried out in fear, her strained voice rising over the wails of her frightened child. "Have the horses run away with us?"

"Nothing to worry about, ma'am," drawled the gunman opposite Jude. He spoke without opening his eyes or straightening his posture into a defensive pose. His statement was calm and even a bit bored. "My advice is you just sit back and let it happen. We're about to be robbed."

Chapter 2

The determined crack of a .44 proved the gunman's theory. Fire was immediately returned by the shotgun messenger in the box above. Screams from the woman in the rear seat joined in shrill harmony over the frightened wails of her youngster. Her own fears in unaccustomed tandem, Jude fought the desire to turn in her seat and slap the near hysterical woman silly in an effort to control her alarm. However, with the way the coach was pitching, that would have required a miraculous amount of balance. Jude was too busy clinging to her own bench to follow through on such an impulsive act.

"Stop it, Hattie," came a strained command from the woman's husband. "You're scaring the boy." Then the screams gave way to a gust of tears and a more charitable murmuring of, "Hush now, darlin'. It'll be all right."

At that moment Jude wished she had someone to hold and comfort her with those tender-toned words. But knowing no one would, she reached down inside herself for the necessary grit, dragging it up by quivering bootstraps until she was sitting ramrod straight on her seat, her lips as pinched as

17

the pleats on the backs of her gloves, her hands gripping for all they were worth. Her knees rattled shamelessly against the gunman's, with which they were laced in forced intimacy. She allowed herself to draw from their pillared strength. They were going to be robbed with only a few miles to go to her destination.

If violence had its way, she might never see Sammy again.

Her terror rose in nearly ungovernable waves. To contain it, she told herself consoling platitudes. Joe Varness was one of the line's best drivers. If anyone could coax a team into outdistancing highwaymen, it was Lucky Joe. Jude sucked a stabilizing breath, forcing herself to hear her own optimistic thoughts as she and her companions were tossed about within the confines of the coach. No stickup artists were going to get the best of Joe. He was known to careen around mountain ledges on two wheels, his whip snapping like pistol shots, without losing so much as a single piece of mail. She began to feel better, holding to that truth. This was the kind of daredevil, razor-sharp handling he was hired to do, the kind for which he lived.

But there came a time when even Lucky Joe's well of good fortune went dry, and it was Jude's ill-timing that it was on this particular run.

A short-clipped cry sounded from above. Through the open window Jude saw the guard's rifle fall, followed by the slack bob of his hand as it dangled down into view, dripping a fearful amount of crimson. A scream wedged up into her throat. Behind her the shrieking began again, and Jude bit down hard to check her own panic.

Passengers and luggage alike were thrown carelessly forward and back as Joe hauled on the reins,

trying to bring the lumbering conveyance to a halt
before his companion toppled from the roof.

"Why is he stopping?" the fretful Mrs. Brockman
shrieked from out of the circle of her husband's
embrace. "We'll all be killed—or worse!"

The gunman opposite Jude thumbed back his hat,
finally taking an interest if not a concern in their
desperate situation. His assurances were soft-
spoken but carried a firm authority that would calm
a nervous horse or a vaporous woman.

"Now, ma'am, don't you worry. They most likely
put a higher stock in your values than your virtue."

Whether it was the circumstance or the insinua-
tion to which she took exception, the woman was
not to be quieted. "I will not hand over everything
we've worked for." Her tone grew querulous, unreasonable in its demand, as the coach rocked to a
stop and their inevitable meeting with the robbers
grew near. "John, you must do something! If you
were any kind of a man . . ." She let that trail off, an
unpardonable challenge to his virility, a goad that
was impossible to ignore.

"I'll take care of it, Hattie," came the expected
puff of foolish bravado, and the gunman groaned in
exasperation.

"Mister, you take care to see that your woman's
mouth doesn't get us all killed."

It was a politely given suggestion, one with which
Jude heartily agreed. This wasn't the time for incau-
tious words, not when their lives were on the line.
Suddenly there was so much for which she had to
live, so many dreams left unfulfilled, as the shock of
her mortality struck home.

Apparently Mrs. Brockman was not of the same
mind. The woman glared at the dapper gunfighter
with the same ill-concealed contempt with which

she'd viewed them all when boarding the coach. She'd stuck her haughty nose in the air then and had insisted the first two passengers vacate the rear seat so she wouldn't be crammed into close quarters with the others up front. Her husband had appeared embarrassed but had said nothing to discourage her petulant stand. He'd smiled with shame-faced relief when the two men gave up their spots to accommodate his wife. And Jude feared he'd succumb now, over his better judgement, to her sharp-tongued orders.

"John, are you going to let him talk to me—"

Pushed into a corner by his wife's outrage and by the expectant lift of his son's gaze, the poor fellow mumbled, "You'd best apologize to my wife."

The gunman smiled narrowly, a dangerous edge creeping in behind the congenial front. "Maybe you should be apologizing for her."

When Brockman hesitated, the woman spoke up impatiently. "John, are you going to take that from a man who's too cowardly to do anything but sit back and wait to be robbed?"

Enough. Jude's temper snapped. She twisted within the tight space, wrenching her torso about so she could glare at the woman with icy menace. "Shut up! I, for one, am not carrying anything that's worth more than my life. Unless you hold your husband and son more cheaply than your trinkets, you'll hand them over and say nothing. Common sense isn't cowardice. One man's been shot already. Doesn't that tell you that these men mean business?"

While the woman sat white-faced and huffing, Jude resumed her seat and found the man opposite regarding her with a twist of a smile. The look implied his admiration if not his thanks for a defense he hadn't felt was warranted.

"Spoken like a veteran of many a robbery."

She gave him a tremulous smile in return. "Just a veteran of living, Mr.—"

"MacKenzie, ma'am. Dalton MacKenzie."

His gaze held hers for a long moment. His eyes were blue, as bright as a Wyoming sky when windswept clear of clouds. He had time to tip his hat to her before the thundering approach of hoof-beats distracted them from their circumstances inside the coach.

Glancing outside, Jude drew a deep breath, determined to back her brave words with a show of staunch backbone, but behind her corseted breast, her heart was thrumming wildly . . . as much from the appreciative look from Mr. Dalton MacKenzie as from the danger at hand.

"You, on top! Throw down your arms!"

There were five of them atop scrawny horses which looked close to collapse from the chase. The men's faces were masked, and Jude took that for a good sign. If they didn't want their identities known, it was because they didn't want survivors to tell of them later, which meant they were going to survive. The knot of apprehension eased a notch within her belly.

One of the men leapt easily from the saddle to the top of the coach. It rocked slightly as the villain went about his work, stripping the upper boot of its valuables, while another of them did the same in the rear. Covering the passengers with an ancient dragoon pistol which looked huge and ominous to Jude, another of the yet mounted men motioned to the coach's interior.

"Everybody out. Step lively now, and keep your hands clear of trouble."

Dalton MacKenzie was the first to leave the Concord. He disembarked with a nonthreatening spread of his hands as the men's gazes were immediately riveted to the fancy pair of irons he was toting beneath the sweep of his open coat. These men who were confident in their craft suddenly grew wary.

"Them's fine-looking pieces, mister. Don't be getting no ideas about puttin' 'em to work."

"You've got your business, I've got mine. I don't see any reason for the two of them to tangle."

MacKenzie's amiable drawl did little to relieve their tension. Keeping the dragoon trained on his middle shirt button, the robber called, "What the rest of you waitin' on? An invitation? Get on out here."

Jude stepped down next. Her concerned gaze went quickly to the box where Joe Varness was binding up the arm of his shotgun rider. The wound didn't appear serious and Joe seemed willing to part company with his cargo, so Jude wasn't one to argue. The only things she carried were peppermint sticks for Sammy and some licorice for their cook. If the bad men had a sweet tooth, she would surrender the candy without qualm. Following the directing nod of the mounted leader, she moved to stand beside Dalton, trying to adopt his air of nonchalance. He gave her a quick close-lipped smile that added starch to her stance, then he returned his attention to the robbers.

The other four who'd been stuffed in front with them were next to climb down, and they hurriedly formed a line on Jude's left. They were as ragged as the bandits' horses, men leaving the hills broke in spirit as well as pocket, from the looks of them. None seemed of a mind to protest the holdup, having nothing to lose but a delay in travel time.

Then came the young family from the rear seat of the coach, and a premonition of disaster to come rippled through Jude. Perhaps it was due to the whipped frustration on the husband's face as he reached up for his son, then his pretty wife. That chill of dread sank home when the prissy Hattie Brockman appeared, her features puckered sullenly, her provoking glare settling upon her husband before she would take his assisting hand. At that same unfortunate moment the robber who'd finished looting the rear boot came around to preempt the offer of aid, his own beefy fingers closing around the female's elbow.

"Watch yer step there, ma'am. I'll help you down, then I'll help myself to that fancy little handbag yer carrying."

"Unhand me, you brute! John!"

A call summoning tragedy.

"Let her be!"

And then everything went to hell in a hurry.

The young husband seized the bandit's shoulder, jerking him back from his wife. The outlaw responded with a lip-splitting backhand. Incensed and forced to action by his wife's foolishness, John Brockman made an unforgivable grab for the robber's gun. Jude uttered a shocked oath, certain she was about to view the ill-advised gallant's death. From the corner of her vision, she saw the massive dragoon level into play. Her shout of warning was instinctive but too late, she was sure, to save the ill-fated man.

Rescue came from an unexpected source. Beside her, Jude felt more than actually saw Dalton Mac-

Kenzie move. With a speed she wouldn't have
guessed such a big man could possess, he charged
the pistol-bearing outlaw, making the most of the
man's surprise. He got as far as gripping the bad
man's forearm and wrestling it upward when the
heavy pistol discharged—not in a harmless shot but
in a devastating misfire. An explosive cloud of black
powder flashed from the rear of the gun, igniting
tongues of fire that took Dalton MacKenzie full in
the uplifted face. His outcry was one of surprise and
pain as he hung tenaciously onto the outlaw's arm
while smoke and fire obscured his vision. He didn't
let go until the butt of the big gun clubbed him
savagely across the brow, dropping him to the
ground without further sound or movement.

Jude forgot all else as she stared in alarm at the
large form crumpled nearly at her feet. His face was
in the dust, and no puffs of it betrayed his breathing.
From beneath the skewed brim of his Stetson, a thin
line of blood began to roll, a trickle that became a
steady stream as it puddled on the dry ground in a
vivid pool. She took a quick step toward him but
found herself facing the rifle point of one of the
thieves.

"Don't meddle in it, ma'am," his growl warned as
his gaze cut from her to the brace of handsome
pistols the downed gunfighter wore. He bent, heav-
ing MacKenzie up just far enough to reach the
buckle, releasing the gun belt. "Guess he won't
have much need for these" was his smug contention.

Jude watched as Dalton flopped back facedown
into the dust. She stood trembling in a paralysis of
anxiety, watching that lake of vital fluid grow.

The rest of the robbery went off with smooth
precision. Valuables were surrendered in a stunned

sort of silence, even from the shaking hands of the cause of all their woes. Pouches of gold were yanked from beneath the driver's seat, and after celebrating that discovery with loud whoops of gleeful greed, the attackers were quick to remount and disappear, rightly confident that the injured guard and passenger would prevent any attempted pursuit.

The instant they were freed from the restraint of the outlaw guns, Jude dropped down in a crumple of skirts at MacKenzie's side. With shaking hands on his massive shoulders, she rolled him with cautious care onto his back. And she gave a moaning epitaph.

The fearful nature of the gash at his temple paled beside the damage done by the discharge of the gun. Even the soot blackening his skin couldn't conceal the raw blisters rising from the scorch of the powder flash across the bridge of his nose and eyelids. She worried about the unseen harm, permanent damage to the eyes.

"I need some water and clean cloths," she called out in a remarkably steady voice. The need for immediate action shut down her emotional instability. A canteen was supplied along with a dubiously fresh neckerchief from one of the other passengers. She smiled her thanks, accepting both, then turned to tear a strip from her own petticoat to use instead. Folding it into a thick wadding, she wet it generously and applied the compress gingerly to his seared flesh.

"How's he doing?"

She glanced up at Joe Varness, unable to keep her concern from tightening her expression. "I don't know, Joe. He's unconscious. He took the brunt of the flash in the eyes. If he survives the blow to his head, I can't guarantee he'll ever see again."

The craggy-faced driver took in the significance of the motionless man's bared hips and the knowledge of his profession. "Could be he wouldn't want to survive crippled up thataway."

Taking his meaning, Jude's purpose took a turn of quiet desperation. "That's not up to us to decide. How's your man?"

"Paining and grumbling, but he'll see it through to the end of the line. How about him? He don't look like he'd stand the rest of the ride."

She made up her mind without applying any real conscious thought. The solution was just there, and she spoke it without concern to consequence. "My station is just down the way a few more miles. If you take it slow, he should be able to get that far at least. I'm no doctor, but I can make him comfortable until you can send one back this way."

Joe scratched his whiskered chin. "I doan know, Miz Amos. That's a lot of responsibility you'd be taking on for not much of a return."

"It's a man's life, Joe. I think that's worth a little inconvenience. Besides, he wouldn't be in this situation if he hadn't been trying to save one of your passengers."

The driver sighed unhappily. "Guess you got me there. Might even be some remuneration in it for you from the line."

Receiving money for her efforts was hardly behind her offer. Nor was it common charity or Samaritan impulse.

It was the way the big gunfighter had made her quiver inside with a warming of female passion.

The coach limped along at a gingerly pace with four of the male passengers lining the rooftop and the two injured men stretched out inside. Jude had resumed her earlier seat, but instead of snatching covert glances at the handsome gunman from across the coach, she had him weighing heavily in her lap. There, she cradled his head in hopes of absorbing any further trauma. He was alarmingly still, looking uncomfortably like a corpse with the swaddling of cloth over his eyes. The bleeding from his head wound had finally stopped. The area was swollen, and angry colors bloomed there like a desert sunset, all purples and blues, reds and yellows. Occasionally she pressed fluttering fingertips to the side of his warm throat, just to assure herself his brave heart was still beating.

Brave. Oh, yes, he was brave. His unexpected heroism made her ashamed of all her earlier assumptions that came from recognizing him as a man who lived by the gun. She'd noted the polished grips that said violence was this man's religion. His dandyish, well-fitting clothes suggested personal pride, but she took that to mean a degree of self-interest not willingly extended to the outside world. And then there was the way he'd handled the harlot on the stairs, with a freedom and disregard that didn't speak well of his attitude toward females. Yet he'd dispelled all her preconceived notions with one selfless act of courage, by throwing himself into the line of fire to save a stranger from his own folly.

And Jude prayed he would not die before she had the chance to ask him why.

Chapter 3

T hey made Amos Station by mid-afternoon, four hours off their regular arrival time. It wasn't as grand as some of the home stations, but it was home to Jude.

After the stage route opened, crude stops sprang up along the trail to meet the needs of the line, but they offered little in the way of comfort or hospitality. They were part store, part hotel, with a long plank bar for the thirsty and the idle of the community. They dotted lonely roadsides and were a part of every town, constructed of whatever was handy, be it log, sod, stone, or adobe brick.

As a good run for a team was twelve miles, swing stations which offered no more than a change of horses averaged that far between them. The home stations marked the beginning and end of each day's journey and were spaced at forty- to fifty-mile intervals to supply lodgings and eating facilities, telegraph, ticket and post offices, a store, a barn with stables and staging equipment, and the best livestock available. Some were ranch houses where dwellers did double duty as agents and cattlemen. The Amos Station fell into that later category of being more home than hovel, and while it wasn't set up as a hostelry, overnight guests who wished to stretch out before the hearth were never turned away.

Set in the Chugwater Valley where perpendicular bluffs formed an unbroken line along the horizon, the Amoses' fair-sized wooden house boasted good stabling and barns a short way off inside their own separate enclosure. A huge vegetable garden, the last legacy of Bart Amos's farm, was planted in neat rows just before a grove of box elder trees opened onto rolling pasture. It was a serene sight which never failed to stir Jude's emotions when she thought of what it had meant to her father before her and to her and her brother now: freedom and subsistence. And loneliness.

As the rocking coach pulled into the yard, a figure appeared on the porch. What lifted Jude's heart then was love, pure and simple.

Sammy Amos was a big, strapping young man with a head of softly curling brown hair, his mother's shining good looks, and biceps that strained the checked cotton shirt he wore. At twenty, with his fair features and brawny physique, he should have been breaking tender female hearts all over the county. But a fluke of nature prevented the growth of mind in normal tandem with body, so Sammy would never develop from little brother to courting beau. He was caught in the perpetual innocence of childhood, with a sweet disposition and willingness to please which made him every bit as devoted as the big, shaggy dog standing at his knee. Both began wiggling all over with excitement as they spied the stage.

"Joseph! Joseph! Stage is a-comin'! Could be Jude's home!"

From out of the shadows of the porch emerged a

wizened Native American with thin, white braids
hanging down almost to his flour-dusted apron. He
could have been in his fifties or over a hundred the
way his leathery features held every wrinkle of
hardship his people had endured. He'd long since
given up a warrior's life to huddle his tired bones
close to the Amoses' cook fire, where he could
continue to be useful. He wasn't their servant, he
was family, an ancient great uncle who enjoyed
telling metaphors about the meaning of life and
wasn't above rapping knuckles with his wooden
spoon when he thought it was warranted. The three
of them had combined strengths over the previous
two years to keep Bart Amos's dream on the isolated
Wyoming prairie alive by making it their own.

Jude had tried and even managed to convince
herself that she'd succeeded until a host of scurrying
emotions controlled her heart and mind as she held
the injured gunfighter in her lap, making her realize
how empty those borrowed dreams had become.

It was then that Joseph's still keen eyesight fixed
upon the bandaged guard and took in the significance of the passengers on top. He started out in a
stooped run to meet the coach with a perplexed
Sammy and the barking hound at his heels.

As soon as the stage jounced to a full stop, Jude
flung open the door to call, "Joseph, one of the
passengers has been injured. Fix up Sammy's bed
for him."

A brief second of relief passed over the weathered
face in recognition of Jude's safety, then Joseph
ambled back toward the house to see to prepara-
tions.

Sammy had stepped up on the front wheel to get
a closer look at the wounded shotgun messenger.

"Holy crow, what happened? Were it outlaws? Were it Injuns?"

"Outlaws, Sammy," Joe Varness explained. He was typical of the stage drivers who, for all their burliness and profanity, held a soft spot for the youngsters living out on the windswept route. Like many of them, Joe carried packages of firecrackers and candy in his pockets to earn delighted smiles from those lonesome children. And all the drivers held a special fondness for Sammy's simple charm and man-sized ability. He had a way with animals like no one they'd seen, and teams hitched at the Amos Station were always groomed and gleaming, as was the tack Sammy spent tireless hours fussing over. He mended worn spots and reattached the tinkling harness bells he always seemed to be able to hear coming long before the stage appeared. He knew every horse by name and every driver's preference, pairing the two together like a diligent matchmaker to find the best combinations. Between Sammy's deft handling and Joseph's flaky biscuits, which were always hot and ready for the road, the Amos Station was an anticipated layover.

"Give ole Harvey a hand down, would you, Sammy? He took a bullet to the arm and is feeling a mite poorly."

"Yessir, Joe." With his Herculean strength, he plucked the guard down from the box as easily as if he'd been a sack of mail, and when the wounded man swooned on his feet, Sammy hoisted him over one broad shoulder. "Where you want I should put him, Jude?"

"Stretch him out on one of the front-room benches, Sammy," she instructed, then directed several of the passengers to assist her with their

injured hero. "Careful now," she cautioned as they
angled Dalton out of the coach. "Mind his head."
She hopped down and led the way up to the house.
Trailing in the rear came the unrepentant woman,
her son, and her shamefaced husband.

The winged guard was groaning his way back to
consciousness under Joseph's care when Jude
brought the slack body of Dalton MacKenzie inside.
Sammy turned in curiosity, then suddenly went
still, his big body stiff, his gentle features going
slack with incomprehensible shock as he stared at
his sister.

"Sammy, what is it?" Jude asked in alarm as she
gestured the bearers toward the back room. Then, as
wetness gathered and gleamed in the boy's dark
eyes, she gave him her full attention. "Sammy?"

He made a soft, guttural sound which rose up into
a wounded wail, a sound so full of pain and anxiety
that Jude rushed to take him into her arms, holding
him tight.

"Sammy? Sammy, honey, what is it?" she coaxed
as his broad shoulder quaked beneath the rub of her
palm.

"Did them bad men sh-shoot you? Is you gonna
d-die like D-daddy an' Mama?"

"What? I'm not hurt, Sammy. Whatever made
you think so?"

"Th-that color there on your dress," he sniveled
against her dusty collar. "Th-that there is blood.
Sammy knows what blood looks like. You ain't
gonna die and leave Sammy alone. Promise you
ain't."

As gently as she could, Jude pried him back so she
could glance down at her travel-stained garment. It
was discolored by blotches of the gunfighter's blood

about the bodice and skirt. Smiling, she patted his damp cheek. "That's not mine, Sammy. That man who's resting in your bed, it's his. He was hurt in the robbery. Do you understand?"

"Not yours."

"Not mine."

His breath gusted out in a huge sigh. Then, like a Wyoming storm, his worries were gone, forgotten as quickly as they'd blown up, and he trotted over to his bedroom to get a look at the man occupying his sheets.

Controlling her own urge to rush in to do the same, Jude stopped first to check on Harvey's progress and was satisfied with Joseph's diagnosis that he would live. Only when the elderly Sioux went into the back room did she surrender to her anxiousness and follow.

MacKenzie was draped across her brother's bed. Sammy was no stripling, but the gunfighter swamped the crude wood frame with the bulk of his sheep-lined coat and long, sturdy legs, making Jude feel uncomfortably overwhelmed by the very size and presence of the man. Not that he was in any way threatening. He was dead to the world—actually closer to dead than alive. Beneath the bristle of his short, dark beard, his face was as pale as the bed linens, except where the robber had bashed his head. That vivid contusion stood out in stark contrast, looking so sore, she winced. Joseph had put a clean, wet cloth over his eyes, so she was spared the sight of the damage there.

"Will he lose his vision?" she ventured in a small voice.

The old Sioux glanced up, his attention piqued by the fragile quality of the question. "It is too soon to say."

"But he'll live?" Again the tentative hopefulness that had the ancient one frowning slightly.

"It is too soon to say."

"How is he?" Joe Varness asked from over her shoulder, his sudden words startling her from her absorption with the injured man.

"Bad," Joseph said in all honesty. "If he lives through the night, it will be a sign from the spirits. If he wakes up, he will have a chance. If he sees again . . ." His thin shoulders gave an eloquent shrug.

"But he shouldn't be moved, should he?" Jude stuck in hurriedly. "I mean, that would decrease his chance for recovery, wouldn't it?"

The old man studied her for an inscrutable minute, saying nothing, while her hot features said all too much. Then he eased her discomfort by murmuring, "He should not be moved."

Jude smiled tautly at the driver, justified by the Sioux's summation. She wouldn't lose her gunman until she had an answer to her curiosities. "We'll tend him here as best we can. If there's a doctor available in Cheyenne, send him on the next stage. If not, and if he's ready for travel, I'll put him on the next southbound coach. It'll be here late tomorrow." *If he's still alive* was what went unspoken.

"Sure he won't be no trouble to you, Miz Amos?"

Jude stood more erect, assuming an air of authority. "Of course not. Joseph is as accomplished at healing as he is at biscuits."

Talk of biscuits had the driver's gaze shifting toward the other room with expectation and his thoughts returning to business. "We shouldn't ought to tarry—just long enough to get Harvey patched fit to ride. The superintendent will want to know about the stickup so's they can get after them varmints. Not that they have a hope in hell of catchin' 'em."

With a reluctance to leave the bedroom that she couldn't hide from Joseph Otaktay's astute eyes, Jude offered, "I'll set you up with some food for the road, Joe."

The driver beamed. "Why thanky kindly, Miz Amos. I'll see the feller's bag is brought in."

Jude tried to keep the bedridden gunman out of her mind as she served up a pan of hot biscuits as well as some dark coffee for the passengers. Harvey had recovered adequately to handle his own cup, but his color was poor and his hand shaking from loss of blood. The single men complimented her on the repast. From the family of three, there wasn't a sound, nor would any of them meet her eye as she poured the boy and his mother glasses of sweetened milk.

"Time to load up," Joe announced at last, brushing crumbs from his drooping mustache. "We want to be making Cheyenne by nightfall. Looks to be some weather blowing in, and I'd like as not to be somewheres dry when it breaks."

There were mumbles of thanks as the weary travelers filed out and headed for the coach. Sammy was adjusting the harnessing, making sure all lay flat and true along the backs of the fresh team, then he waited until Joe climbed aboard for the signal to fasten the left tug of the left horse which would tell the animals all was ready to go.

Jude stood on the porch, watching her fleeting companions board. Soon they would be going about their lives, and she would remain behind within the limits of her own. How suddenly melancholy that played upon her soul. She was surprised when Mr.

Brockman hesitated after handing up his wife, then turned to approach her, hat in hand.

"Ma'am, I'd be obliged to you if you'd tell that fellow how grateful I am for what he did. It may not mean much . . . considering—"

Jude smiled. "I'm sure it will. Thank you."

"Thank you, ma'am." He settled his low-crowned hat and slunk back to the stage where the door stood open, awaiting him. His wife's disapproving countenance framed the window. Jude didn't envy the poor man his lot and, with a sigh, returned to her own as the team pulled away at a gallop.

Except the sameness of her lot had just been altered by the man who lay inside.

Joseph was with him. She could tell the old man had something on his mind by the way he glanced up at her for a brief scrutiny before turning, without comment, back to his care of the injured man. She waited but the silence stretched out, unbroken. She was used to the Sioux's thoughtful broodings. He would sometimes mull something over for days while deciding how to approach it. It was like the fermenting process; one just couldn't hurry it. But finding patience wasn't all that easy.

"Where is Sam?" the old man asked.

"Wiping down the team. They were put to some heavy use when Joe tried to outrun the outlaws." She shivered as she considered all that had happened, and her arms came up to band about her middle to hold in further chills of memory. The movement didn't escape the old man.

"You were not harmed?"

"No. I—I was scared. I know it's always a possibility and I've seen looted coaches roll in here hundreds of times but . . . it's not the same as looking down a rifle barrel at the prospect of your own dying. I had always thought I'd be braver, but I did nothing to save myself."

The old man sighed. "Bravery is knowing when to act and when to wait. This was a time to wait, I think."

"But he didn't wait." She nodded toward the still figure. "And he saved lives . . . maybe at the cost of his own."

Joseph didn't argue, but again that veiled look of speculation touched upon her. "Help me get him undressed." At Jude's sudden flushes, he urged impatiently, "He will rest easier, and I do not believe he will be going anywhere that will require a coat and vest."

Jude's colored deepened. "Yes, of course."

She bent to work the sleeves of jacket and coat down from the impressive shoulders as Joseph held the motionless man in a seated position. His head hung down, causing a stray lock of dark hair to curl upon his brow. Jude stared at it in fascination, compelled by the want to brush it aside with the gentle sweep of her fingers. And she would have if Joseph hadn't been staring at her with that unblinking stoicism. Instead she went to work on the buttons of the gunfighter's shirt. Pearl buttons. Fine material. Custom-made for a man his size. Jude's fingers trembled slightly as she considered that solid breadth and length. Her senses were alive with the scent of him: warm man, starched linen, intimate aromas as foreign to her nose as the salty tang of the distant seas. And just as alluring. She managed to wriggle his shirt over his head, leaving him clad in muscle-hugging long johns. Joseph eased him down to the mattress once more with a grumbled, "I can see to the rest."

Jude straightened, fluttering her hands together

anxiously, not wanting to leave, not sure she should stay. And fearful of the conclusions Joseph seemed to be drawing.

The old man fingered the discarded vest. "What kind of man is this one with his fancy clothes and clean hands? What do you know about this one we have brought under our roof?"

Jude couldn't be less than honest. "I fear he is a hired gun. He wore a cut-down rig, but the bandits stole it off him."

"And you ask that such a man stay with us?" Joseph's gaze was reproachful and she knew why. He hated violence, even the threat of it, for he'd lost his heritage to soldiers' guns and greed.

"I cannot vouch for his character, Joseph, but he was well spoken and his act of courage saved a life, maybe more. For that I cannot condemn him."

"But you did not have to offer to care for him."

Joseph was getting too close to the truth Jude was trying to hide, even from herself. "It was my Christian duty to offer."

"Hummph." Not being a Christian and having little interest in their ways, Joseph refrained from comment.

Just to prove he had no foundation for his suspicions, Jude confronted them head on. "Are you saying you believe I have another reason? Whatever could it be?"

Joseph's black eyes gleamed like reflective stone as he peered up at her. "Have I said anything?"

"Joseph, you don't need to *say* anything. I can read your expression."

This seemed to distress him, for a Native American prided himself on his ability to cloak his true emotions. "And what do you read?" he demanded haughtily.

He had her there. To say anything was, in fact, to condemn herself. Could she tell him that she coveted the care of the injured man to sooth her own loneliness? No. So she scowled and wisely said nothing more about hidden meanings and silent accusations. Instead she asked, "What can you do for his eyes? Shall I get the Frazer's?"

Joseph frowned. He didn't share the belief that axle grease was a cure-all for sores and wounds on man and beast, wondering why white men thought the Native American barbaric when they were so willing to slather their own in vile concoctions. "I think the spirit of clear water would do more to speed his healing. Bring me some gauze that will let in the balm of air and keep out contaminants. Then time and fate will tell the rest."

The storm Joe Varness predicted began to mount at the supper hour. Swollen clouds stacked atop each other, building to tremendous thunderheads. Brilliant flashes played eerily along the edge of the surrounding bluffs as the acrid scent of nature's energy charged the air. For a precaution Sammy stabled the stock and saw all the gates secured before fidgeting at the table like a nervous child. His mongrel dog lay wound about his feet, whining uneasily. They had lamps lit even though it was hours till nightfall as an unnatural darkness settled forbiddingly.

"We got some blow a-comin', don't we?" Sammy asked, eyeing the strobes of light through the partially pulled curtains.

"Just winter giving springtime a last grumble before moving on," Jude assured him with a calming smile. "You can bed down out here in front of the hearth with Joseph tonight."

Sammy brightened at that. "Biscuit too?"

"Biscuit too."

At the sound of his name, the cur dog thumped his heavy tail.

"That sounds like grand fun. You tell me some of your stories, Joseph?"

Joseph promised, secretly pleased by the young man's interest. Sammy never lost his childlike enthusiasm for legends and tall tales, and unlike adults, he never tired of their retelling. Joseph, who had no grandsons of his own to whom to pass his myths along, found a satisfying fulfillment entertaining in the ways of his ancestors . . . even if it was to a *wasichu* instead of one of his own.

"How long is that there fella gonna stay in my bed?"

Jude's gaze dropped to her plate. *Forever* was her guilty wish. But she said, "Until he feels better. Is that all right with you, Sammy?"

The broad shoulders shrugged. "Guess so. What's his name?"

"Dalton MacKenzie."

"Where's he headed?"

"I can't say that I know."

"What's he do? Is he a farmer? A rancher? A banker?"

Joseph gave her a look. Jude understood it and smiled in the face of the boyish curiosity, agreeing with Joseph's unspoken suggestion that they keep the gunman's profession from the impressionable young man. What good would it do for the boy to know they housed a potential killer? "You'll have to save your questions for when he can answer them."

Sammy moaned. "Awww, Jude. I doan know if I can wait that long!"

"Well, there's no help for it. But you can help

clear this table and help Joseph tidy his kitchen before bedtime. If you want those stories, that is."

"Yessum, I shorely do." And he leapt up to gather the plates in an awkward pile.

Jude smiled to herself, watching him, thinking how many blessings were found in what most would consider a curse.

The stories wore down and finally silence was laced by the pop of the fire as its flickers created a muted reflection of the powerful light display disturbing the heavens. From where she sat in a chair angled beside the gunman's bed, the wind-driven rain seemed to echo the restlessness of her own soul. Jude didn't want to contemplate the moody passions rumbling through it. They were too complex for the late hour and she too vulnerable to their suggestion.

Oh, to have a man of her own abed, where she could watch over him with familiar possession rather than in pensive study. To have Joseph regaling *her* children with his fanciful tales until their eyes grew heavy and weariness won out over wonder. The thought tiptoed around her heart, not quite brave enough to march right through its barren terrain. She sighed and smiled at her own fantasy. Usually she didn't indulge in it. Perhaps it was this night of dramatic changes. Maybe it was the man stretched out on sheets she'd washed by hand. Most likely it was the lateness of the day and the exhaustion fuzzing her normal sensibilities with teases of romantic fancy. Whatever, it made for somber company and wistful spirits.

It was past the time for her to retire, and she'd long since run out of excuses to remain where she was. Their guest was resting comfortably, or at least

he appeared to be. The crisp sheet covering his chest
rose and fell with a rhythmic sameness, and as yet
there was no sign of fever or distress. Her own bed
beckoned from the loft overhead, where nightly she
slipped beneath her virgin blankets and settled for
the solitary sound of her own breathing. Tonight
there was something all too compelling about lingering in the near blackness, listening to the soft
inhalations of another. Those rich, deep sighs of life
tempted in a way she could scarcely imagine, making a music that called to her empty heart, a music
she longed to answer by entwining her own in dual
harmony.

Dangerous thoughts to entertain alone in the
darkness with a man who was a stranger. Delicious
dreams to entice a spinster's mind into the untried
realm of passion. Dawning desires that coaxed a
plain woman to consider impossibilities.

And because she was a sensible spinster who well
understood her own limitations, Jude Amos rose
from her musing watch to climb up to her chaste
quarters above, where she would spend the remaining hours of the night, tossing in the throes of
agitated folly.

Chapter 4

Thunder rolled.

It built upon itself with a savage fury from a grumble to a roar until the windowpanes shivered and the wallboards quivered with the force of angry vibration.

To Dalton MacKenzie, stirring to consciousness on the narrow bed, most of the noise was centered between his temples, reverberating there until sound and pain became inseparable, feeding upon one another like hungry wolves in great gulping pulses. He didn't dare move for the longest time, fearing he'd provoke that ravenous misery to even greater proportion. One thought crept in, a familiar repentant litany.

Never again. I'll never touch another drink of liquor as long as I live.

But then, as he lay there hiding from the agony that pounded at his brain, his mind grew more clear, and with that clarity came confusion.

Where had he been drinking? Usually with the punishment came the memory of some previous pleasure. He couldn't remember a saloon, a good meal with wine, or even a bottle in his own hotel room. The last thing he recalled was . . . was . . .

His brow furrowed slightly. Concentration brought an unavoidable shock of discomfort. He'd almost given up trying to drag memory up through the mire of pain when it came back in a surge. The stage. The holdup. The flash of a misfire seeming to cook the flesh on his face and dazzle his eyes in a flood of unholy brilliance, first white, then red. Then black. The same blackness that surrounded him now.

His eyes.

Unsteady fingers groped upward, finding the unbandaged swelling where pain massed like a seething volcano. He couldn't remember hitting his head, but the evidence was unarguable. And also insignificant compared to the connotations of what his exploring touch discovered next. Gauze covered his eyes in loose layers.

Again his mind replayed the pistol flash, the resulting glare, the tremendous burning brightness which became nothing at all. Nothing at all. His fingertips moved over the strip of gauze. *Nothing at all.* His breath shivered noisily, pulling panic up from deep inside until it engulfed all else.

A fierce thunderclap shook the very air around him. *Where was he?* His fingers hooked through the winding cloth, tugging, wrestling, peeling it up over the raw blistering that covered his brow. He scarcely felt the pain as burn adhered to fabric, tearing, opening fresh hurts aplenty. He was busy trying to pry apart eyelids that were fused together in sore, nearly lashless seams. Fear of the unknown and dread of the suspected pushed him beyond prudence, beyond the inner reasonings that said he should leave well enough alone for now. But in that storm-charged, unfamiliar blackness, reason wouldn't hold. He had to know.

He had to know if he still had his sight.

The tortured thrust of his breathing overwhelmed sounds of the wind and rains outside, filling the unknown perimeters of the room with each ragged pull and raw release. His heart beat hard and fast in ungoverned anxiousness, each surge awakening his body to the dangerous uncertainties of his situation. Years of survival in the most hazardous conditions had him struggling to gain control over his surroundings—and over himself. So he forced his eyes to open, ignoring the pain it caused to seared tissues, because the pain of not knowing was far greater.

He waited, gaze wide and directed upward, for something to happen. He wasn't sure what he expected. More of the brilliant lights perhaps. Certainly some sign of shadowy outline as he adjusted to the probable darkness of the room. He guessed it was night from the lack of activity going on about him. That gave him a few seconds of patience as he watched for details to sharpen. Corners of the ceiling. Betraying strobes of light from the storm outside. A sense of orientation within the great well of blackness. But there was nothing, nothing at all.

"No."

The denial moaned from him, rejecting what logic told him even when confronted with its impenetrable evidence because he refused to accept it as truth.

He refused to accept the fact that he was blind.

It seemed to Jude as if she'd just closed her eyes in search of an elusive sleep. Weariness had begun to pull upon the edges of her consciousness with the promise of some much needed peace, and she relaxed to embrace it. Just as that balm of surrender overcame her, her senses snapped back to life at a scuffling of sound from below. Sammy, she thought at first, as she forced her eyes to close in determination. But there was no follow-up noise of the door opening which would mean her brother was making a dash for the privy. Instead there was a rasping sound of furniture on wood, as if someone were stumbling blindly in the dark.

Blindly . . .

Jude raced for the loft's ladder, not stopping to grab her wrapper. She climbed down as rapidly as the tangle of her nightdress about her bare legs would allow. A quick glance told her Sammy and Joseph were still slumbering at the hearth, undisturbed by the noise that had echoed beneath her bedchamber. Even Sammy's old hound lay with paws twitching, oblivious to her passing as she stepped hurriedly on silent bare feet to the room in back.

It took a moment for her anxious gaze to adjust to the deeper darkness of the bedroom. The bed was empty, its sheets in twisted disarray on the floor. A scrape of chair legs across planking drew her attention to a shadowed corner and the massive silhouette of a man. Having lit the lamp, Jude raised it up and sucked a breath as she got her first clear look at him. She'd forgotten how huge he was—appearing even bigger now in just the hug of cotton long johns all draped in heavy shadow. He stumbled again, flanneled knees striking the seat of the chair she'd sat upon while in her vigil over him. Out-flung hands patted the empty air in agitation, seeking some unknown purchase.

"Mr. MacKenzie?" She pitched her voice low so it wouldn't startle him.

His head jerked in her direction, and she could see

he'd torn away most of his bandages. His burned eyes were red and wide with disoriented distress. And obviously sightless.

"Who's there?" he demanded in a growl that was both relieved and defensive.

"My name is Jude Amos. You're at my stage stop. You've been injured, Mr. MacKenzie. You must return to bed."

"I can't see." That truth ripped from him as if by torture.

Jude moved toward him, her steps cautious, her words continuing in that soft, soothing tone. "That's from the flash of the misfire. You interrupted a murder during a robbery on the stage. Do you remember?"

He was panting heavily as his hands still cast about for something of substance. He was wobbling like a majestic oak at the mercy of a crosscut saw. A sheen of perspiration slicked his face, gleaming on taut angles and dotting the vee of his chest exposed by the opening of several buttons on his underwear. Fever, Jude feared, and she wondered frantically if she'd be able to control him if his panic grew any worse. He might have been weakened by his injury, but he was still powerful enough to be a danger, to himself and to her.

"I'm going to take your hand," she told him, preparing him for the contact of her fingers brushing over the backs of his. She gave a gasp of surprise as his hand turned and his fingers clamped about her wrist with the desperation of a man drowning. The pressure hurt but the sudden unexpected warmth of his skin and strength of his grip incited a hurried pulse beneath the tight curl of his possession.

Now that she had him—or rather, he had her—

his other hand waved upward, brushing her hip, skimming her waist, grazing the outer swell of one breast until her flesh burned beneath the thin linen of her gown in a shock of excitation. Of course there was nothing the least bit personal in that awkward fumble, but it was the first time she'd ever felt a man's hands upon her so explicitly and the sensation quite overwhelmed her maiden sensibilities even as other, less giddy reasonings told her she had to get the poor man back to bed before he collapsed. She caught that errant hand and placed it upon the less distracting realm of her shoulder.

"Lean on me, Mr. MacKenzie. You need to lie down."

For a moment he rebelled against that idea, pushing away from her to reel upon unsteady legs. "No."

"Yes." Her tone brooked no argument. It was one she used frequently on her brother when he was in one of his stubborn moods. The no-nonsense crack of it seemed to fare just as well with truculent gunmen, for he tottered briefly, then let her guide him a shuffling step at a time, back to the bed. Even when he was being compliant, Jude was awed by the strength of him. As she coaxed him to lie back, she was startled to be pulled down with him until, unbalanced, she sprawled over him, her scantily covered breasts pressed to his massive plane of torso. There, for one scandalous second, her heart lunged against his in wondrous surrender to the emotions he unleashed inside her virgin body. She let herself revel in the feel of big hands spread against her shoulder blades, compelling her closer still, until his heat scorched her and wilted her will. Her mind spun, so undone by the rush of passion it took her several minutes to remember that the man who held her was an invalid and that he was not seeking seduction but simply survival.

Glad he couldn't see how embarrassed heat flooded into her face, Jude pried his fingers loose so she could put a decent distance between them. Immediately, he was reaching for her again.

"Don't go!"

The tremor of that fearful request held her even as modesty bade her to move away. Very gently she gathered up one of his flailing hands and curled it safely within her own.

"I won't leave you, Mr. MacKenzie, if you promise you'll try to sleep."

He continued to shift upon the rumpled covers, his gaze moving in restless arcs as fever climbed apace with his distress. Determined to control both, Jude settled her hip against the curve of his waist so he could feel her presence. Because the poignant plea in his sightless eyes worked up a knot of unbearable sympathy within her breast, she reached up to readjust the bandages, only to have her wrist compressed in another crushing hold.

"No! Don't do that!"

"Your eyes have been burned, Mr. MacKenzie," she soothed with quiet reason. "They must be kept free of contaminants if you are to regain your sight."

"Regain . . ." He took a hoarse, hopeful breath. "Then I could see again?"

"It's quite possible, but you must let me do what I can to see you heal properly."

His fingers relaxed and his hand fell back upon the bedcovers so she could continue to bind his eyes. She could feel him tense but he didn't struggle and for that, she was grateful.

"Now, have I your promise you'll rest?"

"You won't leave?"

"I won't leave. Have we a deal?"

"Deal."

And as she sat nestled beside him, she could feel him relax in small increments until his hand weighed slack and heavy within her own. She allowed a sigh to escape her. She'd told him there was a chance his sight would return. Well, it could, she argued in justification. It wasn't just a false hope, said to calm a man terrified by the threat of blindness. It would be the truth if she had anything to do with it.

And if she didn't . . . ?

She looked down at the huge figure, no less formidable in sleep, and remembered Joe Varness's claim.

Could be he wouldn't want to survive.

Dalton was ready for the pain when he awoke and, to some extent, was prepared for the darkness as well. But that didn't stop the wash of helplessness from taking him under, nor did it help that his brain was hot and none too clear. He didn't repeat the folly of the night before by trying to get up. What was the point? Everything around him was a dangerous black void of unseen objects and undeterminable distances. Better that he stay where he could monitor his surroundings.

He could hear the rain beating on the wallboards behind the head of the bed and the lonesome wail of the wind that drove it. Though the fury of the storm had abated, it was no less serious in its steady deluge and, in a way, much more damaging, like the inner heat burning steadily as if to consume him. He was thirsty, his fever having cooked most of the moisture out of him. He took a moment to reach out with his other senses, each small discovery lessening his feeling of isolation. He could smell woman, the heat of warm skin sending out a light floral fragrance to tantalize his nose. Lilacs, he thought. He remembered her but had forgotten her name. After she'd kept her promise to remain, he felt bad about that. It was the only knowledge he had of her in his sightless world.

He sent his hand in an inquisitive arc, sweeping over the cool bedcovers where she'd sat beside him. Not there. The fragrance was too strong to be a lingering memory. She had to be close by. Determined to find her, he increased the radius of his search until fingertips made solid contact with fabric over warm flesh.

He was quick to claim what he'd found beneath the cup of his palm: a woman's bent knee, nicely shaped and begging further exploration. No beginning student in the study of female anatomy, he let his touch ease up leisurely, taking desperate distraction in covering familiar ground. A thin layer of material moved above the turn of her thigh where flesh was toned and firm, not fleshy. Intrigued, he followed the upward path again, this time along the inside. She was sitting in a chair at his bedside, deep asleep, her knees in a wanton spraddle of negligence. As his hand climbed, she made a soft sound in the back of her throat, a purring noise of contentment suited to a well-stroked cat, and her legs spread wider in not so innocent invitation.

He was within inches of their tender apex when he felt her come awake, fully and frantically, shooting out of the chair and from beneath his hand as if he'd emptied a scalding kettle into her lap. She didn't flee. He could hear her standing there at the bedside, grabbing for gulps of breath. He didn't know if she was outraged or overcome with shock

because she didn't speak and he couldn't see her
expression. Perhaps she was even aroused. Women
were known to enjoy his touch. But because he
couldn't afford to strain her hospitality, he pretended confusion.

"I'm sorry I startled you. I couldn't recall your
name, and I wanted to ask for a drink of water." His
voice was a dry rasp. That helped convince her of
his harmlessness. He could feel her hesitation, as if
she was still undecided about whether to shriek or
slap him. In the end mercy won out over anger at
the liberties he'd taken.

"Of course. Let me get you some."

He listened to her movements in the room, the
warm burr of bare legs rubbing together, the swish
of her nightclothes. And he could almost imagine
the agitated tempo of her heartbeats. He smiled to
himself, feeling not quite so helpless when he could
stir up such a frenzy in one so seemingly capable.

Her fingers slipped behind his head, and he let
her lift him. The shift of position rewoke the clamor
of distress between his temples, stealing a groan of
protest from his lips before he could catch it. She
paused, giving him time to adjust, waiting for him
to wet his mouth in anticipation before bringing the
cup to it. His nostrils flared at the tempting scent of
water, like a horse brought to a cool stream in the
desert. The tin touched his teeth, then came the
welcome rush of wetness. He swallowed greedily.

"Not too fast or too much," came her warning,
but he chose to ignore it, draining the cup, then
giving way to a spasm of coughing as the cold liquid
collided with the vast emptiness in his belly. She
held him upright until the episode ended, her grip
sure and strong but gentle. When his breath was
back under control, she eased him down upon the

slightly soggy pillow, dampened from his sweat of fever and agitation. He rested there for a moment, wearied by just that small effort, until he heard her step on the floorboards—moving away from him.

"I'm sorry . . . what is your name?" he called, making her pause.

"Jude Amos."

"I thank you, Jude Amos, for taking me in like this, me a stranger and all."

"Any human being of compassion would have done the same thing, Mr. MacKenzie." Was it his imagination, or was there an extra measure of starch to that claim?

"You must know a different sort of human being than I do, ma'am."

"I suspect so, Mr. MacKenzie." Again, the vague air of censure, as if she knew who he was and what he did. "Now, as I said before, you must rest if you expect to recover."

"Oh, I expect to recover. I've got work waiting. How long did the doctor say I'd be laid up?"

"No doctor's seen you as yet. Joseph, my cook, bandaged your wounds. I sent for the physician in Cheyenne, but this weather may delay him some if the riverbanks continue to swell. Roads have been known to be impassable for days when the rains come down this hard." Again, there was something in her voice, some suggestion of something she wasn't saying. Not condemnation this time, but something softer, something like wistfulness, but he was too alerted by her earlier words to wonder why.

"Your cook? I was tended by a cook? But you said my sight would return."

"I said there was that possibility," she corrected, but that wasn't the assurance he wanted to hear.

"Your cook thinks there's a possibility," he all but

sneered. "By God, I'll hold a lot of faith in that claim." His hand came up to feel along the bulk of bandaging, a slight tremor possessing his fingertips.

"It's a faith you must hang on to . . ." she began, but he cut her off curtly.

"I believe in faith about as much as I believe in luck. You make your own luck, and you can't believe in anything but yourself."

A long pause, then, "Harsh philosophies, Mr. MacKenzie."

"They've served me well, Miz Amos. I live in a harsh world." What kind of world did she live in, this angel who'd taken him in without question? Because he was blind, perhaps permanently, and had no way of knowing the answer, his voice was unnecessarily brusque. "Now, if you don't mind, I'd like to get some of that rest you were harping on." And he tossed his head to one side, away from her.

Jude hesitated, not wanting to leave him in such a state of agitation. She didn't believe his bold claims, not really. It was fear talking, and he had every right to that fear. He had no guarantee that his vision would return, and she could make none to ease his mind. Since there was nothing else she could do, she did as he bid and quietly left him to his somber contemplations.

As she washed in her bedside bowl and stripped off her nightdress to don a sensible calico, Jude held the skin-warmed linen a moment longer, her mind in a fever of its own as she recalled the way the heat of his hand had filtered through it. Her insides began that same trembling that overset them earlier . . . when she'd realized it was a man's touch . . . *his* touch upon her leg. The giddiness built until she was certain everything in there had shivered loose.

He'd been touching her while she slumbered. However innocent he might claim his motives, there was no altering that fact. It was shameful, humiliating . . . and so exciting, it hurt to breathe.

Wondering how it would have felt to surrender virgin territory to a stranger, she dressed in the dawning light of her room, while emotions within her brightened and bloomed like the new day.

As much as she tried to begin the day like any other, her brother and her old friend noted the difference in her as soon as they sat down to breakfast together.

"You look pretty as dew on a flower, Jude," Sammy announced unexpectedly. "That a new dress?"

She fingered the fabric. How long had it been since she'd had a new gown or anything else of a female fashion? "No."

"Your hair, you're wearing it different."

She touched the colorful ribbon she'd used to restrain it at the nape of her neck. "Nothing new. Sammy, eat your flapjacks and quit your flattery. It's not going to keep you from going out in that sea of mud to tend the stock."

"Oh, I don't mind doing that," he claimed cheerfully through a mouthful of pancake. "I like squishing around in the mud. I was just remarking on how fetching you looked this morning is all."

"Fetching." A word Jude would never have applied to her own appearance. In a new dress, with her hair styled up and soft about her face, maybe . . . That thought trailed off as she caught Joseph's impassive stare from across the table. For the briefest instant, he allowed her to see what he was thinking through those inscrutable eyes. He was thinking the difference in her was due to their guest in the back room. And he wasn't wrong.

Jude grabbed up her coffee, feeling foolish. Imagine, gussying up for a man who couldn't see, a man upon whom she'd made such a slight impression he couldn't remember her from the stage or even her name. A man who'd placed an unintentioned hand upon her and had her quaking like a silly romantic in desperate search of encouragement. He was her patient, not her paramour, and his only interest was in recovering so he could leave as soon as possible, to get on to the job of danger that drew men of his kind. Men of violence didn't encourage lonesome, homely women to go off into flights of fancy by seeing good in their character which might lead to such things as stability or matrimony. Men like Dalton MacKenzie were better left alone. And that's exactly what she would do.

She stood and began to load an extra plate with the remains of their meal. She met Joseph's gaze unswervingly. "I thought I'd see if our guest has an appetite yet. It wouldn't do for us to starve him. After all, as employees of the stage line, we are responsible for his care."

Joseph made a noncommittal grunt that said she wasn't fooling him any more than she was fooling herself. She gave up the pretense, scowling at the wrinkled old man, then marched across the room, plate in hand, determined to do her Christian duty as if it were an unpleasant chore rather than an anticipated privilege.

She halted just inside the doorway. Dalton had taken her advice and appeared to be sleeping soundly. Though his big body engulfed the bed in evidence of strength and manly power, something about **the strip** of white binding his brow reduced him to **the** helplessness of a child in Jude's eyes. As needy as Sammy, depending upon her care. And there was no way to put a stop to the welling of protectiveness that blanketed her heart.

"He is not the man for you." The claim was stated without cruelty by the ancient Sioux who'd seen more than his share of sorrow.

Jude nodded at that soft-spoken wisdom. "I know that, Joseph."

But knowing it didn't make the slightest difference.

Chapter 5

〜◦◯◦〜

"Step on out, you sonofabitch, so's I can blow you to hell!"

Jude tensed as the fierce epitaph snarled from her patient. Then she gently applied a cool compress to his brow. His head tossed fitfully, denying her comfort, just as his rambling words denied her peace.

By mid-morning it was obvious that aiding Dalton MacKenzie in his recovery was not going to be an easy task. His fever soared, spiking with bouts of restless delirium. He couldn't be left alone, for even in his weakened state he tried to rise. His sightlessness aggravated the situation. He fought the hands that restrained him, unable to comprehend that such care was for his own good. He couldn't remember Jude, where he was, or the reason for his infirmity. And in that disoriented state he became what Jude suspected he was: a dangerous man.

There were times when he was lucid enough to speak clearly. In those moments Jude chased a curious Sammy away, for what came out of his mouth was a frightening stream of obscenity-laced threats directed toward the phantoms of his past. He spoke of deeds that made Jude pale and tremble at

58

his bedside, as he detailed savageries she could scarcely imagine. Some of his tirade was aimed at brothers and sisters. Jude at first assumed he was speaking of family, then it became chillingly clear he was referring to the church and was calling its Catholic relations by name. Such vicious sentiments shocked her even as she mopped his sweat-dappled brow. And she began to wonder if she'd brought a demon under her roof in the guise of this handsome charmer.

"Your food grows cold," Joseph said from beside her. "I will sit with him."

She gazed up through dazed and weary eyes, then nodded, surrendering her seat and the washbasin of water she'd been using to drown his fever.

"Don't bury 'em," Dalton ranted. "Hang 'em up to be a lesson to the others. I want 'em to know hell and Dalton MacKenzie are here!"

Jude stiffened with dismay at the awful outcry. "He doesn't know what he's saying. It's the fever."

Joseph said nothing in response to her weakly tendered excuse.

It was a relief to escape the room with its air so permeated with hateful talk and violent intent. She sat at the table, steadying her cup of coffee with both shaking hands, her mind in a turmoil as she pictured the life Dalton MacKenzie must have led. She pieced together a history of death in which he'd played its darkest angel. How could she be drawn to such a man? It seemed as if her heart was acting traitorously against all she knew and revered.

"Those who live by the gun perish at its whims." She could hear Bart Amos speaking that familiar sentiment along with his immediate conclusion: "A man's worth is not measured by his might but rather by the strength of his beliefs."

Her father had taught her a foundation of peace. He'd lived by those standards and had died for them too. He never carried a gun and was unprepared to defend himself against those who coveted his insignificant wealth when he was in Fort Laramie purchasing supplies. When word reached them, it knocked their world askew. He'd been shot down and robbed, left in a stinking alley like so much trash. The senselessness of it disturbed Jude almost more than the fact of his death. Bart Amos was a man who never would have denied a man down on his luck the price of a meal and a bed. He would have been the first to give all he had to one less fortunate.

"Christian charity, Jude," he was always quick to tell her when impatient willfulness got the better of her compassion. "That's the way to win any battle."

Charity be damned. The unkind thought growled through her. Her father wasn't given the opportunity to be charitable by the greedy creatures who stole his future along with his meager cash. And with that act of violence, they'd stolen Jude's sense of serenity as well.

Now the burden of them all rested upon her.

She wouldn't be stuck here if it hadn't been for that cruel turn of fate.

Jude pressed the heel of her hand to her forehead, too tired to suppress the bubble of traitorous resentment. Death had not once, but twice robbed her of any chance at happiness, and now she had one of its messengers under her roof.

What had she been thinking?

She loathed armed confrontation. To condone it was to defile her father's memory. She refused to listen to the ugly grumblings of her neighbors and stepped down hard on their suggestion that might

just make right turn in their favor. To invite men like
MacKenzie into their troubles was to embrace a
whole other set of problems—problems that ended
in bloodshed—and so far she'd been able to convince the other ranchers that wasn't what anyone
wanted. How would they react to her inconsistency
of having the very bane of brotherhood staying in
her back room like a pampered guest? Was she
encouraging the very danger she despised by keeping this gunman in their valley? Should she have
protected her stand of uninvolvement by letting the
stage carry him on to Cheyenne, regardless of the
threat to his life?

No answers came as she stared into that cold cup
of coffee. She could argue both sides of her decision
from now till next year, and she'd be no closer to the
truth—a truth she suspected had more to do with
her lonely state than with Samaritan impulse.

"He is no better."

Joseph's grim summation startled her from her
thoughts. She glanced up wearily, her own conflicts
there on her face for her old friend to read.

"His spirit is dark from the path he's walked.
Perhaps it is not wise for us to try to save him."

Because she'd been thinking along those same
complex lines, Jude didn't react with surprise to that
harsh suggestion. Instead she gave a heavy sigh. "I
don't think it's up to us to make that decision,
Joseph. He's one of God's creatures, His to claim or
heal. The only thing we can do in good conscience is
the best we can to see he's recovered and on his
way."

"And what if the way he travels is destined to
bring more death and suffering to those who do not
deserve it?"

"Who are we to say who deserves what?" Deci-

sion made, she stood firm on her choice against a
counsel she once would have accepted without
question. "Where he's been and where he'll go are
not our concerns. He's a man fate has placed in our
hands, for what purpose, I cannot guess. I don't like
what he represents any better than you do, but it's
not up to us to judge him for past sins. Let's just do
what we can to get him well enough to become
someone else's problem."

Though he begrudged her dismissal of his advice,
Joseph couldn't argue with that wisdom, for it was
very much in line with what he believed.

"I will make him some bark tea to bring the fever
down. The rest will be up to whatever gods control
his fate."

Dalton MacKenzie had been silent for a long
while, stewing in his fever bed. Jude remained at her
vigil, occasionally leaning forward to apply a cool
towel to his wet brow as she contemplated the news
Sammy had just brought her. He'd ridden out to
assess the rain damage and returned to report that
the Chugwater had overflowed its banks, washing
away the bridge and cutting them off from Fort
Laramie. In the other direction a mud slide blocked
the road, sealing them off from Cheyenne as well. It
would take at least several days for crews to correct
the situation, providing the weather remained stable. Which meant there would be no stage traffic, no
doctor from Cheyenne, no way to rid herself of this
new and potentially deadly burden she'd assumed.
That knowledge toyed with her heart, teasing at its
tender perimeters, taunting with forbidden promise,
whispering a chill of worries like the whip of spring
wind, demanding she brace against them. Dalton

MacKenzie had an unsettling effect, one she couldn't seem to ignore or erase.

"Where am I?"

The sudden rough growl of his voice startled her.

"You're at Amos Station. You were injured by a bandit bent on murder."

"Who are you?"

Patiently, she told him her name yet another time.

"How long have I been here?"

"A day now. You've been quite ill with fever."

And still was apparently, for he began to thrash restlessly, struggling unsuccessfully to absorb his situation.

"I have to go. I have a job waiting. Why are you keeping me here?"

"No one is keeping you here against your will, Mr. MacKenzie. It's for your own good until you recover your strength and regain your sight."

He tossed upon his sodden pillow, breathing in hoarse snatches. His hands rose to chart the bindings over his eyes with a helpless desperation. "Why can't I see? Take these off."

Jude gripped his wrists with a determined show of strength. "No. You mustn't."

"Take them off! I won't be kept in darkness!"

She pitched her tone so it would penetrate his anxiousness with a shock of icy truth. "Off or on, it will make no difference. Do you understand?"

"I'm blind. That's what you're telling me. Is that what you're telling me?" With a powerful twist, her hands were held captive within his, and the pressure was none too gentle as he seethed, "Where are my guns?"

She resisted both the crush of his grip and the force of her own fear to reply levelly, "This is my home. We don't allow firearms within its walls."

"Where are my guns?" He came up on his elbows, jerking her toward him at the same time, so that they were separated by only inches. Jude could feel the hot force of his panted breaths upon her face, and fear of him, of this violent stranger, rose in a weakening surge.

"I don't have them. One of the outlaws took them off you while you were unconscious." Then, hating the quavering of her words, Jude sucked a heartening breath and demanded, "Now release me. You have no reason to hurt me. I am not your enemy."

"Enemies come in many forms, I've found." But he let her go and fell back upon the bed, his frantic energy at an ebb. "I'd say an enemy is one who keeps a man alive when he can no longer be of use to anyone, even himself."

Because his defeated words scared her more than his aggressiveness, Jude's reply was sharp with anger. "Useful or not, you are not going to die here, Mr. MacKenzie. Is that clear? I'm going to see you are strong enough to take the next stage out if I have to tie you down and spoon-feed you. I've promised to care for you, and care for you I will. Once you're gone, you can do what you like, but under my roof you will thrive and be grateful. Is that understood?"

He was silent for a long second, the half of his features she could see still and unreadable. When he spoke, his words were without inflection. "And I suppose you are a woman who takes her promises seriously."

"Yes, sir, I am."

"Then you would be the first of your gender to do so."

"I doubt that, Mr. MacKenzie, but I will be happy to prove you wrong in your opinion. Now then, would you care for some soup?"

"And if I say no, are you going to force it down my throat?"

His tartness made her smile, easing the tension between them. "You've not yet tasted Joseph's cooking. I've never known anyone who had to have it forced upon them."

"Very well then. Feed me, force me to thrive, but I cannot promise I'll be grateful for your efforts," he grumbled sourly.

"Fair enough. You will recover, and I will not hold to any undue expectations."

Damn prickly woman, Dalton thought as he slumped back into the uncomfortably lumpy pillow. He hated opinionated women, especially when they tried to stuff ideals down a man's throat, the way this domineering Jude Amos meant to pour down her soup. Why she should care whether he lived or died, he couldn't fathom, unless she was getting some reward for seeing he wasn't toes up by the time the next stage came through. Dying passengers were bad for business, and his nurse seemed more obsessed with that worry than with his own wishes. Of course she would prefer a docile patient who would cause her little or no distress until the time she could collect her fee. Mercenary little witch, profiting off his pain. He had no desire to make it easy for her, starting with the soup.

But with his first whiff of Joseph's hearty stock, his plan to develop terminal lockjaw was overturned. Savory fragrances teased his nose, exciting his taste buds into a treasonous demand. The loud rumble of his belly echoed a lusty second. Well, maybe just the soup, just so he'd have the strength to rebel against dinner.

He wanted to protest the way his unseen nursemaid bolstered him up on a bank of pillows as if he were an invalid, but to do so would delay his feast upon what his other senses promised would be a culinary delight. He waited, anticipating against his will. A large mug was placed firmly within his grasp.

"No spoon? You'll have a difficult time trying to ram this down my throat."

Her soft chuckle sounded as tempting as the odors rising in steamy tendrils from his cup. "Drink, Mr. MacKenzie. Unless you would like me to hold it for you."

"I can manage, madam, I assure you." And he bent down to slurp loudly, just to prove it was so. It was hot. It burned his tongue. His hands, not being quite as steady as he pretended, cost him precious drops of the flavorful broth. But he drained the cup determinedly, savoring the heat, the taste, and even the tenuous nature of his success in feeding himself.

He couldn't see her, but suddenly he got the feeling she was smiling smugly, as if to gloat, *See, you are not at all useless.* And the fact that she was right, at least for the moment, made him surly as a badger with its paw in a trap.

"How was the soup, Mr. MacKenzie?"

She was smiling. He could hear the odious tone of her amusement.

"I've had better, Miz Amos." Though he couldn't remember when.

She took the bowl from him, and he bit down hard on his wish to ask for more. He was going to see she earned every breath he drew. That was his promise to himself, as he settled down into the covers, stomach begging for seconds against a pride that wouldn't bend.

He fully intended to hold out against supper until he smelled meat roasting and biscuits browning. By the time his payrolled caregiver entered the room, he'd hoisted himself up into a position of readiness, hating his compliance but unable to best his growling appetite. One more moment of weakness didn't mean surrender, he told himself as he allowed her to arrange a tray upon his knees. In his eagerness, he fumbled sightlessly over the fragrant offerings, managing to mire his fingers in mashed potatoes and gravy. His reactive jerk of disgust upset his cup of coffee, sending a flood of nearly scalding liquid all down the front of him. His curse collided with Jude's gasp of dismay, and they bumped heads painfully as both reached to remove the offending tray, now swimming in coffee.

"Let me," she insisted, wrestling the platter from his awkward manipulations.

"Damn it, woman. You are the most careless creature. If you've managed to fry anything I'm fond of—"

Thankfully he didn't finish that rumble, and just as thankfully he couldn't see the heat flaming on Jude's cheeks. In her embarrassment she spoke a curt accusation.

"I am not the one with clumsy hands, sir, so if you would like me to help you clean up this mess you've made, I suggest you show the proper humility."

"Humility be damned! I'm not going to apologize for your nearly cooking me alive."

"Do not swear at me, Mr. MacKenzie."

"Get this *damn* sheet off me."

"I asked you not to use profanity."

"First it's guns and now it's a man's very words that you object to. You are a shrew of a woman, Miz Amos. Is there a Mister Amos who tolerates such bold behavior in a wife? If there is, I pity the man."

She stopped what she was doing and took a deep breath to stabilize the sudden pain in her breast. "No, sir, there is no Mr. Amos. And if there were, I would not allow his curses either."

In his irritation and discomfort Dalton didn't notice how pinched her voice had become; he was too busy trying to untangle the hot wrap of the covers. "I'm not surprised that you could find no one to appreciate that sharp tongue of yours, *Miss* Amos. A man does not hold such skewering wit as a virtue."

"So now you are an expert on all men's values as well as on women's lack of them." She grabbed the corner of the sodden and discolored sheet and yanked hard, jerking it from beneath the press of his hip and nearly toppling him off the bed. When he managed to lie back, grumbling oaths she couldn't hear plainly, her gaze was drawn against her will to that area of his concern. Dampness adhered the cotton flannel of his underwear to his groin in explicit contour, displaying before her wide eyes the bold length of him and every proud curve of which a man might boast. Then that fascination ended when she observed the way his fingers were moving determinedly downward over the buttons on his long johns, tugging the fabric open to expose a broad expanse of masculine frame and curling dark hair. He scowled at the sound of her ragged inhalation.

"If you are easily shocked, I suggest you look away, Miss Amos. You've said there is no mister in residence, but might there be someone who could help me without falling into vapors?"

Jude was paralyzed as material parted at Dalton's waist, showing the hard washboard of his torso and the thick thatch of male furring which hinted at what he was about to bare. Her mind spun. Joseph and Sammy were both out tending the stock . . . no help at all.

Impatient with her silence and too miserable in the steamy flannel to cook within it for another second, Dalton peeled the top away from his shoulders and arms and made ready to stand to complete his disrobing. He underestimated his strength and Jude was forced to step in to steady him, tantalized and tormented by the feel of a nearly naked man bumping up against her maidenly form. He clutched at her as his consciousness ebbed and waned in dizzying swoops, and tremors of weakness overtook the sturdiness of his frame.

"M-Mr. MacKenzie, you must sit down." Her legs were suddenly as watery as his and threatening collapse.

"Not on the bed. It's all wet."

He was hanging onto her, his greater size close to enveloping the sturdy angles of her form. His dark head was tucked in atop her shoulder as he struggled for his balance. His words were a warm, seducing breeze against the hollow of her throat, and her will fluttered.

"There's a chair," she stammered as her palms trembled across the heated plain of his bare back. His long johns dangled from his middle, held up by a single button in front—a button for which he was reaching.

"Get me out of these first. I'm uncomfortably close to stewing."

Because the strain in his voice spoke of genuine distress, she couldn't allow her innocence to overcome compassion. But however noble her intentions, when the button gave, so did her courage. Squeezing her eyes shut, she supported the drape of his upper body as she skinned the wet Union suit down over the rock-hard curve of his buttocks. When the coarse hairiness of his thighs tickled her wrists in a manner so intimate she thought her heart would break free from her ribcage, she muttered, "There. Now let's get you sitting down before we finish the rest."

She had to peek, only for a second, in order to get her bearings. The chair was off to the left, just beyond the long protrusion of his hipbone. She angled him toward that seat, eyes fiercely averted. He dropped down onto it with a grateful groan, and she bent at his feet to shuck the long johns off his firmly muscled legs. Blindly she groped for the quilt which was folded back at the foot of the bed, then breathed a sigh of relief when he was swaddled beneath it.

"Have you another pair of these in your bag?" Was that her voice, so whispery with distraction?

At his affirmative nod, she first stripped off the soiled bottom sheet then hoisted his luggage up upon the dry end of the bed, glad to have something else on which to focus.

There was something very personal about going through a man's belongings, almost like seeing a sacred slice of him to be shared with no other than a life's mate. At least that was how it felt to Jude as she handled his toiletry case filled with brush and comb, shaving paraphernalia, and a bottle of the crisp, manly scent she remembered from her close encounter with him on the stage. She'd hoarded the aroma like she might a treasured memory, where it inflamed her senses in intoxicating doses. Touching the smooth pattern of his vests and the rough nap of his finely cut coats was like sliding a caress over the man who would fill them. Never in her wildest imaginings had she guessed that fondling his apparel would bring a flush to her cheeks and a sweat to her brow. Even his socks held an enticing allure.

That's when she realized fully how desperate her situation had become: standing there, mooning over a pair of socks while a naked man huddled three feet away, clad in just a quilt.

Annoyed by the vapid turnings of her own mind, she snatched out a pair of white long underwear and mashed all the rest back into the bag.

"Here."

Holding the covers together with one hand, he reached out vaguely with the other to receive the clothing. He made a game effort to dress himself, but the instant he bent over to place one foot down into the leg hole, his entire body swayed in a dangerous arc. Jude caught his shoulder and propped him up against the straight chair back, and grimly faced the fact that she was going to have to clothe him.

"I'll do it." Her stern tone didn't deflect the panic banging around inside her. Nor did her determination to think of it as shoeing a horse or dressing Sammy lessen the impact of actually lifting the weight of his foot. She curled her arm around his calf, hoisting with a palm beneath his heel to feed his toes into the leg opening of the garment: a simple action fraught with a host of devastating results. She was sure he could feel her heart flopping like a hooked salmon where her breast was pressed to the corded delineation of his calf. A fine leg it was; she'd never adopted the silly attitude of thinking of appendages as limbs. Limbs were for trees. Whoever heard of saying, "He hadn't a limb to stand on." Unless, of course, "he" was a bird.

Mixing up her metaphors the way he stirred up

her emotions left Jude dizzily contemplating the flannel casing she'd drawn up to his left knee. Something was wrong but she couldn't quite . . . Then she was heating up like a sunrise all over again because if she continued, she'd be buttoning him up the back and his two-button drop seat would be front and center.

"Is there some reason this is taking so long? Have you never dressed yourself before?"

"Of course, I have," she snapped ill-humoredly. "It's just that I—I seem to have gotten the wrong limb—er—leg into the wrong hole and . . ." Her words tapered off in misery. "Oh, hell." The grumble slipped out before she could catch it, and she deserved every bit of his malicious amusement.

"Miss Amos! Such language! And from a lady."

"Do shut up and hold up your other foot. Useless need not be helpless."

His laughter mocked her as she yanked the right leg off his left foot and crammed the other in in its stead. She was too irritated for embarrassment now and had the undergarment pulled up to his thick thighs before she thought to blush again. It was then that she met the loosely draped quilt ends and the shadow of where the seam of his thighs was leading.

"Stand up, please." That choked out of her even as he was choking back his chuckles.

He had to hold onto her shoulders to raise himself to his feet. Once on them, tottering precariously, he remained uncooperative while she snatched the long johns to his waist in one vicious tug. His breath caught as the seam yanked up a bit too enthusiastically, and Jude, to her shame, delighted in his discomfort.

"There. Sit yourself down. I think you can find

the buttons on your own while I get you some fresh bedding."

As she stomped to the door, he taunted, "Not as easy as you imagined, is it, seeing that I thrive?"

"Like tending a sick dog, Mr. MacKenzie, only I fear your bark is worse than your bite."

She could see only half of his face, and that half had stopped smiling when he said, "I'm sure that's what you're counting on, Miss Amos." There was a slight pause and she hesitated in the doorway, tension drawing out as the silence did until he finally concluded with sinister pleasure, "But you'd be wrong."

Chapter 6

He listened for her step.

Dalton told himself it was because he was bored and hungry and Jude Amos's quick, competent footfalls meant both afflictions were about to end. In the four days he'd been under her care, those were the two things he'd learned he could count on within the dark void of his hours. She stayed away unless it was to bring him an always welcomed plate of food, and once he had her in the room with him, it was an irresistible challenge to tease her back up about something, thereby tricking her into remaining longer than she'd planned.

He knew he was going to live and no longer entertained any objection to it. Though the quality of that life was in doubt, once his strength returned, likewise did his will. He'd been fighting his way up and out of bad situations all his days, so it wasn't as if he were used to fate's handing him any favors. This could prove to be his greatest obstacle, and it was easier to pretend he wasn't afraid when he heard those light steps coming. Anticipation pushed away all traces of anxiety. It was one thing to be frightened and quite another to let anyone know of it; for it was terror, pure and simple, that quaked

74

within his heart when he woke each morning to a perpetual night. Worse was the uncertainty of not knowing if that situation was going to change.

It provided him with a rather grim amusement to bait the prickly Miss Amos into thinking he was ready to surrender his soul in a fit of melancholy. She worked herself up into such a frenzy, arguing, cajoling, even pleading with him to have faith. Faith: now there was a word he found as meaningless as her concern. Both implied something personal and strong while they were, in fact, weak with greed and deceit. Yet for some perverse reason he couldn't understand himself, he liked to flirt with a belief in both things, well knowing them to be false. If faith was real, the murmurs he sent heavenward would have been answered decades ago. If Jude Amos's care had any grounding in true emotion . . . maybe it was better he not consider that too closely.

He'd never known pampering at the hands of a woman. Passion, yes, but that was something honestly purchased so he could walk away without any sense of obligation. It had been a long, long while since he'd spent time with a decent woman whose only interest in his bed was in changing the linens. He told himself repeatedly, like one of those childhood catechisms learned with the crack of a ruler, that his fascination with her had to do with her uniqueness among females who had flickered through his past, burning bright for a fleeting moment then gone. She was immune to his charm, even flustered by it, preferring to use her tongue to fillet him rather than turn it to more pleasurable pursuits.

Yet for all her tart words and the fact that she was being paid to show him kindness, there was an exquisite gentleness to her touch. The tender stroke of her fingertips was the first thing he remembered upon waking to his current nightmare, that soft, gliding brush across his brow so much like the soothing mother's caress he'd always longed for and often imagined. Her hands weren't smooth or perfumed; they were roughened by hard living, but they seemed to turn to velvet as they worked a certain magic on his panic and pain.

Helplessness was not something to which he was accustomed. It went against the grain of his determined nature. Forced into a position of vulnerable blindness, all his confidence and control were gone, and the sharp-witted woman who moved in and out of his darkened days was all he had to cling to for balance, both physically and mentally. He couldn't manage anything as simple as cutting his own meat. There were times when the unrelieved blackness swelled in great engulfing waves, smothering him in its embrace until it was all he could do not to scream in terror. And then he'd hear the sound of her footsteps and the waves would ebb. He'd hear her husky laugh, and the indignity of having someone feed him was not quite so hard to bear. He'd come to need her for his sanity's sake.

And his interest in her stemmed from more than boredom.

Helpless as he was, he'd discovered a great deal about his surroundings since he'd first opened his eyes to nothingness. The room that housed him was small and sparsely furnished; not a woman's room. He could smell leather and horse and wood shavings lingering like the scent of Joseph's biscuits. He knew about Joseph, the ancient cook of few words, who was trying to save his eyesight with healing poultices but who never would answer any of his many demands about when he could count on that miracle's occurring. It was the owner of this room, Jude's brother, Sammy, who puzzled him. Signals received from him were mixed. Jude kept her brother away from him most of the time, but he caught snatches of their conversations when the door stood ajar, enough to perplex him. The excitable, careless, rambling words were those belonging to a boy, but the voice that spoke them was deep with years behind it. He got the impression of mass, not meekness, when Sammy managed to creep near. But whenever he tried to coax Jude's brother closer, he would mutter, "Jude says Sammy's not supposed to bother you." Then he'd disappear, leaving Dalton with his curiosity at full gallop.

Jude was another mystery, one he pondered long into the night, as he prided himself on his understanding of women. The fact that he couldn't figure her out intrigued as much as it annoyed him. She was no young girl, not with those worn hands and that whiskey-throated laugh. Both hinted at hard times and heartache. Miss Amos, she'd told him with such haughty defiance. He couldn't help but wonder why she was unmarried when a strong-willed woman was just what a man looked for in a land as harsh as this one. Even a waspish tongue could be tamed, though Dalton begrudged that Jude's rapier wit was one of the features he most admired in her. He had no patience with fragile females who thought swooning was a conversational coup. He liked them to resemble raw silk, sleek yet tough and able to look elegant even after being worn hard. He liked them full of sass and passion. Jude had plenty of the first, and wondering over the latter kept him sleepless more often than he cared to recount.

He listened to her low boot heels tapping up to

the bedroom door, slowing as they neared as if she were garnering her courage. There was a pause, almost as if she had to talk herself into crossing the threshold. Had he made her job that unpleasant? Or was it something else?

She was afraid of him. He could sense it in her reluctant approach. He couldn't see that he presented much of a threat, sitting in bed in his long johns with a naked hip and empty eyes. She had no way of knowing who he was or what he did for a living, yet he could feel her caution. If not his reputation, was it his gender that frightened the bold Miss Amos? On more than one occasion, he'd sensed her naive shock and maidenly confusion over matters that wouldn't cause an experienced woman to blush. The memory of her gentle touch and the picture of her blushes put an odd quiver into Dalton's jaded heart.

"Good morning, Mr. MacKenzie."

She'd come across the room bearing the tantalizing smell of breakfast and lilac water. Each stirred a separate and equally powerful hunger.

"How are you today?"

She said it casually, small talk that didn't really mean anything, so he felt no guilt in tormenting her.

"I'm blind and bored, same as yesterday. How are you?"

"And a touch bitter, I would guess" was her summation, spread just as tart and thick as the wildberry preserves she slathered on his biscuits.

"Kinda hard not to be, holed up in this shabby room with nothing to do but count the drips coming off the eaves, thinking about how I've not only lost my sight but my livelihood as well."

"I apologize if the quality of the room is not what

you're used to, but as for the rest, they are out of my control."

He held back his smile. Lord, she had a delightful tang of vinegar about her. Instead, he arranged his features into deep frowning lines. "You're not going to spill coffee on me this morning, are you?"

"Tempting, Mr. MacKenzie, but it would only make more work for me, and I have quite enough of that, thank you."

"Dalton," he said suddenly, just to judge how she would react. "My name is Dalton. You can call me that, or Mac, but 'Mister' implies respect, and I have a feeling you harbor little enough of that for me. And I'll call you Jude. I think we know each other well enough for first names."

"I don't know anything about you at all, Mr. MacKenzie" came that bramble of a reply. "Only what I can see."

"Well," he drawled quietly, "then you have the advantage, don't you?"

Horrified by her own choice of words, Jude immediately fell silent, busying herself with the arrangement of his tray upon his lap. She nearly jumped out of her heavy stockings when his fingers curled about her wrist in a staying grip. Surely he had to feel the sudden rise in her pulse as her nervousness sent the single service clattering.

"Mr. MacKenzie, unless you desire another hot bath, I suggest you let me go." Her tone trembled as badly as the china.

"That's not what I desire at all" came his alarmingly throaty purr. "What I want is to know what you look like." And his hand skimmed up her arm on a trail of discovery.

How she managed to save him from a second

scalding, Jude didn't know, nor was she aware of anything else save her need to escape his seeking touch. She flinched back, slipping out of his reach. Because he had the tray balanced upon his knees, he couldn't pursue her.

"I am nothing special to look at, Mr. MacKenzie. Now eat your breakfast before it gets cold." And she fairly bolted from the room.

The rest of the morning flew by in a frenzied whirlwind of motion. Jude was afraid to be alone with her thoughts for even a moment, well knowing what would occupy them: her gunman boarder. She repeatedly reminded herself that there was no cause for her distress. Dalton MacKenzie didn't remember her from the stage. What was memorable about her average looks and reticent manner? Now she was in a female fluster because his idle flirtations made her feel feminine and attractive for the first time in her life. Reality was that the handsome gunfighter wouldn't cast a second glance her way if his sight returned. She already knew that for a fact. Why work herself up into a froth of feelings that would never know fruition? Over a man who made his living with a gun? She wasn't anything he wanted and he wasn't anything she needed, so why invest more mooning sentiments over what was mutually impossible?

She'd almost convinced herself to turn a toughened attitude toward their tenant when she happened by his open door shortly after lunchtime and overheard a snatch of conversation, between Dalton and her brother.

She'd given Sammy stern warnings time and again that she didn't want him pestering Dalton, partly to spare the injured man her brother's enthusiastic banter and partly because she wasn't sure she

wanted her innocent sibling to hear anything the
hardened gunman had to say. Dalton lived a lifestyle to which she didn't want Sammy exposed, a
routine of murder and mischief with little or no
morality. Sammy hadn't the capacity to grasp such
concepts, and she didn't want him confused. Nor
did she want him to grow too fond of their temporary guest, only to have his tender heart broken
when Dalton rode away without a backward glance.
She suspected that was the only way a man like
MacKenzie knew how to leave.

So she lingered for a moment outside the partially
opened door, trying to decide how best to wrest her
brother from the evil of Dalton's influence. And
while she hesitated, she listened.

Sammy was going on about his favorite topic:
horses.

"The line gets all its stock from the markets in St.
Louie. You ever been there, St. Louie?" Typical
Sammy, he hurried on without waiting for a reply.
That came from talking mostly to Biscuit, the old
hound dog that never was free with his comments.
"You can't toss together any six horses to make a
team, no, sir. You gotta match 'em by size and color,
pair by pair. The head team, they're the leaders and
the smallest and quickest of the bunch. The swing
team runs in the middle, and they're a hand or two
taller. Then there's the wheelers that pull the load,
weighing 'bout twelve hundred pounds each. Imagine that. Anyways, each team has its own set of
harnesses, and it's my job to keep 'em spick-and-
span. And I shoe 'em too. Once a month, if the
livery in Cheyenne's too busy to see it done. Think I
could ever get to be a blacksmith, Mac? You don't
need to be too smart, you jus' have to know horses
and nobody knows horses like Sammy."

Jude almost burst in then to spare Sammy any scathing opinion Dalton might have, but his answer held her by the heart, knotting about it with a bittersweet compression.

"Why, Sam, I think you'd make a fine blacksmith. Folks are always willing to trust their animals to someone who has horse sense."

"You think I got that—whatcha call—horse sense?"

"Sure. That's the best kind to have next to common sense, and then, of course, there's plenty of folks who've got no sense at all."

The sound of Sammy's happy laughter twisted the knot tighter.

"I'd dearly love more than 'bout anything to be a driver," Sammy sighed when his chuckles wore down. "I'd get me a pair of them buckskin gloves with the fringes on 'em and have me a fine hickory stock whip with a twenty-foot lash on it." He made the sound of rawhide sizzling through the air. "Course a good driver, he don't never so much as flick a hair on one of his horses. He drives 'em with the pop of the lash over their heads. Sounds just like gunfire, I been told. But then them's just wishes."

"How come?"

Jude couldn't believe that gentle probing came from Dalton MacKenzie.

"A driver, he gots to be one smart feller. He has to hold three pairs a reins in his left hand, using just his fingers to tell the team what to do, whilst he uses his right hand to pick up slack and snap the whip. He gots to turn every pair at the right time or they gets all tangled and sometimes hurt. I'd never want to hurt my horses. That's too much for Sammy to remember all at one time."

"The way I look at it, Sam, everybody's got a

talent that God gave to them. Not everyone's meant
to be a good driver, or who'd take care of the
horses? I think God gave you horse sense so you
could be the best at doing what you're doing right
now."

There was a beautiful simplicity to that logic, just
the kind of explanation that got Sammy's shaggy
head nodding.

"Guess you'd be right about that, Mac. You surely
are."

"Sammy, are you wearing out our guest?"

Big guilt-bright eyes turned her way as Jude
crossed the room. "We was just talking, Jude. I
wasn't pestering. Honest."

He found unexpected support from Dalton. "We
were just having a little man to man. Fellas need
that kind of thing once in a while. Right, Sam?"

"Right, Mac." A huge smile split his features,
brilliant as a noonday sun.

"I'm glad," Jude put in. "But Sammy, I think
Joseph is waiting for you to help him with some
chores."

"I didn't forget, Jude. I won't go letting Joseph
down."

Jude couldn't hold to her stern manner; her smile
just got away from her. "I know that, Sammy. No
one's as dependable as you are. Get along with you
now."

"Yessum. Bye, Mac." And he stomped out with
his coltish stride.

Before an awkward silence could settle, Dalton
asked, "What's wrong with him?"

Her hackles flew up in an instant. "Nothing's
wrong with him," she stated with a defensive
bristle. Then she realized how foolish that was.
Dalton had talked to him. He had to have guessed,

even if he couldn't see for himself. She dropped down into the bedside chair, letting her shoulders sag in a weary slump. Dalton was propped up against the headboard, sheets tented over updrawn knees, looking like no threat at all, and suddenly the words started coming, the truth she rarely told to anyone. "I don't know exactly. My mama had a hard time birthing him. Doctors said it had something to do with not enough air getting to his brain. Sammy grew but he never grew up."

"He's seen doctors then?"

"Scores of them when we lived in Albany, as many as we could afford, but all of them said the same thing. He'd never be any different. He'd never amount to anything useful." Then her tone hardened. "They said the best thing we could do was institutionalize him."

Dalton was facing her, and she could almost swear that, behind the swaddling of gauze, he was looking right at her with an unswerving intensity. "But they were wrong, weren't they?"

"Yes, they were wrong." There was no disguising the vindicating pride in her voice. "They said he'd never feed or clothe himself. They said he'd never learn to put together a proper sentence. They said he'd be a danger to himself and others. We never believed it, Papa and I, and we helped Sammy prove them wrong."

"And your mama, what did she believe?" A sudden hush came over his words, as if her answer held some special significance.

"She believed it was her fault, and when the doctors had done all they could and Papa made the decision to keep Sammy at home with us, I don't think she ever forgave him for going against her wishes. She couldn't look at Sammy without being reminded of her blame. I wouldn't have thought someone could die of a broken heart if I hadn't watched it happen to her over the course of the next few years. She just gave up on life, and finally it gave up on her. So that left the three of us out here to start over on our own." Her voice drifted off for a moment as complex emotions got the better of her. She seemed to shake them off at last to murmur, "Sammy's done more than his share to keep our family going."

"It couldn't have been easy" was Dalton's soft observation. His tone suggested he was far away as well, his mind on other things, but Jude was too wrapped up in her long-held private pain to notice his odd withdrawal. She never spoke of it, not to any one, and rarely did she think of that long-ago loss. To deny it was to deny what it stirred within her: feelings of resentment and guilt unbecoming to a loving daughter.

"It wasn't easy," Jude said, breaking the dangerous silence, "but it was worth it. Every day I'd wake up hearing Sammy's laughter, it was worth it. And every time I see him smile over something most people wouldn't even notice, I wonder why she couldn't have loved him for who he was."

"I guess some folks just don't have the ability to accept or forgive."

Then she heard it, that bone-deep resonance of sorrow, but before Jude could begin to wonder where he'd earned it, there was a noisy clamor heralding Sammy's approach.

"All my chores is done, Jude. Joseph said it would be okay if I was to take Mac out for a walk."

"Sammy, Mr. MacKenzie is not a dog!"

Sammy flushed, not quite understanding what

he'd said to deserve his sister's censure. "Well, I know that, Jude. Alls I meant was that since Mac can't see, maybe I could be his eyes and lead him around. You know, like sometimes you have to think for me when my brain don't want to work the way it should."

"Oh." And suddenly Jude felt as though she were the one who should apologize for her gracelessness. "I guess it would be up to Mr. MacKenzie, if Joseph is sure he is able."

"Able and more than willing to be on my own hind legs again," Dalton assured her. "Sam, fetch me some trousers outta my bag. It's there on the floor somewhere. Miss Amos, perhaps you should excuse yourself, since you seem to get all flustered at the sight of my long johns."

"Indeed, I do not," she lied quite aptly, but contrarily she was quick to rise. "I have other matters to attend, is all." And she scowled at seeing Dalton's grin of deviltry perfectly mirrored on her brother's face.

Jude did have things to do, but nothing seemed as compelling as standing at the window, half-hidden by the curtains, watching her brother and the gunman he'd adopted as best friend travel about the yard. They were almost evenly matched in height, both being tall and solidly built. Because of his work with the stock, Sammy had a bulkier upper body, and was able to tote Dalton around with his arm draped across brawny shoulders without any difficulty until the blinded man grew accustomed to moving through his darkened world and required only the tether of Sammy's forearm. Even sightless, he strode with a princely confidence as if anything, man or beast, he encountered should bow down or get out of his way. He was a man to be reckoned with, and the word "dangerous" still applied.

Happily oblivious to Jude's observations, Sammy bustled his audience from stables to storerooms, chattering with an animation that made Jude's heart sore. Watching him, Jude realized her brother was as hungry for a man's attentiveness as she, and she was forced to wonder again if she was doing the right thing in keeping him isolated with only herself, Joseph, and a passel of animals for company. She'd been so concerned with shielding him from unkindness, she'd forgotten how much simple human contact meant to one as gregarious as her younger brother. He was clearly doting on Dalton, gobbling up his encouraging nods of interest with a ravenous glee. The influx of stage drivers and passengers was no real substitute for friends, and she wondered guiltily if she was wrong in depriving him of companionship—and more at fault in allowing him to get too attached to Dalton, who would never be the kind of permanent friend he desired.

Or the kind of permanent mate she coveted.

Her attention was pulled from the two of them by Sammy's excited crow of "Rider's coming, Jude."

Stepping out onto the porch, she followed his squinted gaze down the untraveled road and did indeed make out the shape of horse and rider.

"That there's Tandy Barret. I recognize his bay. Jude, come get Mac so's I can get a stall ready. Looks to be riding hard."

Reluctantly, Jude crossed the yard to take over for her brother, who instantly darted for the barn. Dalton stood adrift for a moment, still as a telegraph pole, waiting for her contact to ground him. She placed her hand upon his sleeve and heard him exhale in relief. With sudden tender insight, she realized how horrible it must be for him in that dark limbo. Just because he was a man of commanding presence and towering physique didn't mean he wouldn't be reduced by normal fears of vulnerability.

"Who's Tandy Barret?" he asked as he fixed a firm grip on her far shoulder. He let his arm lay along the breadth of her back in an easy loop, creating a confining sense of power when she was forced into such close proximity to him.

"He's our neighbor."

"He a close neighbor?"

It wouldn't do to place too much into that casually asked question. Most likely it was prompted by curiosity, not any kind of jealous interest. "He owns a spread to the south, he and his brother, Wade." Unless the question was more pointed, she refused to give away any details of a personal nature describing her relationship to Tandy.

"Sam seems to set store in him, so he must be someone special."

Resenting the way he was cramming an intimate meaning down her throat, Jude said testily, "Sammy sets store in everyone. But unfortunately, Tandy sees him as a bother."

Dalton smiled to himself, thinking that summed up what Tandy Barret was to Jude Amos quite clearly. It took no great mind to determine that the way to the sister was through the brother.

"He must not be much of a friend, then."

"I never said he was a friend. He's our neighbor."

"And he doesn't like Sam."

"I didn't say he doesn't like Sam. It's just that he has no patience with him, not like you—" She broke off, not wanting to continue on that track.

"It would take a pretty sorry son of a bitch not to

like your brother, Jude . . . pardon my choice of words." He hiked her up a little closer, not enough so that she'd protest but enough for him to get a better idea of her shape and size. She fit neatly beneath his arm, solid, womanly, soft in the right places, while still unusually strong of line.

"There are a lot of sorry sons of bitches in this world, Mr. MacKenzie, and if I could, I'd keep them all away from Sammy. He doesn't deserve their contempt. They only see that he's not perfect, and it makes them uncomfortable. I guess that's easier than looking a little harder to discover that he's more perfect than the rest. He doesn't hate, he doesn't hurt others, he doesn't envy or lie. All he wants is a chance to be liked for who he is, not judged for what he's not."

And suddenly her voice snagged on the emotions wadding up about her heart, and her anger at the injustice of it all brought unexpected tears to her eyes. Thinking to hide them from Dalton, she took a gulping swallow and reached up to strike the wetness from her cheeks, but his hand followed hers, his fingertips tracing the path of tears.

And before Jude had time to adjust to the startling texture of his touch, he kissed her.

Chapter 7

⁓~⬩○⬤○⬩~⁓

I t was a long second before anything on earth or in heaven could penetrate Jude's daze of surprise.

By then Dalton had taken full advantage of her slackly parted lips, sliding his tongue along that sweetly puckered seam, then swallowing up the fragile sound that mewled from her with a deep thrust of possession. She didn't respond, but from the way a trembling began to work its way up from her toes, he guessed it was from lack of experience, not from any real objection. So he hauled her in closer, learning what he could of her through that full-length molding of her into him, liking what he discovered.

Then her lips moved shyly, and the taste of her was like the first innocent rain of springtime, so fresh and new it washed away all that came before it. And then he was the one who trembled.

Knowledge of the world around them intruded upon Jude's reverie with a rude shock. They were standing toe to toe, mouth to mouth, right in the middle of her front yard, not exactly the time and place she'd have pictured for her first lesson in love. He was a dangerous stranger, not exactly the

teacher she had imagined in all her maidenly fanta-
sies, and she was bonelessly willing in his embrace.
But for an instant, for a brief glorious fraction of
time, he became her every dream come to life. And
now reality waited. The jolt back from paradise left
her breathless and vulnerable to the emotions swirling through her like hot eddies of late-summer air.
The effect was dizzying and she broke from it,
suddenly frightened by the very thing she desired,
shoving back out of Dalton's arms so she could flee
from what threatened the sterile safety of her world.

He could hear her receding footfalls, rapid in their
panic, as if the very devil was in hot pursuit. Well,
he'd been called that a time or two. What truly
shocked him was his reluctance to appear so in her
eyes. The last thing he wanted was to chase away
the first blush of passion blooming in such a toughly
rooted prairie rose. In doing so, he'd left himself
exposed both to his own inner turmoil and to the
sudden void of external darkness.

It was Joseph who finally took pity on him,
standing there adrift in the vast yard. The old man
curled a gnarled hand about his elbow, offering him
direction as well as a curt snap of advice.

"Your blindness stems deeper than just the eyes.
Take care that you do not stumble into more trouble
than you intended." The threat was subtle but far
from obscure.

"Jude is a grown woman. It's not my plan to hurt
her."

"It does not matter what you plan, it's what she
believes, and in many ways she is more trusting in
her beliefs than even Samuel. You will go away
soon. Do not take part of them with you."

Another surprise was the way Dalton mentally
dug in his heels as Joseph tried to push him out of

the lives of those who lived here. Was it due to his fear of what lay in the darkness beyond Amos Station or because of a real attachment to these people? He wasn't sure he wanted to know as he growled, "And if I mean to stay awhile?"

"Then perhaps you are the one who should take heed. The heart can see beauty the eyes often miss."

With that cryptic statement, he affixed Dalton's hand to his bedpost, abandoning him there to consider what he'd been told.

"Hello, Tandy. What brings you for a visit?" Jude extended that cool greeting along with a cup of coffee. She'd had time to compose herself while Sammy delayed their neighbor in the barn with his endless gab. And now, as she faced the man in her front room, she worried why his features were arranged in such disagreeable lines. Other than the frown creases, he wasn't bad looking, with his weather-beaten face and body like a length of Wyoming whipcord. He was hardworking, with deep-seated ambitions and an unfortunate flash of temper which had been engaging in the boy but not so amusing in the man of near thirty who stood before her.

"It's not a social visit, I'm sad to say. Trouble's coming, Jude, and I'm here to warn you that you're gonna have to take sides."

Though anxiousness ribboned through her, Jude clung to her collected calm. "You know me better than that, Tandy Barret. I'll not support violence on either side. I don't believe there's a situation that can't be solved if two people sit down and talk."

"The time for talk's about gone. I heard tell a big order's been made for fencing, and the minute them posts get pounded in the ground, you might's well touch off the wick on a powder keg. This whole valley's gonna blow."

"Not if you keep your powder dry and your heads cool. There's plenty of room in this valley for everyone."

"There be some who don't think so, and one in particular who won't stop until he has it all."

Jude sighed, having heard this kind of talk too much of late, and she knew well where it was heading. "If you've got something to say, Tandy, come out with it."

"The only way we can come through this with what's rightfully ours is if we all stand together. Your daddy's land sits smack dab in the middle, with water running through it. I heard tell you were entertaining thoughts of selling."

That news surprised her, for she'd been carefully coy about any negotiations. Now wasn't the time to confirm or deny it. "And just where did you hear such a thing?" she accused instead.

"Just never you mind. What I want to know is, is that true?"

Trapped, she had to give something away. "I've no use for the land, that much is fact. I can't afford to stock it, and it's too rich to lie idle. I've been offered a fair price, and I'm considering it." Seeing the way Tandy's face purpled, she was quick to add, "But I haven't made up my mind."

"I've made no secret about wanting those acres, Jude, but you know my pocket situation. I've made you my best offer. Can I hope that you're still entertaining that as well?"

Jude listened carefully and obtained a world of meaning from what Tandy Barret said with his manner of speech. She heard traces of covetous greed and ambition. She heard a tremor of desperation. She recognized the flat reasonableness of a business proposition, but she never picked up a single thread of feeling and that was why her answer now was the same as when he asked the first time.

"I'm sorry, Tandy, the answer's still no and you know my reasons well. I don't think of myself as foolish for holding out for a love match instead of making a business deal. I won't be made a servant to your ambitions."

"You're a stubborn woman, Jude," he declared, slamming down his cup and snatching up his hat. "Have a care or your willfulness is gonna find you out here all on your lonesome, drying up to dust inside." A spinster. He didn't spell it out; he didn't have to. Jude squared up proudly at his ominous summation.

"I'll take that risk, Tandy, and I'll not get pulled into your fight."

All traces of amiability had left him by then, and he scowled at her, his stare hard, his expression soured by her show of independence. "Well, I've nothing more to say to you then. I won't come asking again. It ain't like you're likely to do better'n me any time soon."

The truth of his words hurt because she wasn't likely to do any better than a cold man like Tandy Barret, who wanted her acres, not her affection. Yet in her heart she had the satisfaction of knowing what he offered wasn't enough, and if that was the best deal she was offered, she was better off sticking with the hand fate had dealt her.

And besides, she was no longer an unkissed innocent who would settle for cold seconds. She'd had a wild taste of passion, and to accept less while

her pulse still beat fast and furious seemed uncon-
scionable.

From the darkness of his room and within the
darkness of his mind, Dalton listened in on their
conversation, at first out of boredom, then with a
sharpening sense of curiosity. A neighbor, Jude had
told him. Not even a close friend. Well, what he'd
gleaned from his purposeful eavesdropping said a
lot more was going on than a remote neighborly
relationship. Why had she lied to him about what
this man was to her? A spurned beau? A prospective
fiancé?

What bothered him more than her deception was
the fact that it bothered him at all.

Why should it matter if Jude Amos had one suitor
or twenty? She was being compensated for her care
of him. It was nothing personal, nor did he want it
to be. He didn't like being beholden to anyone.
Debts had to be paid, and he didn't think he'd like
making good on the terms a woman like Jude would
name. Women didn't barter with practical things
like money or services rendered. They went for
intangibles: commitments of time and promises of
fidelity. Those weren't things he felt free to give. He
couldn't afford to involve himself in her problems.
He had plans: a job waiting, San Francisco calling.
His affliction was the only thing holding him back,
and he hoped that was only temporary. The minute
the first coach came through, he'd be on his way to a
real doctor in Cheyenne. If his vision came back
sooner, it'd be "thank you very much" and he'd be
gone. There could be no foolish sentiments weighing him down, like fondness for a simple young
man and respect for his prideful sister.

What happened in the yard was a mistake he seldom made. He'd let the emotion of the moment guide his actions. There was no room in his future for a lonely woman, her needy brother, and an old cook on their lonesomely situated stage stop. And the sooner he made that clear to all concerned, the better. But first he had to make himself believe it.

It was some time before he heard Jude's rapid steps bringing supper to his door. When she stopped to light the lamp, he was bemused because he hadn't known if it was dark or light within the room. No turning up of a wick could bring brightness back into his world. Bitterness made for a festering mood.

Then, after all his self-cautionings, the first thing out of his mouth was, "Has your company gone?" And those four words were laced with enough abrasiveness to tan a hide.

"Yes" was all she'd say, and that gave nothing away. Dalton stewed over her evasion. First the lie, now avoidance. He simmered in his irritation. If she had another lover in the wings, why had she allowed him to kiss her?

And why did he want to kiss her again?

"Trouble in paradise?" he goaded.

"Nothing I can't handle."

And it galled him to think there probably wasn't much she couldn't handle. Shouldn't he have been grateful for that instead of resenting the hell out of her arrogant capability?

She bent close, torturing him with the scent of lilacs as she placed his tray upon his knees. Then she lifted his hand and touched it to each item on the menu as she described it so he would know their location. Flesh warmed to flesh, and it seemed she couldn't release him fast enough. Because of that, he brusquely refused her offer of assistance, growling that he preferred to eat without her hovering over him. Pricked by his unwarranted hostility, Jude stalked haughtily out of the room—or at least that's how he pictured her exit, all irate bristle and bluster. The only maddeningly absent detail was the image of her face. Wondering about it was driving him close to crazy.

Was her hair long or short, wavy or fine as silk? His brief caress of her tear-slicked cheek had left an impression of dramatic height and intriguing hollow. And her lips were full and lush and sweetly ripe, summer berries plump for the picking. He'd spent many an idle moment wondering about the color of her eyes. They would be expressive, full of flash and fire, yet soft and moist as the dew when she was moved to tenderness. He was a man who admired beauty and spirit, and in Jude Amos he imagined the best of both, an alluring Venus with the temperament of a Valkyrie. If he were allowed only one brief snatch of vision which would have to last him the rest of his life, he would choose for the features of his nurse and nemesis to be there before him, a portrait to last for an eternity. For truly he didn't know how much more of the suspense he could stand.

Left alone to his ill-tempered pondering, Dalton awkwardly cleaned his plate without any major disasters, then lay in wait for her return to claim the tray.

Jude entered slowly, wishing she could invent some reason to excuse Sammy from his chores to see to their guest. But she could come up with none, and the truth wouldn't do. The truth was that Dalton MacKenzie, even marred as he was by his injury, was more of a man than had ever crossed her path.

Merely sharing the same space with him made her body hum with unknown vibrations and her mind go giddy with notions of longing she knew to be ridiculous. He was dangerous, a threat to her house and to her heart, but instead of protecting herself, she'd opened both to him with the naive hope that he wouldn't take too cruel an advantage. He was a man just one rung up from the thieves who'd robbed the stage. He killed for a living, accepting blood money without a blink of remorse. Though he dressed nicely and spoke well and smelled good, he was no better than the most base murderers who hung out in dark alleyways awaiting an unsuspecting victim.

She should have held the very thought of him in contempt. His touch should have caused her flesh to shrink away in disgust and horror. She should have devised ways to be safely rid of him, rather than lying awake all night wishing for the means to make him stay.

His head swiveled toward her when he heard her step, and she marveled at how quickly he'd honed his other senses in defense of the one he lacked. He couldn't see her, but he was so aware of her she felt it in every fiber. When she took his tray, she noticed how little of his food had been spilled or deposited on himself or his bedcovers. He was a fast study. It made him a shrewd predator.

He'd grown quite a bristle of dark whiskers since he'd been in her care. They enhanced the image of a cunning desperado. Even the healing gash at his temple cast a sinister shadow over him. Was she mistaken ever to have thought she'd seen something good, something noble in the gunman's smoothly crafted character?

"Why did you put yourself in jeopardy to save

that man on the stage?" The question had nagged at her since she'd witnessed his amazing heroics— amazing because she could not believe such a sacrifice of any man who was not of a pure heart and sterling ethics. So how did a gun for hire fit into that mold? She had to know.

Dalton didn't answer right away. He mulled over her question, reaching inward for a response rather than spouting some superficial platitude. "He didn't deserve to be shot down for protecting his family. If I hadn't acted, he'd be dead right now, and where do you think that would have left his little boy? You think a vain, petty creature like his mother would have made a good home for him on her own? Not likely. A boy needs a family around him to grow up straight and true, like a seedling in a forest needs sturdy trees to buffer it from the wind until it can stand tall on its own. I couldn't let a greedy act snatch away that boy's right to a happy future."

Of all the things he could have said to explain what he had done, the actual reason he gave was one she never would have guessed. But why should she be so surprised? she asked herself, having seen the way he was with Sammy, so kind and fair in his treatment.

"I wouldn't have taken you for a family man, Mr. MacKenzie."

To her surprise, he bristled at her observation, going still and stiff in form and feature. "I'm not, Miss Amos. And don't ever mistake me for one."

His growl of warning effectively scattered the sweet hopes that had begun to nest about her heart. Foolish longings focused on the wrong man, just as Joseph had told her. In a tight, little voice, she replied, "You needn't worry, Mr. MacKenzie." The dishes rattled as she turned away with tray in hand.

"Don't go."

His soft command startled her, making her hesitate. Something in the quality of that quiet "Don't go" touched her. It was an echo of desperate loneliness that reached right to her soul in companion misery, a pebble of uncertainty dropped down a great dark well of the unknown. Without a thought to consequence, she set the tray aside and assumed the chair angled near his bedside.

"You must be bored," she assumed, trying to put herself in his sightless place, left to daily darkness with nothing to relieve it. "I could read to you, if you like. I don't have much of a selection, some Byron, Tennyson, and Shakespeare, if you like such things." She didn't mention the only other book they owned, their big, battered family Bible. "Or perhaps I could write a letter for you. I do that for the drivers on occasion. Is there someone who might be worrying over your absence?"

"No." That word popped like a whiplash. Then he took a breath, and she could see him relax. "Just talk to me for a while . . . if you can spare the time. I don't want to be burdensome."

The prickle of pride in that made her smile. No, of course he wouldn't want to be beholden for any extra consideration from her. "I have some time, Mr. MacKenzie. What would you like to discuss?"

"When do you think the stage will be through?" he asked her.

Her heart plummeted at his choice of topics. Of course he would be anxious to discover how soon he could get away. "I would guess tomorrow, heading in one direction or the other."

Neither said anything for a moment as both reflected upon the significance of that fact.

"I'm sure they'll have doctors in Cheyenne who

can better diagnose the damage to your eyes." She said that to be helpful, because she wanted to believe it was true.

Dalton was silent, his mouth set in a firm, brooding line as his fingertips traced restless patterns upon the snug denim covering his thighs, drawing her attention there. Before she got caught up in admiring how he was made, she continued their conversation with a difficult question. She spoke it because it was what was foremost on their minds.

"And if your sight doesn't return, what will you do?"

"I could pay someone to shoot me."

Jude recoiled in horror, then noticed the slight tug of a smile teasing about the corners of his mouth. She scowled in relief, as her heart beat a fluttering tattoo within her breast. "With your unique sense of humor, you could probably find someone to do it for free."

He chuckled. "Many would line up for the chance, I'm sure." Then he sobered and Jude knew the subject had been preying on his mind. "I have money saved up. I was planning to use it to go to San Francisco to start a new life. This wasn't exactly the change I'd had in mind. I suppose I'll get a room and hire someone to make sure I don't have gravy spilled on my shirt front and to read me the newspaper or maybe Tennyson." He smiled briefly in her direction before completing the stark picture he'd made of his future. "I'll sit on a balcony all day in the center of some town, listening to life going on around me, letting others do what I can't do for myself."

Or you could stay here.

The words flooded up so fast she nearly said them aloud before common sense snatched them off her lips. Stay here. Why, after being sequestered by blindness, would he want to isolate himself further at this lonesome stage stop? Except if he were here, she would no longer be lonesome.

Shamed by her selfish desires, Jude murmured, "Have you no family to go to?"

He was silent for a moment. "No."

Alone and set apart from a normal existence. Jude's heart ached for him as she made the comparison to her own brother's life. Though Sammy was generally cheerful about his lot, there were times when he was acutely aware of a difference between himself and the rest of the world. And oh, how the pain of that knowledge twisted those dear features and how he'd cried huge tears of anguish, asking what he'd done to deserve such a punishment. No one wanted to be a burden on those they loved. But worse, she thought, would be a dependency on strangers, those who took money to provide the most basic care.

Then Dalton shocked her with his next claim.

"I'm sure the stage line will reimburse you well, but if you feel it isn't enough, I'll make up the difference."

She was too stunned for a long moment even to stutter. "What?"

"I appreciate all you've done. If the line doesn't repay you for your list of expenses, present them to me."

"A—a list?" Confusion lifted as a hot flush of temper rose behind it. "You think I was doing this for the pay?"

"Why else?"

"W-why else?" She gave a strangled laugh and stared at him, facing her loneliness and her hunger for his company. No amount of money could buy

what he'd brought into her life, if only briefly and
reluctantly. He'd given her a glimpse of how it could
be, how it was supposed to be when a woman had a
man to love and care for. But this was not her man.
How had she let herself forget that over a little kiss?
"Why else? No, Mr. MacKenzie, I'm sure you
wouldn't understand a motive other than personal
interest. It is probably beyond your belief that such
things as common decency or Christian compassion
exist."

"Oh, I believe they exist, for a price."

Jude steamed at that arrogant summation, hurting
that he should value her integrity so little. "A price.
Yes, I should be considering my price. Let's see,
that'll be three meals a day plus room, linen
changes, doctoring expenses, gauze, maid services,
mopping up spilled coffee, around-the-clock nursing care, not to mention putting up with your
bullying and vile disposition. Why, Mr. MacKenzie,
are you sure you can afford me?"

Furiously, she surged to her feet, only to be
snagged by the upper arm before she could storm
out.

"Release me," she snarled. "You haven't paid for
the privilege of pawing me. That must be an expense that sorely strains the budget of a man like
you."

He yanked hard, pulling her down to the mattress
next to him so they were seated face-to-face. "I'm
sorry," he told her, meaning it. "It wasn't my
intention to insult you." She readied to let go with
another volley of angry words when he said simply,
sternly, "Shush."

Then his questing hand found her. His fingertips
fanned along the flare of her facial bones, moving
lightly in graceful strokes, the way an artist would,

upon the palette in his mind. He palmed the strong angle of her jaw, smiling in confirmation at its crisp, haughty cut. The pad of his thumb rode the soft swells and valleys of her lips, pausing to measure their sudden trembling. His forefinger drew a line up the straight ridge of her nose, following it to the arch of her brows before circling to do a delicate charting of her quivering eyelids. Lashes whispered against his hand like hummingbird wings.

"What color are your eyes?"

"Gray."

"Like steel or the dawn?"

"That depends upon my mood."

He smiled at that and brushed along her brow until fingers sank deep into her hair, raking gently, curling softly.

"And your hair?"

"Brown."

"Like dark honey or sable?"

"Just brown."

"Brown." And the way he said it made it sound like the most glorious shade in the spectrum. "Smooth like silk."

Chills took her body, followed closely by a ferocious heat as he continued to scan her face with his fingertips, as if memorizing each detail, translating texture and topography into an image he could hold within his head.

At last, as his knuckles stroked down the line of her throat, over the jerk of her rapid swallowing, he crushed her dream with a husky pronouncement.

"Beautiful. Just as I'd imagined."

Jude slipped from his grasp and was out the door before the tears upon her plain face betrayed her.

It took a moment for Dalton's aroused senses to relax enough for thought to begin working on what had been said. She hadn't taken care of him for the purpose of reward. Then why? Decency? Charity? She was such an enigma to him. The women he knew were self-absorbed, grasping creatures who expected a return for the most meager smile. And he paid them to anticipate his wants and not complicate his pleasures. What did he know about an honest, gentle female who needed to be taught about her own pleasures, who was willing to sacrifice her own comfort to see to a stranger's?

Looking back, he could see how her barbed words and provoking banter kept him from brooding over his situation. She'd never allowed him to feel vulnerable in her care. She refused to display pity or dismay when he spilled his coffee or fumbled for his fork. It was the way she must have raised her brother, so he would know a sense of accomplishment, not failure, so he would feel surrounded by love, not resentment.

For that was exactly how she'd made him feel.

He, the eternal wanderer, felt at home under her roof. He, who had never had one, felt embraced by family. He, who had never known the benefits, was lost to a tender touch. And the quiet passion of Jude Amos stirred a not so innocent flame inside him, one that would devour if he let it, one that would burn hot and lay to waste all in its aftermath if he allowed it to escape. That he could not do.

He reached up to finger the binding over his eyes, and a cold, sinking fear began in his belly. Blind for the rest of his years. A cruel judgment for the life he'd led but somehow just, all the same. He'd lived by those keen eyes, and now their loss snatched away his unsavory occupation.

He hadn't told Jude about his past or his current purpose, and his reluctance for her to discover them was a surprise. He wasn't one to apologize for his profession. Could a woman so accepting of her brother's imperfections find room in her compassionate soul for one as dark as his?

And as he wondered, he recognized his reluctance to leave this place where he'd found safety and, in a strange way, contentment.

She hadn't taken him in for pay. That novel discovery still amazed.

Then why?

And if it wasn't money she wanted, how could he repay her?

Chapter 8

Explosions of gunfire jerked Dalton from a nightmare into a waking horror. He sat up within his veil of blackness as shots echoed through the night outside. Dalton's first instinctive move was to lunge for the bedpost . . . coming up confused at his empty-handed state. No guns. He never closed his eyes at night without turning pistol butts his way for a quick defensive draw. Then the true depth of his situation sank in as recall came back to him.

Not only was he unarmed, but he was helpless as well.

Hoofbeats and raucous shouts joined in the pistol play as night riders circled Amos Station. From the outer room he heard Biscuit barking over Sammy's frightened cries and Joseph's low reassurances, followed by a scuffle of movement overhead where Jude slept. She was dressing—not to rush into foolishness, he prayed. Not sensible Jude, who shunned violence as a solution. Surely she wouldn't break her own tenets to confront the danger outside. No, not Jude.

Jude, stay put, damn you!

He listened over the harsh sound of his own breathing as she climbed down the ladder, murmuring calm sentiments. For a moment he was able to sigh in relief, believing she would do the smart thing and crouch down out of harm's way. *Smart woman, Jude.* Then he picked up the distinctive clunk-clank of cartridges being fed into a Winchester.

His curse rent the night air. The damn fool woman was going outside to face the marauders with nothing more than an old rifle and a barrelful of grit.

She was going to get herself killed.

And he, the professional gunman and sharpshooter extraordinaire, sat swaddled in his own darkness, unable to do a damned thing to defend those for whom he'd come to care.

Or was he?

Jude stepped out into the glare of torchlight, clutching at the rifle she'd never pointed at another human being. Her hair whipped loose about her features, and her nightclothes snapped snug to her hips and between her spraddled legs. Ghostly shapes swirled about her front yard, masked men on horses. Struggling to contain her terror, she lifted her head, squared her shoulders, and forced her voice to carry a fearless command.

"What do you men want? Be warned that this property is under the protection of the Cheyenne and Black Hills Stage Line."

There was a moment of deafening silence as the riders formed a line, facing her on the porch. Horses tossed their heads and pawed up her yard restlessly. Torchlight bent and bowed in the night's stiff breeze. And a column of masked strangers confronted her, menace plain in their very presence.

Jude was terrified.

"You were offered protection," came a growling reply from one of the shadowy figures. "You were stupid to turn it down."

"Who are you? Cowards, hiding behind masks! You've done your night's work, now get off my property!"

"Our work's not done," came an ominous warning. The hair on Jude's nape stood up as she considered what that might mean, but she couldn't back down, not with her family in the house behind her.

"Are you here to shoot me down on my front porch?" she yelled back, voicing her greatest fear.

"We're here to give you another chance to think about the mistake you're making."

"What mistake?" She brought the rifle up into aggressive play. "You've had my answer. There's nothing to think about."

A vile laugh carried upon the cool air, putting a chill to her very bones as the man drawled, "A woman out here alone—why, terrible things might happen."

A shudder rippled through Jude as her sweaty hands slid upon the rifle stock. They wouldn't dare. *They wouldn't dare!* Uncertainty quivered behind that bold assurance. Why wouldn't they? Never had she been so aware of her isolation. Who would stop them? What was to keep them from taking whatever they wanted under the dark cloak of night? Only her. It was time to display a show of force, but what could she do that wouldn't backfire if they called her bluff? Could she actually pull the trigger, flinging death at her intruders? Was there the slightest chance of her hitting any of them if she found that courage? She was a woman alone, with a brother and an old friend. She was the only one standing in the way of devastating consequences. Backed into a desperate corner, she prayed frantically for an avenue of escape.

"You're wrong, gents," came a sudden declaration from the darkness of the porch behind her. "The lady's not alone."

And none of the men were as surprised as Jude to see a big figure step forward into the erratic flicker of light. Dalton reached out unerringly to take the rifle from her slack grip and cracked it expertly to bring a cartridge into play. He stood at her side, a tower of authority and dangerous determination, his unbound eyes glaring out at the riders as if he were memorizing every detail from trouser creases to dusty tack with retribution on his mind.

"It would be my suggestion that you fellows find a more appropriate time to come calling. It's a bit too late to be entertaining tonight." The rifle swept the group meaningfully. "Unless you insist upon it."

And not one of them had the slightest idea that the threatening man couldn't see out of his own darkness.

"We got no quarrel with you, mister. We just come out to deliver a message to the lady. C'mon boys, let's ride." And as quickly as they had appeared, they rode off into the night.

"Are they gone?" Dalton asked at last, still braced like a sturdy oak to face down an enemy he couldn't see.

Jude's trembling fingers slid over the hand holding the rifle at ready, coaxing the barrel down. "Yes. Thanks to you."

"Boy howdy, that sure was something!" Sammy crowed gleefully.

"Stay in the house," Jude commanded, fear putting a crack in her voice. "They might be back."

"Oh, I doubt that," Dalton drawled. "Their kind are coyotes, sneaking up to sniff around for an easy kill. They won't come back for something they have to work at."

"You're sure?"

"I know their kind well, and you can go back and sleep sound. They don't get paid enough to mix in more trouble than they can handle."

Dalton MacKenzie: bold, selfless hero once again.

An appreciative shiver started in the pit of Jude's belly, displacing the terror that was there only moments ago.

"Thank God," Jude sighed. She took possession of the rifle and let Dalton curl his arm through hers. "You were very impressive. I almost believed what I was seeing."

"As long as they did. Joseph told me to take four steps and stand planted. What they didn't know was to our advantage. And it was to mine that the light was bad. I think I got my shirt on inside out."

It was such a relief to laugh now that the tension of the moment was over. But as Jude led their brawny rescuer inside, she was aware of another tension building: something long smoldering and ready to catch like a grass fire at the slightest spark. There were sparks aplenty where they were linked, hand and arm. Expectation hung between them like lightning-charged air, sizzling with excitement, prickly with want. Dangerous. Jude knew she should pull away and protect herself, find some low ground and take cover before she was consumed by the gathering storm of passions. Yet like the powerful strobes that rent the sky, this untapped desire for the man beside her attracted as well as frightened with its dark and deadly fascination.

"Joseph, get Sammy settled back down for the night while I see to Mr. MacKenzie."

"Awwww, Jude . . ."

She gave her brother a piercing look, and he pulled a sour face as he kicked at his blankets. In the long nightshirt he looked like a sullen little boy. A very big little boy. But Jude didn't worry that he would disobey. Even as she guided Dalton toward the bedroom, he was shoving Biscuit off the center of his pallet so he could crawl in next to the old hound.

Joseph's pensive gaze followed her, but he did not.

As she moved Dalton toward the bed, he dragged back on her arm.

"You didn't light the lamp."

"I don't need it," she told him. "I know every inch of this room. After my father died, Sammy used to have bad dreams and I'd come down here to sit with him. It was easier to get him quieted without the shock of brightness."

"It won't bother me," he said, smiling thinly.

Jude turned up the lamp, bringing a soft glow to the room's interior. In truth, she preferred the darkness, where she wouldn't have to look upon Dalton's face and be reminded that he thought she was beautiful because he couldn't see her.

Without the binding over his eyes, he seemed to watch her, his stare fixed upon her, his gaze tracking her movements though she knew it was just an illusion, that he was merely following the sound and scent of her. Still the effect was unnerving. She'd forgotten how bright and searingly blue his eyes were. The area around them was still raw in spots and sporting new pink skin which was a dramatic contrast to the worn brown leather of his cheeks. Parts of his lashes and brows had been singed away, giving him a ragged, roguish look which deepened his sinister appeal. So handsome.

"Those men, who were they?" Dalton demanded.

"Local bullies looking to frighten us out of our water rights," she told him as she rearranged covers still warm from him between them. His covers. His bed. So close. So tempting. Lord help her, she wanted to give in to it—to him.

"And would you have been frightened off if I'd not been here?"

"No, Mr. MacKenzie. I stand firm on what's mine. I might be persuaded by reason, but I won't be pushed by brute force."

"I'll remember that," he murmured. Then his tone sharpened with what might have been real annoyance. "There's that 'Mr. MacKenzie' again. I thought I asked you not to call me that."

"Why? Is it a title reserved for only your father?" She had thought to be teasing, but a sudden stillness came over his features, cooling the warmth that had been there seconds before.

"I don't know what name that individual goes by, but the title I've bestowed upon him is not meant for polite company." He turned away abruptly, his show of tightly controlled distress making Jude regret her attempt at levity. He shucked off his shirt and gave it a toss in the direction of the side chair. "You don't need to stay, Miss Amos. I'm used to undressing in the dark, and I never have bad dreams."

Even after being so bluntly dismissed, Jude lingered on because she sensed she had somehow

wounded him with her careless words and felt badly
for it. And because the mood of tension was still
between them, compelling her to stay. As he peeled
off his denims, she said very softly, "Thank you for
what you did outside, Dalton. I don't know what I
would have done . . ."

He swiveled back around, still in a half crouch, as
her voice fractured with suppressed emotion. And
he smiled, a rich, rueful smile with the power of a
sunrise. "You would have done just fine, Jude. I've
never known a female with your kind of pluck. You
would have brazened your way out of it and sent
them packing with tails between their legs."

Her answering smile wavered pathetically, but of
course he couldn't see it. "Perhaps."

He straightened then, his greater height overwhelming her within the confines of her brother's
room. "You sell yourself short sometimes, Jude, and
I'm not sure I understand why."

Why, she wondered wildly. Because she was letting him believe a lie, a lie that said she was
beautiful. She wasn't brave. If she were, she would
have told him the truth. Her knees had knocked
together like a trilling cicada beneath the drape of
her nightdress when she'd faced the night raiders.
Her mind had been paralyzed with fear. And if they
came back once Dalton was gone, she wasn't sure
she could stand up to them again.

"Maybe you should think of selling," Dalton
suggested softly, as if he could read the turmoil of
her thoughts. "It's a lonesome life out here for a
woman alone. You could make a new one for
yourself—"

"Where?" she cut in brittlely. "In the city? Where
folks would greet Joseph with hostility and suspicion? Where kids and adults alike would taunt

Sammy on the sidewalks? I won't have them hurt like that, and I won't leave them behind, Dalton. They're my family, my responsibility. So I'll thank you to mind your own business."

"I thought you wanted to thank me for chasing off those hombres tonight."

She paused in her frustrated speech and gave a heavy sigh, her temper deflating with it. "I do. And I'm sorry. I have no cause to snap at you. I do want to thank you for risking so much on our behalf."

"Then thank me from over here."

He extended his hand, fingers beckoning in a slow curl.

And not knowing what he expected, only what she hoped for, Jude went to him, easing her fingers across his broad palm, delighting in the solid, sensual way his closed around them, a gentle binding to hold her fast before him. Not that she ever gave a thought to retreat. Her eyes slid shut as his other hand found her cheek. His thumb locked beneath her chin, lifting so that her face was raised in offering. For a moment she forgot to breathe.

Then he was kissing her, as sweetly as she could ever dream of, as hotly as she could ever desire. And she was answering each slant, each varying pressure, each sensuous slide of his tongue, with her arms wrapped around him, on the very tips of her toes. She arched into him, her breasts hurting inside the binding of her white nightdress and faded robe. At that moment she wished she were garbed in silk and wearing fancy garters and stockings like that harlot on the stairs—anything that would keep her from being quite so plain. Plain Jude Amos, who ached with her need for this dangerous man.

But then his free hand spread wide upon the

curve of her torso and slid up, one rib at a time, until thumb and forefinger supported the weight of her breast. Just that. No hasty groping, no possessing squeezes, as if he knew such aggressive claims might frighten her away. As her heart pounded into his palm, she forgot about not being beautiful because what he made her feel was gloriously so. And because he waited, poised on the brink of bringing her bliss, she lost all patience.

She broke from his kiss, her breath coming in small gasps, seeking some control. None could be found in the hot, urgent world he'd created for her.

"Oh, Dalton," she whispered, afraid of what was happening to her, afraid if she stopped him, she would never have another chance to know . . . rapture. Pure, hot and cold running passion, scalding her senses one instant, then shivering to her toes the next.

He kissed her brow, the roughness of his whiskers scratching her cheek, but even that sensation was exciting like no other. Then his thumb stroked the full plumpness of her breast, the movement maddeningly slow, full of confidence and admiration. By the time he reached the quivering bud of her nipple, it had tightened into a hard knot of raw desire. He made a lazy revolution, and she nearly came apart with pleasure. She buried her face against his shoulder, seeking the same darkness to which he was lost, then marveled at the way her other senses heightened in compensation. Her skin felt hot and liquid; beneath it her blood pulsed hard and fast. She drew in the scent of him with each shallow breath until she was light-headed, intoxicated by the heavy male heat of him.

And while she surrendered to her senses, he

continued to touch her, teasing with his fingertips, toying with her, tempting a pucker into pebble hardness, then pressing her flat beneath his broad palm. She'd never imagined such a limited caress could arouse such a far-reaching host of responses. She felt him all the way to the arches of her feet. And suddenly it was agony to remain passive in his arms.

She reached up both hands to clasp his bearded cheeks, holding him for the voracious assault of her mouth upon his. She tasted the warm textures, even biting gently in her fervor. She thrust deep to explore the inner cavern of his mouth, abandoning herself to a liberating wildness borne of years of caged chastity. She bruised him with her eagerness to learn all that she'd missed.

He let her have her way without protest, merely holding her waist with his hands and bending obligingly so she could take all of him she wanted. Then, gradually, he took back control, overpowering her with his greater experience to become teacher to her impatient student. He quieted her with a slow, deepening pressure, parting her lips beneath his until she felt vulnerably opened to his intent. But instead of a rough, plunging demand, he treated her to a delicate passion play which flickered along her quivering nerve ends until she lay nearly swooning upon him, a jumble of exposed yearnings.

"You should be kissed like this every night for the rest of your life," he murmured as their breaths mated as fragilely as their tongues had. And Jude trembled, too overcome to argue, too weak with delight to ask, *"By you?"*

Then there came a jarring rumble from the doorway as Joseph cleared his throat, and the intimate

moment they'd shared was gone. Jude stepped
down from him to find that her legs had become
embarrassingly unreliable. Her grip on his forearms
was a matter of preservation.

To recover from the way things must have looked
to Joseph, she said rather hoarsely, "Thank you
again, Mr. MacKenzie, for what you did tonight."

And Dalton's hands came away leisurely, just as a
mocking smile touched his lips. "You're very welcome, Miss Amos. For everything."

Flushing at his husky innuendo, she sidled back
and said to the ancient Sioux without ever looking
his way, "Joseph, see to Mr. MacKenzie's eyes. He'll
need a fresh dressing." Then she hurried out of the
room, her hands clutching the front of her robe
together over her breasts as if to contain the frantic
heartbeats that came with the discovery of passion.
She slipped past Joseph, feeling his stare right to the
blush of her soul because of what he'd seen. Where
it all might have led, had he not stepped in to shock
them both back to reality, trembled upon her
thoughts, and she half thanked, half cursed the old
man for his timing. Things could have ended in
disaster, but what she'd been able to sample, however briefly, was enough to sustain her dreams for
an eternity.

Joseph glared at the gunman, knowing he could
feel the displeasure even if he couldn't gauge his
expression. "Sit. I will get clean wrappings."

"Don't bother, Joseph," Dalton countered. "It
feels rather good to go without for a while. The
burns are almost healed, and I was suffocating
underneath all that gauze."

Joseph grunted noncommittally.

"I'm not going to hurt her, Joseph, if that's what's

worrying you. I'll be gone as soon as the stage comes through, and you can have her all to yourself. She'll forget I was ever here."

Again the uncommunicative snort. "If that is what you think, you are better off gone," came his gruff reply. He reached for the lamp and it flared briefly before pitching the room into darkness, then he shuffled back to his welcoming pallet.

But Dalton didn't seek his covers. He stood planted where he was for the longest time, his mouth dry, his pulse racing in fragile hope. Because for an instant, for just a flickering second, he'd seen the vague reflection of light against the blackness of his world.

And he was desperately afraid to hope he'd seen the first shadows of returning vision for fear it was not so.

Chapter 9

Jude expected to toss and turn all night, reliving the excitement of Dalton's embrace. It was almost with regret that she opened her eyes to the brightness of morning with no memory of a single dream. But far from feeling rested, a deep ache of anxiousness pulled upon her heart. Maybe this day, maybe tomorrow, Dalton was going to be gone from her life, and she would never again know those exquisite shocks of sensation he'd awakened with his touch. And never again would a man make her feel beautiful.

She dressed with care that morning, slipping on her best gown of soft, gray wool. It was one of the few she owned that were not patched or altered or worn shiny at the seams and elbows. The bodice hugged the line of her breasts firmly and encased her middle with a molding confidence—the way the spread of Dalton's hands had. But the moment she checked her appearance in the small mirror that had been her mother's, she mourned the gown's unrelieved simplicity. Oh, for a flirty lace collar or a feminine frill at the buttoned front! She'd never thought much of impractical details, choosing her clothing for sensible service, not fluffy appeal. All her choices had been like that, all her life. Never had she selected a bold color or bright calico print. Never had she tried on a foolish hat. Her wardrobe was sturdy and perfunctory, her concern for cleanliness not comeliness. She'd thought affectation ridiculous in the extreme. Why pretend to be what she was not?

Slowly, she wound her fine, straight hair up away from her neck, confining it in a snug web of black netting. And she stared at herself in the glass, thinking how old she looked, how tired. She looked like a spinster, resigned to her staid lot in life. And that wasn't who she wanted to be.

She climbed down the ladder, taking care to move quietly, for Sammy and Joseph were still asleep at the cold hearth. Not even Biscuit stirred as she stood in the room's center, debating whether to go right to Dalton's side. Would he see it as concern or clinging? But that was silly. Every morning she'd peeked in briefly to check on how he fared during the night. To do differently this morning would draw more notice by omission. She sucked in a deep breath and went purposefully to the bedroom where the door stood open. And the room stood empty.

A moment's panic was replaced by the reality that there was nowhere he could have gone. Or at least he couldn't have gone far, not on his own, not without the fancy stitched boots still standing in the corner.

Jude found him on the front porch, leaning back in one of the rockers. His feet were bare and so were his eyes as he sat as if drinking in the glorious shades of the sunrise. But that, of course, was impossible. Perhaps he was enjoying the feel of its increasing heat upon his face or simply the freedom wafting down on the first fresh breath of dew-

softened air. Then he turned his head toward her,
and his searingly blue eyes fixed upon her face. And
as she recognized the signs of his surprise, she
realized that he *had* been watching the sun come up.
Just as he was now taking in the lines of her face.

"You can see."

Her claim was redundant, for she could tell he
was absorbing everything in one sweeping, thorough glance, from her sturdy half boots up the
unadorned tailoring of her gown to features left bare
and plain by the backward scoop of her hair in the
captive netting. Never had she felt quite so exposed
and vulnerable as she waited for his disappointment
to make itself known.

Shock was a lightning flash across his face, then it
was gone. He was too much of a gentleman to let his
thoughts—or his dismay—display themselves
rudely. Instead she watched him garner his emotions behind a smooth smile and an incredible
understatement.

"It will take some time to get used to your face
after a week of imagining it differently." Then his
brow puckered and he asked, "Why didn't you tell
me you were the woman on the stage?"

He remembered.

She was so startled, it took her a moment to
respond. "I—I didn't think you would have any
recollection of me." And more accurately, it was
because that wasn't how she wanted him to see her,
not as that plain, ordinary-featured traveler he'd
found no reason to give a second glance. She'd
allowed herself to take advantage of his blindness,
to let him picture a beautiful woman, so that just for
a little while she could be that woman and be
desired by a handsome man. But now that exagger-

ation was exposed to his unblinking stare, and she couldn't stand the shame of waiting for his disapproval to gather.

None of it was working out as Dalton had planned, none of it at all. When he'd discovered his vision was back, he'd been as anxious as a boy with a secret dying to be told. He'd wanted to share his joy, his victory with one person, with Jude. He'd wanted to snatch her up for a celebratory spin, then kiss the starch out of her right there beneath that glorious dawning daylight. He'd fidgeted in anticipation, expectation like an itch he couldn't reach as he waited for her to wake and find him. The only thing on his mind had been not a return to his career, not a liberating sense of freedom, but a relief from the suspense of not knowing what she really looked like.

He'd been unable to believe what his eyes told him.

This wasn't the woman who'd haunted his dreams.

What cruel joke was being played upon him?

Her face, her form, so achingly unattractive, so impossibly plain. All the churning desire he'd felt for her jerked up to an anguished stillness.

No!

Then he saw the hurt building in her eyes, rising like a flood, and he caught himself before he betrayed his anger at the fates for their twisted humor. He'd fallen in love with an unsuitable woman. The joke was on him, but he owed her too much, this woman with her unappealing features, to let her bear the brunt of it.

So he hid his horror as best he could and hoped she'd never suspect that, at that moment, he wished

his blindness had remained until he was out of her
care so his image of her would have remained in
untarnished purity.

"You'll be leaving now." She spoke firmly. It was
more statement than question.

Still shaken by his discovery, Dalton was slow of
wit in his response. "I suspect so. I've got work
waiting and I'd best be getting to it now that I'm
able."

Jude took a step back toward the house, hating
the sting of hurtful tears burning behind her grim
smile. "I'll go get breakfast started. If you'll excuse
me."

"Yes, ma'am."

Ma'am. After the wild kisses they'd shared, she
was "ma'am" again. Swallowing hard, she turned
and proceeded into the house with all the fractured
dignity she could muster.

Her careless banging of pots and pans woke the
late sleepers and had Biscuit milling about under-
foot, his heavy tail banging into the backs of her
legs. She was slicing off slabs of bacon when Dalton
sauntered in and Sammy nearly swallowed his yawn
whole in his surprise. The gunman sized up the
husky young man and gave a huge grin of acknowledgment.

"G'morning, Sam."

"Mac, you can see!"

Unlike his sister, Sammy Amos was everything
Dalton had envisioned: big yet endearingly boyish,
from tousled hair to puppy-dog eyes. There was
none of the slack dullness about him that Dalton
remembered in those unkindly called "idiots" by
mean members of his childhood circle. Sammy was
bright and shiny as a new penny.

"Hmmph," came a smug sound of superiority.

"And some doubted my ability to help the spirits heal."

Dalton blinked at Joseph. It was a day for surprises. "You're an Indian."

"I know. And you owe me, white man."

And as he dragged his old bones up out of his blankets, Joseph slid a look toward the straight back braced before the stove.

For the first time Dalton joined them at the breakfast table. Sammy could scarcely spare the time to chew as he fired off questions about Dalton's newly recovered vision. And Dalton couldn't keep his gaze from shifting to the quiet figure of Jude Amos as she served up their meal.

Once he'd seen a ventriloquist throw his voice into a wooden puppet. He'd laughed with amazement as the words seemed to come out of that hinged jaw. Watching Jude ask if anyone wanted more coffee was like that; the voice was familiar, but it wasn't issued from the lips that were moving. At least not in his mind. When he'd been a prisoner of darkness, he'd fashioned a face to go with that no-nonsense voice and husky laugh. He'd used the sensory scans from his fingertips like a sculptor and worked up each feature from there, crafting, almost lovingly, what his heart told him must be there: beautiful features to match what he knew of the woman. To be confronted with such an unfamiliar and unspectacular face dealt a startling blow, a stranger who spoke with the words of a loved one. And he mourned the loss of the woman he'd adored within his imagination.

"Mr. MacKenzie will be leaving after breakfast," Jude announced in a constricted tone. "Sammy, will you cut out a good horse for him? He can leave it at the livery in Cheyenne."

"Leaving?" Sammy groaned. "You can't go yet, Mac."

"I'm afraid I have to, Sam. I've got a job waiting, one I've already been paid to do. They must already be wondering what happened to me."

Sammy chewed on that for a moment, looking distraught and sad. "But you'll come back and see us again, won't you?"

"I'll surely do my best." And with that promise, his gaze lifted to Jude's, then dropped away. While she stood in misery, thinking he couldn't bear to look upon her, he was grieving over the truth he hadn't told her, facts that would have him less than welcome under their roof. It was time to take his medicine like a man. "I won't be going all the way into Cheyenne, though. I'm heading out to a local ranch, a place called Sweetgrass. Can you direct me there?"

Jude went still. "You're working for Patrick Jamison?"

"He's the one who hired me, yes, ma'am." And Dalton paused with coffee cup halfway to his lips, sensing a sudden shift in all he'd come to know and enjoy at Amos Station.

Suddenly he was an outsider, an unwelcomed one at that.

"Oh, you won't have no trouble finding him," Sammy chattered on, completely missing the dark overtones that had settled at the table with them. "His ranch is the biggest an' grandest in these here parts. You head out thata way and you can't miss it. Are you gonna punch cows for Mr. Jamison?"

"No, Sammy," came Jude's brittle explanation. "Mr. MacKenzie is a specialist. He doesn't work out of a saddle. He does his business down the sights of a gun."

Sammy frowned, clearly not understanding, but before he could ask any questions, his sister snapped, "Now, you go get Mr. MacKenzie a horse."

"Yessum," he grumbled, pushing back from the table and shooting Dalton a baleful glance which looked ever so much like Biscuit when he was begging for scraps. As he shuffled out, the old hound whined unhappily, torn between a table full of yet-to-be-cleaned plates and his beloved master. Finally loyalty won out, and he trotted after Sammy.

"You never mentioned you were on Jamison's payroll," Jude said as she began gathering up the plates before Dalton had finished what was on his. Her tone was ripe with accusation.

"Had I done so, would I have found myself out on the porch in the rain that first night?"

She looked at him as if the answer were "yes" but muttered, "No, of course not. Those were Jamison's men who came calling last night. Had I known you were going to be working with them—or should I say leading them?—I would have introduced you. I hope you haven't placed your employment in jeopardy by standing them off at rifle point."

"I wouldn't have done any different if I had known who they were."

Her cutting stare doubted him as she turned toward the stove with a snap of her skirts. He watched her stomp away. This was how he'd pictured her: that ramrod posture and haughtily held head. And a slight smile curved his lips—until her next curt words ironed them flat.

"It's time you gathered up your belongings, Mr. MacKenzie. Everything's in your room, everything except your guns, of course, and I can't say I mourn your loss of them, considering."

"I appreciate your taking care of my things and

me." He rose up and couldn't help but notice how she shrank back at his sudden overwhelming stance, as if with the recovery of his eyesight he'd become a threat to her and hers. And maybe she was right. "What do I owe you?"

"I believe we already discussed that," came her tart reply. "Hospitality has no price on it, nor does Christian charity."

"I might argue that with you, Miss Amos. Perhaps another time."

"I doubt that when we meet again there'll be much time for pleasantries." Her gaze lifted to Sammy. "Is his horse ready?"

"I got Fancy tied up out front," he muttered. "Can I help you put your stuff together, Mac?"

"You'll only be in the way, Sammy," Jude warned. She was surprised by the chill of Dalton's glare.

"No, he won't. Come on, Sam."

And the big, sulking figure huddled on the foot of the bed while Dalton repacked his belongings and brooded over why it felt for all the world as if he were leaving home. Running away. Or being evicted. In a short time, perhaps because of his helplessness, he'd grown into an integral part of the Amos household. And he'd liked it, that sense of belonging somewhere. Once he left, he had the feeling that Jude would be right. He wouldn't be back for a visit, at least not for a neighborly one, even if Jude would welcome him, which he doubted. He wasn't the same man to her anymore. He'd seen it in her eyes when he'd announced where he was going. She'd made her opinions clear about the kind of life he led. She had no use for violence or intimidation, and those things went hand in glove with what he did. No, there'd be no stopping back for friendly "howdies." And he only hoped he wouldn't be called upon to make another kind of visit, one that would follow up on the one paid by the night riders.

"Guess that's everything."

Everything except those intangible feelings filling this room, ties of longing he should have known better than to allow. Men in his profession didn't make ties. They didn't have homes. They didn't make friends. No one waited anxiously for their return or waved a sad farewell. It was better that way. But how to explain that to Sammy when he lifted those huge, swimming eyes.

"You will come back, won't you, Mac?"

"We'll see, Sam. That's the best I can do. If I don't get back this way, I want you to promise you'll take care of things here. You're the man of the house."

He blinked in surprise as if that had never occurred to him. Then his shoulders angled back and his chest puffed out proudly. "I surely will, Mac. Don't you worry about a thing." Then he gave a whimpery sigh. "But I still hope you'll come back."

Oh, hell. Dalton groaned right to the soul. It was time to cut and run before things got any worse.

Shouldering his belongings, he strode out into the main room and he knew right then that things were fixing to get a whole lot worse. Jude was standing at the table, her unfamiliar features set in somber lines and her fine gray eyes all liquid emotion. Joseph was beside her, his penetrating gaze calling Dalton on his hastily made vow not to hurt her. Too late. He could read heartache all over the staunch set of her jaw. It wasn't as if he'd made her any promises. She had no reason to hang on his spirit like a solemn vow broken. He'd kissed her. She'd liked it. She'd kissed him. He'd liked that even better. His hands had done some roaming, true, but she wasn't some winsome girl who could cry innocence. Or was she?

It didn't matter what she was. It was all about who he was and what he was off to do. No decent woman had any business attaching herself to a man like him. And Jude Amos was the only decent and deserving woman he'd ever known.

"Thanks again for seeing to me. If ever I can repay you, you've but to ask."

"We won't be asking anything of you, Mr. Mac-Kenzie. That's not why the kindness was offered." Was there an unspoken jibe in those coolly delivered words? Probably, knowing her as he'd come to. She wasn't one to keep her disapproval to herself.

"Well, anyway, I feel beholden. And I am grateful to you, in spite of what I might have said at first." He smiled to remind her, and for a moment she smiled back. The exchange was somehow bittersweet for that shared piece of the past.

What more was there to say? He headed for the door, Sammy and Biscuit dogging his steps. Joseph and finally Jude came later, as he was swinging up onto the big, dark bay Sammy had picked for him. He patted the animal's neck in appreciation.

"Fine piece of horseflesh."

"You can have one of Jamison's men bring him back over. I'm sure your new employer will want to turn you out after his own style." There was a definite bite to that. Dalton smiled in retaliation.

"Nobody turns me out to suit themselves, Miss Amos. You might remember that." He tipped his Stetson to the two on the porch, then tousled Sammy's hair as the young man stood gripping his bridle. Sammy was choking back tears when he let the ribbons go and stumbled back so Dalton could wheel the animal around. He kicked Fancy up into a smart canter.

And it took every scrap of his willpower not to look back even once over his shoulder.

Chapter 10

Dalton rode for miles over rolling plains and grassy hills where not a sign of any living thing appeared. Just when he'd begun to think it was the most lonesome land he'd ever seen, his big bay popped up over a ridge, and before him stretched a rancher's Eden.

Cattle dotted the landscape by the thousands, attended by a scattering of cowboys in their wide-brimmed hats, leather chaps, and big roweled Mexican spurs. He rode through their midst, drawing a few curious gazes from the men moving the placid herd with slow, graceful twirls of manila. Dalton spared them no attention. Eventually he came to Sweetgrass, and there he paused to take in the impressive sight.

The main residence was brick and beautifully situated among a line of box-elder trees, with their stout, crooked trunks and gnarled limbs reaching out like a crew of ancient workers applying the last of the fancy adornment to the wraparound porch. Slanting sunlight glinted off two stories of windows, reminding him of the warning flashes off gun barrels. As he approached, that feeling of uneasiness mounted. True, all was on a grand scale, the buildings and barns all embraced by a huge square of fencing, boasting wealth and conquest, but there was no sign of warmth or welcome, only arrogant domination of the surrounding valley. Nor did he receive a cheerful greeting by the trio of men who rode out, bristling with armaments, to meet him.

"Where the hell do you think yer going?" growled the one in charge. Dalton ignored him, continuing on toward the house. The others gave their leader an expectant glance, goading the thin-lipped ranch hand to follow rather than block, as was his intention. "Hey, I'm talking to you. What's yer business here?"

"My business" was all Dalton would allow, not looking around, as if he didn't consider the others any kind of threat.

Insulted by the stranger's disregard, the top hand kicked his mount into a gallop and jerked it hard so the animal cut in front of Dalton's bay. Dalton had no choice but to rein in or ride right over him.

"I said what's yer business here?"

Dalton leveled a chill blue stare, annoyed by the interference. "My business is bought and well paid for by your boss, and I don't reckon he values you enough to discuss it with you or you'd know the answer. Now, kindly get out of my way." And he prodded the bay forward, forcing the other to wheel about in a tight circle.

The three ranchmen exchanged angry and anxious looks. One of them grumbled, "Who's that sonofabitch think he is?" Someone they didn't want to mess with, was the unspoken answer. They fell in behind the tall stranger, trailing him like mongrel curs all the way up to the porch where Patrick Jamison emerged and confirmed their reasoning with his first accusing words.

"You're late, Mr. MacKenzie."

"I don't recall that I gave you a specific time to expect me." Dalton reined up and regarded the rancher from the superior position of his saddle. His stare was unwavering and unapologetic, demanding a response that Jamison finally gave with a shifting nervousness.

"Well, I guess you didn't at that. Step on down, MacKenzie."

"I prefer that you keep that 'Mister' tacked on in front," came his cool drawl, and he continued to sit atop the tall bay until Jamison fidgeted and flushed uncomfortably.

"Please step on down, Mr. MacKenzie. My men will attend to your horse for you."

Dalton swung down and patted the bay. "He's a fine animal, but he's not mine. Have one of these fellows take him back over to Amos Station with the proper rental fee."

The ranch hands balked at being ordered around by some unarmed stranger, but their boss flipped a gold piece to the fast-lipped leader and jerked his head to the north. "See to it, Monty."

The foreman glared resentfully at the haughty intruder who could cause his employer to dismiss him so roughly to menial work. He snapped a look at one of his underlings and snarled, "Ned, see to it."

Jamison stepped aside, waving his hand toward the interior of his home. "Mr. MacKenzie, I have some brandy in my study that makes an excellent dust cutter. Monty, have his bags brought in."

"Into the main house?" Monty repeated in disbelief.

"That's what I said." And Jamison waited for the big man to precede him inside.

Who the hell was this fellow to ride on in with a chip the size of Nebraska on his shoulder, demanding that the boss call him "Mister" and garnering a room in the big house like an important guest? Hell, as foreman he'd never been invited beyond the leather-scented study, and that was only on rare occasions. Monty's gaze squinted as it detailed MacKenzie's back and he wondered why all at once the man seemed so familiar to him. He wasn't one to give up until the circumstances came back to him.

And he hoped those circumstances would bode ill for Jamison's guest.

Dalton advanced into Jamison's study. He'd been in enough posh homes not to appear awed by the opulent surroundings. He let his gaze idly survey the walls of bound books and buffalo-head trophies as his host moved to a vast mahogany credenza and splashed their liquor into two snifters. Glass clattered on glass. Jamison was unusually agitated for a man of prominence within his own home.

"Let me tell you a little something about my operation here, Mr. MacKenzie. So far I have plans to put thirty-two thousand acres under fence for a herd of close to seventy-five hundred head on some of the best needle grass and bluestem in the Wyoming territory. I've got the best blooded stock in these parts, having mixed imported Herefords in with the breeding herd to bulk up the product. I own four shorthorn bulls with three-quarter blood, worth about seven hundred dollars each. All this is mine, as far as you can see, and I didn't push the buffalo and the Indians off these plains to make room for an invasion of farmers with claims on public domain to chip away at what I worked for."

Dalton accepted the glass and took an apprecia-

tive sip before asking, "And how much of this
kingdom is really yours?"

"Titled? Not near enough. Each cow in this
country needs twenty acres of the best rangeland to
survive at a profit. That means I need close to one
hundred fifty thousand acres to feed what I have,
but the government will only give me clear title to
eleven hundred and twenty acres, enough for thirty,
maybe forty head. I'm not raising milk cows here,
Mr. MacKenzie. I have no choice but to take what I
need."

"Even if it belongs to someone else."

A soft, throaty laugh sounded from behind Dalton. "A man of your profession with a conscience?
Isn't that a conflict of interest, Mr. MacKenzie?"

Dalton turned and was treated to a vision of one
of the most enchanting women he'd ever seen. A
statuesque beauty topped with a mass of red-gold
hair, she wore a starched and lacy shirtwaist which
was feminine in every detail over a pair of men's
trousers so tight they drove the point of her gender
home like a swift kick to the groin. She didn't flinch
at his admiring scrutiny but rather returned it boldly
with an assessing sweep of her own. Over a pouty
smile as inviting as strawberries and cream, her dark
eyes flashed with a shrewd directness as they moved
up the inseam of Dalton's denims from cuff to snug-
fitting crotch. It wasn't the kind of attentiveness a
man was meant to ignore, even if the woman doing
the assessing was barely a woman, probably all of
seventeen at the most.

"Mr. MacKenzie, my daughter, Kathleen. She
harbors the misguided notion that she runs this
outfit." And Jamison smiled dotingly to prove it was
probably true.

"I will some day, Daddy. And you did raise me to

have more of a head for business than for the frivolous accomplishments of womanhood." She advanced into the room, hips swaying like a welcome sign in a high breeze, her stare never leaving Dalton, as her smile grew more predatory and possessive.

Dalton returned the smile. "Ma'am, a woman who's smart and ambitious and looks like you doesn't need much else to fall back on."

"Why, thank you for the piece of flattery, Mr. MacKenzie. If I was a woman who was moved by sweet talk, I'd be positively at your feet."

He grinned. "I think you are a woman who's used to quite the opposite, Miss Jamison."

Her gaze glimmered with appreciation as she took a stand at her father's side. "And from what I hear, you're a man used to getting his own way. Is that in everything?"

"In everything worth having, ma'am."

She pursed those ripe lips in a moment of speculation, then noted, "You are missing a good deal of your eyebrows, Mr. MacKenzie. Careless with your smoking?"

"I'm never careless, Miss Jamison. Just an accident."

"And where are your famous bone-handled pistols? Another accident?"

Having grown uncomfortable with their sensual sparring, Jamison chose that moment to intercede. "Kathleen, Mr. MacKenzie and I have business, and I believe you have studies to attend."

Her pout grew more sullen. "Why do I need to know how to conjugate Latin verbs? I'd be more use to you following the market prices in Chicago."

"I'll worry about market prices, you see to your education. It's going to take more than fluttery lashes to hold this spread together. You need a brain to go with that beauty. Now, no more arguments in front of our guest."

"Mr. MacKenzie isn't a guest, Daddy. And I'm sure he has no use for Latin either."

"Animis opibusque parati. Audentes fortuna juvat."

Kathleen stared at the gunman in astonishment. "Prepared in mind and resources. Fortune favors the bold," she translated slowly, then offered a stunning smile. "Well put, sir. You are, indeed, a surprise. Perhaps you can help me with my studies."

Her father cut in to shake that notion loose. "Mr. MacKenzie is not here to act as a tutor. He has other matters to occupy his time. Now, if you'll excuse us, my dear, we can get to them."

With a haughty toss of her fiery mane, Kathleen strode from the room, pausing at the threshold to cast a calculating gaze over her shoulder, one Dalton had no trouble interpreting. He understood beautiful women. They were no mystery to him, no challenge either. Unlike a certain stage-stop owner he could think of but was trying not to. There was no comparison between Jude and this rancher's daughter. Men would trample over Jude, with her no-nonsense ways and less than spectacular looks, to be near a splendid creature like Kathleen. Was he any different? A man wanted a woman who was confident in her femininity, one who would make an enviable trophy of conquest upon his arm. Kathleen Jamison was such a woman, a female skilled in having whatever she wanted. And what she wanted, at least for the moment, was her father's new gunfighter.

Why should he put up a fight?

Jamison sighed in exasperation when she'd gone,

distracting Dalton from his purely male musings. "Forgive Kathleen. I allow her entirely too much latitude for a child her age."

Dalton could have argued his use of the term "child," but he didn't. There was nothing the least bit childish in her appearance or her overtures. But who was he to open a fond father's eyes?

"Let's get down to business, shall we, Mr. Mac-Kenzie? Now that you're here, I want to waste no time in letting the valley's squatters know about it."

Instead of heading to her room where her boring instructor waited to torture her with conjugations, Kathleen stepped outside onto the porch to draw a deep cleansing breath of air. As she expelled it, a small smile shaped her lips as she considered Dalton MacKenzie. Aside from being devilishly attractive, he had a mind to go with it. A challenge, and she was ripe for a challenge. She may have been just shy of her eighteenth year, but she had no intention of docilely following her father's dictates. If it hadn't been for her insistence, he wouldn't have gone to Deadwood to recruit MacKenzie. He seemed to think the problem of the pests swarming over their land would go away on its own. He was wrong. And he was soft. He never would have issued the order to their men to ride in intimidation under the cover of darkness. Yes, she meant to rule this grassland kingdom some day, and she'd be damned if her father's timidity was going to lose even an acre of it.

"Miz Jamison?"

She glanced in scarcely contained annoyance to where their lanky foreman, Monty, stood, hat crumpled in his hands. He was sweating in nervous lustfulness, as he always did when in her presence.

Though repellent to her personally, she made full use of his chafing desires, the way she would with any means to a end.

"Yes, Monty? What is it?"

He squirmed under the sudden beam of her smile, almost forgetting what he'd meant to say. "Th-that there fellow with your daddy—"

"You mean Mr. MacKenzie?"

"Yep. MacKenzie. I seen him before, Miz Jamison."

"So? Get to your point, if you have one." She was quick to lose her patience with his slow-witted initiative.

"I seen him at Amos Station, you know, the other night."

Her attention sharpened to a razor edge. "What do you mean, 'the other night'?"

"When we went to call on Miz Amos."

"He was there?"

"Yessum. He was inside the station. He come out and chased us off with a rifle."

Lids lowered to a thoughtful half-mast over the glitter of her eyes. "Did he?"

"Yessum. Thought you'd like to know that, and that he rode in this morning on one of the Amos's horses, bold as could be."

"Thank you, Monty. That *is* interesting news." And she wet her lips, musing over what it might mean, the foreman already forgotten as he gazed up at her in rapturous devotion. "And it will be more interesting to hear how Mr. MacKenzie explains it."

After a steaming-hot bath, a shave, and a change of clothes, Dalton took a moment to consider his lot before going downstairs to meet the Jamisons for dinner.

His room was a study in pampering luxury from its mammoth half-tester bed and huge armoire already hung with his belongings to the rich works of art hanging on the walls. Most of the Amoses' frame house could fit comfortably within its papered and paneled circumference. No sleeping on slatted boards and lumpy ticking here. No being served out of pans from the stove. No heavenly scent of Joseph's biscuits or Sammy's laughter. And instead of Jude's dry wit and skittish passion, he'd be facing a prospective seduction from the lovely Kathleen. On the surface things had improved in his favor. Then why was he feeling so melancholy in this lap of plenty? This was the life to which he aspired, being served with deference, drinking out of crystal, while his senses were delighted by things of beauty, one of those things being his boss's daughter. And he was being paid extremely well to enjoy these things.

He stared in his shaving mirror while testing the smooth curve of his cheek: a simple gesture, one impossible only a day ago. A day ago he was considering a sightless life of dependency, and now all was as it had been before. Or was it? Had his stay with the Amoses somehow changed him? Or was it just the abrupt shock of losing, then regaining his planned future that had him waxing sentimental over what could never be?

He smiled wryly to erase his own pensive reflection. Nothing had changed. He was who he'd always been, and that was a man Jude Amos couldn't get rid of fast enough. She'd practically tossed him out her door the moment she discovered he'd regained his abilities to live a life she loathed. Tender kisses exchanged in a darkened room were so easily forgotten when he grew independent of

her care. He refused to believe that his carefully
hidden reaction to her looks was to blame.

So why should he hang on to the memory? It
wasn't as if he'd never kissed a woman before! And
if things went the way they seemed to be progress-
ing, he'd be bedding Kathleen Jamison even as Jude
was reconsidering that farmer, Tandy's, offer.

So why did that perfect solution to everything
leave him feeling so dissatisfied?

A light tap on his door interrupted his moody
thoughts, and when he pulled it open to reveal
Kathleen Jamison, function of the mind was overcome by the reaction of his body.

Kathleen Jamison was every man's dream:
wealthy, educated, young, and beautiful beyond
belief. She stood before him in a revealing gown of
garnet silk, its tucked and gathered lines made to
make the most of her long, fluid form. Her bright
hair was subdued in an upsweep that left her
features unrelieved by distraction. Each chiseled
angle added to the perfection of the whole. Nothing
like Jude. And when she smiled in greeting, that
welcome became simmering invitation within the
dark pools of her eyes, an invitation for Dalton to
enjoy all he saw on a more intimate level.

Dalton was used to women like Kathleen, women
who used their looks to gain control over a man's
sensibilities. And while he wasn't immune to the
effect, he wasn't lost to it either.

"Miss Jamison, did you come to escort me to
dinner? I'm sure I could have found the table on my
own."

Because his opening words held no gush of
flattery, Kathleen's expression lost some of its radi-
ance. Her gaze narrowed into scheming slits. "No,
Mr. MacKenzie. That's not why I've come. I have no

doubt about your capabilities. What I would like to know is more about the time you spent with Jude Amos."

All the rumbling lustfulness that growled along the peripheries was caught up short at that unexpected demand. Dalton gave the young woman a cool glance, not wanting to discuss Jude and her family with her. It seemed disrespectful somehow. "What exactly would you like to hear?"

"I'd like to hear why, after taking my father's money, you were standing off his riders on her behalf." There was nothing soft or fluffy about Kathleen as she made that accusation. She was as dangerous as a newly whetted blade.

"I was injured in a stagecoach robbery on my way here. Miss Amos happened to be on that same stage and took me in so I could recover my strength. I didn't know the politics of that mob of night riders, and Miss Amos was unaware of mine. When we exchanged the facts of the situation, she thought it best I be on my way and I was in full agreement."

It was a sketchy version of the truth, and no fool, Kathleen sensed the gaps in his story. Her slitted stare assessed the healing burns upon his face, which confirmed the fact of his injuries. But that wasn't her real contention. "So, you're saying Miss Amos was your nurse . . . nothing of a more personal nature."

"No, nothing personal at all." Dalton treated her question as if she were a jealous child demanding reassurances. And he made no effort to conceal his displeasure at her curiosity.

Having heard the response she wanted, Kathleen was once more all oozing sensuality. "How silly of me. What else could it have been? After all, you took Daddy's money and I've seen Jude Amos."

Something in the girl's smug conclusions rankled Dalton in the extreme. He wanted to think it was because she implied ownership of him and not because she had insulted the woman who'd cared for him. Neither thing, he decided, could be borne.

"Miss Amos is a very gracious lady, and what did or did not happen between us has nothing to do with what your father is paying me to do. He bought my services, Miss Jamison, not my soul. You might try remembering that the next time you're tempted to pry into my business. Now then, I don't think we should keep your father waiting."

Kathleen's features had gone·pale, each exquisite contour standing out in vivid relief. She stared up at him, at first in disbelief then in tempered fury. Slowly her cherry lips curled into a sweetly vicious smile.

"Why, Mr. MacKenzie, I'm very aware that you are simply my father's hired man. Beyond that there is nothing about you that interests me in the least." And she whirled toward the stairs and fairly stomped away, leaving Dalton to chuckle softly at her tantrum.

She was so young and so spoiled. She was used to having everything she wanted handed over without a struggle. She was little better than a greedy child in a tempting woman's shape.

But he wasn't foolish enough not to see her for the danger she could become.

Chapter 11

Fiddlers squealed like hogs at the slaughter.

No one gathered at the celebration minded the enthusiastic squalling. There had been no occasion to get together with neighbors since the prior year's harvest, and after being isolated over the long winter months, folks were eager to gab and make merry. The Barrets' barn had been swept clean and opened wide to receive those anxious to congratulate Wade Barret and his new bride, Lucinda. They had feared the weather would delay the anticipated event, but that morning had broken fresh and bright as a newly minted gold piece and wagons had rolled down the rutted drive since noon.

Bearing two lemonade pies made by Joseph and a handmade quilt she'd worked on during long, cold eves, Jude approached the noisy building with mixed emotions. She was glad to be out socializing and was thrilled for the younger Barret brother, but there was a nagging fear that the gathering would be used by Tandy as a means of preaching violence to the others in the valley. And she was afraid as well that he would seek her out to press his cause once more in the joyful aftermath of his brother's marriage.

"Ain't this grand, Jude?"

She smiled up at her brother. He was the reason she'd decided to come, leaving Joseph to tend the station. The Deadwood-bound stage had already been through and the southbound wasn't expected until the next day, so she had no qualms about leaving Joseph behind. White men's ceremonies held no sacred significance for him, that was what he always claimed, but Jude suspected he shunned such events because they reminded him too keenly of all he'd lost. Whichever it was, she had too much respect for him to force the issue. She understood loss and wasn't feeling all that festive herself. However, he'd fairly pushed her out the door, ordering them to enjoy their youth and not to hurry home. Jude had gritted her teeth and promised she would do just that. But now that she was here and lantern lights created a glowing welcome within the big barn, she was reluctant once more.

"Why you draggin' your feet?" Sammy wanted to know. He hitched his arm through hers and began a vigorous towing. With his curls tamed back under a sheen of oil and his brawny figure clad in his best white shirt, denims, and leather vest, he looked like any young swain eager to mix and mingle. Only Jude knew that wasn't true. He was more interested in where the children huddled at their games than in where the eligible ladies stood peering over fluttering fans.

"Hey, there's Tandy. Hey, Tandy!"

Too late to do more than smile and advance.

Grinning broadly, Tandy strode over to meet them halfway, relieving Jude of the pies and passing them to Sammy. "Here, boy, take these on over to the food table and help yerself to something," he commanded, his intent gaze never leaving Jude's.

"Mighty nice of you to come, Jude, considering how we last parted."

"I don't hold that against you, Tandy. Besides, I wouldn't miss the chance to wish Wade well."

"Yeah, weddin's have a way of bringin' folks together."

She had to look away from the speculative gleam in his eye.

"You make that quilt? Fine work. Lucinda will love it."

Glad to turn the talk away from Tandy's fruitless hopes, Jude asked, "Will they be living here?"

"Course. House is big enough, at least until they start throwing little'uns. Or until I bring home a wife of my own."

Her jaw tightened in discomfort at his none-too-subtle hint.

Across the cleaned barn floor which would later be used for dancing, she saw Wade and his bride, arm in arm, nodding and grinning at well-wishers. He was stiff in his Sunday suit and she, fragile and lovely in white brocade and plain satin framed by a heavy cloud of white nun's veiling. Both of them radiated joy. A sharp pain of envy lanced Jude's breast and was just as quickly disavowed. She couldn't begrudge them their happiness on this, the first day of their wedded life.

However, she couldn't stop the bittersweet twist of her own imaginings either. The picture of her standing there, herself, in white upon the arm of the man she loved, blushing when others spoke to her of children, not because she was embarrassed but because she was eager to accomplish the fact. A man she loved, a home of her own, children's sweet voices. A dream come true. A distant and impossible dream. Because the man standing beside her in that precious dream wasn't Tandy Barret or any of the other valley men. He was a man who'd already sworn not to be tied down to thoughts of family.

"What the hell are they doin' here?"

The growl of Tandy's tone brought her around to follow his glare. And a jolt of recognition stole her breath away.

Patrick Jamison was helping his daughter, Kathleen, down from their buggy. The conveyance was flanked by several of the ranch hands from Sweetgrass. And among them sat Dalton MacKenzie, as if conjured by her longings. He stood out from the rest who wore their cowboy finery: white shirts and flowing red bandannas. He was clad in black. A brushed Stetson tilted down over the squint of his eyes. He wore a long, black overcoat covering a worsted suit of equally stark color. Both were open to display a black satin vest shot through with silver threads. Though his hips were bare, she could picture the hugging brace of pistols as if they were a part of him. He swung down off a tall buckskin, pausing briefly as his gaze caught hers. He quickly looked away.

Jude's heart twisted.

He couldn't bear to look at her.

"I see Jamison wasted no time trotting out his new killer dog," Tandy snarled. He jumped in surprise as Jude gave him a savage pinch.

"Tandy, don't you dare spoil this day for your brother and his wife with any quarreling. We are all neighbors. They have a right to be here too. No one's wearing any guns, so just relax and don't make trouble."

He scowled at her warning, but she felt the tension ease in his arm. "Guess we'd better go up and say a nice neighborly howdy then."

Jude would have preferred to do anything but.

Still, she hung on Tandy's arm, well knowing her presence had a stabilizing effect on him and the whole situation. No one had to know how emotions were writhing within the simple cut of her blue calico dress as they came up behind the Jamisons and their hired gun while they greeted the newlyweds. Kathleen was extending an elaborately wrapped gift.

"It's a silver tea service," the young woman confided to the round-eyed bride. "Just plated, I'm sorry to say, but it came all the way from New York City. I hope you don't already have one."

The stunned Lucinda shook her head, dazed by the very idea of owning something so fine. Her husband looked equally displeased, though he managed to sound cordial.

"Thank you very much, Miz Jamison. I'm sure we'll put it to good use." He was already wondering how much seed they could buy in exchange for the bit of frivolous extravagance. "So glad you could stop by, you and your"—his gaze lingered over Dalton, summing up his occupation—"men." Beside him, his bride had gone very pale.

Patrick Jamison smiled. He couldn't have been more rewarded by the instant recognition. "This is Mr. Dalton MacKenzie. I've invited him to stay with us as our guest for a time. I hope you'll make him welcome."

Lucinda's fearful gaze touched briefly on the dapper gunman, who met her glance without blinking, then hers sank to the straw-littered ground. "Yes, of course. Please enjoy yourselves." Then she glanced up, relieved to see Jude standing nearby. "Oh, Wade, here's Jude, and look what she's brought us." She passed the ornate gift back to the table behind them and reached out to take the quilt from Jude's arms. The gold of her wedding band gleamed as her hand stroked the soft fabric. "You made this yourself, didn't you? I shall treasure it always."

"Yes, how very lovely," Kathleen commented, miffed at seeing her present passed over without being opened and duly admired. "What a creative and frugal way to reuse old, worn-out clothing."

Jude wanted to shrink back and crawl away in humiliation and horror, but she stood her ground, head high and proud, while inside she was horribly reminded of how she must appear next to the wealthy Jamisons, how they all must appear. To them her gift would look like discards, cleverly made over to another use. They wouldn't see the silver service as an impractical insult to the plainness and poverty of all their neighbors. The fact that Kathleen had mentioned it was plated said clearly it was a trifle in their eyes. It was a matter of different society.

Kathleen stood out among them, a grand peacock amid sparrows. She was garbed in a costume of emerald-colored silk grosgrain, banded with jet gimp where it gathered in back in heavy folds and satin ribbon bows. The young woman's dress was probably a Parisian import, cut just so to emphasize her firm, creamy bosom through a peekaboo of lace between high collar and squared bodice edge, with curves plumped and compressed appropriately by the best catalog corseting available. In comparison Jude felt stout as a stump in her unbustled print, which buttoned demurely down the front to a single tier of pleating at the hem. Her shoulders carried the fabric upon a broad frame, uncinched or fettered by what was fashionable, and she sorely wished she'd forgone comfort for a bit of feminine style.

"Style" was the word for Kathleen Jamison. She wore it draped upon her youthful figure. She displayed it grandly with each practiced flick of her gracefully gloved hand. She toted it with her brilliantly white smile and her perfectly coiffed blaze of curls. If an air of breeding could be bought, Jamison had obviously paid a fortune for his daughter's deportment. A shame he'd not invested as much in her manners.

"Well, now that you've paid yer respects, I suspects you'll be going." That growl came from Tandy.

Surprisingly, it was Lucinda who found her voice to declare, "Nonsense. They've only just arrived. This is a day for celebration, not for airing past grievances. Tandy, Jude looks thirsty. Perhaps you should take her over for some punch."

With a last contemptuous look at their uninvited guests, Tandy all but dragged Jude around and off toward the refreshment table, the first round of disaster avoided. Even so, the presence of Patrick Jamison had a dampening effect upon the gathering, and that tension continued to escalate as the hours wore on. A pint of bourbon found its way into the punch bowl, and the woefully inadequate musicians began to play for reeling partners beneath the lantern-hung eaves.

Dalton stood apart from the merriment, which was nothing new to him. He'd spent a lifetime standing beyond the circle of inclusion, at first by circumstance and then by choice. From that isolated stance he observed the festivities with a dispassionate eye, unaffected by the joyousness of the occasion. He wasn't there to partake, he was there to intimidate, and standing like a dark, looming shadow of foreboding doom on the fringe of the celebration, he was an unobtrusive yet ever-present reminder of trouble to come.

Since spoiling everyone's enjoyment was his sole function for the evening, he was able to let his attention wander. His gaze touched on Kathleen, who was surrounded by an adoring group of young men. Her dark eyes caught his with a smoldering intensity, but his attention moved, restless and indifferent, not marking how her features stiffened at his casual dismissal.

Without his knowledge there was a pattern to his methodical sweep of the crowd. He realized it the moment he saw Jude. It was her solid form he sought among the many. Again he felt that moment of rejecting recoil at the sight of her unexceptional face, that pang of disappointment that was like a jab of betrayal to his gut. He'd expected so much more, and he was brooding over the loss of those expectations like a child who'd anticipated fancy cross-gartered silk hose for Christmas and had to settle for plain wool socks. There was no thrill to receiving socks. They were practical, necessary, yet totally unexciting. So he stared at that unspectacular gift the return of his sight had brought him, and selfishly he mourned the loss of his illusions even as he grew accustomed to the reality.

Jude stood easily in her circle of friends and neighbors. She was laughing with them, exchanging trivial gossip. Her cheeks were flushed to a rosy hue, and the animation suited her. Heightened color accentuated the long hollows of her bone structure and brought a lively sparkle to her eyes. Much of that spontaneous gaiety left her the instant she became aware of his study. Though she quickly glanced away, he could tell by the stiffness of her posture that she was still conscious of his scrutiny.

It hadn't been his intent to smother her mood. He'd only meant to learn more about her by watching her with her peers. And as an experienced student of humankind, he'd already discovered volumes.

Though she stood with many, she was still alone.

The respect the others held for her was obvious in the way they sought her out and deferred to her opinions. Men and women alike seemed comfortable in her presence. Her strength drew them, that and her innate honorability, rare qualities even more unusual in a woman. There was a clear abiding goodness to Jude Amos, a sense of deep-rooted stability that was neither unbending nor easily broken. Men would come to her for trusted council, women for sensible solutions. But to whom did she go? Why did she hold herself so purposefully away from them? He watched and he wondered. Would she turn to that arrogant fool, Barret? He thought not. The man was too set on himself, too weak for a woman of Jude's character, he decided with a somewhat savage pleasure. She stood alone, isolated by the very strength others admired in her. Or did she too have expectations that were unfairly met?

"So serious," came a soft purr at his elbow. Dalton gave a start for rarely did anyone approach him without his notice. But during his pensive study of Jude Amos, Kathleen Jamison had slipped in close, and seeing that she had wrested his attention from the other woman, she smiled prettily and wound herself possessively about his arm.

"Your father isn't paying me to have fun."

"He hasn't ordered you to allow me to die of boredom either."

His smile was narrow in its chiding. "You didn't look bored over there with your bevy of calf-eyed strays."

"You noticed," she murmured with sultry pleasure. "Those are boys, and boys have limited scope. They're content with a smile or a glance or a waltz or two. I like a man who doesn't settle for less than what he wants." Her unblinking stare said he was such a man.

"Such worldly disdain for a woman of your age."

"I don't plan to grow old waiting for my father to tell me what I want out of life. If there's something I want, I snatch it without regret. Regret comes from wanting without the courage to take. I don't want there to be any regrets in my life." Her dark eyes lost their determined sheen beneath the sudden downward sweep of her lashes. The gesture was coy and completely calculated. "Do you dance, Mr. Mac-Kenzie?"

"Yes."

"Would you like to dance with me?" Her gaze came up, simmering with sensual invitation as her body pressed near to let him feel what it would be like to hold her close. Both things were unbearably provocative.

"And what if I decide I want more than a dance?"

She gave a shiver of excitement, both fearing and fascinated by him. "Then I guess you'll just have to take what you want." And her arms slid up over his shoulders to claim him for a waltz.

From across the makeshift dance floor, Jude watched them together, her heart a single mass of leadened pain. They looked well moving in tandem, an attractive couple of sleek sophistication. She

knew little of Kathleen Jamison. They hardly ran in
the same social circle. She knew the young woman
was handed everything she desired by her doting
father, and what she desired was his new hired man.
The interest seemed mutual. And why not? Jude
thought glumly, as she ladled punch, trying not to
be too obvious in her distress. Kathleen was all she
was not: young, gorgeous, charming, rich, schooled,
and unencumbered by responsibility, perfection in
the female form. Yet for all her surface appeal,
during their few face-to-face meetings, Jude sensed
an uncomfortable lack of anything beautiful beneath that lovely veneer. Kathleen was a precious
gem, all flash to catch the eye but lit by a cold inner
fire. Still, men hungered for ownership, simply for
the pride involved in showing off such a jewel.

No one would mistake Jude for a jewel. She was
as common as dirt, but at least, she thought with a
touch of satisfaction, things grew in common soil. It
was nurturing and yielded bountiful rewards to
those who tended it. But if gemstones were scattered upon it, few would cast them aside to possess
its earthy permanence. Foolish men, she concluded,
and turned from the handsome couple dancing to
the awful strains of music to seek the cool of the
evening. She stumbled headlong into a huddle of
discontent: a handful of men gathered just outside
the door, venting their anger.

"He's got some nerve comin' here bold as brass."
That was Tandy, his voice dangerously slurred by
drink.

"And that stranger," muttered another. "He's a
killer, unless I miss my guess."

Tandy jumped on that with vicious pleasure.
"And if he's hirin' killers, it's only a matter a time
before he lets 'em loose. And you know where

they're gonna strike: at your home and mine. Unless—"

"Unless what, Tandy?"

"Unless we strike first."

"How? We're farmers and ranchers, not hired
guns."

"That's why we put together what money we can
and we gets ourself our own gunslick."

"And what then?"

The men turned as one sullen unit as Jude addressed them. Their ranks of perhaps a dozen
parted to let her claim attention in the center, much
to Tandy's disgust.

Having listened to the elder Barret's increasingly
toxic venom, Jude knew she couldn't remain silent.
Tandy was no great leader of men, but he was vocal
in his opinion and one of them, knowing how to hit
upon their greatest fears. They would follow him.
That's what Jude could not allow.

"Then what?" she asked again, challenging each
of them in turn with the direct probe of her stare. All
but Tandy glanced away. "Do you send this killer
after Jamison's men? After Jamison himself? And
once that first shot is fired, do you honestly think
there'll be any turning back? Do you think peace can
be won in this valley at the point of a gun? Who here
is willing to irrigate his next crop with the blood of
those who've fallen? Because it won't stop at hired
guns. It will stop when this valley is in ruin and a
good portion of you are dead."

Silence settled as the men hung their heads,
spirits effectively dampened by the vigor of Jude's
claims. They knew she was right, and none of them
were liquored up enough to deny it. Not even
Tandy. Seeing that, Jude breathed a sigh of relief.

"Go back to your families," she suggested. "Enjoy

the rest of this evening, then get back to your homes and back to your lives. Jamison has done nothing yet but offer to buy our land. If he does more, there are other methods, legal methods, for stopping him. And no one gets hurt. Go on. Dance with your wives, toast the bride and groom, and go home."

Muttering to themselves, they dispersed. The last to go was Tandy Barret. His surly glare warned that he was far from through planting his poison, and as she watched him stalk away, Jude knew with a dreadful certainty that one day, perhaps soon, it would take root.

Perhaps it was time for her to consider Jamison's offer seriously so she could get her family to safety.

But first she needed to find Sammy so they could go home. She'd done all the socializing she cared to for the evening. There was nothing more for her here, under the Barrets' barn roof, not even a reason to hold on to hope.

There was no sign of her brother as she scanned the gathering with an increasingly agitated eye. When last she'd seen him, he was whittling animal figurines for a group of appreciative youngsters. But the children were mostly curled on bails of straw, sleeping soundly beneath the drape of their mothers' shawls. And Sammy was nowhere to be found.

At first she did not pay heed to the sound of low masculine chuckles as she hurriedly circled the outside of the barn, thinking Sammy might have gone to admire the Barrets' stock. Then she heard a harsh tone of cruelty in the laughter, and was alerted to the possible cause for bullies to be gathered in the dark. Her fears were well warranted as she came up upon them where they stood in a tight pack at the far side of the corral. She recognized Jamison's men and, with a sinking suspicion confirmed, saw Sammy's unruly head of hair in the midst of them. When she drew close enough, she could hear the mean goadings.

"Come on, it's only whiskey. Ain't you ever had a drink a whiskey afore?"

"Course he hasn't. His prissy sister only lets him drink milk."

"Whiskey's a man's drink. Ain't you a man, Sammy boy?"

"He were man enough to be lookin' at Sue Ellen Parrish like he wanted somethin' from her. Whatcha want from Sue Ellen, Sam? You afeared to even ask her for a dance."

"Take a sip, boy. You'll find all the courage you need right here in this bottle."

More noxious laughter, as low and dark and dirty as tobacco juice spit upon the ground.

"Sammy?"

The pack of men parted as Jude pushed her way past the outer ring of them. In the center she could see her brother, where they'd backed him up against the fence. His shirt front was stained by dark blotches of drink, but she could tell by the whiteness of his clenched lips that he had yet to swallow any of it. His bright gaze lit with relief when he saw her.

"Sammy, come on now. It's time for us to be going."

One of the men gripped her arm and hauled her back. "What's yer hurry, little lady? We was jus' startin' to have some fun. You want to have some fun with us too?"

"I don't like your kind of fun," she snapped, yanking her arm free from his grasp.

"It don't look like you know what fun is. No wonder you're a sour-faced old spinster. You don't know how to let down your hair. Here, let me help you."

The pins were jerked from her chignon with a good measure of hair in the bargain, but she refused to cry out and give them that satisfaction. She struck out at the rude fellow, then knew a real jolt of apprehension when another caught her elbows, holding her fast.

"Monty, here, wants to see you with your hair down," came a whiskey-fumed voice pressed close to her ear. "How 'bout the rest a you boys? You wanting to see what's under all these prim and proper buttons?"

There was a growl of coarse agreement, and it was then that Sammy realized the threat of their situation.

"You boys let my sister go now, you hear?"

He took a step forward, and one of the cowboys shoved him back, hard, against the rails. "Or you'll do what, dummy?"

"You let her go or else!" His tone roughened as he pushed away from the fence to take a more aggressive stance.

"Sammy, no!" Jude cried, knowing this was what the bullies had hoped for. They were looking for an opportunity to let go with some pent-up rage, and Sammy's feeble confrontation was just the excuse they needed.

"Or else what?" sneered the one they called Monty, the one who still held her hairpins in his hand as if they were daggers.

"Or else you'll regret the day your mother whelped you," came a soft-spoken certainty from the shadows behind them.

Dalton!

Chapter 12

◈

Jude whirled around, huge, grateful eyes seeking out Dalton's figure in the dark. For a long suspenseful beat, all she could see was the glowing end of his cigarillo. As he drew on it, the sudden flare highlighted a gaze that burned with no less heat. The moment he separated from the shadows, the hands gripping her abandoned their hold and she was free to move to Sammy. The encounter had her shaking all over, but she wouldn't let them know how far their intimidation had gone. With her head held high, she looped her arm through her brother's and said with stiff dignity, "Sammy, it's time we were leaving. I've had about enough of this company."

Jamison's men didn't exactly part to allow her passage. She had to elbow her way through them, and she did so with no show of gentleness until she reached the spot where Dalton stood, a large, looming sentinel. She would have strode past him too, except his quiet words shocked her into a moment's pause.

"I'll see you home, Miss Amos."

Pride forced her reply out in a crisp refusal—a pride that wouldn't bend before bullying, a pride that still stung from the sight of him with Kathleen Jamison in his arms. "That won't be necessary, Mr. MacKenzie. I know my way home."

"I insist," came his steel-laced rebuttal.

Jude glanced back at the pack of surly men who'd planned to lay crude hands upon her and fists upon her brother, and her will wavered. It was Sammy who decided for her.

"That's our buggy over there, Mac."

"I'll get my horse."

Jude returned inside only long enough to say her good-byes and convey her best wishes to the newlyweds. She managed to retain her calm front that long, at least. She didn't look for Tandy Barret in the crowd. One awkward confrontation was enough for any evening, and she certainly didn't want the volatile rancher to see her driving off escorted by Jamison's hired gun.

But Dalton had no intention of being a simple escort.

When she reached the buggy, she found him seated at the reins with his big buckskin tethered behind and Sammy contentedly crammed into the boot. She had no choice but to take the hand Dalton stretched down to her. With a single strong tug, he pulled her up beside him, where she settled as if on pins and needles on the suddenly all-too-narrow plank. She could feel the heat of him through the layers of cotton and starched muslin, and it wasn't an altogether soothing sensation even on such a chill evening. She didn't need any extra stimuli for her awareness of Dalton MacKenzie to peak. His nearness had her every fiber thrumming with a nervous sort of anticipation, expecting . . . she didn't know what.

What could she expect of him after the way he'd

waltzed the lovely Miss Jamison about beneath his
charming smile and attentive gaze? Obviously he'd
only stepped in out of some feeling of lingering
obligation. And that was how she was going to look
at it, she told herself sternly as she held her body tall
and tense so the bumps wouldn't push her against
his unyielding form. Oh, she could remember how
those long, hard planes felt . . .

"That's some unsavory company you've decided
to keep, Mr. MacKenzie," she said caustically when
the silence grew too deep and she could find no
comfort in her own wicked thoughts.

He didn't spare her a glance, but she could see the
wry curl of his smile in the near total blackness. "I
didn't choose them. They sort of came with the
job."

"And what exactly is your job?" she put before
him boldly. Let him tell her now that it wasn't to
drive her and her neighbors out of the valley.

"To cast a large shadow, Miss Amos, something I
do very well."

"I'm sure it is."

The tang of her tone had him casting a quick
sideward glance. What was meant to be a glimpse
was held for a long moment, until the treacherous
nature of the darkened path pulled his attention
back to his driving.

"Are you wishing you hadn't tampered with my
fate?"

He'd expected a sharp and sassy answer, not a
soft admission of "no." Then her cadence quick-
ened as if she feared that one word betrayed too
much. "No, Mr. MacKenzie. That's the difference
between me and those you work for."

And as they continued on and the stillness of the
night enveloped them in the chill isolation of its

embrace, Dalton reflected on what she'd said. Yes, that was the difference between Jude and the Jamisons. And, indeed, between her and himself. She did things out of simple goodness, without regard to consequence, even if that act of kindness would repay her with betrayal. The one had no bearing on the other, and that made Jude Amos something outside of his understanding. He'd been brought up to guard his own interests first and foremost, to view everything as to how it related to his own betterment. Unselfishness was a foreign concept, especially in women, whom he knew to be the most treacherous species to walk the plains.

But Jude knocked that thinking askew, and he didn't quite know how to right his world after spending time in her care.

The lights of Amos Station appeared in the distance. Jude viewed them with a sense of thanksgiving and disappointment. However awkward it felt to be in Dalton's company, she didn't really want the chafe of discomfort to end. It made her feel alive.

When the buggy stopped, Sammy straightened from his dozing huddle and with a sleepy murmur of "G'night, Mac," he crawled out of the vehicle and stumbled toward the porch, leaving the two of them in a stalemate on the front seat.

Jude hesitated a moment too long. It gave Dalton time to swing down and to come around to help her alight. She considered the wide spread of his up-stretched hands with an instant of panicked delight, then leaned forward for the pleasure of having them clasp, warmly and strongly, at the sides of her waist. He plucked her from the buggy as if she weighed nothing and turned to let her down. But instead of releasing her once her feet touched solid ground, he retained her in that broad casing of his grasp, and she had no great desire to break away.

In the mistiness of the night, Jude's upturned features held an ethereal beauty that stark daylight disallowed them. Soft, silver light caressed her cheeks and shimmered along the fine strands of her unbound hair like ribbons of silken dross. Her eyes, framed by those incredibly long, inky lashes, were deep secret wells of welcoming moonlight, pooled with dew-drenched longing. He felt himself tottering, tumbling headfirst into their cool, mysterious depths. And the slow, beckoning part of her lips caught him as he plunged, out of control, and held him with their soft, searching caress even as he thought he should struggle to find his balance once more.

It wasn't a lengthy or aggressive kiss, just a slow, slanting reacquaintance with something they both had previously enjoyed. Too soon, Jude was reminded of all that awaited her and of where Dalton was bound once he stepped back from her lips. She made the first move toward separation, but he was able to still it for another long second with the brush of his fingertips along the angle of her jaw.

"Good night, Jude. Tonight, yours was the only company I chose to keep."

"Good night, Mr.—" The press of his fingers halted that impersonal conclusion. Against their broad pads, she whispered huskily, "Dalton."

Pleased with that breathy concession, he gave her a brief closed-lip smile then walked back to where his horse was tied. He was up in the saddle in one smooth move and, just as quickly, gone from her yard, swallowed up by the surrounding night.

For long minutes Jude remained, staring off into

the direction that had taken him, as her fingertips traced the damp impression still lingering on her lips.

The last thing Dalton expected or wanted was to be sensually ambushed by Kathleen Jamison the moment he neared his room.

She must have been lingering in the shadowed bend of the stairs, for he hadn't seen her upon entering or climbing up their graceful curve. Then, just as he reached for his doorknob, her arms ensnared him from behind, tangling about his waist in a silken knot.

"Where did you disappear to?" she cooed. "I thought you had plans to claim more than a dance."

Suddenly annoyed by her aggressive pursuit, he unwound her arms and opened his door, turning quickly to bar her way inside. "Plans change" was his cool comment, which a less determined female would have understood to mean "good night."

Her hands were back on the attack, her palms pushing up the sheen of his vest and curving back inside his coat. He made no move to show how her touch affected him, if it did at all. Kathleen frowned slightly and continued her assault.

"They don't have to," she purred, leaning close until the rounded bodice of her gown flattened upon his chest. She was all scented softness over sharp purpose, and Dalton found that combination unappealing. He had nothing against women who actively enjoyed his attention, but he liked to be the aggressor. With Kathleen he found himself uncomfortably on the defensive as she coaxed, "My father's already retired. There's no one to see or care what we choose to do together."

"Perhaps I should make myself a little clearer, Miss Jamison. I don't choose to do anything more this evening."

She jerked back as if his words delivered a slap to the face. Her intense black eyes studied him for signs of meaning that were beyond her. She couldn't believe he was rejecting the idea of her in his bed, and she was confused by his earlier signals of desire. She smiled uneasily. "You don't have to worry about my telling Daddy. He doesn't know what I do when he's not watching, and that's the way I like it."

Dalton caught her prowling hands and held them away from him, dropping them as if with disgust. And she did disgust him, with her shrewd air of experience, with her overbearing sexuality, with her superior command that he supply what she wanted. He rebelled against it all. And he told himself it had nothing to do with the fact that he could still taste Jude's sweet kiss upon his mouth.

"When I take up with a woman, it's not something I do behind anyone's back. If you have to hide what you're doing from your daddy, you shouldn't be doing it. Grow up, Miss Jamison, and take responsibility for what you want."

She stared at him, dumfounded. Then a dull flush of fury began to climb her cheeks. "How dare you speak to me like that. You work for my father—"

"Yes," he cut in crisply. "For your father. Not for you."

"You might find out that they are one and the same" was her hissed warning.

"I don't think so. I don't think your father brought me here as a paid stud for his daughter. If you think different, maybe we should go right now and ask him about it." He gripped her forearm with a near painful intensity and gave her a propelling yank toward the far end of the hall, where double doors led to her father's suite of rooms. "After you."

Snarling, she pulled away and began to rub her arm reflexively. Her dark eyes shot fire that would pierce steel. "You're a fool, MacKenzie. This is going to cost you your job here."

He laughed. The sound of his amusement had her purpling. Suddenly he leaned in close, so that she was pinned beneath the skewer of his glare. "What are you going to do about it, little girl? Run to Daddy and tell him I wouldn't bed you proper upon your demand?"

"I'll tell him you tried to force your attentions on me," she declared with a vicious smirk of victory.

Again he only laughed as if she were some silly child threatening to tattle. "Tell him. You'll only be humiliating yourself. I don't play those kinds of games, and my rules are my own. I'm here on business, and it's my experience that business and pleasure don't mix. Even when the pleasure is presented in an irresistible package." And he punctuated that quiet claim with the stroke of his thumb over her narrowed lips. The gesture surprised her out of her angry stance and she blinked, overset by her own shifting passions.

Somewhat placated by his display of appreciation, Kathleen assumed her haughty pose once more. "Someday you'll wish you hadn't turned me away tonight."

"Perhaps I will. Maybe even before morning." However, as she undulated toward him hopefully, he added, "But I'll live with the disappointment for now. Good night, Miss Jamison."

And he left her gaping at his closed door.

Once inside he had no regrets about his solitary state. It wasn't his way to take one woman to relieve his ache for another. Then he stopped what he was doing, his vest half off and left to dangle from his elbow, as he considered what he'd just admitted. And he was simply amazed by the notion that he had a gorgeous, unencumbered female like Kathleen panting for his bed and all he could think of was a plain woman of unwavering virtue who scorned what he did and was afraid of who he was.

The knock to the head must have addled his reason.

So he cared for Jude Amos. That didn't mean he had to act upon those feelings. In fact, that would be the most foolish thing he could do. And not just because Jude wasn't the type of woman with whom a man trifled for his own amusement. Jude was a marrying kind of woman, but even beyond that there were the grim facts of the situation, which caught them both.

Jude was one of the people he'd been brought in to silence.

He'd taken pay to clear the way for Jamison's possession of the valley. That meant driving off those who already laid claim to it, Jude among them. And, as in most cases, simple persuasion was not going to be enough.

How could he bully the woman who had cared for him when he was vulnerable and, in doing so, managed to notch a place for herself and her family within his well-hardened heart? Had she taken money in exchange for mercy, his conscience would have been clear. The fact that he still had a conscience was surprise enough. He'd thought he'd lost all sentimental qualms long, long ago, when as a child he'd been forced to realize the harsh realities of life. Living was a work-for-pay situation. Nothing was free. All had to be earned.

He had a job and that job was with Jamison. He owed the man his unswerving allegiance. It wasn't up to him to question the man's motives or rights or even his morality. Money had been taken; services had to be rendered. A debt needed to be repaid. That was the stand upon which his integrity was based. One from which he couldn't stray—not over emotions he vowed would never interfere with his profession.

He finished disrobing and stretched out upon the big, plush bed, staring up at the half tester overhead. His feelings toward Jude Amos could have no bearing on his actions. In a world where few held out for honor, he'd promised never to compromise his own. Honor was what he'd clung to in the worst of times, and he couldn't fail it now. Not over a woman who would never accept what he'd done in the past and what he was prepared to do again. There was no profitable return. It was best to get on with what he'd been hired to do, and if Jude stubbornly wedged herself in the middle, that was her choice and out of his hands. He hadn't created the problem plaguing this valley, but he'd been paid to be the solution.

And if Jude wouldn't budge, he'd have to roll right over her.

Nothing personal.

"Did you see the way they backed right down to him? He didn't have no gun or nothing!"

"Yes, I saw." Jude tried to hold onto her patience as she wrestled Sammy's nightshirt over his head. The last thing she wanted was to listen to more of

Sammy's deification of Dalton MacKenzie. "Sammy, sit still and give me your arm."

It poked through the sleeve, making her job easier until she pulled the shirt down to uncover the bright, revering sheen in his eyes.

"He sure is something, ain't he?"

"Who?"

"Mac!"

"Yes, he's something, all right. Now, go to sleep." She started to push him back but he resisted.

"He sure came right at the nick of time. Yes, sir, right at the nick of time."

Jude had been thinking the same thing in her own mind. How was it that he happened upon the scene at just that precise moment? She hadn't asked. Could be he was just out enjoying his smoke and heard the commotion. Could be. Could be he'd followed her and hung back to see how she'd handle things on her own. She hadn't handled them well, at all, and she wasn't sure if it was the fact itself or the fact of Dalton knowing it that upset her so.

She'd always dealt with her own demons, facing them head on without fear. But tonight she'd been afraid, and if Dalton hadn't arrived when he did, she would have run, far and fast, to escape that terror she'd felt when helpless to defend against it. Terrible things might have happened. Sammy could have been beaten—or worse. She could have been mauled by their rough, uncaring hands—or worse. No one would have heard or come to their aid. She'd been paralyzed before their greater threat, and it wasn't a feeling she would likely forget or forgive. She could run from that feeling of cold, depthless panic by selling out to Jamison's intimidation, or she could confront it by standing firm with the rest of her neighbors. Either way, her loved ones would suffer for her decisions, be they right or wrong.

Was it right to expose them continually to the danger seeping into the valley like an ever-spreading disease? That disease was fear. Had she the right to demand they pull up stakes from the only home they'd known because some wealthy bully said they had to leave? Somehow that seemed less fair.

But if they stayed, it wasn't going to be without a fight. And that meant going along with Tandy Barret and his ideals, unless a peaceful compromise could be reached.

It was late and she was fresh out of ideas.

This time Sammy gave before her determined push, settling down into the sheets that once had held Dalton MacKenzie. It seemed almost strange seeing her brother there in his own bed. The image of Dalton still lingered within the room, haunting her with what she hadn't been able to hold. It was a ghost that made everything all the more empty with its passing. How her heart echoed in its absence.

"I was a-scared, Jude, of them fellas," Sammy admitted softly as she turned down the light.

"So was I, Sammy. They weren't nice men."

"I didn't know what to do. I didn't like the way they was treating you, but I jus' didn't know what to do."

The anguish of guilt weighed upon his tone and squeezed her emotions, making her angrier than ever at the brutes who'd terrorized them.

"But Mac, he knew what to do. Yes, sir, he knew jus' what to do." Smiling his satisfaction, Sammy closed his eyes, ready to accept sleep—a sleep that was to evade Jude for long, lonesome hours.

What troubled her into the wee hours of morning wasn't the harm to which they'd almost come at the hands of Jamison's men. What roamed restlessly through her memory was the unexpected power of Dalton's kiss reducing her to a level of mindless sensation, to a plain where nothing—not who he was, not who he worked for, not the fact that he was disappointed in her lack of beauty—could reach her.

Why had he kissed her? It wasn't necessary thanks. He'd stepped in twice to forestall danger and that more than set the accounts straight between them. It hadn't been out of some loneliness he felt for female companionship. Kathleen Jamison had made it brazenly clear that she was ready and willing to supply the handsome gunfighter with all he could desire in that area.

So why had he abandoned the eager young beauty to see her and her brother home?

And why the kiss, when it would have been much simpler for him just to ride away?

Jude finally managed to drift into an uneasy slumber. She dreamed of dancing, only in her dream, the fiddles were tuned and she was the one turning in Dalton's arms. And in her dream she was truly lovely, with her hair softly curled and her gown shimmering. And Dalton was gazing down upon her uplifted face with a look of adoring admiration, because such things were possible in dreams. The strength of his embrace had the kind of reality to it that only memory could supply. He held her close, as close as he had in the yard, so that her dress and her body melted down the front of him, to mold along every hard line. And in her dream they moved in perfect harmony, twirling slowly until all around them was lost to a blur of motion, until all that remained in her universe was the unmistakable light of love in his eyes.

She was reluctant to surrender that dream to daylight. Because of the late hours she'd kept the night before, neither mind nor body was tempted to hurry her awake. On a distant periphery she could hear Joseph and Sammy coming in from morning chores, and the scent of rising yeast tickled her nose. Finally, when it was apparent there'd be no returning to her state of dreams, she roused herself with a groan and a grumble, tossing on a heavy robe which would serve her well enough on the short walk to the privy.

She was on her way back from the chilly morning necessity when she happened to see a tall buckskin tethered at the porch. She stared at it, her hazy thoughts gathering to place its familiar look.

It was Dalton MacKenzie's mount.

Which meant . . .

She sprinted in through the back door and was up her ladder in a swirl of nightclothes before Joseph could manage the most meager "good morning." Shucking out of her modest gown, she washed hastily and donned a crisp wrapper of printed cambric over a single petticoat. In her rush she forgot her proper stockings and slid bare feet into sturdy boots. There was no time to try to make sense out of the fine curtain of her hair. It wouldn't take so much as a ribbon without fifty strokes of brushing to give it snap and body, so she left it loose about her shoulders and swung down from the loft. Ignoring Joseph's canted brows, she raced for the door, then paused to draw a determined breath to cool the impatient fire of anticipation in her cheeks.

They were standing off to the side of the porch, heads bent together like little boys intent upon

mischief. Dalton's back was to her. In the warmth of
the morning sun, he'd forgone his heavy coat in
favor of a lightweight jacket. It displayed his shoulders like a broad mountain range, and she stood for
a long moment, admiring their height and breadth
until breathless with exhilaration.

About then Sammy took notice of her. His head
flung up and his smile broke wide with excited glee.

"Mornin', Jude. Lookee here at what Mac's showing me how to use."

As Dalton turned toward her, she got an eyeful—
and she saw red.

In Sammy's hands was a Colt .45.

Chapter 13

"**J**ust what in heaven's name do you think you're doing?"

Jude strode across the yard to snatch the offending weapon from her brother's hand.

"B-but Jude, Mac was jus' tryin'—"

"I know what he was trying to do. Get inside, Sammy. Now!"

Because she never raised her voice to him in anger, Sammy stood rooted where he was, his eyes big and beginning to well up in confusion. He glanced to Dalton, but his friend seemed equally surprised by Jude's fierce mood. Finding no support in either Dalton's flat stare or his sister's fury, he broke for the house in a wild gait.

For the first time Jude wasn't preoccupied with her brother's pain. She didn't go after him to soothe his hurt. Instead she swung to face Dalton MacKenzie, her expression as explosive as the firing caps on his metal cartridges.

"How dare you take advantage of our trust and hospitality, then turn around and do something— something like this? I told you how I felt about guns and the violence they breed, yet you ride in here

175

behind my back, bringing the despicable tools of your trade to a boy like Sammy."

Dalton stiffened. Here it comes, he thought with grim resignation, that condemnation of all he was because of what he did for a living. He'd been crazy to think he'd find a scrap of understanding for his motives, even in a compassionate heart like Jude's. It all came down to one thing: he was a man with a gun and she'd never, ever see him as capable of being anything different.

"I wasn't planning to teach him how to earn a wage as a gun slick, Jude. And he's not a boy. He's a full-grown man, a man who's upset because last night he couldn't protect his sister."

Jude hadn't considered that, and for a moment it threw her off balance. But only for a moment. Her fright had been too great, her alarm too overwhelming, for momentum to slow. So she let go with both barrels. "The reason doesn't matter. What matters is Sammy doesn't have the capacity to grasp the concepts of violence. He sees you as his hero, able to step in and scare the bullies away. You give him a gun and he'll think he can do the same. Only he won't know that they were afraid of you because of your reputation, and they'll force him to shoot or be shot. Sammy doesn't understand consequence. He won't realize that if he points and fires, someone will be hurt or killed. Can't you see what you're doing? You're forcing him into a world where he doesn't know the rules and he can't play the game."

Then he did see, everything. It wasn't him and the dark stain of his profession about which she was furious, it was the thought of harm coming to her brother. She was being protective, not condemning.

And something deep inside him gave way at the recognition of such devotion.

"Sammy is all I have," Jude concluded, angry with herself because her voice had adopted a slight shake of emotion. Seeing Dalton at her doorstep had shaken her, just as seeing Sammy with a firearm had jolted her sensibilities to an even greater degree. How could she expect to act rationally? How could she not try to explain what lay behind her panic with her hoarse summation: "I won't allow you to bring that kind of pain into my house again."

Dalton didn't flinch under the deadly bore of her gaze. He was too lost in just looking at her. Worked up into a fiery temper, Jude Amos was something to see. With her cheeks flushed in high color, her eyes dark as thunderclouds, and her hair in a silken swirl about her shoulders, she was an unstoppable tempest in full blow. Like that summer storm, she hummed with excitement and threatened danger, sending out enough electric sparks to charge the air between them. And because it was impossible to resist such a strong magnetic pull, Dalton didn't try.

Jude managed a short blurt of surprise when his arm hooked about her waist to tug her up tight against him. Then he kissed her and all coherent thought fled. Shivers of delight raced down to her toes and back again to pool in the most embarrassing places, places that cried out for his notice. Her breasts throbbed where they were mashed to his jacket. She could feel every one of his brass buttons and wondered, inanely, if they would leave marks upon her flesh, the way the feel of his fingers pulling gently through her hair would leave road maps upon her heart.

"I didn't show him the gun to make you angry,"
Dalton was saying. She felt his lips move as he
framed the words upon her mouth, and she marveled that the act of speech could be as thrilling as
the taste of his kiss. "I was thinking of you out here
alone, and men like that on the prowl. Sammy
asked me to show him, and I guess I just didn't
figure on the rest."

Of course that made perfect sense. He was showing his concern for them the only way he knew how.
She made her arguments with words: he knew how
to put an end to threats with the cock of a .45.

And from out of all that, one idea surfaced.

Dalton cared about them.

He'd ridden out to see them because he was
worried. He had taught Sammy about firearms to
keep them safe, even when the greatest threat was
from the men with whom he rode. Just as the
greatest threat to her was from her own weakness
for him. A sliver of control returned with that
realization, giving her time to accept all that went
with it reluctantly. Care or not, the time was fast
approaching when what he did for a living would
conflict with the man she knew him to be, and her
foolishly exposed heart and the vulnerable trust of
her brother would be caught right in the middle.
How could she be so naive as to think that either
would go undamaged?

She lowered her head, tucking it beneath his chin.
Still, she could feel the tickle of his kiss upon her
hair. Her eyes squeezed shut in bittersweet joy
because what he was making her want from him
was impossible, what they were leading up to
unwise.

"I guess I should apologize for shouting," she
murmured.

He was stroking her hair with his hands, his lips. "No, you don't need to. I'm the one who's sorry."

"Before we have even more to regret, maybe you should go." And she surprised them both by pushing away from what she desired most: his embrace, his touch, his tender concern. When he made no move to leave, she, who made it a habit never to run from much of anything, fled from him again while she could still manage the strength of will.

As Jude hurried for the house, Dalton lingered in the front yard, not wanting to leave yet having no invitation to stay. The pull and push of his attraction to Jude had him warring with himself. It was becoming harder and harder for him to remember any true objection to her looks. She was a fair woman, of strong heart, firm convictions, and honest appearance. There wasn't a trace of artifice to her. Perhaps that was why he couldn't stay away: the novelty of her, of a woman of honor. That was something he never would have believed had he not witnessed it firsthand.

"It was good, what you were thinking."

Dalton glanced about to see the old Sioux standing nearly at his elbow. He hadn't heard the man's approach.

"But it was wrong what you did," the cook concluded just as blandly.

"So I've been told." Figuring the old man had come out to chase him off, he started toward his horse when Joseph's words stopped him.

"He was shot down in Fort Laramie, their father was, by bad men who wanted his money. That is why she hates the gun. It has brought much sadness into her life. She fears you will bring more of it to her door."

He paused, shocked by that fact, though it explained much. Her father murdered. No wonder she hated his profession—a wonder she didn't hate him as well. Still he spoke up in his defense because he hadn't had a hand in that long ago tragedy, any more than he'd started the trouble here.

"I can't stop what's coming from coming. It was on its way before I had anything to do with it."

"You speak of that business with the rancher. Yes. But that is not what has her worried. She worries for you, because she would care for you and will not allow herself to."

Those words confirmed what he'd both hoped and feared in his heart.

"I told you before, I'm not going to hurt them."

"That is what you told me." And he believed it even less now, after seeing what he'd seen. "These two, this brother and sister, they are my family. I lost my people to soldier bullets when the white men with their fever for the yellow rocks tried to drive them from our home. I was not with them when they fell in the snow, bloodied like slaughtered beasts because of this greed for what cannot be owned by man. They were my people, but I was not among them at the end. I was like you, pushed outside my family because of choices I had made."

"What choices?" Dalton asked, wondering what could tie him and this ancient warrior together.

"While my people were yet the proudest upon the plains, I allowed myself to be lured away by the white man's promises. I went to their mission schools, wanting to learn a way of peace with knowledge of them. The road to the mind became a road to my heart when I met my teacher, Lucy Amos, sister to Jude's father's father. When I married her, I became two persons, one of the old ways and one of the new white world. And for a time it did not matter and we were happy."

The old man sighed, his dark eyes softening with remembered pleasures: his lovely bride, the children who blessed their lodge. A time all too brief as clouds gathered darkly on the horizon.

"When white soldiers brought trouble to my people, I thought only of my new family. They were white, but those who had befriended us turned their backs on us in suspicion and hate. I feared for their safety, and instead of standing to be counted as my father and his father before him, I took my family and fled from the hills that were my home. And then sickness came, calling away my wife, my children. It was too late to go back. I, like you, gunfighter, stood alone, with no people who would claim me.

"I came here to this valley, an empty shell with no life inside, hoping that soon I would die. I met this foolish, determined man and his family. They had come west because the pictures painted in letters from Lucy Amos Otaktay led them to dream of freedom in a land of plenty, and though I knew better, I allowed myself to believe their dream of holding on to a home. We found we needed one another. I helped them survive off the land, and they gave me reason to live again within my soul. They became my new family. We are not orphaned when we can claim each other."

Dalton was silent for a long moment, a soul-deep stillness upon him, wondering why Joseph had told him of his past, wondering why the old man had drawn a link between them, as if to pull him in closer when he should have been trying to drive him away. And he wondered what special powers the old Indian possessed to see into his drifting spirit, to read the age-old wounds upon it, then to offer another of his wise cures to make him whole again, to give him a place to belong.

Then Joseph did the unexpected by saying, "Come in. Breakfast is ready and I would send no man away hungry."

Dalton hesitated. Joseph's biscuits were not what he'd grown hungry for. He'd developed an unhealthy craving for the life he'd observed here at Amos Station and the unconventional family it housed. It would be all too easy to become a part of it, if his past would let him.

But that would mean walking away from obligations, obligations he couldn't desert and still retain what was most important to him. Honor was all he'd had to cling to since he'd discovered what it meant to be a man, and he was uncompromising. Here, for the first time, he found himself considering what it would be like to bend. Which was why he thought it might be wise to swing up on the big buckskin before he could be further swayed from what duty demanded.

But in the end he followed Joseph, calling himself a fool for every step he took.

Jude didn't know what to make of Sammy. He was sullen in his refusal to speak to her when she came inside, and would listen to none of her explanations or apologies. It wasn't like him to hold a grudge or to punish her with his silence. It was Dalton, of course, who made the wedge between them, Dalton who was like the father figure Jude could never be, who fired the boy's imagination with his exciting lifestyle and heroic acts. Dalton, who wasn't tied to the day-to-day existence at the station but actually went out to capture the moments of which Sammy could only dream. How could she compete with that glowing image by saying what she'd done was for his own good? How could she repair the rent between them if he wouldn't tell her what moved behind his petulant frown?

Finally Sammy allowed her one brief statement which wounded her to the soul.

"Mac's the only one who ever treated me like a man, and you wouldn't let him make me into one."

Jude gaped at him, speechless. Her first impulse was to deny it, but the words wouldn't come. She didn't know how to answer his accusation because it was true!

She didn't see her brother as a man. In her mind he would always be a child, needing coddling and protecting, not encouragement to grow. She'd convinced herself that, by teaching him his numbers and giving him a limited freedom with the stock, she was fostering a sense of independence, but she wasn't. Her attitude toward him was one of smothering restraint, and that was what made her comfortable. She didn't want him to take steps away from her, and Dalton had encouraged him to take a giant stride. She was frightened and threatened and she wanted to hold on tight. Because without Sammy, what did she have?

And the knowledge that she was stifling her brother's right to manhood out of her own selfishness sat hot and heavy around her heart.

"Being a man isn't about carrying a gun and having folks scared of you."

Both Jude and Sammy turned as Dalton issued that quiet claim from the threshold of their home.

"Being a man is about caring for those who

depend on you to be strong, and not doing anything out of foolishness or pride to hurt those people you love. It doesn't take anything special to hide behind a gun and run whenever things get tough. What's hard is planting roots down deep and seeing that they take. It's always being there when you're needed and knowing when to back down from trouble instead of courting it. It's not about how old you are, or how big you are, or how fast you are. Any fool kid can pull a pistol and take a life, but it takes a man to commit his future to a family. Can you understand that, Sam?"

The tousled head nodded once, slowly.

"I was wrong in what I tried to do because it went against your sister's wishes and she's the one, not me, who's here for you every day. You owe her the respect of abiding by her judgment. And right now you're making my wrong worse by making her feel bad about what she did."

Sammy's mouth quivered. "I—I didn't mean to." And he hung his head the way his dog, Biscuit, did when shamed for bad behavior.

"Sam, you want to be a man, you support your sister in her beliefs. You be strong for her because she needs you there for her just as much as you need her. That's what family's about, or at least that's what I've been told. I'm hardly an expert on the subject."

But his advice rang with a sterling truth, impressing even the simplistic workings of Sammy's mind and piercing deep into the realm of Jude's soul.

As they sat down to Joseph's breakfast, Jude was convinced, right or wrong, that she would never love another man as much as she loved this quixotic gunman, Dalton MacKenzie.

There was little table talk. Sammy wolfed down

his meal to be ready for the morning stage out of
Fort Laramie. Once he'd gone, silence settled over
the platters of food, separating the unlikely couple
whose hearts were filled with one another. In the
small room there was nowhere for Joseph to go to
make a tactful retreat, so he sat at the head of the
table, a reluctant but unmoving chaperon, his presence making intimate conversation impossible
while private thoughts ran rampant.

Dalton snatched glances at the woman opposite
each time he reached for his coffee tin, every time
he picked up one of Joseph's flaky biscuits. Had she
always had such wide, sensual lips with sweet
slopes and swells made to fit a man's mouth? Or
were they still shaped by his own? The bing-cherry
jam on his biscuit paled in comparison to their rosy
warmth. How he longed to lean across the plain
board of fare to grab a taste of that puckered fruit.
She needed to smile more often, just the touch of
sweetening necessary where those lush lips were
concerned.

And her eyes: like a storm one second, then soft
as the underbelly of a dove the next. If a man could
learn to read her passions within the varying hues,
there were no secrets she could hold from him. She
was a woman who liked her secrets; she liked to be
wrapped up tight and close with her emotions.
What did she hide? he wondered. What a pleasure
there would be in watching her mysteries unfurl
before him—or beneath him.

Jude gave a slight jerk, the pupils of her eyes
growing dark and wide as she read his desires in the
chance mingling of their stares. He offered no
excuses, and he did not look away. Instead he held
her timid gaze in thrall, letting it cloud with confused awareness of him as a man, as a potential

lover. And it wasn't fright or reluctance he saw mirrored back; it was wistful remorse.

"If you're finished, Mr. MacKenzie, you should be on your way before you're missed."

"I'm not kept on a leash, Miss Amos. I'm not a dog."

Jude flushed slightly, but still she stood, the movement coercing him to his feet out of gentlemanly habit. Whatever else he might be, someone in the gunfighter's past had taught him manners and had seen to his education. If not family, then who?

Jude led him outside while Joseph busied himself with the remnants of the meal. At the top of the porch steps, she stopped, leaving no doubt of her intent. Time for him to go.

"I should like to see you again, Jude. It was my intention the other night to have a dance from you."

"You were otherwise engaged, Mr. MacKenzie."

The bite of her tone made him smile. "Occupied, perhaps, but not engaged. I've made no commitments in that area, if you're curious."

"What makes you think I am?"

"The way you scowl at me and your eyes spark like flint on steel."

Jude blinked rapidly, startled by his observations—and pleased by them too. It didn't make what she had to do any easier. "You're mistaken, Mr. MacKenzie. As you've warned before, I'd be foolish to turn any interest in your direction. You're a dangerous man. I've known that from the start. We're on different sides, you and I, and I don't think it would be wise for you to come visit us here again. Sammy, Joseph, and I can take care of ourselves, like we always have. We don't need your help."

"Is that right?" His dry-as-dust drawl called her on the times before when his aid was seen as provident rather than as an interference. She was pushing him away, and his instinct was to brace and dig in deep in his defense.

"You may not be on Jamison's leash, but you're bought and paid for just the same. You're going to be riding against my friends, my neighbors, and if he orders it, against me. That makes for a cold welcome under my roof. You've more than repaid your debt to us for taking you in and seeing to your care. I think it's time you got on about your business."

"Good-bye" was heavy in her flatly delivered statement, and suddenly the thought of riding out and not seeing this willful woman again was not acceptable to heart or mind. "And what if I decide to make you my business, Miss Amos?"

A shiver took her, as if that was more threat than tantalizing promise. "You won't. I'm not the kind of woman you want, Dalton, and you've got nothing to offer that I need."

His eyes narrowed in objection to that cold truth—a truth he'd believed up until a few minutes before. "That's not the impression I got before breakfast."

That he would turn her own weakness against her was just the starch Jude needed to stand firm.

"Good-bye, Mr. MacKenzie. I'd wish you well, but you can understand the conflict of our interests prevents me from it. Please don't come back here again. I don't want Sammy confused by your motives." And she didn't want her own heart broken in the process.

No matter how she might deny it, there was plenty that she wanted from Dalton MacKenzie, and the more she saw of him, the needier she became. But he was a walkaway kind of man, and nothing she could say or do would ever change that. "You're an ill wind in this valley, whipping up a storm that's about to blow down upon us all. And I'm going to get safely under cover."

He never betrayed how badly the sear of those words hurt. She was right. He was no good for her, or for anyone, and that had never bothered him before. He made it his motto not to let it matter. But somehow, in this case, his defenses had failed him. How else could he explain the sudden lancing pain the truth of her words drove to the core of his soul? But to let her know of that vulnerability was to invite her to work at that crack in his outer armor until it widened into a cavern, a cavern from which it would be impossible for him to climb out. He knew from experience how quickly tender feeling could be turned against him. Instead he countered her claim with an observation of his own.

"Afraid you'll get swept off your feet, Miss Amos?"

Her gaze tunneled into his, so quiet in its directness, he was caught before he had the chance to glance away.

"Yes, Mr. MacKenzie, I am. And I can't afford to be. Not by you."

Her brutal honesty tore the heart from his chest, making it her humbled trophy as she turned and proudly walked into the house that would never be his home.

Chapter 14

❦

"Time's running out, Daddy. When are you going to stop tiptoeing around and really step down hard?"

Patrick Jamison smiled across the tabletop, offering one of his weak, vacillating gestures in an effort to placate his restless daughter. "Now, Kathleen—"

"You take the same tone to them, like a doting father scolding his children. How do you expect them to listen when they have no respect for who's speaking?"

Dalton watched the interplay between father and daughter over the rim of his wineglass. It was good wine, the best money could buy, just like everything else at Sweetgrass. Just like him. And he had to wonder after all he'd observed if Kathleen was speaking of herself rather than the ranchers when she spoke of respect and the lack thereof.

Jamison sighed with a great weariness. "Kathleen, you're young and full of vinegar. You want to act without thought to consequence. You forget that these people you are so anxious to drive off like unwanted vermin were once my friends. We founded this valley together, helping one another get started."

189

"And so you're willing to let them stay, let them squander precious acres we need for our own stock? Times change, Father. We grew and they didn't. Is that our fault? Are we to rein in our success out of some misguided sense of loyalty you have to folks who despise what you've been able to achieve? Would you be soft-hearted toward a bunch of jealous squatters who hate everything you have because they lack it? Would they if our positions were reversed? I don't think so, do you, Mr. Mac-Kenzie?"

"From what I know of human nature, those who have usually aren't willing to share," came Dalton's quiet claim, making her point and underlining it with his own distaste for her position. She chose to ignore that part of it.

"You see, Daddy, your generosity isn't appreciated. All you're doing is giving them time to mount their resistance. If you struck now, before they were prepared—"

"Struck? You mean fire down upon these people I've known for years?"

"Isn't that why you hired Mr. MacKenzie?"

Jamison flushed darkly at the truth in her sharp perception. Wasn't it? Why else would he want a hired killer on his payroll, if not to do what he did best? Disgusted with himself and at the situation that forced him to such terrible actions, he growled, "And how would you have me direct Mr. MacKenzie, dear daughter? Should I have him pick off the men, women, and children in this valley like they did the buffalo until our way is cleared?"

Kathleen's delicate nostrils flared, scenting the blood and excitement of that suggestion. However, she was too clever to let her father see the lust for violence he abhorred rising up in his own child. She covered it with a soft, feminine smile and a murmur of "Of course not, Daddy," her lashes fluttering down meekly to conceal the hard brilliance of her gaze. "You make me sound like a monster when all I'm thinking of is you and what you deserve after all your hard work. If you're going to be a man of influence when Wyoming becomes a state some day soon, you have to win the respect and awe of those around you. I was just trying to help." And Jamison was easily taken in by her sympathetic show of remorse because he loved her. Dalton had no such blinders to his view, and he saw quite clearly the dark and deadly twists of the lovely Miss Jamison's soul.

Jamison reached out to pat his daughter's slender hand. "I didn't mean to be so cross, my dear, it's just that this whole topic is very distressing to me. If there were another way, one that didn't involve anyone getting hurt at all . . ." His words trailed off wistfully.

Kathleen brightened, seizing the chance to manipulate him. "I might know of a way. It's that woman, Jude Amos, who holds them all together. Without her influence, the rest would fold."

Dalton went still, careful not to let a trace of reaction betray itself to Kathleen's shrewd, assessing stare.

"Jude Amos?" Jamison considered this for a moment. "Of all of them, she's the most likely to sell her land."

"Yes. And if she does, perhaps the others will follow suit. They look up to her and value her opinion." A wry disgust tinged that truth, then Kathleen quickly smiled. "If it would help, Daddy,

I'll ride over and talk to Miss Amos, woman to woman. Perhaps I can enlist her help in swaying the other farmers, or at least discourage her from taking up their cause."

"Would you, Kathleen?" A hopeful relief lightened Jamison's tone as he considered a course that could bypass the use of force.

"I'll ride over first thing in the morning. Perhaps Mr. MacKenzie would accompany me. He seems to have some influence over Miss Amos himself." Her dark glare skewered Dalton, daring him to disagree.

"I don't know that anyone has any influence over Miss Amos," he phrased with care. "Certainly not me. She has nothing but dislike for men of violence."

"I think you sell your charms short, Mr. Mac-Kenzie."

He shrugged, disavowing any interest one way or another.

"I'd feel better if you rode along, Mr. MacKenzie," Jamison entreated. "These times are getting too dangerous for a young woman like Kathleen to go about unescorted, even upon our lands."

Dalton held to his smirk of doubt. Kathleen was about as helpless as a rattler in its coil, and he, for one, wasn't eager to feel the cut of her fangs. "I'll ride along if you think your daughter needs protecting, but I can't vouch for how much help I'll be when it comes to impressing any opinions on Jude Amos. She has a will of her own, and I admire that in a woman." And he canted a look toward Kathleen, enjoying the simmer of fury behind the sweet mask she wore for her father's benefit.

Kathleen surged up out of her chair, her tension telegraphed in the white-knuckled clench of her linen napkin. She gave it a crisp flick to the seat of her empty chair, her smile thin and strained, her glare challenging Dalton's cool pose of amusement. "It's all settled then. I think I'll retire now, if you gentlemen will excuse me."

She swept around the table in a pretty swish of taffeta and placed a swift kiss upon her father's brow.

"Good night, child," he said fondly. "You've lightened the load on my heart."

"It's the least I could do, Daddy. Sweet dreams. And to you, Mr. MacKenzie," she purred with heavy-lidded invitation. Then her scowl returned at his unblinking rebuff, and she flounced from the room.

Jamison sighed in her absence. "Forgive her her impetuous nature, Mr. MacKenzie. She comes by it quite naturally. Her mother was a finely weaned aristocrat at the head of Boston society, used to commanding all in attendance with the slightest lift of her hand. I'm still not sure how I managed the luck to win her heart. She was the culturing influence on Kathleen. Even after we moved west, she continued our daughter's refinement, insisting she never forget she is a Boston Bradshaw."

"And where is Mrs. Jamison now?"

Though the question was reasonable, Jamison greeted it with a tight jaw. "She prefers to stay in Boston. The western elements didn't agree with her. Kathleen visits her often, but I think poor, dear Glenys never understood how Kathleen could prefer the Wyoming spaces to her society soirées." He sounded pleased by that, as if it were a hard-fought battle won in his favor.

Dalton wondered if he had any idea of what he'd

won. Pretty, loyal daughter or ruthlessly scheming deposer, capable of turning on her father as quickly as she would upon the enemy. He wondered too how the man could be so blind to his only child's character flaws. Jamison wasn't a true villain. He was an arrogant, greedy bully, but he wasn't a man without conscience. He wouldn't condone casual bloodshed unless pushed to it . . . by someone like Kathleen. And though Dalton lived by a strict code of uninvolvement, he'd been pulled into the uncomfortable middle of this valley feud by bankrolled duty on one side and by a husky voice and the hint of a home he'd never had on the other. He didn't like it. He hated complications and confused issues. It shaded what he did, made it . . . personal. And to a professional man like himself, nothing could be worse. Emotions made a man second-guess his instincts when often instinct was the only thing that kept him alive. He couldn't afford hesitation when split-second judgment was a necessity to survival.

His interest in Jude Amos and her family dulled his edge. A man without an edge was a man courting disaster.

As he lay back into the embrace of his big bed, troubled thoughts plagued him. Lost to the fantasy of belonging somewhere, he'd let himself forget who he was and what he really wanted. Vulnerable and afraid, he'd been susceptible to the lure of that peaceful existence and to the quiet charm of a plain woman who ordinarily wouldn't have garnered a second look from him. The woman, like the lifestyle, was so different, so appealing because of that very difference. He'd been riding a solitary, self-absorbed path for so long that finding himself in such a foreign clime shocked him from his usual

aloofness, tempting him to flirt with what he'd
never considered: a family, stability, a home, a good
woman.

But those weren't things he really wanted. To be
tied down to a dusty daily grind of labor and lean
means was not for him, not after going without a
single shirt he could call his own for the better part
of his life. He liked to be pampered in luxury with
fine wine, tailor-made clothes, and expensive cigars.
Lumpy beds in drafty cabins held no charm next to
the ready comfort of a good hotel.

What long-lasting pleasure could there be in
waking up to the same woman every morning? One
who had work-roughened hands and wore sturdy
boots when he'd been spoiled by soft flesh scented
by Parisian perfumes, clad in slithery silks and
scraps of lace. One who blushed on the receiving
end of a kiss and had probably never seen a real
man naked. What good was such a woman to a man
of his refined tastes and explicit desires?

The image of Jude Amos's damp lips gently
parted and swollen like a newly blown rose tantalized him. The picture sprang so unexpectedly to
mind, his body responded before his mind could
compensate. He could almost feel her quick, excited
breaths feathering against his mouth.

For a woman inexperienced in passions, she knew
how to twist him up in a torture of desperate want.

Think of San Francisco.

He squeezed his eyes shut, to concentrate on that
far goal. It had been there before him, like a
shimmering mirage, for as long as he could remember: dreams of success and acceptance all tied to
that distant destination. He couldn't allow himself
to get distracted. He'd coolly conclude his business

in this Wyoming valley and move on to his next reward. And one day that reward would be California.

He dreamed of high-pitched streets and a faceless woman with gloved hands smelling of violets.

Jude was crossing the sun-freckled yard from the barn to the house when she saw two riders approaching. In a single, horror-struck moment, she recognized one of them as Dalton.

Why had she picked this morning to muck stables?

There was no time to make a mad dash for the house and a chance to present herself decently to her impending company. All she could do was stand proud and try to ignore the fact that she reeked of manure. For the dirty task, she'd pulled on a pair of Sammy's denims and one of his old, worn shirts. Both garments hung on her, hitched in with the aid of a wide leather belt. Both garments were far from clean. Though she'd knotted back her hair and covered it with a cotton square, wisps had escaped and her constant brushing them aside left streaks of unmentionable origin on cheeks and brow. She didn't dare look down to gauge the state of her boots after standing ankle deep in filthy straw, but she did have the presence of mind to pluck off caked gloves and fling them as far from her as possible.

Bad was Dalton's catching her in such a ragged state.

Worse was discovering his riding companion to be Kathleen Jamison.

Where was a good-sized rock when it was needed? She would have crawled under it to spare herself the shame of their assessing stares. Boldly, she fixed a welcoming smile to disguise her mortification as she hailed them with a cheery "good morning."

Kathleen reined in and her features puckered in dismay. Quickly, she urged her mount to retreat several paces. From out of the sleeve of her form-fitting, dove-gray riding jacket, she drew a lace-edged hanky to press over her mouth and nose.

If one could die of humiliation, Jude would have expired on the spot.

"Good morning, Miss Amos," she muttered through the linen purifier. "I fear we've caught you at a bad time."

The unveiled disdain in the young woman's voice brought a stiffening to Jude's spine. Her smile broadened to a feral show of teeth. "Why, not at all, Miss Jamison. I was just finishing up some chores. Please, step down. You're just in time to join me for some coffee. I planned to enjoy a cup before going back to work."

The suggestion that she meant to sit, oblivious to her own stench, and entertain company boggled the pristinely garbed redhead, but she forced a polite shake of regret and a weak, "Thank you kindly for the offer, but we can't stay."

The intimately crooned "we" didn't escape Jude. Her gaze flickered reluctantly to Dalton, who sat on his tall buckskin with an easy elegance. No emotion escaped the firm set of his features. His steady, blue-eyed gaze regarded her with a blankness befitting a stranger, as if they'd never shared a scorching kiss in the same front yard, as if he'd never accused her of being swept away by her feelings for him.

Those same feelings betrayed her now as she connected his bland stare to the significance of him and Kathleen out for a morning ride. Her spirit nose-

dived into her mucky boots. It hadn't taken him
long to recover from her rejection, and obviously
Kathleen was smugly pleased to rub her nose in it.
Just as Jude wished she could rub the lovely young
creature's in something far less pleasant.

"I'm sure you two are anxious to get on with your
ride. It was nice of you to stop by," she concluded
with a tight-throated dishonesty. Because the message Kathleen Jamison conveyed with her malicious
grin wasn't nice at all: that homely women smelling
of horse dung didn't warrant handsome men like
Dalton MacKenzie as an escort, that poor females
were destined to wallow in barn stalls, pitching
soiled bedding, while wealthy ones frolicked about
in the morning dew. It was a calculated message,
one woman to another, of *I've got what you wanted.*
And Jude refused to give the gorgeous witch the
satisfaction of knowing how horribly that fact hurt.

"Actually, there was another reason for our visit,"
Kathleen said sweetly. "I wanted to urge you, friend
to friend, to take my father's offer for your land. I
fully understand how miserable you must be way
out here with no hope for any . . . happiness. Why
burden yourself with extra property? You could use
the money it brings to buy yourself a new dress,
something neat and serviceable which would make
you more attractive to a prospective husband. I'm
sure a woman as hard-working and resourceful as
yourself needn't live out her life alone, even with
your obvious—ummm—drawbacks."

"Being?" Jude prompted brittlely.

"Well, your situation, for one, of advanced years
and less than average features" was the coyly offered explanation. "And, of course, the unusual
household you keep, what with a half-witted man
and an Indian to boot."

Jude compressed her lips to contain her first furious response to such blatant meanness. Her glance touched on Dalton, hoping . . . she wasn't sure what she was hoping. His denial of all Kathleen said perhaps. But he gave away nothing, his silence a damnable agreement.

"Miss Jamison, thank you for your concern over my situation," Jude began with a chill propriety. "I'm sure you could not understand how anyone could find pleasure in it, but I assure you, I am neither miserable nor desperately lonely. This is my home, a legacy from my father, and I will hold it for as long as I am able or interested. And I can do that without a new dress or a man to advise me. You may tell your father I respectfully decline his offer. My land is not for sale."

"That's not a very wise decision, Miss Amos," Dalton added in his laconic drawl. Her gaze flashed to him with a flinty stubbornness.

"Perhaps not, Mr. MacKenzie, but I'll not change it." And in that moment, pride pushed her to make a choice without deferral to reason, one behind which she would have to stand, whether it was in her best interest or not, because a rich, nasty female had goaded her into it with her offer of smug charity. And because a gorgeous gunfighter with whom she'd fallen in love had failed to come to her defense. "Now, then, I have work to get back to, so if there's nothing more, I'll bid you a good morning."

Just then Sammy ambled out of the barn and, spotting Dalton, broke into a huge grin and a lumbering trot.

"Hey, Mac! We didn't know you was gonna stop by. You come for some of Joseph's flapjacks?"

Then he saw Kathleen perched upon her dainty

white mare, where she'd been hidden from his view by Dalton's shadow. He skidded to a halt, his eyes growing bright and round, his jaw hanging slack in pure admiration of the most beautiful sight he'd ever seen.

While he stood there like a post, gawking in speechless wonder, Kathleen's annoyance with the situation crested. She jerked up her reins, startling a snort from her mount. And to Sammy she snapped, "Get out of the way, you witless moron."

Sammy blinked like a dog struck an unexpected blow upon the snout. All he could think to mutter was "Mac, you ain't stayin'?"

"Of course he's not staying," Kathleen sneered. "Why would he want to waste his time in this hovel with an old maid and her brainless brother? Come, Mr. MacKenzie. It was a fool's errand trying to help these people. They can't even help themselves." And she wheeled her fancy filly away with the saw of its bit and applied her heels smartly, sending the animal lunging forward with a squeal of surprised distress.

Dalton followed. He couldn't bear to linger, tormented by the looks upon the faces of those for whom he'd come to care. It had been bad enough sitting silent while Kathleen cruelly baited Jude. It had taken all his will power not to respond to her wordless appeal for support. He'd wanted to give it. For even standing there, covered in filth, stinking of offal, she stirred his heart like none before her, and to watch her be so abused by Kathleen's cutting disdain left him less a man somehow. Telling himself he was doing his job, fulfilling his obligations to his employer and his future plans, did nothing to lessen the punch to his gut when Jude looked away from him in a daze of betrayal.

But Jude was a strong woman. She knew what kind of man he was, knew she could expect nothing from him by way of commitment or character. It was for the best that she believe the worst now; that made it easier to ride away with the knowledge that he wouldn't be back, that welcome no longer existed at Amos Station. Jude would get over her disappointment because she'd never expected any better from a man of his profession.

But Sammy . . . Sammy was something else again. Sammy had opened up his trusting heart to accept him in as a friend. To witness his hurt at the mean-spirited whims of Kathleen Jamison went beyond what he was prepared to sacrifice. But there was nothing he could do to change what was said, no way to soften the awful anguish in those big spaniel eyes. He'd never kicked a dog before because cruelty in any form disgusted him. He was disgusted with himself as he rode in Kathleen's wake: a hired gun without conscience or care. And he'd never hated a woman as much as he did the coldly calculating Miss Jamison for making him face that lack of soul within himself.

Worse than her own heartache was trying to explain away Dalton's callous behavior to a confused Sammy. He stood watching his friend's dust settle, a woeful look upon his youthful face.

"Is Mac mad at me, Jude? Did I do somethin' wrong? Is that why he wouldn't stay? Is that why he wouldn't talk to me?"

Jude slipped an arm about her brother's sturdy waist, knowing he wouldn't object to the smell or the dirt, and she hugged him tight while trying in her own mind to justify what had happened. How to put such complexity on a level he could understand.

"It's not you, Sammy, it's that lady he was with."

"The pretty lady?"

"Yes. That's Kathleen Jamison, the rancher's daughter."

Sammy sucked at his lip for a thoughtful moment. "She shore is pretty, but I don't think she's very nice."

Jude couldn't disagree. "Mr. MacKenzie works for her father."

"So he has to be mean to us too?"

She sighed. "Something like that."

"Then he's not our friend anymore? He won't come by to see us no more?"

As much as she hated to bring the pain of disillusionment to his tender heart, it would have been crueler to offer false hope where she believed none existed. "I wouldn't count on it, Sammy. Mr. MacKenzie has a job to do for the Jamisons, and that doesn't leave him any time for friends."

He considered that for a minute, then hugged Jude back. "I shore am gonna miss him."

"Me too, Sammy." Jude sucked in a painful breath and released it on a sigh. "Me too."

Chapter 15

"**I**'m against it. I've said it before and I'll repeat it until some of you come to your senses. Violence is not the answer here."

Jude's gaze went from face to face of those men seated at her table, hoping to see that her strong words had made some impression. None of their grim expressions flickered. She threw up her hands.

"What is it you want to do? Meet Jamison head on? That would be suicide and you all know it. He has men and money on his side. What do you have?"

"Right," Wade Barret spoke up. "This is our valley and we won't be driven out of it."

"Wade, surely you don't go along with this insanity," Jude pleaded. "You've got a new wife—"

"Exactly. A wife and a home. And if I'm gonna keep 'em, we've got to put a stop to Jamison's threats."

Jude lifted a helpless gaze to Joseph who was silently refilling the coffee cups. He met her beseeching look with an impassive stare. He alone knew from experience the futility of resisting a man like Jamison. His people had fought a relentless tide, and all but the memory of them had been swept away. He could have told them that resisting such a force was a noble if foolish cause, but these men were ranchers, farmers, white men. They wouldn't listen to an old Sioux's advice.

The eight of them had come to her door at sundown, representing the two dozen or so small concerns in the valley squirming under Jamison's squeeze of power. They had come because the ones not in attendance had asked, "What does Jude Amos think about all this?" So they'd come to find out, and they weren't happy with her response.

She'd called them fools. She had reminded them of their families, of their futures. They hadn't budged. Jake Palmer had been on his way back from Fort Laramie with a load of seed when set upon by a gang of Sweetgrass riders. They'd beaten poor Jake right in front of his wife and daughters and scattered the precious kernels of hope to the greedy Wyoming winds. It seemed Jamison was no longer satisfied with talk. It was time to take action.

And Jude, who sympathized with Jake and his frightened family because she so clearly recalled her own terror at the hands of Jamison's men, was fast running out of reasons to forestall the inevitable. Now that she'd stated her intention of holding her lands, she was committed to whatever these men would decide, be it argument or aggression. Jamison wouldn't pick and choose his targets if he decided on a scorched-earth campaign to rid himself of their presence. No more than Sherman had in his march through Georgia. She'd be as much at risk as any of them, regardless of her personal politics.

"Have you some plan? You can't go up against a man like Jamison without clearly drawn ideas."

Tandy grinned, sensing Jude's surrender. "We've

pooled our money together, seventy-five dollars total, and we're takin' it to Fort Laramie to hire ourselves a fast gun."

"What?" She couldn't believe she'd heard him right. "That's crazy!"

"That's what Jamison did, so we're just followin' his lead. He picked himself a quick draw, now I say we get our own. Then Jamison will know we don't mean to knuckle under."

A fast gun could mean only one thing: a nose-to-nose confrontation with Dalton. Jude's emotions took a savage wringing before she managed, "Who here knows anything about hiring a gunfighter?"

Tandy tipped back in his chair, his smile all cocky and confident. "Figure we'll jus' go bar to bar 'til we find us one."

"Do you think they have regular hours posted for granting interviews?"

Tandy ignored her jibe. "Any bartender worth his salt knows who's the fastest gun in town. We'll jus' drop a coin or two his way and he'll set us right."

"Right down the path to your own foolish end!"

But the men were nodding among themselves, eager to put Tandy's plan in motion, eager to bring death into their valley.

"Are you all set on going through with this dangerous nonsense?" After a unanimous affirmative, Jude drew a resigned breath. "Then I guess I have no choice but to ride along with you to make sure there's one voice of reason amid all this madness."

Having never been inside a hotel bar, Jude approached the room with trepidation. It was midday, true, and there was none of the tinny piano noise

and raucous laughter she'd associated with men at
drink and cards, yet still she felt a deep discomfort,
as if she were treading on unholy ground.

Still weary and worn from the stage ride through
the early morning hours, she'd elected to recover
herself in a sunny eatery across from the row of
disreputable-looking saloons. There she remained
until their anxious scouting party hit on a likely
candidate. It had taken them all of ten minutes,
which didn't say much for the moral fiber of Fort
Laramie and the characters it drew to its bosom.

She followed Wade Barret into the hotel drinking
salon, uneasily aware that she was the only decently
clad woman in sight. Busty creatures with their
attributes spilling over the shoulders of gambling
patrons were every bit as shocking as the nude
portraits brazenly displayed on the wall for all to
see. She kept her gaze fixed in the middle of Wade's
broad back while color burned hot to the roots of
her hair. At least there was no chance of any of the
clientele mistaking her for one of the working
women, not with her square shape and dowdy
gown.

Wade stopped abruptly, mashing Jude's nose into
the satin of his vest when she failed to pull up in
time.

"That's him there. Barkeep said he was one of the
best for hire."

Jude righted her hat and peered around Wade's
bulk to see the other men of the valley huddled
around a small table, paying court to the pistoleer.

At first glimpse he wasn't much to look at, a lean,
lanky fellow of indeterminate age sporting longish
hair beneath the downward tilt of his Stetson and a
proudly groomed moustache . . . and a low-cut rig

on his hip. His expression was mild, even affable, as he listened to the others talk, but when his gaze rose at Jude's approach, she shivered on the receiving end of his flat, black stare. His eyes were chips of coal, fathomless, soulless. This was the man they were going to hire to kill Dalton MacKenzie.

"This is the lady I was tellin' you about," Tandy gushed nervously. "Miss Jude Amos."

"Well now, howdy, ma'am. Cain't say I'm used to havin' a female holding the hiring and firing power." He grinned, lifting the corners of his manicured moustache in a roguish arch.

"If it were up to me, there'd be no hiring at all, Mr.—"

"Latigo Jones, ma'am, dare I say at your service?"

She wanted to scowl, but he was so genuinely charming, a small smile escaped in spite of her opposition. Still she couldn't relax completely because something about Latigo Jones had the same taut edge of danger she recognized in Dalton, a latent violence seeking an avenue of release. And that's just what they'd come to offer him.

"Have a seat, Miss Amos. Perhaps you can give me a straight answer. These here boys have been dancin' around the issue with some mighty fine two-stepping. They done flashed a heap a cash for some fairly routine work. What I want to know is what I have to do that calls for such a price tag. It's got to be more than just facing down a bunch of twenty-five-dollar-a-month wranglers."

"You'd be facing down one of your own kind," Jude told him, fighting to keep her tone even. "The rancher we're up against has his own hired gun on the payroll."

"Someone of consequence, I'm guessing."

"Dalton MacKenzie."

After a beat of silence, Jones murmured, "I've heard of him and folks, you got trouble."

Agitated by the gunman's casual assessment of their situation, the ranchers muttered among themselves until Tandy declared, "That's why we need you, Mr. Jones."

"Yes, sir, you do. But for Dalton MacKenzie, you ain't offering near enough."

From out of the dismayed rumble, Tandy spoke up again, loud and clear. "Yer jus' scared to go up against him."

Jones's black eyes took on a fearsome inner fire while the rest of his features held to an immobile cast. "Are you callin' me a coward, mister?"

"No, of course he's not," Jude cut in with face-saving impatience, wanting to slap the foolish Tandy for his brash and dangerous arrogance. "No one here doubts your courage, Mr. Jones, or that you are good at your profession."

The deadly brilliance faded and Tandy drew a cautious breath. Then he gave a soft curse as his attention was directed to the outer room.

"What the hell are they doin' here?"

His grumble drew all heads around to where Dalton and three other Sweetgrass riders were approaching. They strode up to the bar, Dalton allowing them a brief glance, the others glaring like blazing six-guns.

"Am I to assume that is the opposition?" Jones drawled out.

"MacKenzie and a couple of Jamison's boys," Tandy sneered in their direction.

"Maybe we should invite 'em over for a little friendly talk."

Before the others could object, Latigo called out,

"Barkeep, bring that bottle on over here and rustle up a few more chairs for my *compadres*."

The farmers scattered like hens as Dalton neared the table—all but Tandy, who held his seat.

Under a veil of civility, the two gunmen regarded each other like a pair of wolves, cautiously scenting each other out, bristling over territory, tense and ready for trouble. Hands were held in the open out of professional courtesy as Dalton sank into one of the emptied seats. The rest of them ceased to exist as the two men talked together.

"Jones."

"Mac."

"You taking up their part in this?"

"We're negotiating."

"Heard they were coming here to do some shopping in that area. You'd be backing the wrong side."

"Could be. But right or wrong don't matter to us. You ever knowed me to walk away from a good fight?"

"You might not walk away from this one."

Jones shrugged eloquently. "Guess that don't matter much neither."

The onlookers chafed uneasily as the two men shared glasses of whiskey and a moment of companionable silence—until Tandy Barret broke it. He put his hand on Dalton's shoulder.

"All right, you had yer drink. Now get. We gots business to finish here."

Chill blue eyes focused on the offending hand. "You won't be finishing anything but your prayers if you don't unhand me. Now."

Tandy loosened his grip and eased it away, as if he were releasing something wild that could turn on him in an instant. Once free, he wiped his palm nervously on a pant leg and scowled belligerently at those who would note how his hand was shaking. To remedy that shame, he assumed an aggressive stance once more.

"We're waitin', mister."

Dalton turned his glass slowly within his hand, studying the play of smoky light on its contents as if mesmerized. "Then you can just wait until I conclude my business."

"What business do you have here?" came the challenging snarl.

Dalton rose up from his chair and the ranchers faded back as one, their gazes searching anxiously for signs of a gun. He didn't seem to be wearing one, but that didn't lessen the atmosphere of threat surrounding him when he faced them to drawl a matter-of-fact ultimatum.

"My business is to introduce all of you to hell if you're thinking of solving this situation with gunplay. Like my friend here said, right or wrong doesn't concern me. Either you sell out or I'll see you buried."

The ranchers blanched to a man, hearing it put straight to the point for the first time. Up to now it had been vague threats and bullying intimidation. Dalton MacKenzie had just defined the stakes they were playing for: life or death. And Jude stood among them, equally horrified by that impersonally put claim.

"Or be buried yourself," Latigo amended, smiling as he reached for his glass. It wasn't a pleasant smile. It was full of bared teeth and menace from a man who was more than a little professionally annoyed to be offered so much less than his peer to perform in the same arena. Perhaps he would have to take the job as a matter of pride.

For a moment the gunmen held each other's stares, locked in assessing combat. Friendship ceased to be an issue when reputations were on the line. The others divided by side, flanking their chosen champion with a breath-suspending anticipation of violence to come, expecting it to burst forth perhaps at this very table, hoping it would. All except Jude, who had eyes only for Dalton as her heart pounded a frantic tempo of alarm.

Then the tension eased as Dalton's gaze was diverted to a far table and fixed there with cold certainty. Dismissing them all as unimportant, he strode from the confrontation without a backward glance, heading across the room with a purposeful intent. He stalked between the tables, a raging bull focused on a red flag waving. Those who saw him coming gave him a wide berth, sensing death was his destination.

The men at cards glanced up in irritation as he cast his huge shadow over their play. Dalton's stare leveled on a greasy-haired cowboy holding a prophetic hand of aces and eights.

"You're wearing my guns, mister."

At Dalton's rumbled words, chairs scraped the worn floorboards and cards were abandoned on the tabletop, leaving him and the object of his scrutiny alone.

The cowboy was foolish enough not to look afraid as he noted Dalton's bare hip. He fingered one of the bone handles with a taunting idleness. "Says who?" came his insolent demand.

"Dalton MacKenzie. My name's well-known where you're going. Tell all of them in hell that I said hello."

The seated man's features hardened and his fin-

gers tightened about the grip of the pistol as he
recognized, too late, the gunfighter from the stage
he'd helped rob. He jerked at the pistol but never
had the chance to clear leather.

Dalton reacted with a smooth economy of motion, dipping to one side, snagging a .45 from the
holster of a coatless gambler sitting on his right. The
gun was leveled and smoking with deadly consequence before the bandit's surprise fully registered.
A circle of crimson widening just left of center, the
outlaw dropped face first into the pile of chips he'd
bought with stolen earnings.

Like the rest of her group, Jude stood frozen in a
daze of shock. She'd never seen a killing before, had
never dreamed one could be executed with such
quick, cold accuracy. Her heart beat fast and furious
up in her throat, choking off sound, almost breath,
as a chill of horror shook her unresisting body. Her
gaze followed, helplessly mesmerized, as Dalton
strode to the dead man and unemotionally relieved
him of the pistol belt and pair of bone-handled
Colts, buckling them with a firm familiarity around
his own hips, where they lay like twin messengers
of death. Dalton gestured to the pile of discolored
poker chips beneath the slumped form.

"Those should see him in the ground" was his
casual-to-the-point-of-callous claim. Then he
turned and caught Jude's glazed stare.

Now she knew. Stark horror shaped her expression, a horror at what he'd done, at who he was.
Now there was no need to worry over complications
from Miss Jude Amos. He saw all hope extinguish in
her shiny gaze. And he turned away, striding purposefully out of the barroom into the hot sear of
midday, the tinny taste of death traveling with him.

*   *   *

"Did you see that? Sonofa—" Tandy Barret stood slack-jawed in amazement, unable to move his stare from the dead cardplayer.

Jamison's men mirrored his awe. They were simple cowboys, paid to ride, rope, and brand. They carried arms for defense against the elements, not to gun down their fellow man. Slowly they filed out of the hotel bar on the heels of the man they now feared as well as followed.

Only Latigo Jones remained unaffected by the gunplay. He leaned back in his chair, nursing a whiskey, smiling an amused smile.

"That's what you folks are in for if you go up against Dalton MacKenzie. You sure you got the stomach for it?"

Tandy looked to him with a touch of desperation. "But you're just as good, ain't you?"

Latigo regarded him with a quirk of amusement. "Let's say you haven't offered enough for the privilege of finding out."

He reached out to snag a busty saloon girl about the waist, tugging her in tight between his legs. She put up a token struggle, wetting the table and those gathered around it as her tray tipped and swayed, knocking the heads off the beers she balanced. But when Latigo tucked a gold piece between her ample breasts, she became instantly cooperative.

"If you folks will excuse me, it seems I got myself some other pressing business to attend."

With a tip of his hat toward a blushing Jude, the gunman took his willing armful to the stairs without a backward glance.

Tandy cursed. "He was the best of the lot. Now what are we gonna do?"

"What we should have done in the beginning," Jude said, hoping to put an end to their mutterings so she could escape the acrid scent of cigar smoke and spilled beer and the ever-spreading circle of red. "We fight Jamison on his own terms."

The men grew silent and listened.

"Gunplay isn't going to solve anything. We need the law on our side. We need someone to go to Cheyenne, to talk to the law there. We have legal claim to our properties and Jamison has none. He fancies himself in public office once the territory seeks statehood and he won't go contrary to the law, at least once his doings are brought out in the open and under the scrutiny of future voters. He can be bent to reason if we put enough pressure on him there. And it wouldn't hurt to go before the Cattlemen's Association to state our grievances. They've got enough problems of their own these days and may be willing to use a little of their influence if it means one fewer thorn in their side."

"What she's saying makes sense, boys. Hit him where it hurts."

"Who's gonna go?"

"How 'bout you, Wade? You're good with words."

Wade, who was Jude's choice, shook his head. "I got me a new bride and a whole lot of acres to seed."

"I'll go," Tandy offered. He frowned at the immediate resistance he got from the others.

"You got too hot a temper, Tandy."

"You do your best talkin' with your fists, Barret."

"Well then," Tandy growled in sullen defeat, "who do we send?"

"I got an idea about that," Wade ventured carefully. He waited until the excited prompting of the others quieted, then looked soberly to Jude. "Miss Amos, what do you say?"

"What? Me?"

Jude's voice squeaked with shock. Volunteering her own services had never entered her mind when she suggested a spokesman. Her heart began an anxious palpitation as the men nodded at the logic of Wade's choice. She didn't see it as logical, not at all. It was crazy. Foolish. Frightening!

"So what do you say, Jude?" Wade coaxed with a "put-your-money-where-your-mouth-is" smile that nudged her back farther and farther into the corner she'd made for herself with her own outspoken views. "You're the one touting a peaceable solution. Here's your chance to get it done."

"Me?" came her wobbly echo. "But why would they listen to me, a woman?" It was the only argument that sprang readily to her dazed mind.

"Same reason we all do. 'Cause you make a helluva lotta sense."

"B-but I can't just go off and leave things—"

"Sammy and the Indian can run the station jus' fine for a few days, and we'll take turns lookin' in on 'em. We'll all pitch in for your stage fare and room and board whilst you're in Cheyenne. C'mon, Jude. What do you say?"

There was a host of agreeing murmurs from all but Tandy, who was still scowling over their lack of faith in him. At the moment Jude thought him an excellent candidate and was about to suggest they reconsider him. Then her panic lessened in favor of the common sense that always served her . . . too well, in this case. They were right; she knew it.

And that corner closed in until she had no choice but to step forward or fall flat.

"Well—"

"I knew you'd do it," Wade concluded for her.

Then all she could do was offer up a weak smile

as the others thanked her boisterously for taking up their cause. And Tandy regarded her with a surly frown.

Jude Amos, what have you gotten yourself into?

Chapter 16

O nce she was committed to her folly, Jude saw no need to remain in the hotel's saloon where the other ranchers were busy drinking to the success of their plan. An hour remained before their stage departed, and she didn't want to spend that time in drunken company, not when so much preyed upon her mind.

She stepped out onto the boardwalk, squinting into the late-day sun. What had she been thinking? How had she allowed them to talk her into the job of emissary to Cheyenne? Doubts and excuses flooded her now that the decision had been made and no one was left to hear them. She couldn't go off, leaving her life behind. Who would watch over Sammy? Who would take control of matters should Jamison launch another attack?

What did she have to wear?

Cheyenne. A thrill of excitement trembled through her. A city filled with energy and growth. So many things to see, to do. How she'd dreamed of it, of seeing such a place through a woman's eyes. When her family left the east, she'd been a child, too young to appreciate what she was leaving behind. She'd been denied the chance to indulge feminine impulses in a fancy store. Always the serviceable. Always the practical, cut down, refitted, and ever functional. She'd had no one to teach her the joys of her sex, the pleasures of genteel pursuits, the luxury of admiring herself in the looking glass. Perhaps that was because they'd felt she had nothing of worth to admire. It hadn't been her choice, their lonely destination. No one had asked her if she'd rather live out among prairie dogs or in the company of other giggling members of her gender. Looking back, she realized she'd never had the benefits of young womanhood.

She'd gone right from child to spinster with no opportunity to sample the frivolity of those middle years that also would shape a girl into a suitable wife and mother. The only experience she had was in how to become the head of the family, the master of a station, an independent, slightly intimidating figure to men of courting age—except to those men like Tandy who coveted her land but not her love. She thought of it now, of those things she'd missed, of the shops, the sights, the entertainments found only where masses gathered. And a resentment for her lot simmered, not into a raging boil, but a slow, steady stewing, as if she'd been on the back burner for far too long. Selfishly, she wanted to go to Cheyenne just to see what she'd missed, wanted it so badly she ached inside.

But what of her responsibilities here?

That was always her final argument. Her responsibilities, the anchor that held her in familiar waters when she longed to cast herself adrift with the tide. Sammy, Joseph, her father's dream, tugging upon her tomorrows, refusing to let them free. And that bubble of resentment—resentment for her circumstance and those who bound her to it—built within her breast.

She didn't want to be trapped in a lonely life, defending a home that held her captive from all her hopes and desires or the sameness of her situation, which would never change, would never allow her a taste of happiness or a chance at love. She was dying at Amos Station, withering on the stem like the hearty grasses over cruel winter months. Only for her, no revitalizing spring was coming to stir new juices and encourage fresh growth. And how she rebelled there upon that crowded sidewalk, how angry she became toward all who held her hostage in the name of duty.

Jude took a deep breath, forcing self-pitying thoughts to retreat. Enough. How dare she bemoan her circumstance when there were those needier, more imprisoned by them? How could she begrudge her brother the time and attention he needed, or Joseph the home and family he craved? How could she turn her back on the friends and neighbors who desperately needed her cool head and calm reasoning to hang on to what was theirs? How had she let herself consider them as burdens, when all were obligations gladly shouldered? Enough crying about her lot when much of it was of her own choosing. She would go to Cheyenne, not to serve her own purposes of escape, but to champion those who'd placed their faith and trust in her. And she would return to her life of quiet fulfillment, where pleasures were gleaned from the contentment of helping others. For what else was there to hope, a woman of her age and indifferent appearance? Grand passion? No, not for a woman who wore sensible boots and shoveled horse manure.

And she never felt the trap closing, even as it slowly strangled her on her sense of honor.

Having reconciled her restless wants with the stabilizing facts of life, Jude started for the stage and found herself face-to-face with the only obstacle she couldn't overcome: her love for the wrong man.

"Jude."

"Mr. MacKenzie."

He blocked the sidewalk and shaded her from the sun. She was ever amazed by his dominating size and power but couldn't allow herself to be cowed by it. Not now. She fortified herself with the prickly words of their last exchange.

"I thought you'd be off with your new friends, now that there's no further blood to spill." And she couldn't help her shiver of revulsion when she thought of the life he'd so casually taken over something as trivial as a pair of guns.

Seeing that tremor of disgust, Dalton held to his cool reserve, reminding himself that he'd tossed away the privilege of taking a personal interest here. Jude Amos was no longer an option. There was just his work, and that, he would finish.

"I wanted to talk to you. You're the only one among them who can see beyond pride and temper."

"If that is a compliment, I'm not sure I wish to accept it. I have just as much at stake as any man in our valley, and you with your fast gun and bartered conscience are an enemy to us all."

He didn't react as if she'd just made a rapier thrust to his heart. Instead he leaned a brawny shoulder against one of the porch's support posts and regarded her with a gently mocking smile. "No, Jude. Your refusal to face facts is your only enemy, not me."

She looked for a way around him and, seeing none, confronted him with fearless disdain. "And what facts are those, pray tell?"

"The facts of life, Jude. The strong shall inherit and all that. You can't fight Jamison. He has might on his side even if you have right. He'll crush you."

"And you'll help him do it," she sneered, wishing that particular fact didn't hurt so much.

"It's a job to me, nothing more, but it's your people's lives. There are other valleys."

"And there are other Jamisons. If we don't stand against this one, we run from them all. No one is going to tell me where I can or can't live. This is the land of the free, Mr. MacKenzie, or didn't they ever teach you that in gunfighter school?"

He smiled, a quick brief dazzle of white teeth that prompted a hurried rhythm within her breast. Then his intimidating neutrality returned.

"And it's a land of opportunity too. And opportunity smiles on he who can afford to buy whatever he wants. Jamison is the only winner here, not you, not me. The others will listen to you, Jude. Make them understand that before someone gets killed."

The flutter of attraction seized up in jealous pain. "Oh, I see. You're here to finish pleading Kathleen Jamison's case for her. Well, you can just go back and tell Miss Fancy Face that we won't be bullied by her father and we won't be belittled by her superior airs. We may not have anything that the high and mighty Jamisons consider worthy, but to us it's all we have. And they aren't going to take it from us."

Though Dalton made no physical move, the sensation of potent fury gathering within him overwhelmed Jude. And though she held her ground, it scared her.

"So you'll hire a gun like Latigo Jones to fight

your fight, and when those you hire to spill blood for your cause are through, you'll still lose. Because men like Jamison are the future and they can't be stopped."

"We'll stop him," she argued so he wouldn't guess how shaken she was by his impassioned speech and the unwelcomed truth it held. "I'm on my way to Cheyenne to put a stop to his intimidation." Then, realizing to whom she was spilling her plans, Jude clamped her mouth shut, continuing to glare up at him in wordless challenge.

Dalton's tone softened, but his message remained cold steel. "You may slow him down with your struggles, but you won't stop him, Jude. I know. I've seen it too many times before. It's like trying to stop the railroad, like the Indians hanging on to their sacred lands, like keeping the sun from coming up tomorrow. No matter what you do, it's going to happen. I just don't want to see you hurt in the process." And for the briefest moment he came so close to confessing the rest—that he couldn't bear the thought of her in jeopardy—but she kept him from committing that ultimate folly by pulling away in stiff denial.

"I've already been hurt, Mr. MacKenzie. And I shouldn't have to elaborate the hows and whys of that to you."

No, she didn't. He'd hurt her. She'd taken him in, under her roof, within her family, had healed him in body and had attempted that same miracle in soul. The first had been more successful than the second. How had he repaid her for her kindness? By becoming the enemy she feared most, the one who would wrest away all she valued and loved by means she abhorred. With violence for hire. With loyalty that was bought, not earned. And he had no argument that would stand against her loathing.

"I'm just warning you to be careful, that's all," he concluded with a remote tip of his hat and an impersonal stare which wounded the way no actions ever could.

"I've been warned, Mr. MacKenzie, by you, your boss, by the sweetly insincere Miss Jamison. Now let me warn you. This isn't finished here and it won't be finished by someone like you, who has nothing to lose and only money to gain. You can take that back to Sweetgrass with you. Good-bye, Mr. MacKenzie."

He watched her walk away, her skirt snapping like a wind-ravaged sail, her head held high. And he smiled ruefully, marveling at her stubbornness, at her refusal to yield to the greater flex of muscle. That smile faded when he considered the futility of all that tremendous courage. She would lose. They all would lose.

And when they did, so would he.

Because somewhere along the line, he'd lost his objectivity.

He'd let matters become personal.

"So, what does she expect to gain by going to Cheyenne?" Jamison mused aloud as he poured two snifters of brandy.

"She didn't say." Dalton nodded politely when the rancher handed him the fine piece of crystal. If he drank long enough and deeply enough, he might sleep tonight without disturbing dreams. He drained the glass in a single gulp, savoring the muted burn and spread of warmth through a soul gone cold.

"She troubles me," Jamison continued with his

brooding train of thought. "The others are predictable, but that Amos woman, she's smart."

Kathleen gave a soft refuting sniff from where she sat posed within a waterfall of artfully arranged silk upon the corner sofa. There was nothing soft or composed about the blaze in her dark eyes as she studied Dalton and tried to read behind his carefully presented indifference.

"What about that gunfighter?" she asked to draw the conversation from the detestably clever Miss Amos. "Did they hire him?"

"I don't know."

"You don't know much, Mr. MacKenzie," came her barbed retort. "What good are you?"

"Kathleen."

She retreated behind a pretty pout at her father's warning, but her eyes glittered, chips of coal afire.

"If they hire Jones," Dalton drawled matter-of-factly, "this valley is going to run red."

Jamison frowned at that, a pinch of tension furrowing his brow. "Can you beat him?"

Dalton shrugged. "Possibly. There are no guarantees in our business."

"If they have, I want you to find this gunman and I want you to kill him . . . any way you can. I don't want the people in this valley to think gunplay is the answer."

Dalton smiled wryly at the inconsistency of that. Deter violence with violence. "You want me to bushwhack him?"

"Does it matter to you if it's a fair fight or not?" was the querulous reply.

And considering it, Dalton murmured, "Yes. Yes, it does."

Jamison sighed in aggravation, his distaste for the entire affair plain upon his face. "I don't care how you do it, just do it. In the back or face-to-face. I don't want the farmers to raise any false hopes."

"Then do something about Jude Amos."

Both men looked to Kathleen, who appeared to be distractedly paring her nails.

"Are you asking me to gun down Miss Amos?" Dalton asked with mild disbelief.

"Would that go against your conscience, Mr. MacKenzie?" she taunted, implying either he had none or could afford none. It galled him to wonder if she'd be right . . . if she'd been referring to anyone other than Jude.

"I will not condone the murder of a woman," Jamison said with unaccustomed force. Even Kathleen blinked, taken aback by it.

"Of course not, Father," she demurred. "I was just wondering how far Mr. MacKenzie would go to earn his pay." And her probing glance said she still wondered. "But you must admit, I'm right. Jude Amos is the glue holding their little rebellion together. Without her, the others could be easily influenced to sell. She's the problem we have to deal with and deal with soon."

Jamison nodded his agreement. He ran fingers through rapidly graying hair and closed eyes too long without peaceful sleep. "The time has come to take care of Miss Amos. Mr. MacKenzie, I believe that's why we hired you."

"What do you want me to do with her?" he asked with a flat inscrutability. Behind that stoic question was the fear that he'd finally been pushed into a no-win situation in which his unwise attachment to the Amoses would destroy him no matter which choice he made. He could not—would not murder Jude and her family. That was a step he refused to take regardless of consequence or compromise to his profession or his previous obligation to Jamison. They would have to spell it out to him, that killing was their conclusion, and if that was the case, he would do what he'd sworn never to do: he would return his fee and walk away. Not toward Jude, because how could he face her after casting off the only honor he'd ever upheld? Saving Jude would be the end of him, as a gunfighter and as a man of pride. He waited, wondering if the end was now.

"I don't care, Mr. MacKenzie. Buy her off, scare her off, trick her into abandoning this folly, but see that she doesn't come back from Cheyenne with any more grand ideas about helping these damned squatters."

Dalton knew an instant of indescribable relief as Jamison continued.

"I want this to end before anyone has to die. This is my valley and I will have it. No spinster female, no passel of grubbing farmers are going to get in my way. Take care of it. Now!"

"Do you have to go, Jude?"

It took all of Jude's patience not to snap at her brother's oft-repeated question. She tucked her newest petticoat into the worn satchel and smiled up at him. "Yes, I do. It's very important to all of our friends here in the valley. It won't be for a long time, and you'll have Joseph here to help you take care of things."

"I wish I was goin' with you."

In that instant she saw in his guileless eyes the same yearning expressed within her own heart: to venture out, to sample some of life's excitement, away from the limits of their sheltered world. And again a sense of guilt writhed through her when she thought of how her best intentions had smothered him. She'd been about to give the familiar argument that never failed to tug upon his sense of responsibility: What about the horses? Who'd take care of them if he were gone? And of course he'd back right down from his insisting, just as she always did when confronted with her obligations. She'd moaned at the unfairness those ties could bring and, for the first time, realized how true that must be in Sammy's case as well.

"Next time, Sammy, I promise. I've got too much business to attend to on this trip. Next time it'll be just you and me. We'll go together and see all there is to see."

His grin broke wide, then was tempered with second thoughts. "But who'd take care of Joseph and the animals and Biscuit?"

She placed a gentle hand upon his shoulder and squeezed. "They'll do just fine without us for a few days. The line can send some extra help to stay over a couple of days while you and I explore the city."

"You mean it, Jude?"

"I sure do. While I'm gone this time, you be thinking about what you'd like to see first."

"The train! No, the livery. Maybe the stores. I bet they got oodles of hard candy! And licorice for Joseph." His eyes got all dreamy as he considered the benefits found only in Cheyenne. He gave a start of surprise when his sister's arms encircled him for a tight hug.

"I love you, Sammy."

He hugged back, then got all wiggly. "Shoot, Jude. I know that. Lemme help you pack. The sooner you leave, the sooner you'll be back."

A pain of remembrance pierced Jude's heart because that's what their father had told them when he'd left that fateful day, never to return.

She hoisted her heavy bag, making a promise. She'd be back. Her responsibilities lay here, the foundation of her love and the basis of her life. The lure of the city held nothing in comparison.

Joseph gave her a solemn look when she toted her bag into the main room. He'd said little since she'd announced her decision, and though that was his way, Jude wanted a greater assurance from him.

"Are you sure you can handle things here, Joseph?"

"Why do you have doubts now? All these years you have no doubts and now, you worry. You think Joseph is too old? You think he is ready to go up on high hill to seek his ancestors? You think after all he's been through that making biscuits and wiping up the mud from careless boot soles will wear him down? You have little faith."

Laughing at his huffy indignation, Jude embraced him. The sinewy body was tense at first, then relaxed with the return of her affectionate clasp. "I don't worry about you, Uncle Joseph. You've held this family together for years, just like an honored grandfather."

He pushed away with a sniff of disdain. "Some family. Boy lets dog sleep with him at night, girl runs off to big city and leaves all the work to poor Indian." But Jude caught the glimmer in his eyes as he turned back to his stove and his grumbling.

"Stage's a-comin'!" Sammy yelled, and Biscuit set up a chorus of barking as they both raced out to meet it. Jude followed more slowly, the bag in her hands weighing as heavily as her heart at all she was leaving behind.

And part of that heaviness was her own guilty anticipation at the thought of escape.

* * *

With the arrival of the Union Pacific Railroad in 1867, Cheyenne, Wyoming, became a melting pot of the West. In a few short years' time it went from a hell-on-wheels shantytown to a hub of civilization with Brussels carpets, gilt-edged mirrors, and carved furniture in the new Inter-Ocean and other fancy hotels. After a disastrous fire in 1875, it quickly rebuilt, boasting new brick blocks, thirteen two-story buildings, and a number of masonry residences interspersed between those that still had Queen Anne fronts and Mary Ann backs. Electric lights were making their way down the streets, and stores advertised smoking jackets, plush silk lap robes, and gentlemen's elegant neckwear instead of buckskin underwear. The Magic City of the Plains was as proud of its six miles of water mains and hydrants as it was of the new opera house, which opened with much fanfare and satin-perfumed programs for a performance by the New York Opera Company. From rowdy railroad camp, it evolved into a cosmopolitan hub where only twenty-seven places sold liquor and eight churches anchored the growing community. Instead of rollicking cowboys shooting it up from horseback, young cattle blades rode down the busy streets on high bicycles imported from England and Scotland.

And Jude took it all in with amazement, never realizing such wonders existed so close to her isolated station.

She checked into her hotel with the money the other ranchers provided, trying not to gawk at the dripping crystals of the chandelier suspended two stories overhead. Glossy couples strolled through the lobby arm in arm, swaddled in rich European styles which made Jude grimly aware of her own shabby appearance. She may not have had manure on her boots, but the look of her still reeked of the country. While the desk clerk located her room key, she eyed the fancy silks and satins parading by for her unsophisticated viewing. Never had she seen so many flounces, fringes, loops, puffings, feathers, and frills, all followed by a mass of bunched fabric trailing nearly a yard after its wearer. Such finery paled the elegance of Kathleen Jamison in her eyes.

"Here you go, Miss Amos. Room seven, at the head of the stairs to your left."

She reached for the gold tasseled key, then bent to pick up her lone bag where it rested in faded disgrace at her feet. She paused, startled to see a big male hand close over the cracked leather handles.

"Allow me."

Her body registered the shock, running all hot and cold, before her mind identified the low, crooning voice. Her gaze lifted slowly, traveling up the creased trousers to a coat opened over an elaborately stitched vest.

And a pair of impressive bone-handled guns.

Chapter 17

❦

"Dalton!" In her surprise Jude forgot all formality. "What are you doing here?"

He lifted her bag and offered a heart-melting smile. "I'll be here for a few days on some business. Just like you."

She was so startled to see him, her suspicions failed to surface.

He took the key from her unresisting fingers, checked the number, then led the way to the sweeping staircase with Jude tagging behind him like Sammy's hound, Biscuit. He fit the key into number seven and opened the door for her with a grand gesture.

"As long as we're both here on business, is there any reason we can't combine it with a little pleasure? Say, dinner this evening?" Then his expression stiffened slightly as he added, "Unless, of course, you're not here alone."

Flustered by his question and by his apparent jealousy, Jude shook her head, dazed and delighted. "No, I'm here by myself."

His grin spread wide with confidence. "Then I'll come by for you at seven."

Dinner. With Dalton. In Cheyenne.

231

It was too much to take in all at once. "I—I don't know. I have nothing to wear . . ." Then her blushing modesty was overcome by a dose of cold common sense. Dalton MacKenzie was not exactly the ideal dinner companion, considering her purpose. "I don't think it would be wise for us to socialize."

"Why not? I owe you several meals at least, and I promise not to spoon-feed you in public."

His grin was infectious, and his logic made her protest seem silly. He was a gorgeous-looking man offering to escort her on his arm to a meal in a fine hotel dining room. What objection could she possibly have to that? Other than the fact that they were enemies, probably in the city to further their opposite causes. What harm could come of a single dinner in a public room?

When it was something she wanted so badly, talking herself into it was no great chore.

"Seven o'clock. But under one condition."

"Being?"

"We'll make no mention of the valley. We'll pretend for one night that it doesn't exist."

"Where?"

She responded to his affected innocence with a smile of her own. "I will see you at seven." She slipped past him, grabbing up her bag before he could tempt her any farther, and only once the door was closed between them did she give way to weak-kneed tremors. She indulged herself in a moment of exquisite fantasy, then shook herself back to reality. She wasn't in Cheyenne to enjoy Dalton MacKenzie's courting.

However, as she was hanging away her few best gowns, she could think of nothing else. She fingered the faded fabrics with their absence of adornment.

They'd been fine and serviceable when dishing up a quick hot meal at the way station to hungry travelers who never gave her a second glance. But here, amid the sumptuous silks and crunch of satins, how painfully drab they seemed. She wanted Dalton to give her a second look. She wanted him never to look away. How could she achieve that miracle in her well-worn prairie dresses? She pictured her entrance into the elegant dining room as all the richly garbed patrons turned toward her, wrinkling their noses at the lingering scents of horse and manure. They all would know she didn't belong in such a place, with such a man. And so would Dalton.

Unless she made an effort to fit in.

This was her one chance to fulfill a dream, to be someone other than plain Jude Amos, stage-stop manager of the calloused hands and burden-weighted shoulders. Tonight at seven she could be just a woman freed of obligations, dining with the city's handsomest gentleman.

That would require a little work on her part. Not one to be afraid of hard work, she threw herself into the task, her purpose forgotten in her pursuit of a dream.

At seven o'clock Dalton came to claim her. When she opened her door, she heard his quick inhalation and felt the scorch of his gaze traveling from hem to hairline. This was the moment for which she'd waited, when his assessing eyes finally met and held hers in a simmer of masculine appreciation.

The dress was right. She'd paced nearly a mile, worrying about her choice, impatient with the drag of the train, aghast at the amount she'd spent to earn that smoldering look in a man's eyes. She'd been in every shop along the wide Cheyenne streets, had been poked and pricked with pins, had struggled into a caging corset, had allowed the hair surrounding her face to be cut and frizzed so that when the rest was pulled back in a loose roll, the effect was soft and flattering.

But it was the dress that made the difference. She knew the minute she saw it, the moment it fastened over her constricting undergarments and she beheld the change in the fitting-room glass. The snug basque of rich blue velvet was luxurious gloving to the curve of her torso, hugging the contour of her breasts and inviting a man's hands to rest upon an artificially drawn waist. Long, tight sleeves ended in butterfly bows of lace spilling gracefully over the backs of her hands. Glistened tassels of jet beads dangled, making a beckoning sway with every move she made. A small collar stood against her neck, extending downward in an opened vee to the waist filled in with lace-covered satin which was both discreet and daring, daring her to flirt with the idea of elegance.

Gallantly, Dalton lifted her hand to press a lingering kiss upon it before tucking it possessively within the bend of his arm.

At that moment Jude felt beautiful.

The sensation stunned her, swelling her heart with a proud and frantic beating, bringing tears to prickle behind the rapid flicker of her lashes. And nothing, no matter what happened, could ever take that feeling from her.

The hotel dining room was a fantasy of crystal and silver agleam beneath electric lights. Escorted by the handsomest man in the room, Jude held her head high as they were shown to their table, aware of how the women's stares followed. She struggled

to control her fidgety awe of the surroundings and
the deep inner feeling that someone would discover
her pretense, exposing her for what she was: a plain
spinster hiding in elegant clothes. She tried to
mimic Dalton's ease, admiring the way he took
everything in with a bored acceptance, but all was
too new to her, too foreign, from the parade of
silverware around her china plate and the exorbitant
number of glasses crowding for her attention to the
dapper servers who hovered near, waiting to swoop
down to refill every swallow she took.

Noting her unease, Dalton asked, "Is it the table
that's not to your liking or the company?"

"N-no. It's fine. Both are fine. Really."

His small smile chided her into revealing the
truth.

"I've never been in a place like this. I don't think I
could ever get used to it."

"Oh, you'd be surprised at what you can get used
to." He touched his forefinger to the rim of one of
his goblets, and a waiter instantly appeared to pour
a rich red vintage. Dalton sampled it on a leisurely
roll of his tongue and nodded. The same waiter
filled her glass.

"You look born to such a life of plenty."

He chuckled at her observation. It wasn't a pleasant sound but rather a harsh mockery of mirth. "Far
from it, I assure you. I grew up lucky to have a table
to eat off of, let alone a cloth to cover it."

Realizing how little she knew of him, Jude
prompted, "And where was that, Mr. MacKenzie?"

"It was a lifetime ago, Miss Amos, one I'll never
go back to, not ever." There was an edge to his
voice, preventing any further questioning along that
line, reminding Jude that he wasn't an elegant
gentleman, but rather a man of dangerous profes-

sion and now, it would seem, of hidden secrets as well. He wasn't a civilized beau treating her to a fine meal. He was a gunslinger, a man who lived by taking lives. Her enemy.

She tried to make that matter. She tried so hard to concentrate on it that a furrow raked her brow and pursed her lips, drawing Dalton's notice.

"Is the wine that sour? Or were you hinting for a kiss?"

A hot flush scalded through her, making her heart thrum, her blood race, and her lips ache in anticipation, because Dalton was desire, embodying everything she wanted as well as all she feared. He wasn't safe, he wasn't stable. She wasn't even sure he was a decent man. And he certainly wasn't going to stick around to nurture all the clutching emotions burgeoning within her needy soul. He wasn't a marrying man. She knew she shouldn't settle for less.

But would she?

That scared her and got her remembering the first time she saw him, on the stairs with his harlot. Then it was her mood that soured, bracing her to meet his sultry innuendo.

"Is that what's expected of me, Mr. MacKenzie? Should I be panting for your kisses?"

He laughed, a low rumble of amusement as stirring as a caress upon her senses. "Oh, no, Miss Amos. With you I never know what to expect. But be assured, if you're panting for my kisses, far be it from me to disappoint you."

The arrival of their waiter saved her from having to answer. She vented her annoyance by snapping her leather-bound menu up as a barrier between them. And as she blindly scanned the endless entries, she took a deep breath to flush away the curl of shameless expectation awakened by his words.

Dalton watched the subtle shifts of Jude's expression and wondered when she would overcome her embarrassment and realize the entire listing was in French. The wait was an unexpected pleasure to one so easily bored by predictable female behavior.

He saw her blink and squint at the fancy script before her, reveling in the rosy flush that crept up into her cheeks as she struggled for a way to admit her ignorance.

"Would you like me to order for us?" he drawled out with smooth generosity.

Those bewildered gray eyes flashed up in alarm, then narrowed at his challenge. Her tone was prickly. "No, thank you. I am quite particular in my likes and dislikes."

"Ummmm. So I'd noticed." He flagged their waiter over and spoke his wishes in flawless French, smiling a Cheshire grin as he turned his attention to Jude.

Without missing a beat, she looked up at their waiter to ask, "What would you recommend?"

He rattled off the house specialty while Jude listened to the foreign gibberish in rapt interest, then when he paused, she nodded.

"Sounds divine."

As the waiter bustled away, Dalton leaned on his elbows, grinning behind the tent of his hands. "How do you feel about snails, Miss Amos?"

"Snails? I find them quite disgusting. Why?"

"That's what you ordered."

To her credit, she recovered quickly, only a slight flush of color betraying her. "But they are also delicious. Don't you agree?"

"You are braver than I am. I still feel there are things man was not made to eat. But you have your own particular tastes." He smiled wider as she gulped her wine, as if trying to wash down something extremely unpleasant. "Well, we've discussed your dining preferences and you've placed talk of your valley off limits. I guess that leaves us with only one topic of conversation."

She fell right into it with an innocent blink of her eyes. "And that is?"

"Being a woman of definitive tastes, how do you prefer your kisses?"

As she was still thinking about the snails, Jude wasn't as shocked as she might have been. She met his stare straight on to chastise, "I am not used to such elegant surroundings, but I cannot believe they are so different as to allow such a topic as polite table talk."

He looked momentarily humbled and murmured, "You are right, of course. That's definitely an after-dinner topic of discussion, one I shall look forward to." He let her stew on that for a time, admiring her poise, knowing how false it was compared to the tight thrumming of her pulse against her high collar. He allowed her the dignity of that illusion for the moment, until he drawled, "Ah, here's our meal." He waited with devilish delight as their waiter set Jude's plate before her, whisking off the domed cover.

There was a faint quiver in her eyelashes as she beheld the delicate bits of lamb artfully arranged upon her dish. She studied them for a moment, then aimed a skewering glare across at him.

"Oh," he remarked casually. "My mistake. I must have confused the translation."

"Is everything to your satisfaction, mademoiselle?" the waiter asked, observing their banter anxiously.

She smiled up at him. "Yes, thank you. Exactly to my tastes."

And she dove into her meal without further comment. Dalton might have believed her display of irritation if it hadn't been for the flutter of a smile she tried to disguise behind the dabbing of her napkin.

Lord, he was enjoying himself. His companion was full of surprises: the dress, the hair, the tempting blushes. And the biggest surprise was that the woman sitting opposite him wasn't so different from the angel he'd envisioned within his sightless world. Perhaps she wasn't classically lovely, with the perfect features of a Kathleen Jamison, but there was a deeper beauty to Jude Amos, one that glowed from within and now, on this night, for the first time, shone from without. This was the striking female she'd been afraid to reveal, one of strong, appealing lines encased in velvet, of bold, angular planes softened by a feathery-spun coiffure and dreamy eyes. She wasn't fluffy or delicately feminine, but there was something exciting about a woman who wouldn't break easily.

She seemed unaware that other men were gazing her way with interest, but as they dined, he made sure she was well aware of him. What words didn't say, covert glances betrayed: a longing as bittersweet as the wine. And attraction simmered, steeping into a full-bodied desire about to overflow.

As the dishes were cleared away, Dalton could stand the suspense no longer. Either she was of the same mind, or her shocked modesty would send her running. He had to know which way it was with Jude.

"Thank you for the meal, Mr. MacKenzie. It was wonderful."

A lie. She hadn't truly tasted a single bite. All her senses were channeled to this point, the moment when he would draw back her chair and they would stand close, his cologne tantalizing, his heat scandalizing, while they decided on an end to their evening. She knew it should be as simple as a nod, with her walking away to her solitary bower. It would take only a brief word from her to dismiss all other possibilities. Yet she lingered, enveloped by his scent, seduced by his promising warmth. And she waited, afraid of what she wanted yet not brave enough to walk away without it.

Dalton's hand cupped her elbow, and the polite contact sent a jolt of hungry awareness through both of them. He leaned in closer, not quite touching, but near enough for his breath to stroke her flushed cheek, for his words to feed the fires of her imagination.

"I have an excellent bottle of champagne chilling in my room. I don't like to drink alone. Share it with me, Jude. We can discuss those kisses."

If he hadn't been standing so close, she might have had the presence of mind to chide him for his confidence. Chilling champagne was probably a standard wherever he was staying. She doubted that he spent many of his nights alone. But the thought that he had champagne on ice in anticipation of asking her to his room sent a shiver of pleasure to block out all logical responses from her brain.

Because she couldn't trust her voice, Jude merely nodded, a quick jerk of her head to imply consent. She was thankful for Dalton's guiding grip upon her arm. Without it she would have had a dreadful time convincing her legs to move in any specific direction. She left the dining room on his arm, not daring to glance either right or left for fear that she would see in everyone's faces the knowledge of where the two of them were going.

She was on her way to his bed.

By the time they reached Dalton's room at the rear of the third floor—Jude was surprised to find he was staying in the same hotel—she was in a near paralysis of nerves. Her blood flowed hot and liquid, lamp oil ready to take to flame. Her stomach muscles ached from the tight clench of her anxiousness and trembled with a wanton eagerness she scarcely understood. Then he pushed open his door, and for a moment her common sense cried, *What are you doing? You can't go in there with him. Do you know what that will make you?*

Yes, she did. It would make her a woman.

A deep calm settled inside her, a sense of purpose that both surprised and propelled her forward into the darkened chamber. The curtains were open, revealing the lights of the city beyond, so many and so bright, they muted the stars above. In the corner she could just make out the shadow of a four-poster bed. She looked away from it, swallowing down a lump of maidenly panic. Still she jumped slightly at the sound of the door closing off her escape.

Dalton didn't flick on the blaze of electric lights; instead he crossed the blackness with an unerring stride. Jude smelled sulfur as the scratch of a match brought a flare of light to the room. Dalton lit a branch of candles on the same small table that hosted the silver champagne bucket.

"I must be old-fashioned, but I prefer candlelight to the glare of these newfangled bulbs," Dalton murmured, shaking out the match as the wicks took eagerly and warmed the room with a mellow glow.

The explosive pop of the cork startled her. Her

242   ROSALYN WEST

smile was fixed when Dalton turned, a slender flute in either hand. She took the glass in both of hers, praying they wouldn't betray her with their trembling.

"What shall we drink to?"

The low croon of his voice rippled through her, a heady intoxicant to precede her first sip. Because that shivery effect rattled her senses so, she replied with a snap of wry humor.

"How about public domain?"

"Shame, Miss Amos. You're breaking your own rule."

"Maybe it's one I never should have made." Common sense struggled to surface. What was she doing here, with this man, her enemy? How silly to think she could wipe away all hints of obligation just by saying it was so. Inhaling deeply to clear the clutter of emotion from her mind, she set the glass aside. "I have to go."

Dalton tossed back the contents of his glass with a reckless hurry. Then his big hands were imprisoning her arms in cuffs of velvet-clad steel, giving no pain yet yielding no quarter. His face was near, so near the heat of his breath stroked her skin like a warm summer breeze. She refused to look up into his eyes, afraid of their intensity, that she would surrender to what she'd see there.

"You don't have to do anything, Jude. This night isn't for them. It's for you. Isn't it time you did something for yourself, for no other reason than it's what you want? Or do you think you have to give the world around you every second of your time? Don't you owe yourself this chance to live truly as you'd like to? To be free?"

How temptingly his words entwined about her reasonings, making her believe she had a right to this moment of selfish denial of those who depended upon her. Making her want to push them out of her heart and mind until there was only Dalton. But that would be wrong. She knew it. It wasn't in her nature to act without thought of consequence.

She began to shake her head, only to have it quickly captured between those huge hands. Her fearful eyes darted up and were lost to the penetrating power of his gaze.

"If you can't see that you deserve this night, I guess I'm just going to have to prove it to you."

His kiss conquered her as no other argument could. As she followed its slanting, seeking pressure eagerly with her own lips, her resistance melted away from the sudden fiery intensity building like a new sun at the core of her womanhood. Confused, afraid, then gloriously freed by this foreign urgency, Jude gave up the pretense of not wanting Dalton MacKenzie more than she wanted her next breath. For one had become quite impossible without the other.

She could feel his smile against her mouth when her arms reached up and curled encouragingly about his neck.

"So," he murmured huskily against her lips, "this is how you like it. It would seem for once that we're in agreement."

The tone of their kiss changed then, subtly, so sweetly, she was hardly aware of it until she was weak from the tender onslaught. The taste of champagne on his tongue swirled about her senses. She drank it in deeply. She heard tiny hail drops of sound and realized they were the pins from her hair falling on the hardwood floor. Then her hair was tumbling free of its confining roll in a whispery cascade, caught up in the tangle of his fingers as it flowed about her shoulders. And still he kissed her, deeper, deeper, until rational thought was lost down a well of bottomless desire. And she couldn't frame the words "no" or "stop" or "I must go." Only the desperate plea of "More, please more."

And Dalton had every intention of answering in ways she had never imagined.

Chapter 18

Slowly, so that she would have every opportunity to object, Dalton started down the fastenings of her dress. Protest never occurred to Jude, as she was lost to sensual luxury. He did more than just unbutton; he claimed each inch he covered, his palms soothing along velvet-clad curves, his fingertips drawing erotic circles around each eager swell and aching hollow. His confidence kept her from second-guessing her decision to remain. If he had faltered, she might have had time to come up with some reason to decry what was about to happen between them. But he didn't. And she didn't.

Fabric parted. Jude's sigh echoed that of the sumptuous yards of velvet as they slid to the floor, pooling there, forgotten. His hands glided up her bared arms and adored the slope of her shoulders, touching as if each section of her he uncovered for their pleasure held some special allure. His tongue chased along the ridge of her collarbone, dipping into its recesses to taste the mad thunder of her pulse, distracting her from the fact that he had peeled the hard shell of her corset away so that only a wisp of linen lay between them.

"Delicious," he murmured.

"Ummm. I'm sure your tastes are quite seasoned."

"Only to the finest things, sweet Jude. Only the finest" was his passion-rough reply.

His palms burned through the slight barrier of her chemise, making her gasp and arch into them as they charted the contour of her ribs, as they rose slowly, surely to claim her unfettered breasts. Another gasp escaped her at the hot possessing tug of his mouth upon first one, then the other, wetting the fabric to a sheer cling, whetting her need to have that searing caress upon bared skin.

"A delicacy," he sighed between nibbles.

Her fingers worked at the ties to her chemise. Shock at her own boldness never surfaced as she bared herself to the waist for him. A momentary panic rose as he leaned away just far enough to see her. Her breath caught in suspended anxiousness as the hot blue of his gaze detailed her every exposed inch. The muscles of his jaw tightened and flexed with a slow swallow. Her eyes squeezed shut and she prayed, *Oh please don't let him be disappointed.*

Then she heard him exhale, a raw, shaky sound which said more to her than any hundred words. And for the first time a feeling of pride blossomed within her.

She continued to stand with eyes closed while he finished undressing her. There was something undeniably exciting about the stroke of his big hands down her legs as he peeled away her stockings. He noticed the unsteadiness of her knees, and she was grateful when he suggested in a husky whisper, "Perhaps we should both sit down."

She let him guide her to the bed, sinking down

with him upon its edge without a moment's hesitation. Her fingers shook as they reached for the jeweled buttons of his vest, letting him know in this silent way that there was no reluctance on her part and no turning back. Beneath the open flaps of satin, her hands explored the hard terrain of his torso, riding the smooth material of his finely made shirt at a patient pace. She didn't want to miss anything in her hurry. She was surprised by the pounding tempo of his heart.

His kiss was sudden and swift, snatching away her breath with its ferocity, sending her passions soaring with the deep thrust of his tongue. Just as quickly he gently scattered soul-bruising nibbles along her cheeks to her chin, tracing a gradual line downward to capture a single blushing rosette within his mouth, coaxing it back into its tight bud with the insistence of his attention, leaving it dew-drenched and quivering when he turned to its twin.

Feeling both faint and wildly alive, Jude clutched at her lover's head, her fingers kneading in urgent spasms, mirroring the sensations massing in quaking tandem deep within the heart of her. She'd been unaware that such a place existed but cherished that secret feminine stronghold as longing pooled there and began a tidal throbbing.

Her eyes flickered open when his fingertips grazed along her temples, brushing back the damp strands of hair with an almost revering tenderness. His expression revealed nothing of his thoughts, and Jude's uncertainty returned. She couldn't bear the thought that their intimacy was about to end, not when they'd come so far and yet had such a distance to travel.

Her confusion rose with each second of his silent study until she could stand the uncertainty no longer.

"Dalton, you *are* going to make love to me, aren't you?"

Her fragile entreaty pierced right to his tarnished soul, polishing those time-darkened surfaces to a warm gleam. And what was reflected there was love.

He smiled in the face of her anxiousness. "Until I answer your every dream or the sun comes up."

"It will be the dawn because I have years of dreams to discover."

"Then we probably should get started. There will be no secrets between us. First, I'll learn all of yours." His voice dropped a husky notch. "Then you can learn mine."

Imagining it, Jude sizzled inside like butter swirled in a hot pan.

He scooped one arm beneath her knees, turning her upon the coverlet and placing her back upon the bed. Her naked flesh burned feverishly against the cool fabric of the spread, that heat raging out of control beneath the slow caress of his gaze. She begged him with the lambent glow of her eyes, with the enticing lift of her breasts, with the innocent parting of her knees to come down to her. She had no idea how difficult it was for him to resist the temptation she yielded, but Dalton was thinking of those years of lonely dreams she spoke of and he knew no matter how much either of them were eager for it, no quick conclusion would serve. He'd fled from commitment too many times in the past to leave her with any yearnings unanswered.

He began with a kiss, one ripe with promises, as he sank to one knee beside the bed. A tremor of wondrous delight shivered to the soles of Jude's feet as she waited for him to instruct her in the ways of love. He did so with a languor that had her writhing and restless with expectation.

She was glorious. Dalton was purely amazed by the splendor of her unclaimed territories, aroused by their virgin qualities, by the fact that he was the first to touch her. She was lush as the far Dakota hills, far richer still with discoveries at which none before him had even guessed. Her kisses were wild-berry sweet and luscious, her skin as taut and supple as doe skin over a firm yet feminine frame. He hadn't expected to find that so arousing, but it was. Her response to him fed a man's every fantasy of prideful conquest, and still he was humbled by the very fact of her compliance. She moaned in abandon when he paid tribute to the tender fruit of her breasts and arched up in a quiver upon the balance points of heels and shoulders when his hand strayed to her thighs.

He knew her to be a maiden, had expected her to resist him out of modesty or fright, but as he reached the vulnerable bastion of her sex, instead of closing tight against him, her knees dropped open in full surrender. It was a gesture of trust, not mindless need, and though it would have been easier if he'd mistaken the two, he never would. Jude wasn't a creature driven by bodily urges. She was a woman guided by the tender nature of her heart. And it was that heart she offered along with her body. The latter gift inflamed him. The thought of the first scared the hell out of him, but it was far too late to stop.

Jude was unprepared for the shock of his touch on the most intimate part of herself. Her body jolted in surprise beneath the bold quest of his hand.

Again it was in the back of her mind that she should be protesting, but the sounds that escaped her were low, desperate cries that he continue. She knew about mating but never, never, never had she imagined anything like this. A tight, shuddering yearning began to build at the insistence of his touch, her body instinctively knowing how to react while her mind went numb to all but the invading pleasure.

Just when she was sure there was nothing more he could do to shake the foundations of her soul, he bent up her knee so that her leg curled about his neck and he showed her a new kind of kiss, one that sent a shock wave of primitive power right to her very core.

She cried out. She couldn't help herself. The sensation hit like lightning and rolled through her as thunder while his mouth and his tongue . . . oh, his tongue! . . . pushed her beyond the boundaries of known belief. When he lifted away, the storm settled into a blissful lull of exhaustion and she lay luxuriously limp.

He was smiling as he asked, "And is everything to your liking so far?"

"You have exquisite taste." She sighed.

"In all things."

The touch of his lips upon hers stirred a stronger, more compelling passion and the intuitive grasp for things yet left undone. He stood for a brief instant, long enough to shed the rest of his clothing. Still dazed by her discoveries, Jude gave him a shy glance, then was unable to look away. The sight of his hard body, so full and eager, was enough to encourage a hasty heartbeat. He was strong and bold and beautiful. And she wanted him madly. She lifted her arms in invitation, and he sank into their accepting embrace.

There was an instant of pain, a burning pressure that made her gasp and twist until he was able to force beyond that last barrier of innocence. He soothed her brief anguish away with a wash of kisses raining down upon her damp cheeks. She had no chance to feel ashamed of her naive tears for he began to move, a slow, gliding motion, leading her toward an even greater paradise, one that, once claimed amid her keening cries and his sudden hoarse shout, eclipsed all dreams save one. The one of which she couldn't speak even as they lay recovering in one another's arms. The one in which a man would turn to her to express sweet words of love.

She must have slept. The next awareness Jude had was of a dark, starry sky through the veil of lacy drapery. And the indescribable comfort of being pillowed upon Dalton's shoulder. She was wrapped in the curl of his arm, her bare leg boldly stretched atop the length of his and her hand cushioned upon the heavy furring on his abdomen. She wrinkled her nose at the tease of fragrant tobacco and tilted her head back to see his profile set against the faint glow of his cigarillo. For a long moment she enjoyed just looking at him, possessed by a sudden shyness that forbade words.

She wouldn't lessen the wonder of what had happened with shadows of remorse. He'd given her dreams a spectacular reality. If only for one night, so be it. Dalton MacKenzie was a traveling man. She'd always known that. He wanted nothing more than a passionate way station and, in return, had gifted her with an experience to last a lifetime. She wouldn't complain, yet still she couldn't suppress the ache of tears when she considered their imminent parting.

Dalton took one last draw on his cigar, then twisted to stub it out on the night table. When he resettled and turned his attention to Jude, he knew a moment of terrible distress upon observing her swimming stare. He'd hurt her somehow. Despite all his careful intentions, he'd still managed to bring her pain.

Gently, he rubbed his knuckles down the length of her jaw.

"I didn't mean to make you cry," came his gruff whisper of apology.

Her eyes cleared like a new fresh dawn. "You didn't. You made me a woman."

Your woman. That shone unspoken in her gaze. His first reaction was a floundering panic. Binding them together with permanent ties had never been his plan.

Then, as if understanding his alarm, she snuggled into his shoulder and released his worries with her quietly murmured, "I'll never forget you. You're the only man who's ever made me feel truly—" She broke off then, and he almost could feel the blush heating her cheek. "I'm sorry. I'm talking too much."

His smile was quick and forgiving where it pressed into her hair. "You can say anything you like. No secrets, remember?"

She glanced up and before cowardice could take control, told him, "I love you, Dalton."

Though he tried to betray no reaction, Jude saw a stricken horror stiffening his expression. Nothing could have spoken his reluctance more succinctly or brutally. She forced a smile and touched her fingertips to his compressed lips.

"Please, don't think you have to say anything. I don't fool myself into thinking that could matter to you one way or another. I just wanted to hear myself say it, once. You don't need to worry that I'll repeat myself." He was still rigid and unresponsive, so she gave a strained little laugh. "Please don't look so gut-shot. I guess I should have kept that one secret to myself."

He shook his head slowly, as if punch drunk and fighting his way back to reason. "No, don't say you're sorry, Jude. It was nice to hear someone say that to me, once." Then, before she could question his odd statement, he leaned down to kiss her, using the tender sweep of his lips to convey how much her words had meant to a soul hungry for acceptance. Of course he never would have told her that directly.

Eager to relieve his edge of caution to salvage what she could of their evening, Jude sent a questing hand up and down his chest, turning him toward other distractions, distractions that had him rolling up on one hip so that she could feel the prod of him against her soft belly. He gave an undisguised start of surprise when her hand nudged between them to give him a welcoming squeeze. She looked up calmly and smiled at his blinking amazement.

"You did say we should have no secrets, didn't you?" she reminded him in a spun-honey tone spiked with a sassy bite of warm bourbon. "It's time I learned yours."

He lay back and let her because he was too

stunned by surprise to do otherwise. And because, on the aftermath of her confession, this only drew him deeper into the mire of emotions he was struggling to escape.

By the time her emboldened touch culminated in another round of dusky lovemaking, the candles had flickered out in their own hot wax and the room took on a shadowed intimacy. Darkness had a way of relaxing inhibition with reminiscence of their earlier times together, when Dalton had depended upon her care and she lived in his mind's eye as an angel. Because the illusion of his vulnerability lingered, Dalton was unusually open to her questions.

"Why did you say no one had ever spoken to you of love before?"

His hand paused in its stroking of her hair, then continued the soothing rhythm. "Because it's true. I didn't exactly grow up in the midst of a loving family."

Jude remembered his delirious rantings about sisters and brothers. And she recalled his agitation. But curiosity about this man who vowed to hold no secrets from her pushed her beyond judicious caution.

"You grew up in an orphanage." She felt his start of surprise and added gently, "You spoke of it when you were feverish."

"I suppose I would. The heat making me think of hell and all. Christ's Holy Order of the Covenant Rose. The blessing of my youth." He spoke the name with such irreverence, Jude winced. Though what she'd just done defied it, she had a strong sense of religious harmony, having learned a love of the Scriptures from her God-fearing parents. Hearing Dalton blaspheme with casual contempt evoked those early teachings with their lightning-bolt retributions. If he didn't revere the higher forces of heaven, what kind of man did that make him?

The one she'd always known him to be: dark, soulless, and unrepentant.

But she knew, deep down, that wasn't true and strove to prove it, to herself, to him, because an isolation from inner peace was the loneliest existence she could imagine.

"It couldn't have been terrible living with those who believed in charity and God's love," she ventured hopefully.

His laugh was harsh and black. "Charity. Yes, I found them to be the souls of charity, taking in those whom no one else wanted for the money they could earn off them. As soon as we recipients of their goodwill were old enough, we were sent out to slave at menial jobs, bringing all our pay back to the church, of course, to thank the brothers and sisters for their eternal struggles to save our unworthy souls." He paused, sensing Jude's shock, then continued with an almost perverse want to goad it further.

"Since my soul required the most prayer, I was given three jobs to work. I started by cleaning the streets before sunrise and ended at the docks, unloading cargo in the darkness. The only good that came of it was during the daylight hours, when I was employed by an old judge who had me transcribe his court notes because I had a neat hand. He was a corrupt old bastard, pardon the expression. That's where I learned my reverence for the law. But he did allow me to read when I wasn't busy helping him find some judicial loophole to excuse his thievery, and for that, I guess, I should be grateful. He was always talking about how much

he could earn if he was appointed to a larger circuit
and what he'd have. He measured his life in material possessions, not by the satisfaction of seeing
justice prevail. In fact, he got me started in my
profession."

Dalton fell silent, thinking back to that night
when he'd gone with one of the judge's men to
plant a horse in some poor farmer's barn so it could
be discovered there the next day. The judge
promptly had the supposed thief hanged, and Dalton's disgust for the legal process had been formed
that day when he'd heard the clunk of the trapdoor
and the creak of hemp. It made a huge impression
upon his thirteen-year-old mind and aged his spirit
with the bitterness of bile. He'd gotten over it, the
guilt, the horror, the fear of being exposed for his
part in the deadly sham, but when a five-dollar gold
piece crossed his palm, his conscience had been
quickly soothed. He'd received a beating upon his
return to the home when he refused to turn it
over to the brothers, who claimed it was the price
for his soul. Five dollars. He didn't realize how
cheaply he'd sold himself until his later years,
when his reputation allowed him to demand the
highest dollar for the purchase of his continued
damnation.

"After that night I never went back to Covenant
Rose. I took to hanging around the judge's hired
guns, learning the tricks of the trade, so to speak. I
was a fast study. In the back of my mind, I could
always hear the judge claiming honor and respecta-
bility came with money and power, and that's what
I wanted. I wanted to earn enough to buy back my
soul." He chuckled softly, and Jude thought it was
the most poignant sound she'd ever heard. "Of
course, there isn't enough in the whole Federal

Reserve to buy it back now. I guess I'll just have to settle for respect, not the kind where folks step off the sidewalk and tremble when you pass by, but the kind where they tip their hats to you. That's what I want. That's what I aim to get in San Francisco."

San Francisco. Jude's chest tightened. So far away. She'd always known he wasn't going to stay in the valley, but she'd never actually considered how far out of her reach he would be. In truth, she supposed it didn't matter if it was one mile or a thousand.

"Why San Francisco? Why not here?"

He didn't answer right away, and when he did, she got the feeling he wasn't telling her everything. "No one will know me there. I can start over fresh. I can be anything I want. I've seen pictures of these fancy houses set on a hill. I want one of those. And when I pass by, folks will tip their hats to me."

San Francisco. What would it be like to pull up roots in Wyoming and head west with Dalton? Were his dreams so different from her own? She considered that, and her answer had to be a reluctant "yes," they were different. Because Dalton hungered for things to own, just as she yearned for someone to whom to belong. Their needs were on different planes, and he gave no indication that a woman to love and a ready-made family fit anywhere into his plans.

Her thoughts were interrupted by his sudden fierce kiss. He made love to her again, but this time with the compelling forcefulness of all she'd stirred up with her innocently asked questions. She couldn't complain of not being satisfied—she was all of that and more, but there was a subtle change in him that made her ultimate pleasure bittersweet. Because she sensed he was concentrating on himself rather than on what they could make between them: taking, giving, but not sharing. And when at last he rolled away from her, Jude felt like that abandoned harlot leaning against the rail, watching him walk away. And there were tears in her eyes as she closed them upon the knowledge that she would never have more of him than that bartered creature of the night.

Chapter 19

J ude awoke to a luxury of sensations: cool, slippery sheets wound about her like a lover's caress, the sweet scent of the dawn's breezes, rich coffee tantalizing her nose. And the hot memories of Dalton MacKenzie brought back the wonderful achiness of a body now experienced in love. She longed to linger in that blissful place, on the edge of awareness and dreams, but slowly the fact that she was alone in the big bed stirred her from her lethargy.

Rubbing at her eyes, she sat up, the sheet clutched modestly to her bosom, for she was naked as the day she was born. The room was filled with sunlight, and she had a terrible moment of dread when she thought about being confronted with evidence of the night's doings here in the stark reality of a new day. She expected to see clothing scattered in a testament to their unbridled passion, the remnants of champagne and candle wax as cold reminders of that romantic mood, now gone with the night's shadows. Instead she discovered a breakfast cart set with an elegant meal and several parcels wrapped in thin paper upon the foot of the bed. There was no sign of her clothes and, at first, none of Dalton. She wondered a bit frantically if she was going to have to sneak to her own room clad in his sheets.

Then her host came in from the adjoining area, announced by the crisp, clean scent of shaving soap and his spicy cologne. He was dressed in black trousers and a white shirt so sharply creased, she could have cut her toast on it. His groomed appearance made her aware of what her own must be, and she cringed within the tangle of linens.

He stopped when he saw she was awake, and for a moment the hot blue glow in his eyes brought back every wicked detail of their night together. Then he smiled a polite greeting which was both neutral and effective in extinguishing the desire in his gaze.

"Good morning. There's a bath for you in the other room and some fresh clothing there on the bed, though I have no objection to dining with a woman wearing my sheets."

Never had Jude felt quite so naked. His jest was humorless, delivered with that flat, remote smile— the one he must have supplied for the numerous woman who woke in his bed under similar circumstances. He treated the whole matter casually, lessening the special sentiments she'd hoped to attach. But, of course, she realized with all practicality, that was his intention. He didn't want her to attach anything to what had happened. That's why he'd denied her the pleasure of waking within the circle of his arms, why he'd put on impeccable and impersonal clothing along with that bland smile. And never had she felt so despairing or ashamed.

By surrendering to their passions, she'd acted like a common tart, and now he was treating her like one.

"I think I should like to wash up and dress," she murmured in a tone as void of tangible feeling as his own. Draping the sheet into a concealing toga before picking up the parcels, she walked like a Grecian queen to the far dressing area. Once out of his sight, her starched will wilted and her tears salted the water of her bath.

Dalton remained where he was standing, his posture going stiff as he listened to the splashing from the other room. An achy tension possessed him as he imagined her in the tub, all slick with scented oil as cascades of water caressed her naked form the way he wished to. It took every scrap of his determination not to intrude upon her bath with sponge in hand to turn the act of cleanliness into one of passion. But he'd worked too hard to set the tone of things between them to ruin it with carelessly loosened emotion.

He knew his cool attitude hurt her. She'd wanted more from him this morning, some validation that their night together had moved him as it had her. If only she knew the truth of it; that he'd lain awake for the better part of an hour, watching her sleep, fearing to touch her lest he break his cardinal rule and confess to all the tumultuous feelings beating madly within his chest. He couldn't allow her that power over him. Not because of the job he was here to do, but because the memory of her claim of love still shivered along his every nerve in a fever of futile hope.

She'd gotten the drop on him, and he was too much of a professional to feel comfortable with that. Her vow had taken him totally by surprise, but it was his own reaction to it that had him in an anxious quake. For one insane moment he'd wanted to reply in kind.

Having never placed his love wisely, he was reluctant to admit to it now. Not to this special, tender woman who would use his claim to destroy his will and crush his ambitions. He didn't want to live at a dusty way station on an island of isolation, spending the rest of his life with the smells of horse and sweat up his nose, laboring for others with dirt beneath his nails. He wanted more than that for himself. And he wanted more for Jude and her family. He'd tasted the good things life could offer, and after having so little for so long, he couldn't go back to nothing. He wouldn't. A man was nothing unless he controlled his own destiny. The judge had taught him that. Otherwise he'd always be a puppet to another's plans.

As it stood, he picked his own jobs, set his own rules. He was free to walk away when he'd earned his pay. Except for this time. He'd let down his guard, and Jude had snuck in like a sucker punch to the gut, robbing him of his wind, his balance, and his claim to rational thought. She was a cog in the machinations, and he had to pry her loose so things would run smoothly again. But she was lodged so deep, right in the middle of everything. He couldn't roll forward without crushing her, and he couldn't go back without damaging his pride. He was stuck and it was time to do something about the situation.

He reached into his trouser pocket and ran his thumb over the time-worn surface of the five-dollar gold piece he carried like the burden of a cross. It was his reminder of the path he'd chosen, of the man he now was and always would be.

San Francisco. He would think of San Francisco. That goal was in sight if he could only solve his current troubles. And the source of trouble took on a capital T as Jude Amos emerged from the dressing room.

He'd chosen the gown with her in mind, something elegantly understated yet ultrafeminine, something that would display her attributes without apologizing for any less-than-perfect qualities. Something soft yet confident, something like Jude. He'd chosen well.

The graceful gown of pale salmon-colored silk was shaped to her torso, softening and accentuating her bosom with a fichu of lace and a red Bengal rose pinned at the junction of its high-standing collar. Frills of the same lace fell from elbow-length sleeves, making her arms seem long and slender. The overskirt was drawn up in a rounded crunch of fabric, held at either hip with deep-red rosettes which heightened the illusion of a dramatic hourglass shape over a snug cylindrical skirt of pale green patterned with ruby-colored swirls of embroidery. The total effect was one of style and unaffected glamour.

Jude's fingers plucked at a swag of silk. "This is beautiful," she whispered in an awed tone.

"Yes." How could he disagree? "I couldn't resist when I saw it. I couldn't imagine anyone but you wearing it."

"How much—"

He held up his hand. "A gift. And that other there on the bed is for Sam. I didn't want him to think I'd forgotten him." He turned away before she could argue and so missed the moistening of her gaze. "I took the liberty of sending your dinner gown out to be pressed. It will be brought to your room in plenty of time."

"In time for what?"

"To attend the opera with me this evening."

"I've never been to the opera," she mused in a husky little voice that cut right to his heart. So many things she'd never experienced. So many things he longed to show her.

"Then you must go. It's an acquired taste not everyone enjoys but everyone should sample at least once. We'll have dinner first."

Dinner. The opera. With Dalton as escort. Her dazed and dreamy thoughts went beyond, to the possibility of returning to this room, to more of the delicious pleasures to which he'd introduced her the night before. It was so easy to be swept along by this long-sought fantasy, she nearly forgot her other purpose. With a shake of her head, Jude called herself back to it.

"I would love to attend the opera with you, but I might be busy for dinner. I'm here on business, as I told you, and I've put it off for too long."

Dalton turned toward her, his gaze intense, his voice compelling. "Put it off forever, Jude."

"What? I'm afraid you don't understand."

"I understand that you're here in Cheyenne to stir up a hornets' nest of trouble. Leave it alone, Jude. It doesn't have to be your trouble."

"It already is, Dalton," she corrected quietly, not wanting this wedge to come between them now.

"Why? Because a bunch of foolish farmers told you so? You don't need to carry their crusade. The valley has no hold on you. You could live here, in Cheyenne. You could go to the opera, wear fine clothes, discuss Tennyson, Byron, and Shakespeare with other literate minds. There's a school here for those like Sammy, where he could get help. A job for him at the livery. Even Joseph wouldn't find

himself unwelcomed after a time, and I know of
several eateries that would fight over his biscuits.
Think of it, Jude. No more struggle, no more back-
breaking hours, no more threats."

And she was thinking. Her mind was swirling
with the possibilities he planted there. It sounded so
good, so perfect. A solution to her every dream.
Until he concluded his persuasive speech.

"With Jamison's offer, you could have it all,
Jude."

The mention of Jamison was a cold slap to wake
her from her daydreams. Jude blinked away the fog
of fancy and looked at Dalton, really looked at him,
where he stood in his dapper clothes, his features
remote, his stare carefully veiled. And she realized
he'd made no mention of his place in these glorious
plans.

But, of course, he wasn't supposed to share them
with her. He was only supposed to woo her with
them. Right into Jamison's hands.

What a fool she was!

How clear it all became. Dalton had been sent
after her to distract her from her business and to
bribe her into abandoning the valley's cause. And
what an exquisite bribe it was, a night of passion to
sway a lonely spinster into believing anything, followed by ample funds to escape the pressures of her
life. How well they knew her every weakness!

Well, Dalton had pointed out the inadequacies in
her existence. He'd taken advantage of her desperation, coaxing her into believing his ardor was real.
And she'd almost caved in to his virile persuasion.

"You paint a tempting picture, Mr. MacKenzie, all
on Jamison's canvas. But I wasn't supposed to see
that until it was too late, was I?"

He didn't even blink. And because he made no attempt to argue the point, she believed it completely, to her utter heartbreak.

"You must be incredibly well paid for what you do," she said with a tortured smile. "How else could you make it seem so convincing?" The quick breath she took sounded harsh and raw, but the words that followed were strong as steel. "Tell Jamison thanks, but no thanks. He'll have to come up with a more believable argument."

Holding up her head with the sheer power of wounded pride, Jude strode past him and out the door.

Dalton let her go. He could have stopped her with the truth, the truth that it wasn't Jamison's cash but rather his own care that motivated him. The very last thing he wanted was Jude and her family in the middle of the valley's shooting gallery. But he kept silent and let her rip his heart out with her leaving. Because in order to convince her that he wasn't Jamison's puppet, he would have to tell her the whole truth—that he was so crazy, blindly in love with her, the money didn't matter. Even the walls of his reputation were beginning to crack under the strain.

However, it wasn't money and it wasn't professional honor that kept him from admitting what weighed upon his soul. It was fear. A deep gut-gnawing fear that she would fail him as all others had before her.

So instead of going after her to mend the rip of faith he'd allowed, Dalton sat down to breakfast, eating mechanically as the nuns had taught him until the last morsel was gone. Then, before packing his bags, he spent long minutes gazing at a faded picture postcard of gorgeous houses marching up a steep street, postmarked San Francisco.

Upon entering her room, Jude's first impulse was to strip off the lovely silk gown and return it to Dalton in ribbons. But as she kneaded the sleek fabric in her hands, a calmer logic kept her from destroying the sophisticated garment. No, she wouldn't ruin it; she would use it to further her own cause. She had to flush her mind of folly and concentrate upon the matters of importance . . . as she should have been doing from the start. Now was not the time to mourn her weakness for the wrong man. She could punish herself later with how wonderful things had seemed—if only for a moment, and if only a pretense. Dalton had distracted her from her purpose for long enough. She would put him behind her and move forward with her plans. That would be her best revenge against the heartlessly handsome liar and his scheming boss.

She washed her face, cooling the flame of humiliation from her cheeks. If only there were a means to extinguish similarly the burn of betrayal from her heart. She drew a deep breath and her will faltered. The pain of disillusionment was immeasurable. The loss of her dreams left a huge hole in a spirit bereft of hope.

How could he have done such a thing? It would have been kinder for him to just shoot her and be done with it.

Jude squeezed her eyes shut, determined to get past the awful pain. There would be many lonely nights ahead in which she could drag out her sorrow. For now she had to collect her wits and will and get on with the business that had brought her to Cheyenne.

Revitalized by her goals, Jude forced the misery
down deep where it burned, a constant ache of
remorse, a constant reminder of how much it hurt to
dream.

Jude sat nervously in the dining area of the
Cheyenne Club, aware of the hostile glares from its
white-jacketed bartenders and waiters imported
from Chicago. She wasn't sure it was because she
was an unescorted female or because they'd gotten
wind of her reason for requesting an interview with
Tom Sturgis, the demigod of the Wyoming territory.

It had taken her all morning to finagle Sturgis's
routine from one of his lesser-paid underlings eager
to exchange the information for a weight of coins.
She wouldn't bother going back to the law to plead
her case. The Wyoming Stock Growers' Association
not only controlled the law, she had discovered after
a brief and futile inquiry at the marshall's office, but
it *was* the law. And association policy was formu-
lated, directed, and enforced by its secretary, Sturgis. The effete and arrogant young New Yorker was
also founder of the WSGA, president of the Boston-
financed Union Cattle Company, and first president
of the Stock Growers' National Bank. An audience
with him carried more weight than the favor of the
president, at least in the Wyoming territory.

Jude waited, mentally rehearsing her speech, but
the moment she saw Sturgis enter the room surrounded by his entourage, the carefully phrased
petition disappeared from her mind. She stood as
the group approached and, seeing her chance, acted
quickly.

"Mr. Sturgis, might I have a minute of your
time?"

He paused. "Ma'am?"

"My name is Jude Amos and I represent the small ranchers in Chugwater Valley."

The polite attentiveness vanished from his features when he guessed the direction their conversation would take. "I'm sorry, Miss Amos, but my time has been promised elsewhere today. If you'd like to make an appointment for, say, sometime early next week—"

She held her frustration, masking it with her sweetest smile. "I'm sorry, sir, but I'll be leaving Cheyenne later this afternoon, and it is vital that I speak with you."

He recognized her determination, and rather than make an unpleasant display in the crowded dining room, he gestured to one of his sycophants. "Kilgore is my personal representative. He'll listen to your grievances, and you can be assured they will be relayed to me." Then, before she could protest being shifted off to a lower rung, he turned and began to shake hands with the occupants of nearby tables, working his way steadily away from her.

Jude regarded the whey-faced little man who remained behind, blinking at her through thick spectacles. Better than nothing, she sighed to herself philosophically.

"Mr. Kilgore, won't you join me?"

For the next hour Jude laid out all the concerns of the valley's landowners. She expressed her worry over possible bloodshed, questioned the legality of Jamison's threats, and outlined the potential repercussions should he try to apply muscle to move them out. Sturgis's proxy sat listening to her, nodding in apparent agreement at the appropriate times without interruption. When she spoke of airing their situation in the Cheyenne *Leader*, the most important paper in the territory, he didn't so much as flinch. And that was when Jude began to fear her efforts were ineffective.

Having heard all her complaints, Kilgore took a moment to arrange his thoughts, then began with clear, concise diction to cut her arguments to shreds.

"Miss Amos, the competition for land and water brought the need for cooperative action by ranch owners of the territory. Our Stock Growers' Association operates in five states, controlling some two million head of cattle, recording legal brands, supervising roundups, settling claim conflicts, obtaining railroad rebates, and lobbying in Washington for the good of many."

"I know all that, Mr. Kilgore—"

He held up his slender, white hand to stay her comments until he was finished. "It is our job to stabilize the beef industry by preventing stagnation in the marketplace and by combating chaos whenever it threatens our stand. Mr. Sturgis is very concerned at the moment about the position of your farmers. It's not the first time he's heard complaints voiced in that valley. He is especially interested in how your friends happened to obtain stock of their own with no apparent income to provide for such purchases. You are familiar with our Maverick Laws, are you not? That is what should concern your farmers, not Mr. Jamison's right to operate in his valley as he sees fit."

Jude knew a terrible chill. "Are you threatening us, Mr. Kilgore?"

"Oh, no, Miss Amos. I have no need for threats. Another benefit of belonging to our organization is our support when members are forced to hire outside help to enforce our edicts. We never intercede directly."

"You mean hired killers," Jude spat out.

"Call them what you will, but they get the job done. As for protesting in the *Leader*, please be aware that Mr. Sturgis's opinions are those of the *Leader*. You will find no sympathy for your cause here or anywhere in the territory where cattle is king and nesters are a plague to be exterminated by any means possible. My suggestion to you, Miss Amos, is that you return to your valley and you advise your friends to move elsewhere before the association turns a more personal interest their way. Thank you for the coffee, ma'am, and good day to you."

The little viper unwound from his chair and returned to where Tom Sturgis held court. Though dazed with disappointment, Jude's acuity sharpened when she beheld one of the men seated at that influential table. There was no mistaking the broad shoulders or the elegant cut of his coat. Or the brace of bone-handled pistols.

It hadn't taken Dalton long to throw in with the power in Cheyenne.

Jude stood slowly, her carriage proud yet defiant, despite the crippling blow she'd just suffered. She was aware of Kilgore murmuring in his boss's ear and of that man's piercing glare, measuring her as a future threat. She didn't flinch under the harshness of his stare. Then Dalton twisted to follow their intense scrutiny, and Jude's pulse gave a miserable leap at the sight of his handsome face. His features never flickered in beholding her.

It was as if they'd never shared an intimate moment, as if he'd never heard her confession of love.

She'd thought before that the impassive set of the gunman's features was a mask to cover his inner emotions. Now she knew that assumption to be false. The hard, blank glaze was Dalton MacKenzie:

cold, unreachable, and totally without feeling. Who should know better than she?

Without so much as an acknowledging blink, Jude walked out of the dining room. There was no reason to remain, howling protests into deaf ears.

In her room she found her velvet dress all cleaned and neatly pressed. Next to it lay the gift for Sammy. She packed both without allowing her thoughts to question why. And when she departed Cheyenne on the late-afternoon stage, she left more than her innocence behind. Her naive dreams of how wonderful love could be remained there as well, wrapped as tightly as the salmon-colored silk gown delivered to Dalton's door.

Chapter 20

〜〜〜✦〜〜〜

"They're stringing wire, Jude, miles of it," Tandy Barret growled as he paced the main room at Amos Station. His brother, Wade, stayed seated at the table, but his expression was no less grim after hearing Jude's disheartening summary of what had happened in Cheyenne. They were on their own, and the entire valley was running scared. Especially now when Jamison was making his first truly aggressive move.

"So far," Tandy continued, "they're sticking to unclaimed public lands, but we've got to be prepared for the fact that property boundaries ain't gonna stop 'em. They're gonna go for the water, and the crow-flies route is across my land and right up to your back door. What are we gonna do about it, Jude? You planning to just let 'em come knocking? Well, I don't, damn 'em to hell. I don't!"

Jude was only half listening to Tandy's tirade. She knew he had to blow off steam before he would be ready to hear reason, and that time was far from coming. What distracted her wasn't so much Tandy's chest-beating antics. Since her return she'd been preoccupied with more personal matters she tried to block out of heart and mind.

273

She was wondering about Dalton's reaction to her return of the dress. Would he consider it a childish gesture?

She was tormented by the image of his reunion with Kathleen and writhed in shame when she thought of what he might tell the other woman. Would he boast of her eagerness to fall into his bed? Would he laugh when he spoke of how easily she'd believed his lies? Would he be lying with Kathleen Jamison tonight and joke about the comparison of that lovely creature to a silly, awkward spinster? And she died a little inside every time she pictured the gorgeous redhead on the receiving end of Dalton's kisses.

Oh, how she'd enjoyed them! How she'd enjoyed all he'd offered!

Huge angry sobs she'd held at bay since leaving Cheyenne threatened to rise up and choke her as she thought of him, of Kathleen with him, of the two of them laughing at her expense. Jealousy tore through her soul, yet worse was the truth from which she tried to hide, the fact that, even now, knowing what she did, she still wanted him.

Worse, still, was that if he'd asked her from the heart, she would have turned her back on everything here to have him for herself. Her shame in that knew no bounds.

"Jude, what do you think?"

Her head shot up, and her unfocused gaze found Tandy's riveted to it. He was waiting impatiently for her to comment on something she hadn't heard. Scrambling mentally to avoid admitting her own distraction—and its cause, she said, "What does your brother think? Wade, you haven't had much to say so far."

Wade, unlike his volatile brother, wasn't given to

rash decisions. He was a man who carefully weighed consequence, a man whose opinions others respected. He was Jude's last hope of support when it came to holding out against bloodshed. And it was to her that he addressed himself.

"I can't see any way around it. If they bring their fence onto our land, we'll have to stop 'em. If the law won't back us, we'll have to do what we can on our own. A man just don't give up what's his 'cause somebody bigger and stronger says git outta the way. There comes a time when a man has to stand firm. I'm sorry, Jude. That time has come."

She listened with a heavy heart, seeing the valley soaked in innocent blood as he spoke those fateful words. No matter what she said now, once Wade expressed his view, the others would fall in behind him. All was lost. Nothing could halt the inevitable confrontation. Now she had to make a decision of her own. Would she stand with them and risk losing all? Or would she take what Jamison offered and escape the valley with her family, carrying the shameful guilt of abandoning her friends?

Jude never had a chance to mull over those options, for just then Sammy burst in from the porch, his eyes wide and wild, his speech next to incomprehensible.

"Jude . . . Jude, the sky, it's so all-of-a-sudden dark. What does it mean, Jude? Sammy's scared of all them dark clouds. Come look. Come look!"

"We don't got time to go looking at no storm clouds, you fool," Tandy grumbled, but Jude, alarmed as was Joseph by Sammy's frantic gesturing, rose and hurried to the door.

"Oh, my God!"

Her anguished cry brought Tandy and Wade up

behind her. There was a moment of awful silence as they took in the significance of the darkness coloring the horizon. Smoke, black and relentless, poured skyward.

The Barrets' ranch.

"Oh, God," Wade moaned. "Lucinda!"

Jude was running toward the barn, yelling, "Joseph, ride south. Sammy, you ride north. Stop at every place you see and tell them to hurry to the Barrets'. There's a fire."

Jude and the Barrets rode hard over the rolling hills. Lush green grasses glowed silver and fluid in the moonlight, almost like a breaking sea. The riders didn't speak. They held tight to their own thoughts and fears as anxious eyes beheld the ever-spreading cloud of destruction. All were afraid of what they'd find when they crested that last hill.

Heat lightning, Jude told herself. That could have started the blaze. A moment's carelessness with a lantern. But she knew neither of those to be the reason. It was Jamison, striking his first fierce blow at those encroaching in his valley. Terror beat hard within her chest, an anxious fist pounding as if to escape. First the Barrets', then where? Would she and Sammy and Joseph awake some night to find the timbers ablaze above their heads? Panic ran away with her as fast as her mount's four flying hooves. What had they been thinking? What had any of them been thinking? They couldn't stand against a man like Jamison, a man who would burn a family out just for the grass that grew on their land. It would be slow, sure suicide.

They cleared the final hill and it was like peering down into hell. Heat struck them in an invisible wall, just behind the stench of smoke, making them pause on the summit to get control of their frightened horses—giving them a long, horrible moment to view what damage had been done.

The Barrets' barn, the one in which Jude had longed to dance within the circle of Dalton's arms, was blanketed in flames. Its opened doors were a yawning maw to an inferno. Nothing could have survived inside. Jude sent up a quick prayer that there had been time to get the livestock out. Already the fire had spread to the house. Tongues of hungry devastation raced along the porch roof in wicked glee and snaked as if alive about the support posts. Curls of smoke billowed through the broken front panes, dashing the hope that the fire hadn't gotten inside. Above the ravenous crackles and the pops and groans of surrendering beams, it was quiet. Too eerily quiet.

There were no signs of life.

Wade flung off his saddle, screaming his new bride's name. Tandy caught him before he cast himself recklessly into the ferocious flames now licking at the ominously closed front door. And Tandy had to yell to be heard above the roar of the blaze, above his brother's wails.

"Wade, stop. It's too late. It's too late. There's nothing you can do to save her now."

That truth broke Wade down completely. He sagged to his knees as all his dreams went to raging ruin about him.

Jude sat atop her horse, her vision skewed by smoke and loss. She saw the wavery image of Tandy dashing for the windmill to dredge up a bucket of water. She knew she should dismount and help him, but a whisper of logic moaned, *What was the use?* They couldn't save the house or the barn. Nor could they save the happy new bride, who only a few days before had been clutching joyously at her husband's arm as she heard the good wishes of their friends. Now the next gathering would be over her grave, and Jude was helpless with remorse.

As Tandy ran a wobbly race between the windmill and the flame-engulfed porch, Jude's teary gaze caught another movement through the black haze behind him. Riders, help arriving too late. With numb surprise she recognized them as they came through the roiling smoke. It was Ned Farrel, one of Jamison's hands, and Dalton. More of a surprise was when they both leapt from their saddles and went to line up in a hasty bucket brigade with the Barret brothers. Finally, seeing their determination, Jude climbed down and formed the link between the gunman and the cowboy.

Jude swung pails, full and empty, until her arms felt stretched and nearly torn from their sockets. Her hands grew raw from the chafe of the narrow handle and her damp skirts clung, adding to her misery. Still she labored to keep up with the ebb and flow. Gradually their sparse brigade was padded as neighbors arrived and quickly joined in. Jude's every breath was strained through smoke and streaked down her throat still afire. She coughed violently with every other inhalation, and her eyes were blinded by soot, heat, and tears. She would have continued to her last breath, to her last ounce of strength, but her endurance was never put to that test.

It was Wade who finally stopped it all with a weary cry. "It's gone, boys. There's no use in keeping it up anymore. There's nothing left to save."

The last full bucket fell to the ground, overturning, as each one in the line slumped in reluctant defeat. With a victorious snap and rumble, the roof caved in, turning the fire in upon itself to consume eagerly what was left of the Barrets' lives.

As they stood, wheezing and dispirited, awareness grew of the two in their number who did not belong.

Hostile, angry eyes turned on Jamison's hand and his hired gun. Both men stood in their shirtsleeves, black with ash and splotched with water, as exhausted in body and spirit as all around them.

"How dare you come back here?" Tandy rumbled hoarsely. "Did you have to come back and see your handiwork? Did you want to make sure you'd destroyed it all? You sons of bitches! Somebody get a rope!"

"It wasn't us!" Ned cried in genuine alarm, his reddened eyes fixed in morbid fascination upon the length of manila one of the men was uncoiling from his saddle. "I'd just gone to meet Mr. MacKenzie at Bear Creek Ranch and the stage was late getting in. We heard the bell and saw the smoke. We had nothing to do with this."

Tandy snatched up the curl of hemp. "Why the hell should we believe you two murderers?"

Dalton, who kept his hands carefully clear of his guns, looked only to Jude. His gaze was piercingly direct. "It wasn't us."

Jude didn't want to be part of any illegal neck stretching, although her heart ached for Wade's loss. She believed in justice even for those who didn't deserve any—even for Patrick Jamison, who she believed was guilty as sin. But when Dalton held her stare unblinkingly, a part of her, a foolish part which refused to learn its lesson, believed him.

But already the cry had been taken up by the others gathered at the smoking rubble of the Barret ranch. Fear drove out good sense, the fear that it could have been any one of them counting their losses and burying a bride.

Fear made men ugly.

"Hang 'em," came a gruff growl, one that was echoed quickly by all the black-faced men in the scorched yard.

"No!" Jude stepped in, herself a damning sight with singed skirt hem and soot-streaked cheeks. "You men can't do this. There's no proof. You have to wait for the law."

"Law?" Tandy sneered. "What law is that, Jude? The law that says it's all right for men like Jamison to snatch up what we've worked hard for? The law that'll say it was okay for him to strike the match that killed my sister-in-law? And roasted our stock in the barn? Is that the law you're countin' on to see justice done? This is justice." He held the rope high. "And tonight we're seeing it's done proper."

Jude's gaze flashed to Dalton, whose hands had begun to edge closer to the bone handles of his guns. His features were dark and tense, signaling he had no intention of taking a short drop off a tall horse for something he didn't do. Her heart was beating a wild objection to what was about to happen, each anxious throb demanding she do something to stop it. Despite all his dirty tricks on Jamison's behalf, she was still in love with the man who'd sat out on her front porch, engrossed in the sight of the sunrise. She turned her appeal to Wade.

"You can't let them do this," she petitioned frantically. "It's wrong."

Wade stared at her through hollow eyes, a glazed look on his face, that of a man whose spirit had died. "As wrong as my Lucinda dying alone," he intoned flatly. And he reached for the rope.

"You can't do this!" Ned cried again, his gaze flashing from one neighbor to the next. "Mr. Jamison didn't order it done!" No one listened as his scruffy pony and Dalton's buckskin were led toward a smoldering box elder and positioned beneath two gnarled branches that looked strong enough to snatch away a man's soul.

"No!" Jude shouted again, but as she stepped forward to intervene physically, her arms were pinned by one of the men. She writhed like a wildcat in his grasp until he yanked her elbows high enough to subdue her, all the while muttering apologies.

"Now, you quit that wiggling, Miss Jude. I doan want to hurt you. You can't stop this from happenin'. If you wants, you jus' turn your head away until it's over."

Over. They were going to hang Dalton!

Shrieking like a madwoman, she redoubled her efforts to escape, sobs of distress clogging her already raw throat and burning her eyes.

But it wasn't her protests that halted the forward surge of determined men. It was the sudden click of a revolver brought to full cock and the boom of a stern, masculine voice demanding, "Stop right there. I don't want to hurt nobody, but you ain't hanging my friend. If Mac says he didn't do it, he didn't do it."

Jude's struggles ceased in amazement as she watched Sammy separate himself from the angry crowd to take a firm stand in front of Dalton, a pistol directed at his neighbors. His usually jovial features were set in grim lines which aged his demeanor to match his massive size. Just as surprising was the sight of Joseph stepping in beside him with an ancient flintlock in hand. Joseph, who hated violence, standing staunch as his warrior ancestors, his thin, white braids and withered face suddenly noble and strong.

A tense stalemate ensued, with no one knowing exactly what to do about it. Until a new intrusion drew their attention, a slight figure staggering up from the rear of the smoking barn.

"W-Wade?"

The rope fell from Wade's fingers as he stared for a long moment, disbelieving. Then, with a hoarse cry, he ran to catch the soot-blackened figure in his tender embrace.

"Lucinda! My God, I thought you'd died. I thought you were in the house." He was sobbing, clutching the limp form to him. "What happened, honey? Where were you?"

Neighbors, friends, and enemies alike, gathered close to hear her raspy explanation.

"I—I was in the privy. I heard riders so I stayed where I was. I smelled the smoke and I waited until I was sure they was gone. I tried to get in to save the horses, but the smoke was so thick and it was so hot." Her words choked off in a moment of remorse before continuing. "I heard riders again and I thought it might be them coming back to finish me, so I ran to the root cellar. Only my eyes was all full of smoke and I took a wrong step. I must have taken a tumble down the ladder an' hit my head. Next thing I heard was shouting."

Wade hugged her tight. "It's all right, Cindy."

"Oh, Wade. We've lost everything."

"Not what really matters, honey. Nothing that really matters."

With the focus turned from them, Dalton laid a calming hand on Sammy's tense shoulder.

"You can pocket that piece now, Sam."

Sammy exhaled shakily, and all his surprising fortitude flowed out on that gusty breath. "Be happy to, Mac. Are you okay?"

An odd smile played about his lips as he observed the anxious man/child. "Yeah, Sam, I'm fine. Thanks to you."

Shy pride lit Sammy's features. "Jus' doing what you told me, Mac. Standing up for them that I cares for. I was right, wasn't I, Mac?"

Dalton's hand squeezed the broad shoulder tightly. "Yes, you were, Sam." And he had to turn away from that shiny, adoring gaze before he choked on the boot-sized chunk of emotion wedging up into his throat. "What about you, chief?"

Joseph looked indignant at having his motives questioned. "I care for him," he announced pompously, nodding toward Sammy. "It has nothing to do with you, gunfighter."

Dalton's grin called him liar. Then his expression sobered as he glanced over at Jude. Jude, who'd fought like a she-devil to save his life. She regarded him with a wellspring of feelings he didn't even want to recognize, there for anyone with eyes to see. He averted his gaze. What the hell was he going to do about these folks who loved so unwisely?

With the reappearance of Lucinda Barret, the crowd, even Tandy, lost its taste for killing. Though none truly believed their claim of innocence, they were willing to let things go as Tandy growled, "Get the hell off our land. You ain't accomplished nothing here. We ain't leaving. We'll live in the root cellar until we rebuild, but you ain't drivin' us off. You hear? You ain't drivin' us off!"

There was a mutter of consensus from the other ranchers as hard eyes bid Patrick Jamison's men to get while the getting was good. Dalton wasn't one to pass up that opportunity. His neck had come too close to a pattern of hemp twists. He grabbed up the reins to his stallion and swung aboard, seeing no reason to voice his uninvolvement yet again to those who had already condemned him.

Now that the direct danger to Dalton was at an end, Jude's terror for his safety eased back into a warring confusion of want and angry distrust. She was frightened by the way Sammy, and even Joseph, had jumped into the fray to take his part. She'd embarrassed herself by flying to his defense, and now he and his new mistress would probably laugh over that too. By the time he angled his horse over to where she was standing apart from the others, her resolve was as grimly set as her features.

"I had no part in it, Jude."

She believed him but, at the same time, realized it didn't matter. "Maybe not this time, but you would have been here, torch in hand, had Jamison ordered it. Just your being on his payroll starts more fires than we can control."

His gaze darkened with undisguised turmoil, and for a moment she dared consider that he really might care. When he spoke, his tone was low and rough as a riverbed.

"What do you want me to do about it, Jude? I've

an obligation I can't just walk away from. You know about obligation or you wouldn't be here."

"This isn't obligation, Dalton. It's caring, one neighbor for another. One human being for another. But you wouldn't know anything about that, would you?"

He didn't address that attack nor did he flinch from it. Instead he restated his only argument. "It's my job, Jude."

"Then go do it."

And she stepped to the side, slapping her palm down upon the flank of his buckskin to startle it into a forward leap. She walked back to the circle of her friends before he could get the animal under control to continue their terse conversation. She didn't look around to see him ride off. She would never look back again.

Dalton rode back to Sweetgrass on an anxious Ned's heels. He purposefully tried to block all thoughts of Jude, her family, and the valley's plight from his mind, but that was hard to do when his lungs were filled with the taste of smoke and his heart burned from the cut of Jude's blaming glare.

There was no reason for the events of this night to have such a strong effect on him. He'd seen it all before: the burned-out ranch homes, the weeping women, the shouts of impotent men angry over their inability to stand against a more powerful force. It wasn't even the first time he'd been fitted for a noose. Death by dangling was a common risk in his profession. Yet the sight of the grieving husband's face haunted him. There were so many ghosts on his soul, why did this one, one for which

he wasn't even responsible, torment him so? He had
no reason to care about these people's misfortunes.
None except that their pain affected Jude, and that
violence directed at them brought danger closer to
the Amoses' door.

He still choked up when he thought of Sammy
coming to his rescue. And Joseph too. And Jude,
even after their harsh parting. He'd expected her to
be the one slipping the rope over his head. He
wouldn't have blamed her if she had. Revenge, he
respected. Outright demonstrations of care spooked
him. They'd been willing to stand against their
friends for the sake of a paid gun, an enemy. He
didn't understand it, and that confusion was a
plague upon his mind. He hadn't asked for them to
take up his cause. There was no profit in it. He was
sure they hadn't stepped in in order to make him
feel guilty enough to ride away. Blackmail never
occurred to folks like the Amoses. So why? Why risk
so much with no hope of return? He wouldn't have
stuck his neck out for them.

Or would he?

Not being sure, one way or the other, made him
surly as a man with a bad tooth.

One thing he did know was that Jamison had
been behind the raid on the Barrets'. Perhaps not
directly, for the man seemed too genuinely upset by
the idea of bloodshed to be involved. Could Monty,
the spineless foreman, have been behind the destruction? Somehow he didn't figure the man as one
to take that kind of initiative. He was a sullen
follower, not a shrewd leader. And though he knew
her to be capable, he couldn't quite picture Kathleen
Jamison behind a mask and a torch. She gave
orders; she didn't act upon them.

All his questions were soon answered as they

arrived at the big prairie mansion. Curious hands took their winded horses but didn't ask about their sooty appearance. As Ned headed for the bunkhouse to fill in his anxious associates, Dalton went silently inside, bringing the pungent odor of devastation with him.

Kathleen met him in the hall. Her surprise was real enough. She stared at Dalton, her dainty nose wrinkling at the stench of smoke.

"Goodness, what have you been up to, Mr. MacKenzie?"

"There was a fire at the Barrets' ranch. That young woman whose wedding we attended nearly died in the blaze."

Her eyes glittered with malicious amusement as she drawled, "How terribly unfortunate."

"I can see you truly mean that" was his sarcastic reply. "I almost expected to see you covered with soot."

"Really, Mr. MacKenzie, I don't involve myself in the dirtier aspects of the business. Besides, I've been busy entertaining our new guest."

And she turned with a smile for the lanky figure appearing behind her in the doorway.

"Mr. MacKenzie, I believe you already know Mr. Jones."

Chapter 21

❧◦◦◦◦◦◦❧

Latigo grinned in the face of Dalton's stunned silence.

"Well, howdy, Mac. I told you I'd see you again soon."

Kathleen waved a lace-trimmed hankie beneath her nose as she eyed Dalton's soiled appearance. "I met Mr. Jones on my trip to Fort Laramie yesterday. It seems the two of you share the same occupation. He was already well versed in our situation and offered his expertise in solving our little problem with the squatters."

"You hired him?" Dalton surmised. "Without consulting your father?"

"A terrible thing occurred just this morning," Kathleen confided, turning back into the room so he couldn't read the truth of her emotions upon her lovely if treacherous face. "My father and I were out riding when one of those damned squatters took a shot at us. Fortunately he missed, but Daddy's horse was spooked and he got thrown."

An icy premonition settled in Dalton's belly. "How badly was he hurt?"

"Nothing horribly serious. Thank you for your concern. He twisted his knee quite badly in the fall and has to remain in bed for some time. Until he's better, I'm in charge." And she revolved slowly, her black eyes ablaze with dizzying power and dire consequence as they fixed upon Dalton's. "I know my father would expect you to show me the same allegiance you owe him. You don't strike me as a man who would welch on a debt, Mr. MacKenzie, especially when the debt owed is your life."

"This was your doing tonight, wasn't it?" Dalton commented quietly.

Kathleen regarded him with a coldly calculating smile. "Of course. Do you think dear Daddy would have condoned such an attack on his nester friends? Friends who tried to ambush him? I couldn't ignore such a thing. Let's just say Mr. Jones proved himself to my satisfaction, which is more than I can say for you, Mr. MacKenzie. Mr. Jones is here to see that you don't get distracted from what you were hired to do. From what I gather, things were less than successful in Cheyenne."

"She didn't get any help from the authorities or the association."

"And you, obviously, had no great success in discouraging her."

"As I said, she's a strong-willed woman. I would think you'd admire that, considering it's a shared trait."

"Not in an enemy." She gave her head a regal toss of disdain, then smiled sweetly at her new hired gun. "Anyway, Mr. Jones will be much less dainty in his dealings with her. Once she folds, the others will quickly follow."

Dalton experienced a prophetic chill. "And what if your father disagrees?"

"He won't be making those decisions for a while. This is my valley, and he will not lose it because of

his weak fondness for a batch of fools." She ground
one delicate fist into the other as if it were the might
of her holdings crushing the smaller landowners to
powder. "I'm in charge here. That's the one lesson
my dear mother taught me. With absolute power
comes freedom. She was never able to control my
father the way I can. She let him manipulate her life
and make her miserable, and in the end it drove her
away. Well, he won't do that with me. I'm taking
what I want. No man will control my destiny. And
no man works here unless he's willing to take my
orders."

Latigo grinned widely. "I got no problem with
that. You, Mac?"

Dalton said nothing. His refusal to capitulate both
annoyed and impressed Kathleen. Because she was
an aggressive female, the fact that he withheld his
homage made her want it all the more. She liked a
fight, and Dalton MacKenzie put up an intriguing
struggle—though she had no doubt of her ultimate
victory. She gazed up at him, pouting for a moment,
then rewarding him with a beguiling smile.

"I know you won't let me down, Mr. MacKenzie.
Men of your reputation don't take defeat easily. I
know you and Mr. Jones will work together to give
me exactly what I want. Won't you?"

She swayed toward him in an inviting undulation.
Her palms pushed up over the bulge of his muscular
thighs. Dalton never blinked.

"That's what your father paid me to do, Miss
Jamison."

His cool reply brought a stiffening to her features,
then she laughed and stepped away. "Yes, it is. Now
see that you earn it. Mr. Jones, I assume you've
made yourself comfortable?"

"Oh, yes, ma'am." He grinned widely, his eyes sparkling with humor. "Snug as a bug in a rug. You've seen to all my needs quite nicely."

"Then I'll bid you both good night." She turned with a haughty toss of her curls and started upstairs. Both men watched the hypnotic twitch of her skirts as she climbed, and both were sure she was well aware of their scrutiny.

"Interesting woman," Latigo mused. "Makes you want to bed down at night with your boots on."

"A real scorpion," Dalton agreed.

Latigo slapped his back. "You look like you could use a drink. C'mon and tip a few with me." He gave his friend a compelling push toward their boss's study, and because he was bone weary and brain dulled, Dalton gave in. Once glasses were full, they assumed comfortable seats in Jamison's big red leather chairs. Latigo took a deep drink and sighed. "Ahhhh, the good stuff."

Dalton merely held his glass as he observed the other gunman. "Kind of a quick change for you, isn't this?"

Latigo shrugged. "You know me, Mac. My only loyalty is to my fee up front. Miss Jamison was more than generous with that." Again that sly smile, suggesting she'd included more than money in her offer. "I must say, I do prefer to be on the winning side. Better chance of walking away alive."

Dalton regarded him then through different eyes, seeing not his longtime friend but a dangerous and deadly killer who wouldn't think twice about burning a building over a family's head. Or gunning down a woman and her brother and their elderly cook if the job demanded it. And several months ago he wouldn't have either.

"You're backing the wrong side with Kathleen. I say we wait until our orders come down from her daddy."

Latigo stared at his companion as if he'd suddenly gone loony. "What?"

"Jamison doesn't want those people hurt, and if we do what the daughter tells us, we're going to get caught up in an ugly family feud."

"So? Why should we care about that? We got paid up front. What difference does it make who gives the orders? Mac, what the hell is wrong with you?"

"I almost got lynched tonight after risking my life fighting that fire you started. I know Jamison never would have ordered it. I don't want to get knee deep in blood and then have him pull out, saying it was all a mistake. Without his daughter pushing for it and us there to back it, he'd be over there right now, negotiating some kind of deal with his neighbors."

"Peace don't pay our bills, buddy-boy. We ain't in the negotiating business." He tipped his head to one side, studying his friend in perplexity. "I ain't never known you to get squeamish about a fight, and I surely can't believe I'm hearing you talk about dragging your feet." He gave Dalton a curious once-over, then cocked an amused brow. "Oh, ho! You getting ideas about the beauteous Miss Jamison?"

Dalton snorted. "Not hardly."

"I thought sure it must be a woman. Only a woman makes a man forget where his loyalties lie." Latigo thought some more than he stared, plainly shocked. "It ain't that homely stage-stop woman, is it?"

When Dalton glared at him, Latigo let go with a whooping laugh.

"I can't believe it! Why, Mac, I seen you wine and dine the most gorgeous women north and south,

and none a them ever made you go to mush in the
head. What's so special about this one? She ain't
even nothing to look at!"

Dalton couldn't explain it to a man like Latigo, a
man who judged by surface appeal and pocket
worth alone. Hell, he couldn't even explain it to
himself. And he didn't waste the effort to try.

Latigo gulped the rest of his drink and leaned
back, chuckling. "Lordy Lord, if you don't beat all.
So you fixing to hang up your guns and go throw a
bunch a homely kids with that woman? You gonna
be a farmer? You gonna give up the taste of fine
whiskey like this and sassy women like our Miss
Jamison to hang on the apron strings of that old
spinster? What about San Francisco? You givin' up
on that too?"

Latigo's amusement dwindled at the sudden stillness of Dalton's expression. He'd stared death in the
eyes before, and looking at his friend now gave him
that same crawly chill.

"C'mon, Mac," he coaxed. "Drink your drink and
forget about getting domesticated. That ain't for
you. Men like us, we can't be tied down to that kind
of drudgery. Hell, in a month or two, she'd have you
helping her pick out curtain material. You'd never
last, so why be tempted? We ain't the settling kind.
If we was, we'd a picked a different line of work.
C'mon. Drink up and let's talk about some of the
good times we've shared and some of the pretty gals
we've laid down with."

Dalton set his untouched drink aside and fingered
his filthy clothes. "I'm going to get out of these
things and wash up. I smell of smoke and sweat,
and neither is exactly my favorite perfume."

Latigo smiled at the return of his friend's wry
humor. "You do that, Mac. Me, I think I'll help

myself to a little more of this fine liquor. Then, come morning, you an' me an' Missy Jamison, we got us some plans to make."

Dalton watched his fellow gunman amble to the sideboard and pour a stiff whollop of bourbon. He was watching a reflection of himself: hardened, solitary, prideful, and money motivated, scoffing at things like family and settled roots and obligations to another human being. His same philosophies. Life was held as cheaply as a grain of gunpowder, and the future was as far as one could see at any given moment. Home was the hotel where you hung your hat and slept with your guns on. Happiness was as foreign as hope. Neither thing had any business in their business. And that's the way they liked it.

That's the way he'd liked it.

Until Jude.

He watched Latigo Jones, and he saw a man who'd turned his back on humanity, a man who had no ties, no morals, and no ambition other than to inspire a respectful fear in others. A man who laughed at things he couldn't understand, who hated those who had what he would never hold, and destroyed what he secretly coveted. A man riding toward a brutal and lonely end with an unmarked grave and no one to mourn over it. His future too. His life was a selfish, meaningless race toward an ugly death along a path where he dragged down many innocent others in his violent passing. And nothing mattered. That was why men like he and Latigo Jones made such a big fuss over reputation, because behind that prickle of pride, there was nothing.

And suddenly Dalton hated it.

* * *

The night was longer than any Jude could ever remember. After coming home and washing off the smoke and sweat, she'd seen Sammy to bed with Biscuit curled up on the floor beside him. In the main room Joseph had taken to his pallet, exhausted by the vigors of the evening . . . or maybe just giving her time to think about things.

She was tired of coming up with all the answers. And as she began turning down the lamps within their humble home, she had a harsh curse for the father who'd left such a burden on her. And nothing but resentment for the mother who'd deserted her without teaching her how to be a woman.

If her mother had been stronger, she might have been here this evening, she might have known what advice to give regarding Dalton MacKenzie. She could have answered all Jude's questions involving the way her heart was aching, breaking over a man she shouldn't love. She was her mother! She was supposed to be there for her!

Jude rubbed at dry, smoke-reddened eyes, too weary to hold the truth at bay.

She resented her absent father for being so prideful in his humility, for not being prepared when fate confronted him in the darkened alleyway. For leaving her alone, condemned to a spinster's lot. She would never see an opera now. She would never know an occasion to dress up in velvets. And she would die with only Sammy for a companion, out in the middle of this windswept hell, with only dreams of one night to sustain her.

And for one awful moment she resented Sammy as well, for without him she would be free. He was the one who'd broken her mother's spirit. He was the one who tied her to this desolate place, where nothing grew but loneliness and sorrow wailed on the incessant winds. If she wasn't burdened with his constant care, she could travel, she could experience life, she could . . .

What was she thinking?

Jude clapped her hand over her mouth as if to silence the words of angry discontent she'd never spoken aloud. Horrid, ugly things that left her close to weeping with regret. And as she swayed in the center of the darkened room, hating the mean-spiritedness dwelling equally dark within her, a tap on the door called her from her self-flagellation.

Jude answered the knock clutching her wrapper together with the same hand holding an old revolver. She couldn't have been more surprised to find Dalton MacKenzie on her front porch. He was bundled in his heavy fleece-lined coat, his Stetson tipped down to shield his eyes. His stubble-darkened face was unsmiling. About him swirled an aura of smoke and dangerous excitement. Jude began to tremble. A moment of glorious delight was quickly shadowed by a more cautious distrust. She didn't lower the pistol.

"What are you doing here? It's the middle of the night," she hissed, casting a glance over her shoulder to where Joseph was sleeping, a motionless bag of bones before the fire. "I don't believe we have any further business with each other."

"I'm not here on business."

Before she could utter a squeak of surprise, Jude was mashed up to his chest for a will-bruising kiss.

Chapter 22

By the time he lifted off her lips, Jude hung limply within the circle of his embrace, her head thrown back, her hair streaming like a curtain of dark silk over the curl of his forearm. Then her eyes opened, gleaming like wet slate. Dalton stared down into them, reading the pain and hope, seeing the tears tracking her cheeks. And he was lost. He bent so that his mouth brushed hers. Her lips quivered beneath that gentle touch, and a sob snagged in her throat. He said her name, the sound of it a throb of longing.

"No," she moaned, turning her face away. "Don't do this, Dalton. Please." But at the same time her palms were pushing at his chest, her fingers were clutching his shirt, the conflicting gestures a mirror of her emotions. Because she knew her will was melting as fast as grease on a hot axle, she grabbed for a desperate defense.

"Did the Jamisons send you to try again?"

Hurt pulsed in her tone. He felt it clear to his soul. He stroked her hair, trying to tame the shudders that claimed her body even as she tried not to weep. He pulled her closer so that she was tucked up under his chin, so he could kiss her brow, her temple, burying his mouth in the softness of her hair.

"You know better than that, Jude," he chastened tenderly.

And she believed him. She did know better. She'd known in his hotel room that he hadn't been using her as part of his duty to Jamison. But it had been easier to believe the worst of him than to think a man like Dalton MacKenzie, a man who could have any woman he wanted, could actually care for, let alone desire, a woman like her. She'd forced herself to doubt him because she doubted herself and her own ability to make a man love her. She'd pushed the question of trust between them because she was afraid—no, she was terrified!—that what they'd experienced together was genuine magic. Loving a man like Dalton was dangerous business. Having him return even a portion of that feeling proposed a host of unknowns she would have to answer, and she'd run rather than face them. Just as she wanted to run now, except he wouldn't let her.

His hands were no longer still. They prowled the slope of her spine, wrapping around the curve of her torso, fitting to the flare of her hips. Her body arched against him, a traitor to her resolve. They were pressed together as snugly as a sheet on a bed. Though he was still giving her slow caresses, where he pushed against her belly, he was rock hard and beating with a wild, explosive need. A need she shared as uncontrollably.

"We can't," she argued faintly. "Joseph— Sammy—"

"Step out with me, Jude," he coaxed, sultry as a summer eve. But unlike his heated tone, the night was cool and Jude stepped back, aware of her

inappropriate dress. Without a word Dalton
stripped out of his bulky coat, wrapping it about
her. The weight of it pulled upon shoulders that
supported so much without complaint, but the
fleecy lining cuddled up to her like a baby's bunt-
ing, still warm from the heat of his body, still full of
his scent. Jude inhaled deeply, reveling in both.

"Walk with me, Jude," he urged again. "Hear me
out. Then, if you want me to go, I will."

She never made a conscious decision. He took a
step back and she one forward in an unwillingness
to separate from him. When he began a slow stroll
across the moon-drenched yard, she fell in beside
him, feeling safe inside the cocoon of his coat, while
the chaotic state of her emotions was anything but.
He'd come here to see her, after all her harsh words,
after all that stood between them. He'd kissed her
the way she'd always imagined a man in love would
kiss a woman. Was he a man in love? With her? The
improbability of it was a long-felt ache in a well of
emptiness. The possibility was there too, a rope
dangling down into that hollow depth, offering the
means to climb out. But the rope was frayed and the
climb dangerous, and she didn't know if it would
support her weight. Would she be a fool to trust it?

Would she be a worse fool if she didn't try?

"You asked about my family," Dalton began
suddenly. He didn't stop walking nor did he look
down at her to see if he had her attention. He knew
he did. "I don't know who fathered me. My mama
was a singer who had great dreams of being on the
stage. She was beautiful and had an angel's voice, if
you can take the word of a little boy who was crazy
about her." A small poignant smile shaped his lips
in an expression of rarely displayed and almost

forgotten fondness. "It was a hard life for us, a lot of saloons and cheap rooms, a lot of moving around so she could find work. A lot of different men."

He said that casually, but Jude felt an almost imperceptible tension in him, as if old wounds festered beneath a hastily healed surface. Her tender heart broke for the pain of the boy he'd been, forced to accept such things about his mother.

"An acting troupe passed through one of the little towns we were in. Their manager heard Mama sing and did his best to talk her into joining up with them. His persuasion settled in under her sheets and he became her lover. She fancied him and convinced herself that, in time, he'd do right by us and marry her. I never heard him mention it though. He and I had no great feeling for each other—no, that's not true. We had a lot of feelings, mostly jealousy. He didn't like the way I took up so much of her time, so when the time came for the troupe to move on, he asked Mama again to go with them. The only catch was, there wasn't room for me."

His memory still burned with the picture of her bending down at his bedside, begging him to understand her choice. This was their chance, she told him. This was her opportunity to make it big, to be somebody. She was going to be sought after for her voice, with money showering down upon her. And her lover was going to make an honest woman of her. She was going to get a proper surname for him, and a real house where they could be a family. They already were a family, he'd argued angrily through the tears, but his pleas had no affect. His last image of her was through the iron gate of the orphanage. They'd had to shut it to keep him from racing after her. She was wearing white, like an angel, and her eyes held such sadness when she turned to promise she'd send for him . . . soon.

"I got a picture postcard from her. She'd sent it from San Francisco. That was the only time I ever heard from her. I waited. I waited years for her to keep her promise. I waited in that horrible place, watching the other children being adopted by good homes. But I waited because I had a mama who was going to send for me. She sent money for my keep for a month or two, then that stopped too. The good sisters told me something terrible must have happened to her, perhaps she'd even died. The not-so-good sisters said she'd made a good life for herself and had forgotten all about me. After a while it didn't matter which it was. All I knew was that she never kept that promise and I never forgave her for it."

He stopped his aimless walk and simply stared off into the darkness. His features were immobile. The blue of his eyes glittered like moonlight on a cold mountain stream. Though he was remote and forbidding in both mood and stance, Jude couldn't help reacting to his wordless grief. He flinched slightly at the feel of her palm, warming where it rested on his lower back, but he wouldn't look at her.

"She would have sent for you if she could have," Jude intuited. He answered her with a soft snort.

"I spent a lot of years trying to believe that. I don't anymore."

"Is that why you want to go to San Francisco? To find her?"

"No," he protested a little too quickly for complete honesty. "I want to go to find out what was so special there that she wouldn't come back for me."

The sadness of it struck a deep personal chord in

Jude. A boy's lonely quest carried on by an angry, unforgiving man who'd guarded his heart against all others who might fail him. She wanted to hold him, to stroke his troubled brow the way she did Sammy's, to vow to him that she wouldn't be like his faithless mother, that she would always be there for him. But she dared not, not at this fragile moment of confidence—his first, she was positive.

"You mustn't hate her for things she couldn't control." Her tone was tender. If he could soften his heart to the woman who'd betrayed him, perhaps there was hope for her as well.

But Dalton MacKenzie had steeped in the poisons of bitterness for more than half a lifetime, and absolution, for his mother or for himself, wasn't going to come quickly or easily. He gave a wry chuckle.

"No, I guess I shouldn't hate her. She taught me a valuable lesson in life. She taught me the importance of standing behind a promise once made. I've lived by that simple rule because I couldn't stomach the thought of doing to another what was done to me." He glanced at her then, his gaze a turbulent sea of sorrow and rage. "But then, you know about honor, don't you? That's why you're here, hanging onto this land you don't want, trying to satisfy a dream that's not yours. Are we fools, Jude, me running from responsibility, you hiding behind yours? Have those we loved made a cruel joke of our devotion?"

Surprisingly, she laughed too. It was better to laugh than to bemoan what he said as truth. "I've often wondered that myself."

And somehow their hands got tangled together for a comforting squeeze, and a heartbeat later their tongues were tangling for a taste of consoling passion. Quickly, the moment heated out of control, dry tinder touched by greedy flame. In that urgent rush of breaths and moans of capitulation, all the frustration, all the pain and pride of past sins were forgotten.

He caught great hanks of her hair as the moment escalated beyond the need for gentleness, and held her head still for his plunging, slanting plunder of her mouth. She heard a raw, plaintive sound and was shocked to realize it had come from her. Desire for him, hot and still unfamiliar, rose up in her, swelling painfully. She moved against him, seeking surcease for those intimate aches. Finally she could stand it no more.

"Love me, Dalton," she moaned into his wild kisses.

He paused, almost telling her that he did.

Instead he looked about them, at the house and its impossibility. "Where?" His voice was packed with impatience.

Wordlessly she took one big hand in hers and guided him toward the stable. The well-maintained door opened without a sound, and pungent scents of hay and warm animals enveloped them. She stepped inside, releasing him for only as long as it took to light a single lantern. Then she looked up at him, her gaze wide and vulnerable. And hungry. He smiled, encouraging that last part.

Boldly, Jude reached up for his Stetson, giving it a toss toward a bundle of loose straw. She ran her fingers through his hair. He wore it short and neat, regardless of the current style. She noticed it was thinning slightly and wondered how his vanity would take to the weathering of age. She wanted to discover that for herself at his side. She wanted to grow old with him. She didn't want to miss another moment of his life.

He stood still and a bit bemused while she charted his features with a gliding touch. She rubbed his temples, then stroked along the slash of his brows, now thickening with new growth. The burns were but pale memories blending in with the untanned creases about his eyes. She lingered down the lean plains of evening stubble to the squaring of his jaw. Her thumbs traced his smile.

"Anything you like?"

"Everything I see" was her husky reply.

"Not all of it's good," he warned, punctuating that with sucking kisses to her palms.

"I'm not afraid to take the bad with the good, Dalton. You should know that by now."

His eyes darkened with unspoken pleasure, promising her paradise in return.

She wasted no time. Stripping off his heavy coat, she spread it over the clean bed of straw. He was there, undressing her even as she turned back to him. Her plain wool wrapper pooled to the floor, followed by her unadorned gown. And he kissed her like a starving man while his hands roamed desperately over her body. She moaned, loving his touch, his kiss. Loving him.

Her hands hurried over his buttons and fastenings, tugging, pushing, wrestling aside anything that came between the hot excitement of flesh on flesh. She molded to him, absorbing his heat, glorying in the hard power of his frame, so beautifully muscled and now tense with anticipation. His manhood was thick, proud, and eager, and she throbbed wetly in ready welcome.

He bore her down to the cushioning sheepskin of his coat's lining. His mouth came down hard on her lips, grinding, probing, then fixed upon her nipple,

where his intense suction pulled white-hot spears of
longing through her yearning body. She clutched at
his broad back, digging in with her nails, knowing
with a thrilling certainty that he wanted her as
much as she did him. That he'd missed her, as she'd
missed him.

There was no time for finesse or careful courting.
Jude didn't need it . . . didn't want it. She was alive
in every sense, thrumming with expectation. She
was ready when he parted her with his knees, was
already straining upward to catch his first enjoining
thrust. And it was a frantic, all-consuming reunion.
Fast, too fast. Dalton slowed their pace, wanting to
savor the sensations, the woman. He trembled with
the effort of restraint, but Jude's soft moans of
pleasure were a reward not to be missed.

"I'm sorry about Cheyenne," he told her, his
words interspersed with kisses, rough with the
struggle for control. "It wasn't supposed to be like
that—end like that. It wasn't meant to be business
between you and me."

"Don't tell me. Show me."

How could she fail to believe him when he was
demonstrating it so beautifully? And as Jude thrilled
to his masterful possession, she vowed to make him
believe as well, with each returned kiss, with each
accepting bow of her body, that he could put the
past behind him. That he could believe in love
again. Her love. She wanted to make him believe
that he could find something special here, with her,
in her arms as they enfolded him, within her heart
as it beat a quickening tattoo against his breast. She
wanted to promise that she would never desert him,
never hurt him, but desire flared, engulfing thought,
drowning all in a tidal pool of passion. The assur-

ances went unspoken, their claim expressed instead in an all-satisfying flood as the lovers took their simultaneous release in an explosive instant.

They lay entwined, drained, dazed, and deliriously pleased with themselves and each other. And for a time the outside world consisted of only their immediate surroundings: the soft shuffle of hooves in the hay, an occasional nicker. With the gradual slowing of their thundering pulses and lull of their breathing into lazy sighs, contentment seeped into two separate and needy souls, making them one.

Eventually the tickle of straw beneath Jude's calf made her shift reluctantly, and Dalton moved to one side, braced up on his elbow. He was looking at her. In the lantern light his eyes gleamed all liquid silver. She lay still beneath his scrutiny, not trying to hide herself, not minding because there was something almost worshipful in his stare. When she said nothing, he stroked her, a possessive sweep running from placid breast to slightly bent knee and back. By then a pert nub appeared to delay his attention. Heat gathered along her skin, shimmering, pooling to the points where they touched: at the ankles, where her thigh rested atop his, where his hip bumped hers, where one breast was flattened beneath hard chest and where his clever fingers teased a helpless response.

"Oh, Dalton, I could lie here with you forever," Jude confessed breathily.

"Could you?"

She glanced up at him because his question was deceivingly flat. Tension provided a network of angles to his face—sharp, intriguing, and puzzling—considering their mood of moment's ago.

"Yes."

Her candid reply woke a flicker of disbelief in his pale, impassive eyes. "You'd be happy with a gunman? With an ill wind?" She had the good grace to wince at the return thrust of her own words.

"I'm afraid of what you do, Dalton, and I'm afraid for you." She hesitated a moment, then stroked his face, the tenderness of that gesture turning his heart over within his chest. He caught her hand and kissed it hard, impressing his passion upon it as he was trying to impress his reasonings upon her.

"I've told you how it is for me."

"And you told me you were thinking of retiring. Why not now?" She garnered her courage to add, "Why not with me?"

He was motionless for a long moment and Jude waited, nervously, unsure of his reaction to her last question. Had she pushed too far behind the boundaries he'd placed around his heart? She knew he cared for her and for her family. She just didn't know where on his list of priorities such emotion lay.

"We have to talk, Jude."

There was something ominous in the way that was said. She swallowed hard and began to tense for the word "good-bye," vowing not to cry when it came, as she'd always known it would.

"I know I said I wouldn't talk business, but there's no way around it now."

"Business?" She blinked, confused. This wasn't about them and their future or lack thereof?

"Kathleen Jamison has hired herself another gunfighter. Latigo Jones. Remember him?"

"But—I don't understand."

"He's in it for the money, Jude, and that's an advantage the Jamisons have over the rest of you. The old man's down in bed, and his daughter is running the show. She's a bad one, Jude, and Jones is working for her. I know this man, Jude. He's good and he's thorough. If Miss Jamison wants you out of this valley, he won't stop until you're gone. Or dead."

She paled dramatically. "And you're going to ride with him?" No matter how hard she tried, she couldn't make that sound like less than an accusation.

"I'm hoping I can keep him from any real bloodshed. We go back a long way. Maybe he'll listen to me."

"But if Miss Jamison says kill us all?"

Dalton's jaw flexed. He didn't have to answer.

"Oh, my God," she whispered despairingly. He gathered her up close when her tremors became apparent.

Dalton pressed a hard kiss to her hair and hugged her crushingly. His voice was raw with feeling. "Jude, I want you to take Sammy and Joseph to Cheyenne. I want you to stay there until I join you. Once I'm finished here, we can start over anywhere you like. Don't worry about the money. I've got plenty of that. If you don't want to sell to Jamison, you can wait for a better offer, maybe from the railroad. I heard they might be running a spur up to Deadwood. Your land could double, even triple in value. Whatever you want, Jude. Just, please, get out now."

Jude heard him out, but her thoughts caught on one word out of all of them. *We.* "You'd stay with us?"

His taut expression didn't alter. "Forever. Isn't that what you said?"

"Forever." Her mind was so dazzled, the consequences of the rest of his speech didn't sink in.

Dalton MacKenzie was going to be part of her family. Hers to love and with whom to grow old. Forever. It seemed like a dream. She couldn't help but question it. "Are you sure that's what you want? Sammy and Joseph? And me?"

"That's all I've ever wanted, Jude. You're all I've ever wanted."

A feverish flush came over her, followed by a bout of lightheadedness. Her heart was beating madly, which didn't help matters much. She'd longed to hear a man tell her such things; she'd prayed to hear *this* man say them. And now it was almost too much to comprehend. A future with Dalton. A strong male figure for Sammy to emulate. A younger warrior for Joseph to school in wisdom. A lover to share her heart and her bed for the rest of her days. It was perfect, all of it.

Except he hadn't said the one thing she needed to hear.

He hadn't said why.

He hadn't told her he loved her.

That got her mind working again, mulling over the remainder of his words. And her joy froze in her veins.

"'Finished here'?" she echoed in a tight little voice. "Killing my friends, you mean? Is that the 'finished' you're talking about?"

"Jude—"

She sat up, shivering in the wrap of her own arms. When he rose and tried to hold her again, she jerked away. "No!" Then she turned a desperate gaze upon him. "We'll leave now. We can be packed and gone by daybreak." She gave him no chance to express his relief before delivering the rest of it. "But you go with us, Dalton. We'll go if you ride out now."

Dalton balked. "I can't."

"Can't or won't?"

"It doesn't matter. I told you how things are with me. This is a job I've taken on, and I'll see it through. I've a debt to pay to Jamison. I'm honor bound—"

"This isn't about honor! What you're doing is wrong. You're hurting innocent people. And wrong is wrong no matter how you wrap it up in pretty words like 'honor.'"

His jaw firmed into granite, his eyes to steel.

"Dalton, please. You wanted a fresh start, a home, a family. Leave with us and you can have all those things. Please!" She watched him, studying his eyes for any telltale sign of weakening. When none appeared, she grew more alarmed. And she tried to force him with a shaky ultimatum. "If you don't go with us now, don't come back here at all."

"You don't mean that."

"Don't come to me with the blood of my neighbors on your hands."

"Then just go, yourselves. Forget about me. Just go and keep yourselves safe." He met her gaze and read the undisguised hurt, the bitterness and the fear, and he knew her answer before she spoke it sadly.

"No. This valley is the only home I've ever known. I won't leave it. I have responsibilities . . ." She trailed off helplessly.

A deep, desperate panic touched off inside him. His first crazy thought was to snatch her up, obliging or not, and tote her to Cheyenne, hog-tied if he had to. Couldn't she see that he was half mad with worry over her and her loved ones? Didn't she understand that he no longer felt uninvolved with the fate of the others? He'd save them all if he could, but he wasn't in the rescue business. His profession was ruin. And he'd never been ashamed of that until this very minute.

She was asking too much and she knew it. And he resented the hell out of it.

"I came clean with you about my reasons. Isn't it time you admitted your own?"

"I—I don't understand."

"That's the sad thing, Jude. You truly don't. You don't realize that the only thing holding you here is your own fear. What are you afraid of? Living? Or do you feel the only way folks will care about you is if you play the martyr for them all? Those who love you won't stop just because you take a stand for yourself and what you want. You can't be perfect, Jude. No one is."

Hurt and shocked by his words, she countered, "You don't need to tell me how imperfect I am. I'm well aware of all my faults."

"Then stop hiding behind them, damn it! Is it that hard for you to believe that I care?"

"Yes!" The cry tore from her in humiliation and shame.

And it was that shame and his own fearful aggravation that made him hide behind a veil of angry pride as he got to his feet and shrugged into his clothes.

"Fine, then. Keep your sainthood for all the good it does you. Wallow in your loneliness, feeling sorry for yourself. The only one who pities you, Jude, is you."

Jude watched him, unmoving, until he'd put on all but his coat. She didn't dare try to respond in her own behalf, not with the turmoil raging inside her. Then she stood, proud and straight, to don her nightclothes before bending to lift up the warm sheepskin with its dusting of hay. She extended it to him, not saying anything, the stiff gesture saying everything. He took it, equally silent, equally dismayed, but unable to bend his path to hers.

Perhaps that was the way it was meant to be.

"Jude—"

"Just go," she told him flatly, fighting against the wetness welling up in her eyes. She wanted him gone before she gave way to tears.

But he couldn't just leave her. She didn't struggle against his sudden strong embrace. She didn't resist his kiss; in fact, she returned it voraciously, with an unquenchable thirst for the taste of him. Her fingers tore at his hair while devouring his mouth.

Then, with the same fervor, she shoved away from him and started across the yard toward the darkened house. He watched her for a moment, loving the fierce determination of her stride even as he cursed her stubbornness. He blew out the lamp, then went to his horse, wheeling it about with a rough jerk so that he was heading away before he saw her gain the steps to the house.

He never saw the way she collapsed against the porch post, her body shuddering with silent anguish as she listened to the sound of hoofbeats carrying him and all hope away.

A sudden soft voice intruded upon her pain.

"You let him ride away. I must be getting old. I thought you wanted him to stay as much as he wants to remain."

Jude glanced up to see Joseph's image glimmering through the sheen of her tears. "Men like that don't stay around when you need them," she cried out bitterly, "not unless the money's good."

"What good is that kind of man?" He seemed to agree.

"No good," she sniffed, hauling herself upright in an attempt to reclaim her self-respect.

"Who wants a man who thinks more of his work than his woman?" Again the casual question echoed the angry wails of her heart. "Better that he's gone."

She nodded, trying to convince herself that was true. Joseph nodded too, appearing to support her decision. "A gunfighter. No good for me, just like you said."

"A man who kills for pleasure. A man without honor."

"No," Jude argued, coming to his defense without thought. "That's not true. Dalton isn't like that. He is honorable. It's that pride that keeps him from walking away from what he knows is wrong."

"Unreasonable pride," Joseph provoked.

"He has a reason. He has a reason." And her voice faltered as she heard herself speaking his case so vehemently. Looking at things through his point of view changed her attitude considerably. If not for that sense of unswerving honor, Dalton would be just like his friend Jones, and she wouldn't be weeping over him now. She slumped down onto the top step, wrapping her arms about tented knees.

"Oh, Joseph, I asked him to toss aside everything that's given his life meaning. He said awful things about me and—and I think he was right to say them. I insisted he make a choice, then drove him away when it wasn't the one I wanted. I was angry because he wouldn't walk away from his word once given, but am I any better, claiming this piece of land is worth more than the man I love?" She looked up at the old man to claim staunchly, "Yes, I do love him," as if she needed to defend herself. Joseph only nodded, his gaze knowing and steeped in sadness.

"My people valued the land above their lives. And now they are no more. But they died with their honor."

Jude wiped her eyes on her robe and mourned. "He asked me to leave, to take you and Sammy to safety, but I wouldn't go. I don't want to die here, Joseph. He was everything I wanted and I let him go. What am I going to do? I'm never going to see him again. He's never going to come back."

Joseph didn't answer. He was an old man, a wise man. He'd seen young people in love do hurtful things to one another, do desperate things to deny their hearts. He'd done many of them himself for the love of a woman not meant to be his own. He knew about that kind of heartache. And he understood more about Dalton than Jude ever would if she thought she'd never see him again.

About that, she was terribly wrong.

Chapter 23

❦

The hardest thing Jude had ever had to do was get up the next morning without arriving at any solutions.

She'd tossed and turned away the remainder of the night, trying to think clearly about the future while the scent of Dalton clung to her skin, a constant torment to her senses. His claims echoed, both cruelly and kindly. She could find no way to resolve this conflict. She wanted Dalton and all he offered, but she couldn't take it when the price was the lives of her friends. Dalton was right. The land, the station, they had never been her dream. If not for loyalty to her father, she would have sold them in a second. But if she sold now, it would be an abandonment of her neighbors. She would be breaking the strength of their stance for her own sake. She'd acted for the good of others all her life. It was a hard habit to break. And see what it got her: a lonely life she didn't like in a place she didn't want to be, risking everything for a cause she didn't support. Sacrificing the man she loved for someone else's principles.

She was a fool, but she'd have her honor to cling to.

She was no different than Dalton, caught in the snare of pride.

And he was right as well about her fear. How much easier it was to act for others than to make a decision in her own behalf.

Would it be so bad to think of herself and the needs of her family just once? She wasn't responsible for the situation in the valley. She wasn't her neighbors' guardian. They had the same choice to make as she did. Was she supposed to feel guilty if they chose to stay and die and she to live? Only what kind of life could she have, knowing it was built upon their blood? And how could she be happy with Dalton, knowing he was the one to shed it?

As she dressed, Jude wondered why none of her choices were ever easy. And when she climbed down the ladder from the loft to the buttery smell of Joseph's baking and the rich scent of oil and leather from the harness Sammy was repairing, she wondered how everything could be so familiar and unchanged when all, in truth, was now different. Biscuit lifted a shaggy head and thumped his tail to announce her to the two men.

"Morning, Jude," Sammy called cheerily. "I just about got this belly strap mended. Now it won't be a-chafing General Sheridan no more." He held up his handiwork for his sister to admire, but she never gave it a glance as she came up to put her arms around him. He hugged her back for a confused minute, then began to squirm in her tight embrace. "Yer squishing my innards, Jude," he complained uncomfortably.

"I'm sorry." She leaned back and brushed the dampness from her cheeks before he could see it and ask a host of awkward questions. Pasting on a smile, she laid a paper-wrapped parcel in his lap. "Here. This is for you."

His eyes grew round with anticipation. "For me? Is it my birthday?"

Her hand rumpled through the tousled locks. "No. It's a gift from Dal—from Mr. MacKenzie. He gave it to me when I saw him in Cheyenne. I forgot about it until now."

Sammy frowned and looked from the package up to her impassive features. "I thought you was mad at Mac."

Her smile grew wry at his innocent intuition. "No, I'm not mad at him. We have a difference of opinion about things is all. That doesn't mean I'm mad at him."

Sammy beamed. "Good." The subject was closed to his thinking, and he returned to the gift eagerly. "Can I open it now or do I have to wait for a special day?"

"This is a special day," she told him through a sudden thickening in her throat. "Open it now."

The brown paper was quickly shredded, and Sammy sat back with a wordless sound of awed amazement. From the wrapping he lifted a pair of gauntlet-style buckskin gloves. Heavy fringe danced from the wrists as Sammy turned them over and over in his hands. They were the same type of gloves worn by the drivers on the stage line.

"Oh, my" was all he could think of to say, but his eyes brightened with joyful emotion.

"Try them on," Jude urged gently, sharing a smile with Joseph who'd come to admire the gift.

Sammy tugged on the stiff gauntlets, flexing his fingers and turning his hands to marvel at the swinging fringe. "Oh, my," he whispered again.

Jude had to look away or risk breaking down

altogether under the pressure of tenderness swelling within her breast.

"How do they feel?" Joseph was asking.

Sammy grinned up at him. "They feel just grand. I can't wait to tell Mac how much I like 'em. When do you think he'll come by again, Jude? Jude?"

Her shoulders trembled, then firmed and her head came up to its usual chin-high position. "I don't know, Sammy. I don't know if he'll be back at all."

The joy drained from the young man's face. "What do you mean, he won't be back?"

Before she could come up with an appropriate answer, a tremendous ruckus rose from the yard, the sound of mounted men and frightened horses. Uttering a dire oath to cover her own fear, Jude grabbed up the ancient rifle and headed for the door.

It would seem Dalton had returned sooner than she'd anticipated.

Dalton MacKenzie was deep into a bottle of Patrick Jamison's bourbon. He'd poured his first glass upon his return from Jude Amos's arms. That had been hours ago, when shadows hung heavily across the elegant parlor room, shrouding its corners the same way they did the niches within his soul. He hadn't lit a lamp, preferring the impersonal blackness as an echo of his mood. He'd closed the door so he wouldn't be disturbed in his brooding, unwilling to share such personal reflections with a mocking Latigo or a cruel-tempered Kathleen. Glass followed glass as he sipped slowly, not really savoring the smoothness and glowing heat of the liquor. The movements were mechanical, his intention not to enjoy the finer things Jamison offered, but to block all from his mind as darkness gave way to dawn.

He didn't want to think. He wanted a cushion of numbness to separate him from the visions flashing through his mind—some from the grim past, some a sure intuition of what was to come. He could close his eyes and still see the brightness of flames as the Barrets' house went up in a pyre of one man's greed. True, he hadn't had a hand in that, but was he any less guilty than those who had tossed the first torch? Guilt by association. Jude was right to damn him with her accusations because he was no innocent. He had the blood money to prove it. Money that could yet buy him his dreams but no longer his desires.

He took another sip as daylight penetrated the lacy draperies. He could hear the ranch stirring to life but felt no spark of it within himself.

The situation in the valley was grim. Dalton knew the farmers wouldn't survive it no matter how brave a fight they staged. Death was coming on the first round discharged, and once it started, there would be no stopping it until all were dead, buried under the cinders of the homes they'd hoped to hold. It couldn't go down any other way, not with Kathleen Jamison taking over in her father's stead. There was nothing he could do to halt the inevitable.

It was the final picture that taunted his imagination, of Jude with all burned down around her, her proud spirit broken in a battle she'd never had a chance of winning. He was still tortured by the desperate hope he'd seen in her eyes when she'd asked him to come away with them. As she looked to him for a sign that he cared, for something—anything. But he'd turned her down cold. He couldn't absolve himself by saying he'd tried to save her. He hadn't sought compromise; he'd demanded she give in. Those actions weren't honorable. They'd cost him nothing and committed him to less. And she'd called him on them, seeing them for the shallow gesture they were. He'd ridden away then, as always. Except this time he'd done the unforgivable. He'd left ties to pull him back.

Honor, he'd claimed so righteously. Where was the honor in destroying a home, in frightening a family out of their dreams? In slaughtering innocents like sheep? What right had he to steal those things he'd longed for all his life? For money? For pride? Because of a debt owed in repayment for his life? What kind of life could he have if things went down as they were bound to? What would it be worth?

Without Jude.

He listened to the cadence of hoofbeats as the early shift of range hands went about their business. Tiring, thankless work for little enough wage, but at least it was honest pay. Could he say the same of his?

He was about to take another drink when a sudden fierce anger took flame inside him: at Jude for her stubbornness which forced things to this avoidable point, at Latigo and his men for their eagerness to go about their remorseless work, at Jamison for his greed, and at the ranchers for their stupidity. And mostly at himself for his cowardice in not standing by Jude when she'd asked him. He was no better than the pack of dumb, dangerous beasts controlled by Kathleen's fervor. In fact he was worse because he did know better. He did know that what they were doing was wrong. And there was no honor in it.

Dalton cursed and shoved his glass aside, finding no answers, no solace there.

"Mr. MacKenzie? I see you're enjoying my best whiskey."

Dalton glanced up to greet his employer with a wry twist of a smile. "The best money can buy. Just like me."

Jamison advanced into the room slowly. His color was bad, his balance a bit precarious as he limped across the carpet with the aid of a gold-headed cane. But even worse for wear, he was impeccably garbed and groomed, proof positive that a man of means could rise above all things. Even murder.

The rancher gestured to the nearly empty bottle. "Pour yourself another. It's a taste you'll not likely find in any saloon. You look to be a man of taste, Mr. MacKenzie."

Dalton's smile crooked even more. "Funny thing about good taste, Jamison. Any man can learn to affect it, but not all of them can really appreciate it."

Jamison frowned slightly, not sure if he was being insulted by his hired gun. He thought better than to take issue as he moved to the sideboard. He took in the quantity of liquor that had been consumed and the still steady appearance of his employee, wondering which told the truer story.

"Don't you have things to do, Mr. MacKenzie?"

Dalton stared up at him for a long, silent moment, his scrutiny unblinking in its intensity. Jamison fidgeted under the unwavering study. Finally Dalton heaved himself up out of the chair to remark with a deceptive quiet, "Yes, sir, I believe I do. Something I should have taken care of a while back."

"And what's that?"

"I've got your banknotes up in my room. I'll be returning them to you after I pack up my things."

Jamison blinked, cocking his head in confusion as if doubting it was Dalton and not the liquor talking. "What?"

"You don't need me to win this war of yours. You'll have your victory written in blood, but I won't be signing my name to it. I've seen enough blood spilt, mine and a whole host of innocent others'. You might say I've lost the taste for it."

And while Jamison gaped in disbelief, Dalton headed toward the door, turning his back on all the things that blood money could buy. Because he'd just discovered it couldn't purchase him anything of value.

"Now you just hold on a minute!" That exploded from Jamison when the impact of Dalton's decision struck him. "You can't just walk out in the middle of this."

Dalton paused to stare back at him. "Why?"

"B-because you took my money and I took your word."

"Just paper and so much talk. Nothing that matters."

A dull crimson fury began creeping up in the pasty cheeks as Jamison blustered, "You owe me, MacKenzie! I snatched your neck out of a noose!"

"In case I forgot to say so, thank you. But I didn't ask you to. I didn't sell off any part of myself when you bought my way off those gallows. Besides, if it weren't for Jude Amos, I would have been back to swinging on your behalf." While Jamison's brow puckered at that, Dalton continued in the same tightly clipped tone. "You don't own me, Jamison. I'm not like that fine bourbon or those pure-bred cows, and it's pretty damned arrogant of you to think I am. Or that any man is. And that's why the people in this valley will fight you to the last drop of their blood. You don't own them and you don't own their land, and that annoys you something fierce, doesn't it?"

Jamison had gone all tense and puffing with indignation. "Who do you think you are to talk to *me* like that?"

"I'm just as good a man as you are, Jamison. I guess I just figured that out. Our accounts are settled here. In fact, I owe you a little something for breaking the terms of our agreement." Dalton reached into his coat pocket and drew out a coin. He gave it a flip. Jamison caught it in his good hand then studied the well-worn five-dollar gold piece.

"What's this for?"

"The price of my soul," Dalton told him. "I just bought it back."

The rancher looked from the coin to the stoic face of the gunman. His gaze narrowed. "Go on, then. Get. I don't need your kind to get what I want."

"No, you don't. Not when your daughter can get it for you by burning the roofs over your neighbors' heads. But I guess that won't keep your kind from sleeping nights." He settled his Stetson on his head and gave the brim a mocking tip. "A pleasure, Mr. Jamison."

"Wait. MacKenzie! What do you mean? I'm not burning them out."

"No? Tell that to the Barrets while they sift through the ashes of their house to find that fine silver tea service you gave them for a wedding gift. But I don't think it'll be worth enough to buy off your guilt."

The rancher went very still. "I didn't order that done."

"Your daughter did, after she conveniently arranged for you to be out of her way."

"It was them, those squatters," Jamison argued. "They took a shot at me . . ."

"Are you sure? Did you see who was behind the trigger? Or who arranged for it to be pulled? Your little girl was real quick to step into your shoes. One would almost suspect that she's been waiting to try them on for size for some time now."

"What the hell are you suggesting? That my daughter—that Kathleen—" He broke off, terrible emotions working his features.

"I'm not suggesting anything, Jamison. Just want you to consider if the shoe fits . . ." He smiled, thinly and coldly. "But then maybe you don't want to consider it. Give her a couple of days to run your men and you won't have to wonder anymore. All your neighbors will be dead, so it won't much matter if it was one of them, will it?" He gave a soft snort of disdain. "A respectable man? Mister, you don't know what the word means."

As Dalton turned toward the stairs, a winded Ned Farrel burst through the front door.

"Mr. MacKenzie," he wheezed in breathless agitation. He spared a quick glance at his employer, then looked back to the gunman. "I watched 'em, jus' like you tole me, and I listened good. There's gonna be trouble out at Amos Station. I just heard 'em talking about how they were gonna set her place a-fire."

"Who?" That was demanded by Patrick Jamison as he hobbled to the door. "Who ordered it done?"

Ned swallowed hard but his words were clear. "Miss Kathleen. She and that Jones feller rode out with a dozen or so of the men. They all had guns,

Mr. Jamison. I don't think they were going to just light a few fires, if you know what I mean."

Dalton did.

They were on their way to destroy the one obstacle they hadn't been able to go around.

That obstacle was Jude.

Chapter 24

～◯C◯～

The yard was full of galloping cowboys, whooping as if it were Saturday night in town as they flung their lassos over corral posts and began to drag down the fences. Others trampled through the neat rows of Bart Amos's big garden, tearing up the tender shoots of what was to be their winter stores. While Jude watched in helpless horror, one of the men tied a hay bale behind his horse and towed it, ablaze, through the open barn, touching off the bedding in each empty stall. Thankfully, Sammy had already released the stock into the corral where they milled about, eyes white-rimmed in terror.

She stood on the porch watching, one woman with an old gun, no defense against so many, so well armed.

And on the outskirts of this willful destruction sat a pair of stony killers, stoically observing the carnage. One of them was Latigo Jones, doing what he was paid for. The other was Kathleen Jamison, there to enjoy the fruits of their labor.

Barking furiously, not one to consider the odds, Biscuit hurtled off the porch into the midst of the

326

riders, snapping at heels and growling ferociously in defense of his property. Until one of the cowboys swung his rifle butt, catching the old dog in the ribs and tumbling him head over heels with a yelp.

"No!" Jude raced out, mindless of her own position of danger to scoop up the winded animal and bear him back to the protection of the porch. She crouched down on the front steps, hugging the shivering dog to her. He was quick to recover and wriggled wildly in her arms, snarling and yapping at the intruders. Jude feared to release him lest he be trampled or shot by the marauders. She ducked down over the dog's hackled back as glass exploded behind her, feeling Biscuit's frantic heartbeats pounding next to her own as they shared the same sense of panic. Then more windows shattered as bullets and potatoes from their garden went through them until not a pane remained whole.

When Jude dared look up over the old dog's quivering head, her mind was dazed by the ruin they'd managed to reap in such a short time. The barn was burning, their storehouse had been smashed, and its provisions were scattered. Bits of sliced-up harness littered the yard. She glared through the skew of withheld tears to where Kathleen and her hired gunman sat and damned them for directing such devastation. Dalton wasn't with them. She was both surprised and relieved. And bitter that he'd chosen to sit out this particular visit. Perhaps he thought she could forgive him in his absence. She didn't know that she ever could, not when the mill of marauders' horses trampled across her father's grave, knocking its headstone facedown in the lovingly tended soil.

Rapid movement closing in on her tore Jude's gaze from the desecration of her father's resting place. Her head flew up in alarm as one of the riders headed right toward her, torch in hand, intending to force his mount up onto the porch where he could fling the blazing brand into the house.

Clutching Biscuit to her, she cried out and tried to struggle to her feet just as Joseph leapt off the steps into the path of the charging animal, waving his arms wildly to frighten it off course. As the horse swerved, its shoulder caught the ancient man a hard glancing blow, knocking him down at Jude's feet. With one hand still curled around the dog's collar, she crouched down over the old Sioux warrior, holding him down when he struggled to rise in her defense.

"No, Joseph, don't. It's not worth it. Please!"

He quit fighting, his tired old eyes tearing at the sight of his second home going up in flames before a vicious conquering force.

"Sammy. Where's Sammy?" Jude's desperate gaze raced over the yard, searching through the chaos of horses and riders for her brother's familiar form.

He was at the corral, trying to catch the squealing horses as they bolted over the broken fence in a stampede toward freedom from the pistol fire. Jude watched in terror as the big animals swerved to avoid hitting him. Realizing he couldn't stop them, Sammy turned toward the cause of their panic, shocking Jude when he reached up to drag one of the pistoleers out of his saddle. Then he had the cowboy's revolver in his hand and began waving it in threatening arcs at the circling riders.

"Sammy, no!" Jude cried, but she was a world away from where time seemed suspended.

Out of the corner of her eye, she saw Monty, the malevolent foreman, reach downward in a slow, purposeful move. As she stared, her throat too clogged with horror to allow even the smallest sound of warning, she watched his blued gun clear leather. A slow, thin-lipped, sneering smile curved upon his face.

Without thinking, Jude surged up off the porch steps and started to run toward her brother. Through a glaze of frantic tears, she saw the mean-spirited foreman carefully level the barrel.

"Stop!" The scream tore from her, raw with fear and desperate pleading. But she knew, deep down in the quaking pit of her belly, even as she called for it, there would be no mercy, not from the gunman, not from the smirking Kathleen Jamison who watched the tragedy unfold through eyes ablaze with deadly pleasure. This was the answer to her prideful stance, a quick, violent death at the hands of soulless others. Over land, useless acres she had never wanted, never cared about. A meaningless sacrifice to one man's ambition. And she saw so clearly, as she raced with an impotent lack of speed toward an event she couldn't hope to halt, that Dalton had been right. It wasn't worth it. Not when the price was her brother's life.

Why hadn't she listened?

"Sammy!" His name ripped from a heart that would be irreparably broken the moment that fateful bullet struck home.

The sound of the shot was so loud, it peeled like vengeful thunder, rumbling in her ears, shaking to her anguished soul. And for a moment she squeezed her eyes shut, unwilling, unable to watch as her dear brother's life, his good, gentle life, was cruelly snatched away.

She'd come to a stop somewhere in the middle of the yard, an easy target for the next fatal round. But no other shots followed. As the sobs roiled up from the depths of her grief, Jude dared open her eyes, steeling herself for what she would see.

What she saw was Sammy, standing by the corral, fringes waving on his new buckskin gloves, a confused look in his eyes, the beginnings of a grin shaping his lips.

Confused herself, Jude turned toward Monty. The gun was still in his hand, not smoking, unfired, as he toppled with a strange boneless grace from out of his saddle, his expression of malice replaced by one of infinite surprise.

And that's when she followed the startled stares of his crew, who'd gone suddenly still. And she saw Dalton MacKenzie bearing down on them at a full gallop on his big horse, Stetson tipped down to cast his face in all-business shadows, one pistol dribbling powder smoke and the other held at ready.

"Hold your fire!" came his authoritative shout. "You boys leather those guns. There'll be no more killing here."

He reined in his lathered mount to stand between Sammy Amos and the hesitant cowboys, who were still shaken by the lightning-fast demise of their foreman and in dreadful awe of the man who'd called down that killing thunder. Dalton took full advantage of that caution by growling, "Put 'em down, or be planted beside your partner." And he thumbed back both hammers to punctuate his intentions.

The crew was made up of range hands, not gunmen. They were used to taking orders, to herding cows and mending fences. Murdering wasn't something they were used to, and the majority of them were grateful to be directed off the course of Kathleen Jamison's wrath. Most of them responded out of instinct to the command of a man's voice, not a woman's. So they began to holster their guns even as their boss's daughter railed at them.

"What are you men doing? Kill them! Kill them all!"

But the men continued to hesitate, intimidated by Dalton's guns, by his reputation. By the fact that he was the one their boss had hired to lead them. And with Monty lying dead on the ground, all the malicious fun had gone out of things. Where was the sport in shooting down a woman and her half-witted brother and an old man to boot? That was MacKenzie and Jones's stock in trade. So they were content to look at the two pistoleers to see who would make the first move.

"Mac, you're interfering in things," Latigo called out calmly. "Things'll get messy if you don't move on outta there."

From her vulnerable position in the center of the yard, Jude almost forgot to breathe as she watched the tense interplay between the two men. Then slowly, Dalton shook his head.

"Not here. Not now. It's over. She's the one who's done the interfering, and her daddy's on his way to set things straight."

Kathleen sucked in an anxious breath. "He's lying!" The strident quality of her voice undercut her credibility. "You work for me. All of you work for me!"

The men didn't move.

She turned her fury on Jones, exclaiming, "Shoot him! Kill him! You damned coward, do what you were paid to do!"

For the first time in his illustrious career, Latigo Jones, who considered himself to be above all personal entanglements, hesitated too. "Now, ma'am, I don't think that would be the best of ideas. I think we oughta wait till your daddy gets here."

"He's not in charge here. I am!"

Latigo stared unblinkingly into the face of her fury. "Miz Jamison, you ain't the one paying me, and what I'm getting ain't enough to do what you're asking. Men in my profession don't make friends, but that man's my friend. I'll square off against him in a fight if the job calls for it, but I'll be damned if I'll exchange lead when we're both on the same payroll."

Jude saw it coming a beat before the others. Perhaps it was because she was a woman and understood the passions of a woman's heart, no matter how darkened by ambition and hate. She knew in an instant that Kathleen wasn't going to let it go just like that. And Jude began to run toward Dalton, ready to put herself in the line of fire when Kathleen let loose her rage.

"Dalton, look out!"

The cry had no sooner escaped Jude's lips when Kathleen jerked her carbine free and leveled it with deadly intent.

However, Latigo was no stranger to the black twists of vengeance either. He caught her movement from the corner of his eye and was quick to knock the barrel heavenward with the upward thrust of his forearm. The shot roared harmlessly toward the heavens. The carbine was wrenched from her hands before she could recover, then rested easy across Latigo's thighs, pointed meaningfully in her direction.

"Ma'am, don't be deceived into thinking that I wouldn't bust cap on a woman if the need arose," he drawled most pleasantly, but the dark obsidian gleam of his eyes held no trace of any softening. He nodded beyond them. Patrick Jamison was approaching fast on horseback with his man Ned Farrel riding at his side. He lifted the carbine, touching the barrel sites to his hat brim in a mock salute.

"Stand down all you men," Jamison ordered as he rode into the path of any potential fire. "What the hell is going on here?"

Kathleen's near manic behavior vanished behind a sweet demeanor of concern. "Daddy. I'm sorry you were disturbed by all this. I didn't want you bothered." And she shot Ned a venomous glare.

" 'Disturbed'?" Jamison echoed in disbelief. " 'Bothered'? The only thing disturbing me is your handling of this behind my back."

Kathleen grew agitated at the evidence of his temper. "Daddy, I was taking care of things just fine. Surely you can't expect me to show them any compassion after their murderous intentions."

"Whose intentions?" Dalton interjected. "Mr. Jamison assumed it was one of the farmers who took a shot at him, looking to even the score, but it wasn't, was it, Kathleen?"

She glared at Dalton while trying to adopt a bewildered look. "I'm sure I don't know what you're talking about. I was right there with Daddy, in case you've forgotten."

"No, I haven't forgotten," her father murmured, the pain of understanding pinching his brow. "I seem to recall you were the one who insisted upon that particular spot for our sudden ride. And you who wanted to stop there on that particular rise. Why was that, Kathleen?"

"So Mr. Jones could get a clear shot, I would guess," Dalton surmised.

"Is that true, Jones? Did my daughter give the

order to have me killed? You'd better speak the truth or you'll be speaking before a judge!"

Latigo was one who knew when to turn with the tide. He cast a halfway apologetic glance toward the fuming Kathleen and shrugged before looking back to his employer. "Not to kill you, just to make it look like an attempt on your life. I'm not one for doing away with them that pays me."

Kathleen clamped her jaw shut defiantly, seeing no point in denying the obvious. She'd gambled for control and she'd failed. For now. Her glare cut between the two gunmen, promising a suitable revenge.

By then Jude had angled over to where Sammy was standing. The hug they shared was tight with relief. Family squabbles between father and daughter didn't concern them. All they knew was providence had intervened in the form of Dalton MacKenzie. No brutal end would find them on this day.

"I've been a fool," Jamison mourned wearily. "I've let my arrogance and greed provoke me beyond common decency. No more. The people in this valley were once my friends, and I was proud to be theirs. We founded this land together, and I've allowed my hunger to have all of it push that fact aside. No more. Neighbors don't murder neighbors."

"You're a fool," Kathleen growled with all the pent-up hatred she'd been hiding. "You are weak and sentimental, and I am not going to let you give away my inheritance. This is my valley! No one is going to take it away from me! I'm in control here—"

"No, Kathleen," her father cut in curtly. "You will never have control, not of my fortune, not of my

lands, not of my trust. Never again. I should have
learned my lesson from your mother. Since you
seem to favor her instruction over mine, that's
where you shall go, back East to live with her."

"B-but Daddy, you can't—"

"I just did. Get home, girl, and start packing. Ned,
take a few of the boys and ask our neighbors—
politely—to join me at my home. We have things to
discuss if we're going to bring peace back to our
valley. One of you take care of Monty."

Kathleen held her ground for a long moment, her
proud, angry gaze going from one face to the next,
seeking some show of support. She found only
disgust and, worse, pity. With a sob of fury, she
wheeled her mount toward Sweetgrass and headed
off.

As his men filed away to do his bidding, Jamison
surveyed the damaged station with a mixture of
shame and sorrow. His shoulders bent for a moment under the weight of his daughter's betrayal,
then he straightened with a cleansing sigh. "Miss
Amos, I trust no one was hurt."

She stepped out from behind Dalton's tall horse,
her arm curled around Sammy's middle. Her chin
tipped up with a shaky display of gritty accusation.
"There was no time, thanks to Mr. MacKenzie's
intervention."

"I'll make up for your losses. You just let me
know the amount and I'll—"

But she was walking away from him, not interested in hearing of his absolving offer, her focus on
the glass-littered porch where Joseph and a tail-
wagging Biscuit waited. Her family. Dalton looked
after her, suddenly uncertain if he would be readily
embraced into that fold now.

Jamison distracted him by asking, "What about

you, Mr. MacKenzie? Now that our debt is paid in full, I could sure use a good man with a cool head to run this outfit."

"Our accounts are settled, Jamison. I'm not for hire anymore. I've changed my line of work." And his gaze lingered on the empty doorway through which the others had passed.

"Mr. Jones? What about you?"

"I haven't changed mine, sir. So if there's nothing more for me to do here, I'll be on my way soon as I pick up my gear." He tipped his hat to Jamison as the rancher gathered up his reins. "Been a pleasure." And, as his former boss headed back toward Sweetgrass, Latigo urged his horse over to where Dalton still sat astride. He looked over the smoldering ruin of the barn to the uninviting isolation of the house. "Mac, are you sure you want to stay here?"

"I'm tired of fighting other people's little wars. I finally found something worth taking a stand for." His mouth bent in a wry smile. "Why aren't you laughing at me now?"

"Somehow it don't seem funny." They'd been friends a long time, which was a rarity in their business. He'd listened and laughed in the past when Dalton spoke of retirement because he knew the other man wasn't serious about it. But now, this time, there was a deeper determination to Dalton, something far back in his eyes, something lurking behind his faint smile. It was good-bye, and Latigo hated to see it coming even though he'd known it was inevitable the minute he'd seen his friend and the stage-stop woman together. He grinned. "You'll make a lousy farmer, Mac. You'll be back in business in no time."

"No."

Latigo chuckled. "We'll see. Our kinda life ain't that easy to walk away from."

"It is when you've got some place better to go."

"Send me a picture card from San Francisco."

Dalton smiled. "That's not where I'm headed. I don't need to go there anymore" was his cryptic reply.

"Retired and leg-shackled all in one jump. Mac, you sure you know what you're getting into?"

He gazed toward the house, his eyes going all warm with longing. "I'm sure."

Still chuckling, Latigo gathered his reins. "Of the two of us, I'd say you're in for the more dangerous line of work. See ya, Mac."

"Watch your back."

"And you, yours." With a jaunty wave, he was gone, off to find another problem to solve with his own brand of expertise.

Jude knelt on the floorboards, picking up pieces of glass. She was able to find them by the way the shards prismed through her tear-filtered gaze. Bit by bit, she gathered up the remnants that as a whole once provided protection from the elements. Even as she worked at the arduous task, she knew the glass would never be replaced, that the pieces could never be made whole. This would never feel like her home again.

She gave a start, flinching as a piece of glass sliced into her thumb. She dropped it and stared dully at the oozing crimson, unable to respond to the sight or the pain. Her chest felt so tight, she couldn't draw a decent breath. Tremors of delayed shock were fighting for expression, goaded by the memory of Monty's gun scraping leather. She pushed them down farther, refusing to fall completely apart, not in front of Sammy and Joseph, who would be looking to her for direction. There was too much to do for her to lose control now. She had to think of where they would go, what they would do.

She moved in her isolated daze to a wall shelf in the kitchen and began collecting the pieces of a sugar bowl that had been smashed by one of the raider's bullets. Fine white granules had spilled all over the stove top. If Joseph had still been mixing up his morning batter when those shots were fired . . . Her breath gave a small hitch before she could clamp down on the image. Her eyes squeezed shut, and she swayed in the throes of sudden knowledge. So much could have happened because of her pride and insecurities. Things could have been so much worse than burnt timbers and spilled sugar. She clutched the edge of the stove with white-knuckled hands as spasms of guilty consequence shook her. She could have lost everything . . . everything because of her vain stand.

Visions of Sammy and Joseph sprawled dead in the yard swam dizzily through her head, quickening a renewed sense of panic. She would never, ever feel safe beneath this roof again. She couldn't stay here. Her fight was over. It was over the moment she'd been forced to realize the dreadful price she'd almost had to pay. New tears balanced on her lashes. She was tired, so tired of fighting back the fear, of holding to a brave front, of being so alone. She gasped for breath in weak, pathetic little snatches, like old Biscuit when he was dreaming of younger days and rabbit chasing. Her mind was so giddy, she thought she was imagining it when she heard his voice.

"Jude?"

She heard the crunch of his boots on glass. Then came the sweet knowledge of his tender touch as his broad palm skimmed beneath her jaw, drawing her around to face him.

He'd been watching her from the open door, afraid to enter, afraid he wouldn't be welcome. He'd deserted her once, and it was presumptuous of him to believe she'd forgive that. She'd told him she loved him, and he'd gone into a fretful panic of denial. Why should she believe he felt the same way about her now?

So he'd hesitated, agonizing over how best to mend his fences. Then he saw her brave shoulders shake, and there was no holding back.

Tears welled and wobbled in her eyes, spiking her lashes and making her eyes appear as transparent as the glass littering the floor. There was no trace of the feared accusation in them, no glint of anger, just an overwhelming gladness that cut to his soul.

"Oh, Dalton."

He scooped her up, pulling her in tight until he could feel the jerk of her breathing against his chest. She felt frail and small, vulnerable despite her size, and an anguished protectiveness swelled within him. He spread one hand wide to cradle the back of her head while the other rubbed between her shoulder blades. Dalton kissed her hair and began a slow rocking motion. "It's all right, Jude. Cry it out. I got you and I'm not going anywhere."

It took a long while for the sobs to work their way out of her system, but he was patient, holding her through it all while Sammy and Joseph tactfully went out to gather up what stock they could find. Only Biscuit was there to witness their embrace. Dalton didn't speak as she leaned, drained and exhausted, against him, limp as a length of wet leather. He would have stood there for days, for as long as it took for her to conquer the fright and assemble her phenomenal courage once again. He had nowhere else he wanted to be.

Finally her desperate clutch eased, and one palm moved anxiously up and down his tear-sodden shirt front. Her voice was raw with a painful hoarseness.

"What are you doing here, Dalton?"

"Taking care of you for a change. Is that all right?"

She wasn't put off by his gentle evasion. "Why did you come back?"

"I came back to tell you I was wrong, Jude. Wrong in what I was doing and wrong in what I didn't tell you."

She sniffed softly. "What didn't you tell me?"

He cupped her chin, raising it slightly. His gaze was all brilliant blue fire. "I didn't tell you how beautiful you are to me. I haven't had a clear thought since you kept that noose off my neck. I can't close my eyes without seeing the way you looked in Cheyenne in that dress I bought you. I kept it, you know."

She swallowed hard. "Why would you do that?"

"Because I couldn't stand the thought of not seeing you in it again, of not taking it off you on some special night, like a wedding night or something."

She stared at him, amazed that he hadn't stumbled over that last part but unable to answer as Sammy's giggle announced that they weren't alone.

That fact didn't seem to bother Dalton for he continued. "I love you, Jude. I've been fighting it because, quite frankly, the idea scares the hell out of me, but not as much as the thought of you up against those guns. I'm sorry. I should have listened to what you were saying, to what you were asking, instead of feeding my pride."

"When I think of what could have happened . . ." Her voice thickened and closed off completely. She cleared her throat noisily and said, "None of it matters now. Dalton, take us away from here."

"I will." His fingers stroked her cheek, brushing away the silvery traces of moisture. Her eyes began to close as he leaned forward, and her breath sounded in a soft sigh as his lips touched hers.

"Are we going somewheres?" Sammy interrupted.

Dalton straightened away from Jude's kiss with reluctance, then smiled to put the other at ease. "Someplace nice. Someplace you can work with horses. That be okay?"

Sammy frowned for a worried minute, then nodded. "I guess. What about Joseph and Biscuit?"

"They'd be coming too."

"And you'd be coming with us? That'd be swell." Sammy beamed. "We'd be like brothers."

Dalton smiled. "Like brothers."

"Jude, Mac's gonna be our new brother. Ain't that grand?"

"I wouldn't be Jude's brother, Sam," Dalton corrected with a deep gaze into Jude's tranquil eyes.

"What would you be then?" Sammy asked, purely puzzled by the whole thing.

Dalton read the question in Jude's eyes. *What would I be then?*

"I'd be marrying your sister," Dalton answered, posing the question at the same time. "That would make us brothers and Jude my wife. If she'll have me."

"Sure she will!" Sammy shouted before she had a chance to reply. "A brother! Holy crow, that's grand!"

But he still hadn't heard Jude's answer. Dalton looked down at her, waiting, an unfamiliar anxiousness curling in his belly at the thought of her possible refusal. He searched her stare, feeling his world shake beneath him.

Then Jude smiled and warmth sprang into her gaze, searing him to the soul.

"We'll be family," she told him. "Sammy, why don't you and Joseph see what's left of our belongings. I'd like to get started for Cheyenne as soon as possible. There's nothing left for us here."

Once they were alone, Dalton leaned down once more to taste the yielding heaven of her kiss. His possession was wooingly slow, seeking her soft, surrendering sigh. His arm curved around her waist, tugging her up closer so they could enjoy the tease of fully clothed tension that chafed the will. He lifted his head at last, and they shared a breathless moment when control teetered and ultimately steadied as they gazed into each other's eyes and saw forever there.

"I've never told another woman that I loved her. Even if I had, it wouldn't have been true, till now. Having nursed me and reformed me, are you sure you want to keep me?"

The hint of unexpected vulnerability in his tone made her smile with a burgeoning tenderness. "Yes, Mr. MacKenzie, quite sure. And you need never worry that I will fail to keep my promises to you." She touched his parted lips with the caress of her thumb. "Where to, Dalton? San Francisco?"

"No. I've got everything I want right here." And

he bent to kiss her, using the lingering crush of his mouth to prove it was true.

How could she doubt it when he put it like that?

Avon Romances—
the best in exceptional authors and unforgettable novels!

WICKED AT HEART   **Danelle Harmon**
78004-6/ $5.50 US/ $7.50 Can

SOMEONE LIKE YOU   **Susan Sawyer**
78478-5/ $5.50 US/ $7.50 Can

MIDNIGHT BANDIT   **Marlene Suson**
78429-7/ $5.50 US/ $7.50 Can

PROUD WOLF'S WOMAN   **Karen Kay**
77997-8/ $5.50 US/ $7.50 Can

THE HEART AND THE HOLLY   **Nancy Richards-Akers**
78002-X/ $5.50 US/ $7.50 Can

ALICE AND THE GUNFIGHTER   **Ann Carberry**
77882-3/ $5.50 US/ $7.50 Can

THE MACKENZIES: LUKE   **Ana Leigh**
78098-4/ $5.50 US/ $7.50 Can

FOREVER BELOVED   **Joan Van Nuys**
78118-2/ $5.50 US/ $7.50 Can

INSIDE PARADISE   **Elizabeth Turner**
77372-4/ $5.50 US/ $7.50 Can

CAPTIVATED   **Colleen Corbet**
78027-5/ $5.50 US/ $7.50 Can